Linda Gillard lives on the Black Isle
been an actress, journalist and t
novels, including STAR GAZING wl
Romantic Novel of the Year and *The*
writing that promotes the Scottish I

CW00376398

HOUSE OF SILENCE became a Kindle bestseller and was selected by
Amazon as one of their Top Ten *Best of 2011* in the Indie Author
category.

Also by Linda Gillard

Emotional Geology
Star Gazing
House of Silence
Untying the Knot
The Glass Guardian

www.lindagillard.co.uk

A LIFETIME BURNING

Linda Gillard

Originally published by Transita in 2006
First published as a Kindle e-book in 2012
This paperback edition 2013

ISBN 978-1482637359

Cover design by Nicola Coffield

For Debbie Robinson,
publicist and pal

Prologue

2000

The Dunbars are a good-looking family – even the old ones – and massed in black, as they are now, impressive. Clearly the gene pool has never been muddied with inferior stock. Was it in fact ancient in-breeding that produced such refinement of feature, such acute sensitivity, such intelligence? The Dunbars aren't telling. We're a canny and a clannish lot, loyal to a fault – even when we hate each other. A Dunbar will stand by another to the bitterest of ends – even the black sheep. Especially the black sheep. (And I should know – flighty Flo, dear Aunt Flora, poor Reverend Wentworth's mad wife who, for everyone's sake, really should have been kept in the attic.)

The Dunbars have an effective way of dealing with miscreants. You could call it assimilation, I suppose. We simply pretend the black sheep is white. As Hugh once said in one of his sermons, 'There's none so blind as those who don't wish to see.' There was a lot the Dunbars didn't wish to see.

And so we didn't.

Theodora Dunbar, matriarch, known always as Dora, is ninety-three. Only my mother could manage to look commanding in a wheelchair. The entourage helps of course: a bevy of attractive and attentive men hovering, pandering to her every wish. Dora has loved us all in her own peculiar way and the Dunbars have returned that love with loyalty and devotion. Only I stepped out of line. And of course Colin, but he was instantly forgiven on account of his extreme youth and my extreme wickedness.

Dora's wheelchair is manoeuvred by one of her grandsons, Colin. My ex-lover. My nephew. My brother Rory's son – like Rory, but much darker. The awkward boy has matured, as I (being something of a connoisseur in these matters) always knew he would, into a handsome man. But today Colin stands, as ever, in Theo's shadow.

1

Theo. My son. At thirty-four, a few months older than Colin, taller, fairer, finer-featured and always said to favour me. Everyone agreed Theo's Apollonian good looks owed little to Hugh. Theo is a Dunbar through and through. Nevertheless, Hugh and Theo are close – to spite me, perhaps. Theo adores Hugh, protects him, supports him – at the moment quite literally. At nearly eighty, Hugh's tremendous height and bulk are bowed. Leaning heavily on Theo's slender frame, he droops, like an ancient, gnarled tree, his thick black mane now white as a wizard's.

There has been much love in this family – some would say too much – and not a little hate. The most unlikely love has been Hugh's for Theo and Theo's for Hugh. Against all the odds... I doubt Hugh ever contemplated revenge since he regards himself as even more of a black sinner than me, but if he'd wanted to settle old scores, loving Theo and making Theo love him would have been a masterstroke.

Rory weeps. My brother stands between his wife Grace, as plain and four-square solid as Grace has always been, and Colin. (My niece Charlotte is not present. She is on the other side of the globe, the distance she thought necessary to put between herself and my son.) Colin fidgets, clearly embarrassed by his father's tears. My husband and son are dry-eyed; my mother, stunned by grief, is stoically composed; my sister-in-law Grace can barely disguise her relief.

Grace hated me. I can't say I blamed her. She had good reason. Several, in fact. But if you asked my gracious sister-in-law why she hated me, she'd say it was because I seduced her precious firstborn, relieved him of the burden of his virginity, chewed him up and spat him out on to the admittedly sizeable scrap-heap marked 'Flora's ex-lovers'. That's what Grace would say. But she'd be lying. That isn't why Grace hated me. Ask my brother Rory.

Rory and I haven't spoken for thirteen years, but my twin brother, my childhood companion, the other half of my life, the other half of my self weeps, weeps for me, his dead sister, who burns.

Burns...

Like a witch.

~

'It is better to marry than to burn.'
The elderly man bearing a marked resemblance to an Old

Testament prophet appears to be talking to himself.

'What?'

'Paul's first Epistle to the Corinthians. Chapter seven, verse nine.'

'Oh,' Theo replies vaguely. The younger man, though tall, is still shorter than his companion. He is thin and his delicate, almost feminine features are drawn. He appears young at first but closer examination reveals many fine lines about his eyes and mouth suggesting a greater age, or at least a fondness for the outdoor life. His thick, fair hair, brushed vigorously in honour of the solemn occasion, is being coaxed by a gentle summer breeze into its natural state of unruly curls.

As the men wander round the parched crematorium flowerbeds, Theo finds himself wishing his mother had died in the spring. July has little to offer apart from blowsy hybrid tea roses and vulgar gladioli. Not Flora's flowers at all. He tries to think what she would have preferred. Something blue perhaps, to match her eyes. Delphiniums. Larkspur. Cornflowers. Theo finds the botanic litany oddly comforting.

Hugh resumes his grumbling. 'Trust St Paul to take a dim view of marriage. What did *he* know about it anyway? Lifelong celibate! Homosexual, probably. Poor bugger...' The old man loses his footing and leans more heavily on Theo.

'Take it easy, Dad. The paving's uneven here. I wish you'd brought your stick.'

'Don't need it, my boy.' The old man halts and breathes heavily, giving the lie to his claim. He speaks eventually and in quite a different tone. 'I *did* love your mother.'

'Dad, don't upset yourself. It's all over and done with. Long ago. Let's go home.'

'I tried to love Flora. But my kind of love wasn't enough. She needed more than I could give her and, God knows, I needed more than she could give me. Mutual misery should have brought us together. It was one of the things we had in common.'

'Dad...'

Hugh draws himself up to his full, imposing height so that Theo has to look up into his face. The remarkable brown eyes are barely dimmed; there is passion still. *'But if they cannot contain, let them marry: for it is better to marry than to burn.'* He snorts and raises a finger to admonish the absent saint. 'In this – as in so many things –

3

St Paul was wrong.' He shakes his white head. 'Flora and I married *and* burned...'

Rory is now composed. As Grace drives them home she steals a glance now and again at his profile and wonders if her husband will ever age. At fifty-eight, there is something of the superannuated schoolboy about Rory. His sandy hair is now threaded with silver but it still flops across his forehead when he moves his head suddenly, which he is inclined to do. His thick fair brows have become untidy but his face is still lean, the skin almost unlined. Grace scowls at her own furrowed brow reflected in the rear-view mirror and envies the blessing of Dunbar genes.

Rory, staring straight ahead, announces suddenly, 'You know, Flora always thought she'd burn in Hell.'

'She didn't really believe in all that mumbo-jumbo, did she?'

'I think she did. She was a vicar's wife. Goes with the territory.'

'How horrible.'

Rory is silent for a while, then resumes. 'I don't think she saw it like that. Hell wasn't a place she was afraid of going to, you see. My sister spent most of her life there.'

Grace lifts a hand from the wheel and lays it on her husband's. Despite the summer heat, Rory's long fingers are chilled.

In a Sydney wine bar a young woman sits alone with a briefcase and a bottle of wine. There is only one glass on the table but the bottle is nearly empty. A folder of documents lies open in front of her, unregarded as she fingers a dog-eared postcard, tapping the table with it nervously. One side of the postcard is covered in a black, uneven scrawl. The other shows a botanical print: *Fritillaria meleagris,* the snakeshead fritillary, checkered purple and white. Her favourite flower. She wonders how long it took to find a postcard of it and drinks again, turning the card over and over, as if rotation might eventually generate a different message.

Charlotte Dunbar – at thirty-one she hasn't married and believes she never will – steels herself to read the postcard again. The message is unchanged.

Dear Lottie

I've asked Grace to forward this to you. She won't give me your address. I don't expect you to reply but I wanted you to know that my mother has been found, but she was dead. The cremation will take place on July 21st. I'm OK but my father took it very badly.

All love, as ever,

T.

PART ONE

Chapter 1

1942

Dora Dunbar had given up hoping for a child. At thirty-five, after fourteen years of marriage, she'd come to terms with her barrenness. Archie was equally sanguine. He apportioned no blame and kept his disappointment to himself. The painful subject of prospective parenthood was no longer discussed.

Dora's faith in God was vague but unquestioning, as befitted an Anglican in wartime. She assumed quietly, with little fuss, that the confirmation of pregnancy, followed some months later by a diagnosis of twins, was nothing short of miraculous. Dora prayed in her modest way that at least one of the babies would survive. She didn't pray for a son, partly because she feared to tempt Fate (a pagan deity who co-existed comfortably and just as inscrutably alongside her God); partly because she simply didn't care about the babies' gender. A baby, any baby, something to hold in her arms, to present to Archie, a piece of himself, a Dunbar scion, was all Dora asked. But Dora refused to pray mainly because she knew prayer didn't work.

As a child she'd prayed nightly till she wept for her adored brothers to be spared in the last war. God had shown Himself to be deaf or indifferent and had taken Henry in 1915 and Roderick the following year. Dora had consoled herself with the infant Henrietta, had petted and spoiled the baby as if she were a treasured doll. Dora's parents were grateful for the distraction of a new life in the family and, praising the resilience of children, marvelled at how young Dora cared for little Ettie, as she came to be known.

Dora would chatter incessantly to the infant long before she could understand anything she was told. Dora's parents, bereft of both their sons and numbed by grief, paid little attention to Dora's prattle. As she leaned over the cot, they assumed Dora told the baby stories.

She was indeed telling stories – stories of her adored brother

Henry, dead at twenty. Dora, aged nine, told stories so that she wouldn't forget Henry and so that little Ettie, who had never known him, wouldn't forget him either.

When the twins were born – a pigeon pair: Roderick Henry and Flora Elizabeth – Dora wept copious tears. Archie assumed it was relief; the midwife said it was the milk coming in. Nobody asked Dora why she cried. She might not have known, but when two live babies were placed in her arms Dora found herself suddenly overwhelmed with grief for her two brothers, dead more than twenty-five years.

Ettie, hovering outside the bedroom door not wanting to intrude, might have understood but if she had, she would have said nothing. Ettie said little but perceived much. It was Ettie who, when Dora remarked anxiously that Roderick seemed such a mouthful for a tiny baby, suggested he be known as Rory. Dora looked up and smiled gratefully.

Rory settled to his feeds better after he'd been re-named. He fed well and slept soundly, unlike his older sister who, to Dora's distress, seemed perpetually hungry, perpetually wakeful. The midwife on one of her visits cast a professional eye over Rory sleeping in his cot and Flora fussing at the breast and announced harshly – but prophetically – that Flora was 'a naughty, greedy girl'.

1987

Tea sat untouched in bone china cups as brittle as the preceding silence. Dora sighed, then said firmly, 'It's wrong, Flora.'

'Says who?'

Dora flinched at the sharp retort but continued evenly. 'I do. So do Rory and Grace... And Hugh. Not that you care what Hugh thinks.'

'Too bloody right, I don't.'

'Please don't swear, Flora. It isn't necessary and it doesn't help.'

'Well, mind your own damn business, Ma!'

'I do usually. You know I do. I always have. But I think I have a right to speak here. You are making my grandson very unhappy.'

'On the contrary – I appear to be making him deliriously happy. Ask him.'

'Don't be glib, Flora. There's more to life than sex. Don't pretend you think otherwise.'

'There's more to Colin and me than sex.'

Dora gave her daughter an appraising glance. 'Yes, I dare say there is – for Colin.'

'How dare you judge me!'

Dora fixed her daughter with faded blue eyes, still astute, still steely. 'I may be very old but I am not yet a fool. Colin is twenty-one and you are forty-four. At best it's mutual infatuation. Put an end to it now before Colin is hurt.'

'Why should I? It's not as if he's a child. Or particularly immature. He wasn't even a virgin, actually.'

Dora winced and held up her hands in protest. 'Please! I don't wish to hear details of Colin's private life. Or yours for that matter.'

'So why is it wrong? Tell me. He says he loves me. And I– I'm terribly fond of him.' Her voice faltered. 'We have a lot of interests in common,' she added quickly. 'And we enjoy sleeping together. Why is that wrong?'

Dora looked down at her hands, registering the throb of pain in her arthritic knuckles. The ugliness of her once beautiful hands never failed to repel her. She looked up into Flora's still lovely face and, against her better judgement, relented. 'I don't know if it's wrong, but I do know that one day you'll regret it. I think you will feel...' Dora cast around for a word and seemed almost surprised by her choice. 'I think you'll feel ashamed.'

Flora laughed, a high, barking sound that had nothing to do with mirth. 'Oh no, Ma! That's one thing I won't feel. I was inoculated against shame a long time ago.'

I don't remember my mother as a young woman. She was thirty-five when we were born and in my earliest memories she already seems old. Our father was sixteen years older than our mother and so it was as if we'd been born to grandparents.

When I think of my mother, I see her in the garden wearing an old straw hat and a moth-eaten fur jacket that for all I know might have been fashionable in its day. I was crucified with embarrassment on the rare occasion when I brought a friend home to tea. They could barely stifle their giggles. Other people's mothers wore pretty dresses, high-heeled shoes and took trouble with their hair. Mine wore galoshes.

The resemblance between Dora and my son Theo was astonishing – the same remarkable blue eyes, the high cheekbones and silky curls (except that Dora's were, from her mid-forties, pure white.) She was pretty, tiny and doll-like. When she became crippled with arthritis, Hugh would lift her out of her battery-driven cart, kiss her pale, powdered cheek and carry her indoors. Dora was unperturbed by the lack of ceremony. I think she relished the attention, especially from Hugh. She'd cling on round her son-in-law's neck, continuing her conversation over his shoulder. (Except that Dora didn't really do conversation. She waved a twisted but regal hand and gave you an audience.)

When Theo was placed in my arms as a newborn I finally felt I was no longer a child. At twenty-three, I was free at last from my parents' jurisdiction and disapproval. But as I cradled my beautiful son, I was struck by the sickening realisation that I hadn't the faintest idea how to be a mother to this child.

1945

Rory didn't speak. By the age of two he had uttered no recognisable words and very few sounds. He would cry out in pain and laugh out loud but he had no language other than a low humming, chaotically melodic, that accompanied his play and to which Flora appeared to respond, sometimes antiphonally, sometimes in unison. When Flora babbled to Rory's droning hum, it was as if the two toddlers were making music together.

As the twins' third birthday approached, Flora was speaking in whole sentences but Rory was still verbally silent. Dora worried aloud that he was deaf or mute although she knew he was neither. Ettie pointed out that Rory scarcely needed to talk with such a vocal twin to interpret his every wish. Rory had only to look up, point at a toy and Flora would interpret: 'Wor want his teddy.'

Flora observed her brother closely as if he were an object of fascination, like an animal at the zoo. She kept up a kind of running commentary on his every move. If Rory rubbed his eyes Flora would announce, 'Wor tired now.' If a look of pained concentration stole over his face, Flora would exclaim, 'Wor want his potty! *Quick!*'

Flora could pronounce neither of their names and they emerged as 'Wor' and 'For'. Sometimes the two monosyllables were indistinguishable and it was unclear whether Flora was talking about herself or Rory. Since she eventually seemed able to interpret most of his needs without even looking at him, it was often unclear which twin she was referring to, or even if she herself made a distinction.

The family tended to address Flora as spokesperson for the twins. They tried to talk to Rory through her but eventually they just talked to Flora. Rory retreated still further into his impenetrable musical world. Dora fretted but Archie said it was mere laziness and cited an older brother of his who hadn't said a complete sentence before starting school but who'd made up for lost time by becoming an MP. Dora was not reassured.

Ettie suggested separating the twins for a day to see what happened. Only then did it occur to Dora that the twins had never been apart for more than a few minutes at a time. She agreed readily. Ettie took Flora out in the pushchair doing her best to ignore the child's increasingly frantic cries as she looked at the empty space beside her, aghast.

'Where's Wor gone? Aunt Ettie, where's *Wor*?'

Dora sat on the hearthrug with Rory, surrounded by a battery of toys including a new wooden xylophone. He looked round the room, his eyes darting, his head swivelling at the slightest sound, his ears cocked for Flora. Dora tried to distract him. Rory's head movements increased in their rapidity, taking on the appearance of a nervous tic. His droning hum began, soon punctuated by heartbroken gulping sounds as he cried in his own distinctive, almost silent way. Dora picked up the small hammer of the xylophone and picked out a tune, singing unsteadily.

'Three blind mice...
Three blind mice...'

Rory took no notice and started to make a new sound, pressing his lips together and blowing, as if he would burst. The sound that emerged was 'Fff... Fff...'

Dora paused, the little hammer in mid-air. 'Flora? Are you trying to say Flora, Rory? *For*?'

The boy looked round the room and pointed at the door, still puffing at his lips. 'Fff...'

'Flora! Say "Flora", Rory!'

His head jerked back and he sobbed, a terrible groaning sound that appeared to come from his stomach. Dora felt uneasy but lied cheerfully about Flora's imminent return. She beat out *Three Blind Mice* again, singing the words loudly in an attempt to drown Rory's cries, then, dropping the hammer, she gathered him into her arms, unable to bear his distress. She rocked him back and forth, stroking his thick fair hair back from his forehead until he seemed a little calmer. The child pointed to the hammer on the floor, then looked round for Flora. As he started to cry again Dora reached hurriedly for the hammer and put it into his hand.

Rory looked at the spherical head of the hammer, his silky golden brows twisted into a frown, as if the hammer itself had been the source of the music, now fallen strangely silent. He turned his head quickly and looked up at Dora. Another jerk of the head as he stared at the door, then his eyes settled on the hammer again. He heaved a deep, shuddering sigh. His mouth opened but at first there was no sound. Then to the tune of *Three Blind Mice* Rory sang, 'Where – For – gone?' He looked up at his mother, startled, as if it were she who had sung. Dora was too astonished to answer and Rory sang again. 'Where – For – gone?'

Breathless, Dora sang tentatively in reply, 'For – gone – out.' Then, more confidently, 'For – back – soon!'

Rory smiled and chuckled. Dora hugged him tight and kissed his cheek. 'Clever Rory!' She grasped the hammer and beat out the four notes of Big Ben's chimes on the xylophone, singing boldly, 'Where – has – For – gone? – She'll – be – back – soon!' Rory laughed again. Dora repeated her improvisation to Rory's increasing delight. He nodded his head vigorously to the beat of the music. As he grabbed the hammer from Dora the front door slammed. Rory's head jerked upwards, catching Dora painfully under the chin. He fixed his eyes on the door, scarcely breathing. The handle rattled and Flora charged into the room, her face grubby and tear-stained. Ettie followed, looking exhausted. 'I'm sorry, Dora. She was quite inconsolable. I thought we'd better come back. She was making herself sick with crying. Did Rory fare any better?'

Flora threw her arms round her brother and squeezed. 'Wor!' She caught sight of the hammer in his fist and snatched it away. 'What's this for?' She tapped him on the head with it. Rory beamed.

Dora whispered, 'Give it back to him and he might show you.'

Reluctantly, Flora handed the hammer back to Rory. He stared at the end again, then at his sister. Grasping the hammer tightly, he opened his mouth and sang softly, to the tune of Big Ben's chimes, 'Where – you – gone – For?'

Flora's jaw dropped and her eyes widened. For the first time in her short life, she was speechless. Rory laughed delightedly and tapped her on the nose with the hammer.

Rory and the xylophone were inseparable thereafter. His speech, once started, developed quickly but it was many months before he could speak without singing. Thus, at the age of three he started to compose his own music so that he could talk. When many years later he said in an interview that he had learned to compose music before he had learned to talk, the claim was dismissed as artistic licence on the part of an eccentric musician, but in fact the statement was quite true.

They said that was when I started to feel jealous of my Wunderkind *brother. Attention-seeking Flora, little Miss Look-at-Me couldn't cope with the competition. But that wasn't it at all. Jealousy wasn't the problem, but they didn't have the words to describe what was really going on. It was the first time Rory had seemed separate from me and I couldn't handle it. My brother was me and I was him, we came as a package, an indivisible whole. Or so I'd thought.*

The tantrums and spitefulness weren't sibling rivalry or even just plain naughtiness as my benighted father thought. It was a form of grief. They'd probably call it "separation anxiety" nowadays. I was trying to cope with having half my self amputated, without anaesthetic. I was a Siamese twin forcibly separated when I'd thought we'd been doing quite nicely, thank you.

Rory survived the operation. I didn't. I just took a long time – a lifetime – to die.

1948

Flora's performance as the Virgin Mary was perhaps the first and last time she felt herself to be the star of the show that was to be her life. With her fine, pale blonde hair, her large blue eyes and air of intelligent composure, there was no question but that Flora Dunbar should play Mary in the St Ethelred's Elementary School nativity play. As Miss Stapleton remarked in the staff-room, puffing on her Craven A, 'That child has *presence* – and she will look lovely in blue.' She didn't add that unless they put the Dunbar girl centre-stage in a spotlight, she would find some other, less acceptable way of drawing attention to herself. Damage limitation was a concept that hovered on the outskirts of Miss Stapleton's mind, but she was too kind-hearted to acknowledge it.

Equally easy to cast was her brother Rory as the Angel Gabriel. Apart from his golden hair and an appropriately solemn expression, Rory had a beautiful singing voice and would cope well with the angelic solo Miss Stapleton had in mind, informing Mary of her impending happy event.

The staff all agreed they'd be sorry to lose Rory. 'A crying shame,' was the general consensus. That some of the best boys were sent away to public school was neither kind to the boys nor fair on the girls but, as Miss Stapleton pointed out philosophically, brushing ash from her lap, that was the way of the world for those who could afford to choose.

But she did wonder how the Dunbar lad – strangely aloof, yet somehow vulnerable – would cope with the rigours of boarding school. It was hard to imagine him separated from his more robust sister. Miss Stapleton, with her many years' experience of young children, thought there would probably be trouble.

1949

Rory was making his preparations to run away from school.

His letters home had been censored; his painted measles had failed to convince Matron and had simply earned him a stern lecture from his Housemaster. Refusing to speak had disconcerted staff and pupils alike for a week but had achieved nothing beyond an even sterner talk from his Housemaster, to which Rory had made no reply. He'd refused to make a sound even when being beaten.

So there was nothing for it now. He was going to have to run away if he was ever to make them understand.

~

Dora answered the door to a police constable accompanied by an urchin whose face and clothes were so filthy she stepped back in alarm. Then she recognised the badge on the boy's blazer and gasped. As she enveloped Rory in her arms the constable explained that the boy had evidently been sleeping rough and had collapsed in a neighbouring village. A doctor had been summoned and pronounced the child to be suffering from exhaustion and dehydration. Rory couldn't – or wouldn't – speak and had nothing on his person to identify him, but someone at the surgery had recognised the school badge. The receptionist had rung to enquire about absconders and Rory had been identified at once. Matron, much relieved, confirmed that there had been 'a spot of trouble' recently. She'd suggested the boy be sent home for a few days to recover from his ordeal.

Later, when Rory was in the bath, Dora asked him why he'd run away. He was silent for a while then said, with a croak, 'Because they found the tunnel.'

'Tunnel?'

'Yes.'

'You were digging a *tunnel*?'

'Yes. Me and Parsons. So we could escape. But Mr Abbott – the gardener,' Rory explained, 'fell into it with his wheelbarrow.' Rory's thin frame heaved a sigh. 'It was taking far too long anyway... Parsons was *useless* at digging.'

'What I actually meant, Rory,' said Dora, as she applied plasters to his blistered feet, 'was why did you feel the need to run away from school? Why did you want to come home?'

Rory blinked at his mother in astonishment. 'To see Flor, of course. I thought she'd be missing me.'

1987

Flora sat on the stairs, clad in an old pair of pyjamas and a raincoat, waiting. A mouse appeared from behind the skirting board and scurried across the hall floor. She watched it without interest, her eyes unfocused. The rain had started up again and she could hear the penetrating drip-drip as water fell through a hole in the roof and landed in the bucket. She rubbed at her knee. The damp was making her joints ache. Pulling her raincoat around her more tightly, she poured the last of the vodka into a grubby tumbler. Beyond the heavy rain Flora thought she heard a distant car engine. She stared fixedly at the front door.

A car drew up outside the house, braking suddenly. Flora listened for the door opening but there was no sound apart from the accelerando of dripping water. Eventually a car door opened and shut. A firm knock on the front door sent it swinging on its hinges.

Rory stood on the threshold, his hair and clothes unkempt, his face drawn, his features blurred by a two-day growth of beard.

'Hello, Ror.'

'Hello.'

'You look as if you've been sleeping in ditches.'

'No... In the car. I didn't want to stop.'

'You've driven straight here? From *Suffolk*?'

'Yes.'

'Jesus! Have you eaten?'

'I had something...' He cast his eyes upwards as if trying to remember. 'Yesterday.'

'Well, there's not much here. Only tins.'

'I'm not hungry.'

'Did you bring booze by any chance?'

'No.'

'Pity. There's no kindling left either. It's bloody cold. How did we use to bear it here?'

He shrugged, his shoulders tense. 'We were kids.'

'Yes, I suppose so.'

'Flora...'

'Yes?'

Rory's gaze was level but his chest rose and fell as he tried to control his breathing. 'You know I will never forgive you for this.'

'Yes, I know,' Flora said mildly. 'But you see, Ror, I'm past caring if anyone forgives me. Even you. The only thing that matters to me now is that you're here. Come in and shut the door. Mind that hole in the floorboards. The dry rot's got a lot worse.'

Rory pushed the door shut behind him and stood shivering on the worn coconut mat. He looked down at the filthy floor and said absently, 'Those are bat droppings.'

'Yes. We've got bats, mice, a barn owl and a nest of robins. And that's just indoors. Outdoors we have a pine marten.'

'Really?' Rory's face was slashed by a sudden bright smile.

'Yes. I put scraps out for him and he comes out of the woods at dusk... It can't be the same one, can it?'

Rory shook his head. 'After thirty-odd years? No, of course not. It's probably a descendant. Can it peel hard-boiled eggs?'

Flora smiled, her face radiant. 'Yes.'

'There you are then.' And with that Rory covered his face with his hands and started to cry silently.

Flora rose unsteadily from the stairs, raised her glass and said, 'Welcome back, Rory.'

Chapter 2

1953

Flora slapped her book shut, irritated. Rory's playing didn't usually annoy her, she didn't usually even register it, but today he was playing scales, faultlessly but repeatedly, shredding her nerves. *The Naughtiest Girl in the School* could not compete. Flora leaned back in her armchair and put her fingers in her ears but she could still hear the relentlessly ascending and descending octaves. She jumped to her feet and, for want of anything better to do, decided she'd go and annoy Rory.

He didn't look up as she entered the music room. As Flora approached the grand piano she could just see his eyes above the music stand, concentrating fiercely. His head swayed slightly as his hands travelled back and forth over the keyboard. Flora walked round and stood beside the piano stool. On the music stand in front of Rory was this week's copy of *The Eagle*, open at a double-page spread of Dan Dare's adventures in outer space. Flora wasn't surprised. Rory quite often read while practising. She began her inquisition.

'How can you read and play at the same time?'

Without breaking his rhythm or moving his head Rory replied, 'Easy. I'm not thinking about the scales. My hands do them on their own.'

'How can you talk and play at the same time?'

'How can you talk and breathe at the same time?'

Flora thought for a moment. 'Don't know. I never think about breathing.'

'Exactly. It's different parts of the brain. What I'm doing with my hands is just mechanical. They've got a life of their own.' Flora watched his hands moving up and down like elegant crabs and could see what he meant. '*I'm* not doing it – *they're* doing it.'

Flora hated it when Rory talked like that. It gave her the creeps. His hands continued relentlessly and she thought briefly of slamming the piano lid shut, of smashing Rory's fingers. She laid her hand surreptitiously on the lid, luxuriating for a moment in her power, in the possibility of wickedness.

'Turn the page for me, Flor.'

Startled by Rory's voice, she did as he asked, automatically, because in the end Flora always did what Rory wanted. The moment to destroy her brother's hands seemed to have passed and so she left the room, consoling herself with delusions of power and her own magnanimity.

1950

Flora was never sure exactly when she realised she was bad. She couldn't actually remember ever having thought she was *good*. 'Flora! You bad girl!' was a phrase she'd grown up with, had heard so often it had come to seem like an additional name, like her middle name, Elizabeth. Flora wasn't sure what it was about her that was so very bad but it seemed clear she was worse than Rory, who didn't often do bad things, largely because he could get Flora to do them for him.

Some of the things that made Flora "bad" didn't seem fair at all. Rory would come in from playing football, covered in mud, even bleeding sometimes, but he was never told he was "bad", yet when Flora fell over on the grass when she was skipping and got grass stains on a new frock, she was told she was a bad girl for spoiling it. Flora didn't understand.

Once, on a rainy day, she'd accepted a ride home from the park from a nice man in a car and her mother had thrown up her hands in horror and shouted. When Dora asked if the man had touched her Flora said no, he'd just given her a sweet. This wasn't true, but Flora hadn't wanted to upset her mother any further by saying that the man *had* touched her, had laid his warm, rough hand on her bare legs and slid it up her skirt and touched her knickers. Flora hadn't understood why the man had done this, but it hadn't hurt and the sweet – a barley sugar – was very nice, so Flora hadn't really minded. But when her mother shouted, she felt bad.

Dora had said the friendly man was bad, but she didn't say why. She'd said he might have hurt her, but as he hadn't, Flora couldn't see what was so very bad about him, especially as he'd given her a sweet. Flora thought that seemed *kind*, not bad. It was all very confusing. But Flora could certainly see that if the man was bad, she must be worse. He hadn't actually done anything bad, but Flora had. She'd told a lie.

One Saturday morning when Flora was out Christmas shopping with Ettie, they came upon a brass band in the square. Flora could see they were soldiers because they were all wearing uniform. There were several lady-soldiers singing and shaking tins that rattled like Flora's money-box. Ettie stopped and reached into her handbag for her purse. Flora wondered what she was going to buy. Her aunt handed over some money to one of the ladies who was wearing a bonnet tied with a big bow like Bo-Peep. The lady smiled at Flora, then moved away, shaking her tin without giving Ettie whatever it was she'd paid for. Ettie didn't seem to mind, but stood watching the band play.

Flora's legs were starting to ache. One song finished and another started. It appeared to be about laundry.

Are your garments spotless? Are they white as snow?

Flora thought guiltily of the grass stains on her frock. She looked down at her feet and noticed that her long white socks were splashed with mud from the wet pavement.

Lay aside the garments that are stained with sin...

Flora wondered whether it was sin staining her socks. She wasn't sure what sin was, but she knew it wasn't nice. People didn't talk about it, like the thing the man in the car might have done, but didn't.

When the Bridegroom cometh, will your robes be white?

Flora felt certain hers wouldn't be. Just look at her socks – clean on this morning! She sidled behind Ettie and hoped the soldiers would be too busy singing to notice her stains.

Will your soul be ready for the mansions bright
And be washed in the blood of the Lamb?

Flora wondered what 'the mansions bright' were. They sounded pretty. She knew that rich people lived in mansions. Perhaps 'mansions bright' were houses decorated with candles and paper chains, like Christmas all year round? Flora wished she could go and see them, but she doubted *her* soul would be ready. She knew for a fact that she hadn't been washed in the blood of a lamb, but with smelly Wright's Coal Tar soap. But she couldn't see how being washed in lamb's blood – *any* kind of blood – could possibly get you clean. Whenever Rory grazed his knees the first thing their mother did was wash them with soap and water, even if it made Rory cry. Then Flora remembered the time Rory had been running with a bottle of lemonade and had tripped and broken it. The shattered glass had gashed his hand and there was a lot of blood, but Ettie had said calmly, 'Let it bleed for a while – the blood will wash out any tiny pieces of glass and dirt.' She and the twins had sat on the back doorstep, watching blood well and then drip from Rory's hand. After a minute or two Ettie had wiped the cut with disinfectant and bandaged Rory's hand. She'd kissed him and said he was a good, brave boy.

Flora thought this was really unfair. If Rory hadn't been running with a bottle in the first place the accident would never have happened and Flora had been *just* as brave as Rory. She'd watched the horrible blood washing his hand, while Rory looked the other way.

1949

After Rory ran away from boarding school, Dora suggested to Archie that their son should go back to the Elementary School with Flora. She voiced her concerns about Rory's welfare to an indifferent husband. The product of a public school where large quantities of cold water and small quantities of food were considered to be of educational benefit, Archie had little time for his son's nervous sensibilities, being of the opinion that the boy could come to no real harm. Looking up briefly from his horticultural journal, he intoned cryptically, 'Who is born to be hanged will never be drowned', his harsh words softened by his Highland burr.

Dora drew no comfort at all from this gnomic utterance. Irritated, she pointed out that if Rory were unhappy he might stop speaking again. The school would not tolerate it and her nerves could not bear it. Tears appeared to be imminent, so Archie yielded with good grace, relieved to be able to give his full attention to the fine single malt in his glass and the pests of greenhouse cucumbers.

Dora broke the happy news to Rory but insisted he now sleep in a room of his own, not in the old nursery he used to share with his sister. She said he was too old to share a room with Flora and claimed the room was in any case far too small for two growing children. She ignored Rory's indignant protestations – echoed by Flora – that neither of them minded. Dora wouldn't explain but talked vaguely about them both growing up – Flora into a young lady and Rory into a young man – and assured them that they would appreciate having more space and privacy as they grew older.

Rory's bed was removed and a desk put in its place. He was given a small room that had hitherto been used by Ettie as a study. Rory thought this a shocking waste of space and told Ettie she could use his room any time she wanted because he'd always be playing outdoors or in Flora's room. He cleared a shelf for his aunt's personal use, carrying his belongings back to the bookcase he'd shared with Flora until he went away to school.

At night Rory lay awake in the dark, missing the heavy breathing, the coughs, the muffled weeping of a dormitory of small boys. He'd thought he'd never get used to all the noise, but this silence was even worse. Just when he thought he was never, ever going to get to sleep he woke crying, thrashing about in the bed. His heart thumped against his ribs and he lay still in the dark, terrified, trying to understand what had woken him. When he felt brave enough, he sat up and switched on his bedside light. He got out of bed, pulled the eiderdown on to the floor and opened his bedroom door quietly. He padded along to Flora's room, turned the handle and crept in, closing the door carefully behind him.

'That you, Ror?'

He walked over to Flora's bedside, dragging the eiderdown. 'Yes. I'm back.'

'Goody.' She sat up in bed and switched on her bedside lamp. 'Was it you crying?'

'Just a bit. I had a bad dream. A nightmare.'

'What about?'

'I dreamed you were on fire.'

'*Me?*'

'Yes. You were burning up. Your hair was on fire. Like a halo.'

'Did you put it out?'

'What?'

'The fire. Did you send for the Fire Brigade to rescue me?'

'No.'

'Why not?'

'I woke up. That's when I cried. I came in here to see if you were on fire.'

'Well, I'm not.'

'I can see that *now*.'

'What made you dream such a horrible thing?'

'Oh, I don't know. History, I expect.'

'*History?*'

'We were doing the Tudors. At my old school. Mary Tudor burned witches.'

'Why?'

'Don't know really... 'Cos they were bad, I suppose.'

'What did they do, the witches?'

'They kept cats. And they used plants called herbs to make medicines. People didn't like that.'

'Is that all?'

Rory thought for a moment. 'I think they turned milk sour as well.'

Flora frowned. 'Doesn't seem fair that you got burned to death just for *that*.'

'Well, they must have been bad people as well.'

'Or somebody *thought* they were.'

Rory nodded. 'Mary Tudor. She wasn't very nice. Elizabeth was better at being Queen,' he explained. '*And* she beat the Spaniards.'

'We're doing the Romans. They were horrid too.'

'Did they burn people?'

'No, they crucified them.'

'Like Jesus?'

'Yes. *He* was a nice person... Did you say your prayers, Ror?'

'Yes,' Rory lied.

'Night, night, then.'

'Night, night.'

Flora switched out the light. Rory shivered, wrapped himself in his eiderdown and lay down on the rug beside Flora's bed, careful to keep his bare feet off the cold linoleum. He arranged his arm under his head, making a mental note to bring his pillow tomorrow night.

'Ror?'

'Mmm?'

'They don't burn witches now, do they?'

'There aren't any witches, silly!'

'But do they still burn bad people?'

'No.' Rory yawned. 'Not any more.'

1950

As a Christmas treat Dora and Ettie took the eight-year-old twins to Covent Garden to see the ballet *Cinderella*, with Margot Fonteyn in the title role. Rory was not enthusiastic. Ballet was something girls did and he couldn't see why he had to go. Ettie assured him that not only did men and boys dance, but that if he came on the outing, he'd see that orchestras consisted almost entirely of men and that the conductor would also be a man.

'Does he sell the tickets?' Rory asked sceptically.

'I beg your pardon?'

'The conductor. Is he the one who sells the tickets for the show? Like on a bus?'

'No, my dear! The conductor is the man who directs the orchestra. Everyone has to watch him, even the dancers. He's terribly important. You'll see.'

Rory did see. Leaning over the red plush balcony throughout the performance, he stared down into the orchestra pit below, barely glancing up at the stage. He couldn't believe his eyes and ears. The man with the stick waved it and the theatre was instantly full of music, music so loud, Rory almost wanted to put his hands over his ears, especially when the clock struck twelve and Cinderella had to rush home. He thought it sounded as if the theatre was splitting in two. When Cinderella ran down the stairs, shedding a glass slipper as she went, the noise was so exciting Rory thought he was going to cry or need the lavatory, but instead he laughed out loud and clapped his hands together. A lady sitting behind him leaned forward and said, 'Sshhh!'

On the train going home Rory was very quiet while Flora

26

chattered with her mother and aunt. Dora said she thought the Ugly Sisters were very amusing and did Flora realise they were actually played by men? Ettie said her favourite character was the Fairy Godmother because she was so kind to Cinders. Flora wished *she* had a magic wand so she could go to parties in a silver coach and have a new dress whenever she wanted.

Ettie turned to Rory and asked if he too would like a magic wand. 'Yes. But not one like the fairy had. I want a real one.'

Flora assumed a wise and patient expression, the one she used to try to convey that she was years older than her brother, rather than forty-five minutes. Rolling her eyes she said, 'There's no such thing as a *real* magic wand, Ror!' She looked up at Dora and Ettie for corroboration. 'It's just pretend, isn't it?'

'Yes, darling,' Dora said, smiling. 'It's all just pretend. Unfortunately, there aren't any magic wands in real life.'

Rory stared up at his mother. 'Yes, there are. The conductor had one. I want one of those.' He turned his face to the window and stared out at the Suffolk countryside as it sped past.

We were born at home, at Orchard Farm near Saxmundham in Suffolk. The house was eighteenth-century in origin, whitewashed, with tiny windows outlined in black and an erratic, red-tiled roof. In front of the house lay lawns and flowerbeds; to one side and behind there were glasshouses and outbuildings; on the other side was an apple orchard with paths mown through the tall grass.

Dunbars had lived at Orchard Farm for several generations. Our father had inherited it from an uncle whose grandfather had bought the property as a working but not prosperous farm. In those days they'd made cider from the small, inedible apples that grew in the orchard and were a source of constant disappointment to us as children. Archie sold off a lot of the land but kept enough to lay out a garden on a grand scale. There was even a decent croquet lawn till the moles got at it. It became too hopelessly uneven for croquet, but Rory knew all its slopes and dips like the back of his hand and would trounce anyone foolish enough to challenge him. For some reason croquet brought out Rory's killer instinct, perhaps because it was one of the few sports he could engage in without having to worry about damaging his hands.

The farmhouse itself was gloomy but large, comfortable and brim-full of treasures. Every shabby surface was littered with objects, all of them precious to their owners: snuff-boxes, Staffordshire figurines, china dogs, inlaid wooden boxes with secret compartments, ivory carvings and a patchwork quilt with one thousand and four pieces (which Rory counted), the accretion of many lives displayed not to impress, simply to comfort or commemorate. There were countless photographs in silver and leather frames depicting cherubic schoolboys with over-large ears who might have been Rory, Theo or even Colin, but were mostly our late uncles, Roderick and Henry. The family face gazed back at us down the years in all its themes and variations.

I suppose the Dunbars were what nowadays you'd call asset-rich, cash-poor. There was a grand piano but the only holidays we ever had were spent with Dunbar relatives in a ramshackle house on the west coast of Scotland. When Rory wanted to incense Dora he claimed he'd auction his half of the inherited antiques and furniture and donate the proceeds to the Musicians' Benevolent Fund. She liked to think he was joking but I was never sure. Rory had no time for sentiment or even possessions. It was me who wouldn't part with our toys, who insisted they stay in the room we called the nursery, with its paper frieze of farm animals and chipped blue paint, the room where we played and slept for the first seven years of our lives.

We were very lucky. We had so much and we grew up surrounded by lovely things. But Rory was beaten up at school and ridiculed for his love of classical music; I was teased and bullied because I wasn't like other girls. I had no interest in boys – I loved Shakespeare and God, in that order. Rory and I didn't have friends. We just had each other.

1957

Rory had finished his piano practice and it had not gone well, at least not well enough to meet his exacting standards. He slouched into the sitting room, hands in pockets, in search of Flora. He found her lying on the hearth rug in front of the fire, her head pillowed in her hands, listening to the wireless. Rory flung himself full-length, which was now almost that of a man, on to the sofa. It was clear to Flora that he wanted attention but before he could open his mouth she said, 'Be quiet, Rory.'

'I haven't said a word!'

'No, but you were about to.'

'What are you listening to?'

'*Ssh!*'

Rory was obediently silent and listened. 'It's a play,' he announced after a few moments.

'Clever Rory!'

He was silent again for a while. 'Nothing much seems to be happening.'

'That's the whole *point*,' Flora explained with a withering look. 'It's Chekhov.'

Mystified, Rory listened again. Eventually he said, 'If nothing's happening, how can the play come to an end?'

'Ssh! I'm trying to listen.'

'Well, if nothing's happening, you won't miss much answering my question!'

'Please go away, Rory.'

He was silent again, his expression becoming more and more puzzled. 'Will they just drivel on until the BBC decides it's time for the news?' Flora glowered, silencing him again, but not for long. 'You know, you couldn't have music where nothing happened.'

'Don't be ridiculous!' she snapped. 'Nothing *ever* happens in music! Not in music without words anyway.'

'Things can be happening in music without there being any words.'

'Such as?' Flora sneered.

'Arguments. Violence. Passion. And sexual intercourse,' Rory added for good measure. 'And you can't do *that* in a play,' he said, wagging a finger at her. 'It's against the law.'

Flora experienced a familiar sensation of wading in out of her depth, but she persevered. 'How can all those things be happening in music? Who says they are?'

'Nobody. But they could. *Anything* could be happening in music. It's up to you. It's in your ear, in your head. But when it comes to expressing emotion, music's more precise than words. There's less scope for interpretation.'

'That's rubbish!'

'You're only saying that because you don't understand. Look, it's quite simple: words are the things we use to *describe* what music *expresses*. So words are at one remove from the experience itself.'

'So is music,' Flora said, regarding him suspiciously.

'Well, yes, in a way. But there's nothing between you and the composer. Take a piece of piano music by Schumann... He thinks or feels something, he expresses it as sound, and you, Flora, have to decide how you feel about it. The meaning doesn't have to be filtered through words.'

'No, but it's filtered through your fingers.'

'How do you mean?'

'*You* have to decide how to play it. That's like using words.'

'No, it's not.'

'Yes, it is.'

'No, it's *not*,' Rory said firmly. 'Music is closer to the original because the words in a play have still got to go through the actor's mouth before they get to your ear.'

'I still can't see that music is any closer!'

'It *is!* Look.' Rory sat up and spread his fingers, counting off the points as he spoke. 'The composer has an idea. He expresses it in notes. I play it. You listen and decide how you feel about it. That's four stages. Now the playwright, this what's-his-name – Chekhov? He has an idea. One. He expresses it in words. Two. The actor speaks them. Three—'

'And I decide how I feel about them. Four!' Flora said triumphantly. 'It's the same! Four stages.'

'No,' said Rory, shaking his head. 'Before you can do that you have to decide what Chekhov's words *mean*. Not a lot, if you ask me. That's four. *Then* you have to decide how you feel about them. *Five.*' He held up a hand and wiggled his fingers in Flora's face.

'Oh...' Flora knew she'd lost but her sense of defeat was mitigated by a grudging admiration for her brother's mind.

He jerked a thumb in the direction of the wireless. 'If this play was being broadcast in Russian you wouldn't have the option of interpretation. The meaning would stop at the actor's mouth. But I could *play you music in Russian* and you'd understand it as well as a Russian! Well, *you* wouldn't,' he said scornfully, 'but a musical person would. That's the big disadvantage of words, you see. They only work if you speak the language. But music works in any language because it doesn't *have* a language. It's faster, more direct. Like mainlining.'

'What's that?'

'Oh, it's to do with drugs. Heroin addicts inject the drug into their veins. It's called mainlining. It hits you harder than smoking opium because it goes straight into your bloodstream.'

Flora stared at him, awestruck. 'How do you know all that?'

'Dave Potter's brother went to university in Paris and came back a drug addict,' Rory explained, as if this were a natural consequence of studying at the Sorbonne. Flora didn't understand but was too shocked to seek further clarification. Rory continued. 'Music goes straight into your emotional bloodstream, bypassing the brain. Words have to go the long way round.'

'So you're saying music is better than drama?'

He grinned. 'No. That's what I *think,* but it's not what I'm saying. I'm just saying music is more intense, faster-acting, a stronger drug. Drama is a more dilute form of emotion. It's at one remove.'

Flora considered for a moment. 'Then presumably, performing music is even closer to the source than listening to it.'

Rory frowned. 'I hadn't thought of that... But, yes, it stands to reason. If I'm playing the piece I'm probably feeling it more strongly, more deeply than anyone in the audience.'

'Well, if that's the case, the composer wins.'

'How do you mean?'

'He feels something and then he expresses it in lots of dots and squiggles. Whatever you play only exists because the composer felt it. Your playing is just a dilution of what he felt.'

'Oh, yeah...' Rory said softly.

'Am I right?' Flora asked, astonished.

'Yes, I think you are.' Rory looked at his sister and said thoughtfully, 'You know, Flor, you're a lot cleverer than you look.'

'Thank you,' she replied, trying not to preen. 'I hope you realise you've just talked all the way through the end of my play.'

'*We've* just talked. You shouldn't have argued. Anyway it wasn't very interesting.'

'How would you know?'

'I was listening.'

'You weren't.'

'I was.'

'While we were talking?'

'Yes. I can listen to two things at once. At least.'

'How did it end then?'

'Oh, I don't know… It was all much the same. People complaining, sounding depressed. God, why would anyone listen to such stuff?'

'You see, you weren't listening really.'

'I *was*. I'm just trying to remember.' He leaned back on the sofa and closed his eyes. 'There was a woman talking, but she wasn't really saying anything. And there was a band playing. A military band. The woman kept repeating, "If we only knew… If we only knew." '

'Knew what?'

'I don't know! The play ended, didn't it! Why they were all *suffering*, I suppose. She said something like, if we wait, we'll find out why we live, why we all suffer.'

'Oh, that's *beautiful*.'

'It's just a load of words, Flora.'

She ignored him, wanting to indulge her emotions. 'It's so sad… but sort of hopeful at the same time.'

'No, it's not,' Rory scoffed. 'But the *band* was – the brass band playing in the background. That was sad, but sort of hopeful.' Flora's eyes filled with tears. '*Now* what?' Rory asked, exasperated.

'Oh, you wouldn't understand.'

'Tell me – what's the matter?'

'It's just – well, it's just I don't know who I'm going to *argue* with when you go away to college!'

'Oh.'

Flora hugged her knees and buried her face in her arms. At a loss, Rory looked down at her bent head, at the back of her neck, exposed where her long blonde hair divided and fell forward over her shoulders, revealing pale skin that rarely saw the light of day. He wanted to comfort her, to lay his hand gently on her neck, but instead he shoved his hands into his pockets and said, 'You'll find someone, Flor…'

I didn't. Rory was wrong. I never spoke to anyone else the way I spoke to him. I discussed theology with Hugh, poetry with Ettie, Method acting with fellow students and I discussed sex (exhaustively) with Colin, but it was never the same. There was always the need to explain. It wasn't like thinking aloud, like talking to myself. And no one ever took my breath away, pulled the rug from underneath me, made me laugh like Rory did.

He was a hard act to follow.

1959

Flora had never felt so terrified in all her sixteen years. She sat in a waiting room presided over by a benevolent middle-aged woman who occasionally looked up from her typewriter to smile encouragement at Flora and the two boys sitting opposite her on the other side of the room.

The three young people took it in turns to glance furtively at a clock on the wall. From time to time one of them would retrieve a folded piece of paper from a pocket, study it briefly, then put it back. The lips of all three moved occasionally, as if in silent prayer.

Flora was indeed praying. When she wasn't praying she was mouthing the lines she'd learned from *Saint Joan*, alternating them with a speech of Viola's from *Twelfth Night*. She stared fixedly at the clock and prayed to the trinity of God, Shakespeare and Bernard Shaw that she'd be called upon first to audition and preferably soon.

Flora and her mother had arrived in London early. Dora insisted that Flora eat something as she'd refused breakfast and so they went to the Lyons Corner House where Flora forced down a cup of tea and a Chelsea bun, which did little to relieve her nausea. She still arrived early for her audition, before the two boys, both of whom appeared to have travelled even further. The taller boy was darkly handsome in a black polo-neck sweater and spoke with a Lancashire accent. Flora found it hard to understand him when he spoke to the receptionist who had no such difficulty. Flora watched him from beneath her illicitly mascara'd eyelashes and tried to imagine him as her Orsino. He certainly looked the part, but Flora couldn't imagine the immortal opening lines of the play – *If music be the food of love, play on –* uttered in a broad Lancashire accent. She decided that, sadly, his northern vowels must surely count against him.

The other boy arrived clutching a small battered suitcase. He was stocky, with an appealing, animated face. Not an Orsino – far too short and his ears stuck out slightly – but Flora could imagine this boy playing Shakespearean clowns. She decided he had nice eyes – dark brown and trustworthy, like a retriever's.

He directed a strained smile towards her as he sat down and Flora attempted to smile back. She didn't, *couldn't,* speak. Finding this faculty had deserted her, she started to panic, wondering what she'd do if, when they finally asked for her Saint Joan, she opened her mouth and no sound emerged. Flora decided to alter her petition to the Almighty. She ceased praying to be admitted as a student to this illustrious drama school and asked if He would simply ensure she survived today's ordeal without fainting or bursting into tears.

The receptionist, who had seen a lot of suffering in her time, broke an electric silence with, 'Shouldn't be much longer now,' and gave Flora another kind smile. Glancing at the clock again, Flora hoped her mother hadn't exhausted the shopping possibilities of nearby Oxford Street. Dora had been given strict instructions to wait outside the building, but as it was now raining Flora feared she might venture through the hallowed portals in search of shelter. Public humiliation might ensue if Dora were to notice the mascara and comment. Flora modified her prayer yet again. She requested the Almighty keep her mother at bay, standing on the pavement in the rain until the ordeal was over. Her clammy fingers groped for the now crumpled sheet of paper on which she'd typed Joan's final soliloquy and her eyes scanned the page, settling inevitably on the last line: *How long, oh Lord? How long?*

1961

The door opened and a cello case appeared, followed by its owner, a young girl of about eighteen, her face masked by a curtain of long dark hair. She slammed the door behind her, leaned against it and burst into tears.

Rory looked up from behind the grand piano, appalled. Eventually he decided to cough. The girl didn't hear, so he coughed again. She jumped and stared, her damp face plastered with tendrils of hair. Rory opened his mouth, his jaw twisting as he worked at the words. 'I'm sorry – this practice room is booked.'

'Oh... Sorry.' The girl searched for a handkerchief. 'I listened outside. I couldn't hear anything.'

'I've been studying the score.'

'Oh. Sorry.' She blew her nose thoroughly. 'I was just looking for somewhere to cry actually.' She gestured towards the case. 'It's a bit difficult getting a cello into the ladies' lavatory.'

'Yes. I mean, it must be.'

She heaved the cello case on to her shoulder and turned away. Rory looked down at his score and picked up a pencil. 'I don't mind. If you want to cry in here.' He waved his pencil in the air, vaguely. 'Stay. Till you feel better. I'm just looking at a score.'

The girl blinked at the strange young man and sniffed. 'You're Rory Dunbar, aren't you?'

'Yes.' He looked at her warily. 'I don't know you.'

'Grace Bridgewater.'

'Oh.' He nodded, a jerky movement that dislodged his long fair hair on to his brow. 'Pleased to meet you.'

Rory saw a sturdy, brown-eyed girl with strong features and ugly, workmanlike hands. Her tight-fitting jersey drew his attention to her large breasts, which he admired for a moment before dropping his eyes hurriedly to the open score in front of him. He looked up again, aiming his gaze at her face. No one could call her pretty, but it was an arresting face: the mouth and nose too big for beauty, but her long thick hair, tumbling over her shoulders and across those breasts, was magnificent.

'Why were you crying?'

'I just had a lesson with the Nazi Kommandant.'

'Toller?'

'Yes.'

'He's vile to everyone. Don't take it personally. He sees it as his mission in life to put as many young people off music as possible."

'Well, he's making a pretty good job of it. He says I'm *hopeless*.'

Rory smiled and spread his hands. 'Translation: you don't play like he does.'

Her face brightened. 'Yes, that's it! He doesn't *teach* me, he just wants to *show* me. I think he plays more in the lesson than I do.'

'Just say yes and copy him. Don't let him break you. He hates girls anyway.'

'Yes, that's the impression I get. But why?'

Rory hesitated and looked down at his score again, blushing. 'Toller prefers boys... If you know what I mean.'

She giggled. 'Oh, Lord.'

Rory looked up and grinned. 'So you see, you don't really stand a chance.'

'Well, thanks for the advice! I'll clear off now and let you get on with your practice. Sorry I disturbed you.'

Rory decided Grace was much prettier when she smiled. 'Do you feel like playing a duet?'

'What, *now*?'

'Yes.'

Grace approached the piano. 'Have you got any music?'

'I think so.' Rory rifled through a shabby leather music case. 'Brahms? Beethoven?'

Grace's eyes lit up. 'The sonata in A?'

Rory nodded.

'Do you know it?'

He nodded again.

'Oh, I'd *adore* to play that! Shall we give it a go?'

Without waiting for an answer she arranged a chair. Rory fetched her a music stand, adjusting the height as she took her cello out of its case and tuned. Grace watched him from behind her curtain of hair. He must have been eighteen or nineteen but seemed older. He wasn't tall. Slim. Sporty-looking. His fair hair unbrushed, if not unwashed. His large grey eyes moved constantly, rarely settling for long. When they did she thought they looked serious, almost sad. As he arranged the music on her stand, she looked at his beautiful hands: smooth and pale, with very long fingers, the little finger almost as long as the third. Useful for a pianist.

Rory sat down at the piano, turned and looked at her, his fair brows raised in enquiry. Grace wished she'd worn slacks or a longer skirt to cover more of her splayed legs – far from her best feature. 'Ready when you are,' she said cheerfully.

Rory looked at his music for a moment, then asked, 'How did you know who I was?'

'People talk about you.'

'Oh? What do they say?'

'That you're good.'

'Oh.'

'The *girls* say you're nice.'

'Oh.' Rory looked surprised. 'What do the boys say?'

'That you're weird.' She laughed. 'Which probably has a lot to do with being good and nice, so I wouldn't worry about it. Shall we play?'

~

Grace liked to tell people that she fell in love with her husband the first time they played together, somewhere during the scherzo of Beethoven's Cello sonata in A, Op.69.

So romantic.

It took Rory rather longer to reciprocate, but he never told people exactly how long. Well, apart from me. The fact is, Rory didn't fall in love with Grace until he'd been married to her for years.

Better late than never, I suppose.

Chapter 3

1957

Ettie Sinclair, to no one's real surprise, had never married. She'd lost her sweetheart, Geoffrey, in the war and had subsequently thrown herself into the arms of the Church, finding consolation in the words, music and arcane rituals of High Anglicanism. Now aged forty-one, her orderly life was divided between family, church and an undemanding job in the local bookshop. What little leisure time she had, she devoted to reading poetry and her duties as secretary of the Poetry Society. (Her talk on the dramatic monologues of Robert Browning had been very well received and the chairman had asked her if she felt up to tackling Keats, a prospect that both thrilled and daunted her.)

If asked (though nobody tended to ask questions of Ettie) she would have said that her life was fulfilled, that it was happy, that she knew the love of God and therefore had little need for the love of man – any man in particular, that is.

When Reverend Pym retired from St Edmund's, Ettie was sad but bore the loss with her usual fortitude. The minister had heard her brief and uneventful confessions and helped her come to terms with the loss of Geoffrey, but faced with new and stimulating possibilities, the departure of the elderly priest didn't seem quite such a cross to bear. Used to making the best of things, Ettie looked forward to sermons delivered by a younger man with perhaps more go-ahead ideas, the product of a mind more incisive than Reverend Pym's, which had displayed a worrying tendency to wander over the last few years.

The new vicar of St Edmund's was the Reverend Hugh Wentworth, a young man of thirty-six, with a pretty wife called Miriam. The parish took the new incumbents to its bosom, not least because they resembled film-stars. Miss Thompson, who organised the flower rota, was heard to comment to her helpmate, Miss Cartwright, that young Mrs Wentworth bore a striking resemblance to Vivien Leigh. Miss Cartwright didn't disagree but remarked that Mrs Wentworth's beauty was of a superior kind, being as it was 'all natural', a reference, Miss Thompson assumed, to the actress's fondness for powder and paint.

Mrs Wentworth's being of childbearing years was yet another point in her favour, although, as Miss Cartwright pointed out to Miss Thompson, the Wentworths hadn't long been married, so it was premature to talk of christenings. Instead, they talked of Reverend Wentworth. Miss Cartwright – wont to find fault even with the likes of Vivien Leigh – could find nothing to criticise in the new clergyman, although she did remark cryptically that he was a mite too handsome for his own good. The other flower ladies and most of the female congregation perceived no such flaw or, if they did, were prepared to overlook it.

Father Hugh, as his affectionate congregation called him, was an imposing figure. Miss Cartwright might have claimed that at six feet three inches he was also too tall for his own good, but she could find no fault with his upright bearing, his ready smile which displayed a fine set of large white teeth, or his head of black hair which was perhaps a trifle long for a clergyman. Father Hugh the preacher was of no less interest to the congregation than Father Hugh the man. His voice was deep but clear, a firm musical baritone, and he declaimed the scriptures with passion (but not, Miss Cartwright noted gratefully, *too* much.) His sermons were short (which endeared him to many) and interesting (which endeared him to all). He was never thrown off his stride when babies cried. On the contrary, he was quick to bestow one of his winning smiles on the mother of the offending infant.

Father Hugh was a success in the parish and the congregation of St Edmund's thanked the Lord for sending them such a splendid new minister. Ettie too gave thanks for the advent of Father Hugh and never failed to mention him in her prayers. She never missed Sunday communion now and took to attending evensong more regularly, a change of habit she ascribed to a newly acquired enthusiasm for psalm-singing. When poor Miss Thompson slipped in a puddle of water in the Lady Chapel and broke her hip, Ettie was only too happy to take her place on the flower rota.

Her research on the metaphors of John Keats fell quite by the wayside.

Father Hugh, passing through the church on his rounds one Saturday, stopped to chat with the flower ladies and to admire their efforts. Ettie, a little flustered by the attention, adjusted her spectacles and remarked that she hadn't realised how much pleasure and satisfaction might be derived from the arrangement of flowers to the glory of God. Father Hugh smiled, bending his leonine head to one of Ettie's arrangements. (Miss Cartwright had thought it a little on the exotic side, with its Turk's cap lilies and bourbon roses. She'd urged more greenery, but Ettie stood firm and ignored the advice.)

Father Hugh closed his eyes and inhaled deeply. 'Glory indeed, Miss Sinclair! Such colours. Such scents!' He cupped a full-blown rose and plunged his aquiline nose into its luxuriant petals. Upright once again, he looked down at the flower ladies from his lofty height and pronounced, 'Our senses are God-given and such displays as these allow us to revel in them! Take advantage of your opportunities, ladies. Hedonism is not always the work of the Devil,' he added, flashing them another of his smiles.

'What a very odd remark,' Miss Cartwright whispered as Father Hugh headed towards the vestry.

Ettie watched him disappear through the door. 'Did you think so?' she asked, a little breathless. Extending a finger towards a lily and stroking its firm, waxy petals she said, 'I thought it was *wonderful!*'

1958

When at the age of sixteen Flora decided she was going to be an actress, her parents were relieved. This ambition seemed slightly less appalling than Flora's previous aspiration, which was to be a nun. Dora could not for the life of her see how the two vocations could possibly co-exist and queried Flora's latest decision. Her daughter had replied impatiently, 'Oh, you just don't understand!' and flounced off to her room, but the truth was Flora didn't understand either.

One thing she did understand was that she wasn't prepared to spend the rest of her life being Flora Elizabeth Dunbar, skulking in her brilliant brother's shadow. It was all very well for Rory who was obviously going to be a famous musician with his life mapped out for him. He'd never had any doubts and nor had anyone else, but no one, it seemed to Flora, much cared what became of *her*. It was assumed she would marry and have a family (even by Ettie, who hadn't managed to achieve that happy state herself.)

Flora knew she was clever, if not as clever as her brother. Her best subjects at school were English and Scripture. She spent many happy hours reading Shakespeare and the Bible and writing passionate love poetry to an anonymous love object – anonymous because Flora had not yet managed to fall in love, except possibly with Jean Seberg whom she'd recently seen at the cinema playing Saint Joan. Flora's love poems were not dedicated to Miss Seberg, but she felt a strange desire to emulate her. Or was it Saint Joan she wished to emulate?

Flora became confused when she thought about what she wanted to do with her life. What she really wanted to be was a better person, but she knew in her heart that would be tremendously hard work. She thought she might settle instead for being a *different* person.

'Are you sure?'

'Of course I'm sure! Get a move on, Ror. Ma will be back soon.'

Rory picked up the dressmaking shears, weighed them in his hand and looked at Flora doubtfully. 'How short do you want it?'

'Really short. Like yours.'

He picked up her long blonde pony-tail and pulled it slowly through his hand. 'It seems a shame...'

'Oh, give me the scissors – I'll do it!'

'You won't be able to do the back. Sit still if you don't want to lose an ear.'

Rory gathered the pony-tail into his hand and started to shear through it with the scissors. The rhythmic crunching sound sent shivers down his spine. Seated in front of her dressing table, holding her breath, Flora watched his frown of concentration. When Rory had finished cutting he held up the hank of hair as if it were a dead animal. 'What shall I do with it?'

'Put it in that shoebox.'

Rory laid the hair gently in the box, coiling it round like a question-mark, then he looked at Flora's reflection in the mirror. 'You're sure?'

'It's too late to ask me now!' said Flora, who wasn't sure at all.

'You look very strange.'

'That's because it's lop-sided. Hurry up, Rory! She'll kill us if she comes in and finds out what we're doing.'

Rory burst out laughing. 'You don't suppose Ma's not going to *notice*, do you?'

She turned and held out a trembling hand. 'Give me the scissors.'

'No, I'll do it. Sit *still*.'

Carefully and methodically, Rory lifted locks of hair all over Flora's head and cut them so they were about three inches long. He took particular care with her fringe which he cut a little longer ('otherwise you'll look like a boy'). He stopped frowning and smiled at her now and again as if he were enjoying himself. Once he accidentally scratched her cheek with the scissors, but by then Flora was glad of an excuse to cry a little. Rory apologised, licked his thumb and wiped away the blood, saying, 'I think it looks nice. You look older... Sophisticated.'

'I look like you,' Flora said gloomily.

'No, you don't. Well, a bit, I suppose.' He stood behind her and looked into the mirror, comparing their reflections. 'Our eyes are different colours. And you don't have freckles.' He wanted to say she was pretty and he wasn't, but he thought that sounded stupid.

Flora groaned. 'I look *awful*.'

Rory felt unaccountably guilty and started to panic. 'Well, why did you ask me to do it then?'

'I didn't *know* I'd look awful, did I?'

'You *don't* look awful. You just look... different. Anyway, it's too late now.' He patted his handiwork, ruffling her hair. 'It *feels* nice. You try.'

Flora raised a tentative hand to her head and stroked her hair. 'It feels like an animal. Like a cat.'

'Or an otter. Very smooth and sleek. Not like mine. Mine feels...' He reached up and touched his own hair, as if to remind himself. 'Mine feels rough.'

'It wouldn't if you brushed it more often.'

'No, mine's different. Feel.' He grasped her hand, bent his head and laid her palm against his hair. 'See? It's not silky like yours.'

'No.' She raised her other hand and stroked the fine down on his upper lip. *That's* silky.'

Rory didn't answer but stood quite still as Flora gently touched his mouth. The front door opened and closed with a slam. He jerked his head away from his sister's exploring fingers. 'Now we're for it.' He looked down at the floor and then at himself, both covered in snippets of hair. 'Crikey! Look at the mess!'

'Don't worry about that. I'll deal with it.' Flora stood up and started to brush hair from the front of his shirt. 'You clear off and leave me to deal with Ma.'

'Rather you than me,' he said with a grin.

'What can she do to me other than scream and shout? And I've heard it all before,' Flora said, rolling her eyes heavenwards, 'many, *many* times.'

Since my mother had refused to take me to the hairdresser's I took matters into my own hands and Rory took the dressmaking shears into his. It was the wickedest thing we'd ever done, but even then I took all the blame. When she'd finished being hysterical Dora asked if I'd cut it off myself. I lied and said yes, mainly because I wanted to take all the credit for this wonderfully subversive act, but by then I was used to protecting Rory, covering for him. It was just habit.

1958

The Reverend Hugh Wentworth was in church one evening tidying hymnbooks and reorganising the parish notices on the board. He looked up from the back of the church towards the altar to admire the elaborate flower arrangements which, he noted gratefully, distracted the eye from the vulgar Victorian stained glass in the windows. His eye was caught by a head bent low in a pew. A worshipper deep in prayer, perhaps even asleep. The hair was short, very fair and rather untidy. Hugh's heart was gladdened to think that a boy had chosen to come into church to talk to God. Most of his regular churchgoers were women, many of them elderly. Hugh saw young parishioners when they were christened and married, hardly at all in between.

As he shuffled notices about the Brownie pack, the Mothers'

Union and a whist drive, Hugh thought how much he still missed his old life in the monastery. He knew he'd made the right decision in leaving and he loved his work as a parish priest, but he missed the companionship and spiritual commitment of monastic life; he missed even more the intellectual stimulation of his training at the seminary. He could see that, on the face of it, the Anglican Church had little appeal for boys unless they aspired to be choristers or priests. Hugh had spent a lot of time thinking about how this might be changed and had discussed with Miriam setting up a youth club. She hadn't been keen on the idea, viewing such an undertaking as yet another drain on her husband's precious free time.

As he studied the boy's bent head Hugh wondered whether a Bible study group might appeal to the youth of the parish. It would certainly require less organisation than a youth club, which would please Miriam. Yes, a Bible study group would be a good idea and if some youngsters could be persuaded to come along, so much the better. They'll ginger things up a bit, Hugh thought with a smile.

As he turned to leave he caught a faint sound of weeping and glanced across at the boy again. His immediate impulse was to offer comfort, but then he wondered about the etiquette of intruding on prayer. Quite possibly the boy didn't even know Hugh was present in the church. He decided to make his presence felt, as discreetly as possible. He dropped several hymnals on the floor, offering a swift apology to God for irreverence in a good cause.

The head shot up. There were sounds of fumbling, then a nose being blown vigorously. As Hugh watched the hunched, narrow shoulders, the head above them turned round and looked at him. He was astonished to see that this was no boy, but Miss Sinclair's niece, Flora Dunbar, who attended church regularly. The child was transformed. Her long blonde hair was shorn. With her red eyes and mournful expression, she now looked like some Dickensian waif.

'Flora! I didn't realise it was you. I'm sorry if I intruded on your prayers.' She gave him a faint smile, but said nothing. 'But... if you're in need of spiritual comfort,' Hugh spread his large hands, opening his arms towards her, 'I am here.'

It wasn't a bad chat-up line. I certainly fell for it. I fell for the whole classic package: older, married man – and a priest, to boot. I didn't stand a chance. At sixteen I thought Hugh was the nicest, kindest, most handsome man I'd ever met.

Actually, I still do.

Hugh was the first man I'd met – apart from Rory, who didn't count – who talked to me, asked me what I thought about things and actually listened to my answers. Rory had practically stopped talking to me by then anyway. Things just weren't the same any more. He was sullen and moody and spent all his spare time playing the piano or shut up in his room. He didn't have a girlfriend, although several of the girls at school were keen to go out with him. I could never quite see the attraction. He wasn't tall and never seemed to be all that clean, but my friends raved about his soulful eyes and his beautiful hands. I told Rory he could take his pick, but he just shrugged and said he hadn't got time for 'all that rubbish'. Rory thought women were a lower form of life.

Actually, he still does.

1958

Hugh genuflected towards the altar and sat down next to Flora in the pew, dealing with the lack of leg-room by turning his body to face her. 'These pews weren't built with men of my height in mind,' he joked mildly. Flora smiled but remained silent. 'I wonder if you'd like to tell me what brought you into church?'

'I was asking for guidance.' Hugh nodded and waited. Flora screwed her damp hankie into a ball. 'I've got to make a decision, you see. I was going to go to drama school. To train as an actress,' she added shyly, 'but I think I've decided that, actually, I want to be a nun.'

Hugh maintained his composure, frowning hard to stop himself from laughing. 'A *nun*? Now what makes you think you'd like to be a nun?'

'Well, I'd really like to become a better person. Dedicate my life to God. *Help* people, that sort of thing. And... I think living in a convent would be... nice and peaceful. I think I'd like that. I think it would help me to be good.'

'I see. Have you ever met a nun?'

'No.'

'Or visited a convent?'

'No.'

'Ah.' Hugh folded his hands together and rested them in his lap. 'You know, people tend to think life in an enclosed order is somehow easier than life outside. Quiet. Contemplative. But actually it's jolly hard work. I know because I used to be a monk, you see.'

Flora's lips parted as Father Hugh assumed even more ecclesiastical glamour in her young eyes. She swallowed. 'I've talked to Ettie about it and she said I should pray for guidance. She said God would make His plan for me clear but,' Flora sighed, 'He's taking His time about it.'

'Miss Sinclair is right, of course: prayer will certainly help to clarify things in your mind.'

'She's the only one who doesn't laugh at me wanting to be a nun. Or an actress.'

'It's a big decision to make. Certainly no laughing matter.'

'I've been thinking about it for *years*.'

'But you still don't feel certain?'

'No. Well, yes, I *do*. I feel absolutely certain that I want to be a nun. Then I change my mind and feel absolutely certain that I want to be an actress.'

Hugh suppressed a smile. 'Tell me, how do you feel about being Flora Dunbar?'

Flora stared at him. 'Well, I don't have a choice, do I? That's who I *am*!'

'My point exactly. You see, whether you become a dedicated nun or a celebrated actress, the fact remains you'll still be – will *always* be – Flora Dunbar. Although in either case,' he said with a twinkle, 'you could at least change your name.' Flora laughed. Hugh felt moved as he saw her anxious expression lift, some of the rigidity drop from her shoulders. 'You see, I suspect the problem – your biggest problem – is how you feel about being *Flora*. If you could just sort that out, it might not matter quite so much whether you become a nun or an actress.' Flora looked down and said nothing. 'You know, God will love you whatever you decide to do with your life. He won't love you any more for being a nun and He certainly won't love you any *less* for being an actress. Think of the parable of the Prodigal Son.'

Flora looked up again and said cautiously, 'I never really thought that story was very fair.'

'No, quite right! It's extremely *un*fair. But it's not a parable about rewards for being good. It's a lesson on the infinite forgiveness of God, how it's never too late to be sorry for what we've done. If you look at the story in that light, it's enormously comforting to all of us sinners.'

'I hadn't really thought about it like that.'

'As children we tend to grow up seeking approval. We think by being good we will earn our parents' love and very often we do. But we don't have to be good to earn our Heavenly Father's love. He does, however, expect us to be good for *goodness'* sake.' Seasoned preacher though he was, Hugh was disconcerted by Flora's steady, enraptured gaze. He changed the subject swiftly. 'I don't think I know your parents, do I?'

'No. My father's an atheist and my mother – well, she isn't anything really. They don't come to church.'

'So there's only Miss Sinclair to discuss these matters with?'

'And my brother Rory. But he thinks being a nun is a really stupid idea. He says I worry too much about things, things that don't really matter. But *he* never thinks about anything apart from music.'

'I see. Look, why don't you come round to the vicarage one day next week and have a cup of tea and a chat? My wife, Miriam, will be there of course,' Hugh added hastily, though Flora wasn't sure why. 'We could talk things over and...' He put his head on one side and smiled at her, 'perhaps say a prayer together? How does that sound to you?'

'Oh, yes, I'd like that very much! Would it just be... you and me?'

'Our conversation will be quite confidential, you need have no worries on that score. But I'd prefer you to tell your parents where you're going.'

'Oh, yes, I will.'

'Would Wednesday at seven suit you? I'm afraid I don't have a lot of spare time, what with parish council meetings, confirmation classes and so on.'

'Mrs Wentworth won't mind me taking up your time?'

'Not at all. She's quite used to it. My time is not my own in any case. It's all dedicated to the service of God and my parishioners – of whom you are one!'

Flora tugged nervously at the short hair above her ear, unsure how to thank Father Hugh for his generosity and understanding. She wanted to throw her arms round the enormous man and give him a hug but as soon as the thought entered her head she chastised herself for her childishness. She murmured, 'Thank you, Father Hugh—' then clapped a hand to her mouth and blushed. 'I mean, Reverend Wentworth!'

Hugh laughed loudly, revealing his white teeth. 'Oh, everyone calls me Father Hugh! Without exception.' She pulled at her hair again, embarrassed. His smile lasted a long time. Eventually he said, 'I wonder if I might ask you a personal question, Flora? It *is* related to what we've been discussing.'

Her initial reaction was to be thrilled to be asked a personal question, but then she wondered what it might be, whether answering it might entail telling a lie. Flora had done a lot of bad things and she knew God would forgive her, but she didn't think His forgiveness would extend to lying in church, let alone to the vicar.

'What did you want to ask me?' she said anxiously.

'I was curious to know if you'd cut your hair as part of your plan to become a nun?'

'Oh! No, not really. I used to have quite long hair.'

'Yes, I remember.'

'But I got fed up with it. I saw a film...' Flora decided not to mention the title. 'The actress had very short hair – and I liked it. So I got my brother to cut all my hair off. But I don't think he made a very good job of it. Looks terrible, doesn't it?'

'No, I don't think so.'

'My mother says I look like a boy.'

'No, not at all! I think it looks rather... *chic*,' Hugh said, savouring the foreign word.

The large blue eyes widened. 'Do you? Do you really? *Thank you!*'

Hugh had only a vague understanding of the word *chic*, but he saw that his intended compliment had hit home and was pleased he'd been able to reassure this troubled girl. It was, after all, hardly appropriate for him as her minister to point out that she was so utterly disarming in her manner, so ravishingly pretty, that it scarcely mattered what she did with her hair.

Chapter 4

1959

Despite her many blessings of youth, beauty and a handsome husband, Miriam Wentworth didn't appear to be happy. Within a year of moving into the spacious but gloomy vicarage she'd lost her bloom and rarely smiled. Instead she arranged her features to suggest a professional cheerfulness, the kind expected of clergy wives, whatever their personal circumstances.

Miss Thompson felt sure that Mrs Wentworth's discontent was caused by having to watch other women's babies being baptised at the font every month, 'And her with all those empty bedrooms up at the vicarage'. Miss Cartwright narrowed her eyes and declared that she thought there was more to it than that, but wouldn't be drawn into hypothesis.

For reasons not entirely clear to her, Ettie observed Mrs Wentworth closely and noticed she occasionally looked red-eyed, as if she'd slept badly. Those eyes were restless too, moving round the congregation, avoiding contact with parishioners. Ettie noted too that Mrs Wentworth's eyes rarely settled on her husband, even – and this surprised Ettie – during the sermon. Instead, Miriam Wentworth would look down at the prayer book clasped in her hands, her face impassive.

Suitably hatted and gloved for a formal visit to a minister, Dora sallied forth to the vicarage for what she feared might be a difficult interview. As a precaution she'd selected one of her older, larger handbags for moral support and had applied an authoritative shade of red to lips that seemed nowadays to be pinched in permanent disapproval of her teenage daughter.

The front door was opened by Mrs Wentworth in an apron, clutching a potato-peeler. She looked harassed and a little dishevelled, lifting a damp hand to pat an errant lock of hair into place. She ushered Dora in, avoiding her eye and began to speak in a monotone.

'Mrs Dunbar, how do you do? Do come in. Hugh's in the study working on his sermon. Let me take your coat for you. It's a little chilly today, isn't it? But much better than yesterday. Would you like some tea? Or perhaps you'd prefer coffee?'

As she listened to this mechanical recitation of pleasantries, Dora decided she'd heard more animation issuing from an *I speak your weight* machine. She requested tea and hoped she wasn't disturbing the vicar. 'I did telephone earlier to make an appointment.'

'Oh, yes, he's expecting you,' Mrs Wentworth replied listlessly. She opened a door and, without looking in, announced, 'Mrs Dunbar to see you, Hugh. I'll bring some tea.'

The phone rang. Mrs Wentworth froze and then said wearily, 'I'll bring it as soon as I can.' She hurried down the hall where she picked up the telephone and began another litany of platitudes.

Hugh was already on his feet, looming over Dora and shaking her hand firmly. Dora was taken aback and by more than his height. Flora had neglected to mention that the minister was both young and handsome. As Dora adjusted her prejudices along with the handbag on her arm, it occurred to her that as Hugh was twice Flora's age, he wouldn't seem young to her and therefore couldn't possibly appear handsome. Dora, now into her fifties, was old enough – and still young enough – to appreciate attention from a younger man, particularly one with a dazzling smile. She began to relax a little.

'Mrs Dunbar, do come in and take a seat. I'm pleased to meet you at last. Flora has told me so much about her family.'

'A lot of it uncomplimentary, I'm sure,' Dora said smiling.

'No, not at all! I think Flora realises that her unsettled state of mind is creating difficulties for everyone, not just her.'

Dora clutched her handbag on her lap. 'Reverend Wentworth, I'll come straight to the point as I know you are a very busy man. You are – as I'm sure you're aware – in a position of some influence over my daughter.'

'Yes, and I take that responsibility very seriously.'

'I'm sure you do. But I'm concerned whether or not there might be a conflict of interests.' She hesitated. 'Oh dear, this is all very difficult...'

'Please take your time, Mrs Dunbar. And speak freely. I'm sure

Miriam will bring us some tea soon,' he said doubtfully, cocking his head to listen. The sing-song soliloquy still echoed down the corridor.

Dora took a deep breath. 'Whilst I'm not a churchgoer, Reverend Wentworth, I am a believer – of sorts. My husband is a rabid atheist and it would incense him if I followed my inclinations, which would be to attend church with Flora and Ettie now and again. When Flora started to develop her religious enthusiasm I was pleased in a way. I thought it a healthier way to spend her time than hanging around in coffee bars, wasting her pocket-money on the juke-box. Flora is a dear child, but she's grown up in a rather strange way, I'm afraid, trying to be like her brother. They are twins,' Dora explained, 'and absolutely devoted to each other.'

'Yes, Flora has told me a lot about Rory. I'm under the impression that he's not just her brother but also her closest friend?'

'Undoubtedly. But I'm not sure a seventeen-year-old girl should have a seventeen-year-old *boy* as a best friend – particularly not one like Rory! He's a law unto himself,' Dora muttered in an undertone.

Hugh smiled amiably and said, 'I'd very much like to meet Rory. I gather he's a gifted musician?'

'Oh, yes. He has his heart set on playing the piano professionally and he'll be going to music college. Which is partly why Flora wants to go to drama school, I think. She won't have Rory stealing all the limelight. She does have *some* theatrical talent – she was a charming Titania in the school play – and her English teacher speaks highly of her ability. She's very pretty of course, so I don't doubt she has the makings of an actress, but whether she does or no, I wish to encourage the idea because the alternative...' Dora clicked open her handbag and plunged a hand into its depths in search of a handkerchief. 'The alternative would appear to be entering a convent.' She dabbed at her eyes. 'I'm here to ask you, Reverend Wentworth, if you would please do your best to dissuade Flora from this idea. I'm hoping that your judgement and experience in these matters will have convinced you that she has no sense of vocation, no natural bent towards the contemplative life. On the *contrary*,' Dora said with feeling, 'she is temperamental, self-centred and argumentative! And horribly spoiled,' she added with a warm smile. 'In short, Flora would make a *dreadful* nun.'

Hugh, who had listened to this long speech with his head bowed in thought, looked up at last. 'You will be relieved to hear, Mrs

51

Dunbar, that I'd already come to much the same conclusion myself.'

'Oh...' Dora relaxed her bulldog grip on her handbag. 'Oh, I'm so glad!'

'I've said nothing of the sort to Flora, of course. Instead I've been regaling her with anecdotes about my own experience as a monk and the difficulties of the cloistered life. I've tended to dwell on the lack of physical comforts, the simplicity of the food, the hard discipline of many hours of daily prayer.' The corners of his mouth twitched. 'I'm ashamed to say I've quite neglected to tell Flora anything at all about the spiritual rewards of such a life... May God forgive me,' he added, with a smile Dora thought nothing short of roguish.

'Oh, *bless* you!'

'I thought it best to treat Flora's soul-searching with the utmost seriousness. She deserves no less. At the bottom of it all lies a sincere wish to be a good person, a good Christian, and that's to be applauded and encouraged. I think Flora is aware how problematic her behaviour is for her family. She is full of the best intentions, I can assure you.'

'Oh, yes,' said Dora. 'The *intentions* are there. But as my father used to say to me – when I was much the same age, as a matter of fact! – the road to Hell is paved with good intentions.'

My mother abdicated responsibility to Hugh for saving me from a life of poverty, chastity and obedience. In this he was entirely successful, though Hugh's diversionary tactics turned out to be rather more radical than Dora had envisaged.

Dora and Hugh became great friends, much to my annoyance. She started going to church now and again, I think to show her gratitude. (To Hugh, not God.) I even suspected her of flirting with him. They shared a passionate interest in gardening and swapped cuttings and seeds. The exchange of horticultural catalogues generated such excitement in the pair of them, you'd have thought they were sharing pornography. Aged seventeen, I found their alliance incomprehensible and embarrassing. I was also jealous, so I took myself off to drama school in London where I hoped I would become the centre of attention.

1960

'Flora, darling, we can't *hear* you.'

The disembodied male voice rang out from the back of the stalls. In the silence that followed Flora looked up and stared blindly into the darkness, a hand raised to her eyes, shielding them from the bright lights.

'Oh. Sorry.'

The voice approached down the centre aisle of the tiny theatre and slapped a clipboard down on the front of the stage. Clipboard and voice belonged to an elegant young man dressed in a corduroy suit, silk shirt and flamboyant cravat fastened with a diamond pin given to him, it was said, by Gielgud. Toby Tavistock leaned on the stage, folded his expressive hands into a cat's cradle of digits and assumed what senior students referred to as his 'patience on a monument' look.

'Flora, sweetheart, I know you're meant to be raving mad, but don't you think the audience ought to be able to *hear* the words of the immortal Bard? After all, *Hamlet* is generally considered to be his greatest play – probably the greatest play in the English language.' Toby put his head on one side and arranged his mobile face in a travesty of a smile. 'So, ar-tic-u-late, darling.' He tapped his propelling pencil on the clipboard. 'Remember: eyes, tits and teeth and *sock* it to the gallery. That's all there is to it.' He broadened his gaze to include the rest of the assembled company who stood, motionless and attentive, in Tudor tableau. 'Can't imagine why we have to spend two whole years drumming the basics into you lot. It's all so bloody *obvious*.' He yawned, then with a sudden spasm of facial muscles, the smile was displayed again. 'Can we run it again, please, everybody? From the top, Act Four, scene five. And Flora...'

She spun round, startled, her legs unsteady beneath her thin white shift. Toby ascended the small flight of wooden stairs that led up on to the stage. 'Don't look so terrified, duckie! I'm not going to bite your head off – well, not if you do as I *say*.' He put his arm round Flora's narrow shoulders and drew her to one side of the stage. 'Look, sweetie,' he said, speaking in an intense whisper. 'It's all perfectly lovely, but could you possibly sing a little more... *lasciviously*?'

Flora didn't know what this polysyllable meant. Playing for time, she adjusted her coronet of artificial daisies, then said, 'Yes, of course.' She smiled in what she hoped was an accommodating way.

'Good girl! You see Ophelia has lost her *mind*. And she's lost it because...' Toby patted Flora's tummy in an explanatory way. 'She's up the spout.'

Flora gazed at him blankly, her eyes dull with exhaustion.

He persisted. 'She's got a bun in the oven...'

Shivering, Flora wondered how many hours it was since she'd last eaten.

'...And that bun is Hamlet's.'

At least four. Possibly five.

'And now she's taken refuge in *madness*. But you see, her madness is a manifestation – pre-Freud, of course! – of her troubled psyche, of her guilt and frustrated libido.' Behind Toby's gesticulating figure, Flora saw the student playing Laertes produce half a squashed Mars Bar from his doublet and swallow it whole. Toby, who appeared to be waiting for a response, sighed and took Flora's hand. 'She's singing dirty songs, darling, because she's *damaged goods*. So could you sing less... beautifully? She's not auditioning for the Elsinore Christmas panto.'

Flora heard sniggers behind her back and thought perhaps she was meant to laugh, so she obliged. 'I'll certainly try,' she added gamely.

'*Thank* you, sweetheart. Appreciate it.' Toby patted her on the cheek and turned away, clapping his hands. 'Places everybody, chop, chop. May I remind you, ladies and gentlemen, that the curtain rises in three hours. This rehearsal was meant to be a run-through not a *stagger*-through.' He descended the stairs at a trot and the blackness of the stalls enveloped him once again.

The ensuing scene – tragic in every sense – became the stuff of legend within the walls of that institution. Flora's fellow students had been unprepared for her to enter with a jersey hastily bundled under her shift, her belly thrust forward as if in the final stages of pregnancy. They were caught unawares by her improvised leers and lavatorial giggles. Laertes was unmanned by a nudge in the ribs followed by a hearty slap on his buttocks. Gertrude's tears of grief turned to tears of laughter and had to be stifled in the folds of her embroidered handkerchief. As Flora sidled towards the King, making lewd gestures with a bunch of drooping daffodils, the student actor's look of dread was genuine. These movements hadn't been rehearsed. His worst fears were confirmed as Flora climbed on to his knee, put an arm round his neck and began to sing tunelessly into his ear while toying with his cod-piece.

Toby would have stopped the scene sooner had he too not been helpless with silent laughter, laughter that abated only when he reflected that this was a final dress rehearsal and the paying public would shortly attend. Undoubtedly the wretched girl had a bent for comedy, but what *imbecile* had ever thought this dim but endearing little blonde was the stuff of tragedy?

Flora was hiding in her grave. The rest of the company were eating sandwiches and drinking cups of tea in the Green Room, but after the brief notes session with Toby, she'd fled to the only place she could think of where she might be alone, since even the peace of the girls' toilets had been disturbed by a steady traffic of female students, jittery with nerves, loud with high spirits and the pressing problem of how best to pee in a farthingale.

Flora had gone backstage in search of the coffin-like structure that formed Ophelia's grave in Act V. She climbed in, set Yorick's skull carefully to one side with the Gravediggers' shovels and abandoned herself to the luxury of tears.

She had failed.

She'd failed but she didn't understand how or why. She'd done what Toby asked (and everyone agreed that she hadn't misunderstood his direction) but nevertheless the entire company had laughed at her and Toby had forbidden her to incorporate any of the new elements into her performance. He had patted her yet again, said it had been 'a very interesting experiment', that laughter had been *just* what everyone needed. Even Dinah the wardrobe mistress, whom Flora adored and who could always be relied upon to furnish downcast students with a mug of tea and a chocolate digestive, had said a disastrous dress rehearsal was a good omen. 'The worse the dress, love, the better the first night. Always the way!' Flora had found this no consolation at all. Depressed, she'd declined the proffered biscuit tin.

Weeping in her surrogate grave, wishing she were in fact dead, Flora didn't notice a dark figure approach, eerie in the blue backstage light. A knock on the wooden wall silenced her. She held her breath.

'Flora? Is that you in there?'

'Jack?'

'What on earth are you doing? I came to look for you. Some of the girls were worried.'

Jack's face hovered, moon-like, above black velvet. He made a splendid Dane and Flora was half in love with him even before he'd donned his sombre costume. Thin and sensitive, Jack alone of all the boys in her year treated Flora with respect and took her acting ambitions seriously. Jack kept his hands to himself and was more interested in talking to Flora than removing her clothes. Having a chat with Jack didn't turn into a wrestling match. The other girls teased him and so did some of the boys. Flora heard one of them describing Jack as 'queer' but she didn't think he was all *that* strange, just different from the others. She liked him all the more for it. Flora felt safe with Jack and although she believed herself to be a little in love with him, she also felt sisterly towards him, as if he were more like a big brother than a potential boyfriend. Flora liked their relationship. It was straightforward and comforting. She'd passed an idle moment wondering if she would rather have Jack for a brother or a boyfriend. He would certainly have made a much nicer brother than Rory. For a start he was kind to her. *And* he loved Shakespeare. What more could one want in a man?

'You should go and eat something, Flora.'

'I'm not hungry.'

'You should still eat. Can't do a show on an empty stomach.'

'You sound like Dinah.'

'Well, she's right. Is it nerves?'

'No. Not really. I mean, I *am* nervous, but... No, it's not that.'

'Was it everyone laughing?' Flora chewed her lip and nodded. 'Thought so. You know, people only laughed because they were... *surprised*.'

'You weren't there.'

'I was watching in the wings.'

'Were you?'

'Yes.'

Her face brightened. 'Watching me?'

'Not just you. Everybody. I like to watch scenes I'm not in. I love the play.'

'Yes, so do I. It's my favourite. At least, it *was*.'

'What you did with the scene, Flora, I think it was right. And terrifically brave. Shocking, actually, but in the right way. It wasn't like you at all – it was as if you were *possessed*. You seemed *really* mad. I think that's why people laughed. Because it was quite scary and all so unexpected. But I don't think it was wrong.'

'Toby told me not to put any of it in tonight.'

'He said to keep the tuneless singing. And he said you should flirt with Claudius. With your eyes. That was your own idea. And it was brilliant.'

'Do you really think so?'

'Yes, I do. Toby just wanted you to... tone things down a bit. Well, quite a lot, admittedly, but he's kept your basic idea.'

'He thinks I'm an idiot. They all think I'm an idiot.'

'I don't. I think you're a jolly fine actress. And I just wanted to say... that I don't think you should give up.'

Flora looked away, shocked that Jack had divined her thoughts, thoughts she had hardly acknowledged, even to herself. She picked up the skull and stared into its eyeless sockets. 'Acting's awfully hard, isn't it?'

'Yes. It is. Harder than people think.'

'It's confusing. You forget who you're meant to be. I mean, *sometimes* I think the person on stage – Flora the actress – seems more real than *me*, Flora the student. I know who Ophelia is, what she's like, who she loves, I even know how she dies, but the funny thing is, I don't feel I know myself at all. Because I haven't got a script, I suppose.'

Frowning, Jack shook his head. 'What on *earth* are you on about?'

'Oh, I'm not explaining it very well. You know that dream everybody has – where you walk on stage and find you're in the wrong play? You don't know the lines and you don't know the moves and all the other actors *do* and they're waiting for their cue and hundreds of people are watching. That's how I feel. Not when I'm on stage – that's how I feel when I'm *living my life*. As if I'm in the wrong show. As if I've been in the wrong show for years and years and *still* don't know my lines. I don't mind telling you, Jack, there are times when I think I'll just do a bunk in the interval.'

'Can't do that.'

'Why not?'

'You know what they say: "The show must go on." '

'I suppose so.' Flora sighed then rose up out of her coffin, extending a regal hand towards Jack. He took it and handed her out, then made her an extravagant bow.

'The fair Ophelia!'

Flora curtsied deeply. 'Hamlet the Dane!'

'Break a leg tonight, Flo.'

'You too, Jack! Break a leg.' She squeezed his hand. 'Break *two*!'

He laughed and shook his head. 'You know your trouble, Flora?'

'No – what?'

'You never know when to stop.'

Chapter 5

1959

The source of Mrs Wentworth's discontent never came to light for in the summer of 1959, within a mere forty-eight hours, she sickened and died of poliomyelitis. The parish was shocked but rallied quickly. The flower ladies surpassed themselves with their heartfelt but tasteful arrangements for the funeral. Father Hugh was inundated with home baking and casseroles, few of which he can have touched to judge by the rapidity with which he lost weight. His hair grew longer; his face was strained; sometimes he even forgot to shave, an oversight his parishioners readily forgave in view of his tragic circumstances. Their minister bore his loss heroically but it was many weeks before anyone caught even a glimpse of his famous smile.

Ettie prayed hard to understand why such a good man should have to sustain such a terrible loss. To lose one's sweetheart in wartime was a tragedy, but not entirely unexpected. In any case, Ettie told herself, the loss was tempered by the knowledge that the loved one had died making the ultimate sacrifice. One was consoled to some extent by pride and patriotism. Moreover, the loss did not have to be borne alone. Everyone knew people who were in the same boat. No family was untouched. Just look at the Sinclairs and the Dunbars. Two fine young sons lost in the first war; Archie's brother and Ettie's Geoffrey killed in the second. But to lose a young wife to polio in the course of a weekend... It would be enough to cause a lesser man to question his faith.

Ettie grieved for Father Hugh and tried hard to think of some personal gesture of condolence she could make. After much deliberation she settled on the purchase of a copy of Eliot's *Four Quartets*. She very much wanted to inscribe the volume but hesitated lest this seem over-familiar. In any case, how should she sign her inscription? 'Ettie'? She doubted Father Hugh knew her Christian name was really Henrietta, referring to her as he always did as 'Miss Sinclair'. Should she write 'H. Sinclair'? Or perhaps 'Ettie

Sinclair'? Ettie settled for the last, believing it struck a balance between warmth and formality. She wrapped the book in sober brown paper, tied it with string and set off for the vicarage.

Ettie claimed she was happy with the face God had given her, but that wasn't strictly true. She wasn't prepared to tamper with it, but she was aware there was plenty of room for improvement. In an earlier age, with the help of horsehair padding and punitive corsetry, Ettie might have been described as a handsome woman. Her dark, luxuriant hair would not have been tortured into spurious curls by home perms; her large, myopic eyes would not have been screened by unflattering spectacles; her thick, well-defined brows might have seemed alluring, not mannish; her height might have seemed imposing instead of awkward; flowing drapery would have concealed a multitude of sins, including thick ankles and large, turned-out feet.

Ettie bore no resemblance to her pretty, blonde relatives. Her dark features and athletic physique (even Rory admired her tennis serve) harked back to the male Sinclairs whose photos adorned Ettie's dressing table in place of the lipsticks, powder puffs and bottles of scent so cherished by Dora and her teenage daughter. Three uniformed men, dead war heroes all, gazed solemnly at Ettie from silver frames as she brushed her hair: Henry and Roderick Sinclair, killed in action in the First World War and Geoffrey Summers, pronounced missing, presumed killed in 1941, aged twenty-four.

Ettie was not much given to regrets, which she considered self-indulgent, but if there was one regret in her virtuously uneventful life it was that her strict moral code had ensured young Geoffrey died a virgin and that, in all probability, she would too. For herself, she was not troubled by either curiosity or passion. She'd read several novels by D. H. Lawrence and had concluded that the satisfying of carnal appetites must be both enervating and undignified, but she regretted that she'd not felt able – as many other girls had – to make a gift of her virginity to Geoffrey before he went to the front. At the time it had seemed too great a sacrifice to make, but afterwards, in the light of Geoffrey's own, ultimate sacrifice, her moral scruples had seemed petty, almost a kind of selfishness.

Ettie was never sure if she'd done the right thing. She'd abided by her religious principles, but it wasn't at all clear to her whether that was quite the same.

Ettie barely recognised the man who opened the door to her. Stooped, unsmiling, hollow-eyed, Father Hugh seemed to her physically diminished. The strong bones of his face showed beneath his skin – skin that had lost its usual ruddiness. He was dressed in a dark woollen jumper and black trousers and it occurred to Ettie that she had never seen Father Hugh without his cassock before. There was something surprising, almost unseemly, about seeing his legs at last. They were remarkably long and ended incongruously in tartan carpet slippers. Casting her eyes downwards, taking a moment to collect herself, Ettie registered the red-and-yellow tartan as Buchanan, one of her favourites, then immediately chided herself for her frivolity. She wondered whether the late Mrs Wentworth had given her husband the slippers. Recalled finally to the sad purpose of her visit, Ettie held out her parcel.

'Father Hugh, I do hope I'm not disturbing you. Would you please accept this small gift? I wished to...' She faltered as he gazed at her blankly. 'I wanted you to know that you – and Mrs Wentworth – are in my prayers. You have my deepest sympathy.'

As if dazed, he appeared to take a moment to recall his visitor's name. 'Miss... Sinclair?' Ettie nodded confirmation. He didn't reach for the parcel and she began to feel both distressed and embarrassed. She couldn't leave until Father Hugh had relieved her of the gift, but clearly she was simply adding to his present difficulties. Her extended arm began to ache.

'It's a copy of Eliot's *Four Quartets*,' she said, waving the book slightly in the hope of drawing his attention to it.

'Oh?' He looked down at the parcel.

'You said once that you admired Eliot. We were discussing the Amateur Dramatic Society's production of *Murder in the Cathedral*.'

'Were we?'

'Yes,' Ettie replied, increasingly desperate. 'You said you wished you knew his work better.'

'Ah.' He reached out slowly and took the book. 'Thank you, Miss Sinclair. Thank you very much indeed. Such a thoughtful gift. I'm very touched.'

'Really, it's nothing. I just wanted...' All the tactful and encouraging words Ettie had planned to say evaporated and she fell silent.

'You lost your fiancé, didn't you, Miss Sinclair? In the war?'

Ettie was taken aback. 'Yes. I did, as a matter of fact. How on earth did you know that?'

'Flora told me. She said God had comforted you when your fiancé died.'

'Yes. He did. My faith was a great help to me. In fact, it was strengthened by my loss.'

Father Hugh nodded slowly but said nothing for a moment, then he sighed and spoke with what appeared to be an effort. 'I don't suppose you have time for a cup of tea, do you, Miss Sinclair? It seems rather a long time since I talked to anyone about anything other than death... and funeral arrangements.' His face was contorted suddenly by an attempt at a smile. 'Bereavement is a kind of plague, isn't it? People leave you alone to get on with it, but sometimes all one wants is to hear another human voice. I've been talking to God, of course... non-stop.' Father Hugh raised a hand to his forehead and rubbed his temple slowly as if his head ached. 'But so far He hasn't... responded. Either that or I simply can't *hear*.'

His distress was so palpable, Ettie felt her own composure begin to crumble. She said briskly, 'A cup of tea would be very welcome! But do, please, let me make it for you while you sit down. You look absolutely done in.' She moved forward into the doorway, past Father Hugh and headed along the dismal hall towards the kitchen. The musty smell was not the odour of death, Ettie told herself, merely rising damp and an accumulation of stale air occasioned by closed windows. Aware of Father Hugh's shuffling footsteps behind her, she breathed a short and fervent prayer for guidance.

The sink was full of dirty dishes and after filling the kettle Ettie insisted on tackling them. Father Hugh seemed either too weak or too relieved to protest and sank down on to a kitchen chair, staring at his parcel, as if trying to summon the energy to unwrap it.

Ettie rolled up her sleeves and glanced round the kitchen looking for an apron. She picked up a frilled, floral garment and then hastily replaced it on its hook. She felt sure Father Hugh would not relish the sight of a woman in his wife's apron standing at the kitchen sink. As she washed she talked about Eliot, then the last meeting of the Poetry Society. There was no response, nor could she hear the sound of her gift being unwrapped. Unable to bring herself to turn and look at the poor man, Ettie was debating whether to launch into the topic of the next Poetry Society meeting when Father Hugh said quietly, 'Miss Sinclair, what do you consider to be the worst sin?'

She spun round, dishcloth in hand and stared at him. 'The worst sin? Good heavens... Murder, I suppose. There's nothing worse than murder, is there?'

'No, indeed, but murder is a crime as well as a sin, isn't it? I was thinking more of the lesser sins we all commit in the course of daily life.'

'Oh, I *see*,' Ettie said, although she wasn't really sure she did. Turning back to the sink she scrubbed thoughtfully at a stained teacup. 'Well, deceit is pretty bad in my book. There's simply no excuse for it. And I've always found it well-nigh impossible to forgive cruelty. A weak soul might believe deceit is occasionally expedient – the lesser of two evils, perhaps – but cruelty of any kind is quite unnecessary.'

'I've always told my parishioners that God will forgive anything. If we will only repent and refrain from sin, He will forgive. Deceit. Cruelty. Even murder.'

'Yes, indeed. Christ died for us so that our sins might be forgiven. *All* of them.' Ettie placed the clean cup on the draining board and fished around in the bowl for sunken cutlery.

'But what about anger?'

'Anger?'

'Yes, anger... Anger with God.'

'I'm afraid I don't quite understand.'

Father Hugh's voice sounded uncertain, as if he were groping for meaning. 'He won't forgive me until I cease to be angry with Him. So I'm lost. In the wilderness. Not fit to serve God or guide my parishioners.'

She stared at his hands, clenched in tight fists, resting on the table either side of her still-wrapped gift. 'Are you saying you're angry with *God*, Father Hugh?'

'Yes.'

'For taking your wife?'

'No. I'm not angry with God for taking Miriam. I'm angry that He hasn't let me understand *why*.'

Poor Ettie. Poor Hugh. He thought she was safe. Just a friend. She was only five years older than him but he thought of her as a middle-aged spinster who shared his love of poetry. Which of course she was. But Ettie didn't see it quite like that. She didn't see Hugh for what he was. (But then which of us did?)

Hugh was looking for the ideal woman, the woman who would make him whole, the woman who would hold the key to his happiness, who could solve his puzzle. He had made a mistake with Miriam, whom he worshipped but could not love. He resolved that next time – if ever there were a next time – he'd marry for love and love alone. It was simply a question of finding the right woman.

And that certainly wasn't Ettie.

The irony was that Ettie, who asked so little of life, might have been happy with Hugh. A life of skivvying for my mother and feeling beholden to relatives meant that her expectations of life were low. Her world fell apart the day after her sixteenth birthday and it was shattered again when she got the news about Geoffrey. After that Ettie made a life out of scraps, like the horrible patchwork quilts she used to make for orphanages.

Ettie wouldn't have made Hugh happy and she certainly couldn't have prevented him from falling in love, but she might have turned a blind eye when he finally did.

1962

'*What?*' The saucepan slipped and fell crashing on to the draining board.

'Ssh, Rory – Ma will hear you! I said I'm going to be married.' Flora took another wet plate and dried it carefully.

Rory stood with his rubber-gloved hands plunged in the sink and stared at his sister, stupefied. '*Why?*'

'Because I'm in love! Why else would anyone get married?'

'Who to?'

Flora braced herself. 'The Reverend Hugh Wentworth.'

'The *vicar*?'

'Yes.'

'Flor, are you out of your tiny little mind? He's ancient!'

'You've never even met him.'

'I've seen him. He came to our school once, years ago, to give a talk. About leprosy. He's old enough to be your father!'

Flora sighed but was relieved to find herself on well-prepared ground. 'Our father was old enough to be our mother's father. Anyway, I really don't see what age has to do with anything.'

'Have you told Dad?'

'No, not yet. I haven't told Ma either. Hugh wants to ask formally for my hand in marriage, so at the moment we're just unofficially engaged. It's a secret,' she said, smiling shyly.

Rory scrubbed viciously at another pan with a Brillo pad. 'You can't seriously be thinking of marrying a *vicar*!'

'Why ever not?'

'Because... because you just aren't cut out to be a vicar's wife! I thought you wanted to act?'

Flora thought of her brief, inglorious career as a student actress and the gauntlet of importunate male hands she'd run. She flushed and rubbed at the pattern on a teapot, for all the world as if she expected Aladdin's genie to appear and grant her a wish. 'Oh, that was just me being silly. I don't suppose I would ever have been very successful,' she said wistfully. 'Anyway, I'd much rather be doing something *useful*, something worthwhile. Like parish work.' Flora couldn't help noticing how vague, even lame, the words sounded as she uttered them. 'You'll like him, Rory, I know you will! He's a wonderful man. A *good* man... and funny... and so handsome! We talk and talk, about everything under the sun – not just religion.'

'Have you slept with him?'

Flora caught the teapot as it slipped. '*Rory!*'

'Have you?'

'Of course not!'

'Then how do you know you love him? How do you know he loves you?' He turned his head and looked at Flora, puzzled. 'Doesn't he want to sleep with you?'

'There's more to marriage than sexual relations,' Flora said with the calm conviction of one totally ignorant of both marriage and sexual relations.

'How far have you let him go?'

'Rory, for goodness' sake! He's a minister of the Church of England!'

'Well, he's also a man – I presume?'

Dawning realisation diverted Flora's mind from the tart reply she was about to make. 'Have you slept with Grace?' she asked in a shocked whisper.

'Yes,' Rory lied. 'Well, practically… We've slept together but we haven't… *done* it yet. But I know she wants to.' Rory pulled the plug with a flourish and watched the dirty water spiral down the sink.

'How do you know?'

'I just know.' He peeled off the rubber gloves and tossed them on to the draining board. 'There are ways of *telling*.'

Flora was disconcerted at the thought of her brother in bed with Grace and briefly visualised them both naked. Feeling a blush rise suddenly from her neck she said firmly, 'Well, I want to be a virgin on my wedding day. I'm saving myself for Hugh.'

'Why?' Rory turned round, leaned against the sink and folded his arms. He stared, uncomprehending. 'If you're going to marry him anyway, why do you have to save yourself? What's the point?'

'Because sexual intercourse outside marriage is fornication. It's a sin.'

'Oh, don't give me that!'

'Hugh says marriage is a sacrament.'

'And what's that supposed to mean?'

Flora did know, because Hugh had told her, but she had difficulty now recalling precisely what he'd said. She tended to get distracted from *what* Hugh said by *how* he said it. She could remember looking into his kind, brown eyes and listening to his soothing voice talk about matrimony as a remedy against sin. This had sounded comforting at the time but she didn't think it would satisfy Rory who was clearly trying to confuse her with his awkward questions. He didn't seem the least bit pleased for her and hadn't even said congratulations, so she took refuge in resentment.

'I wish I'd never told you! I wanted you to be the first to know. I thought you'd be pleased for me.'

'Pleased you're making the biggest mistake of your life?' he replied with a cruel smile. 'You must be joking. You are joking, aren't you? Tell me you're just pulling my leg.'

Flora folded her wet tea towel carefully and hung it over the rail of the Aga. 'No, Rory. I am more serious than I have ever been in my life. In fact your cynical attitude, your flippant remarks have helped me see the rightness of what I am doing. They have strengthened my resolve.'

Rory snorted with laughter. 'Here endeth the first lesson!'

Flora ignored him and lifted her chin. She spoke in the clear, ringing tones she'd cultivated for her audition speech as Saint Joan. 'I feel even more convinced now that Hugh is the right man for me and that our marriage will be blessed by God, if not *you*, Rory Dunbar. I'm sorry you aren't happy for me. I'm sorry and very disappointed, but I shall pray for you. And,' she added primly, 'for Grace.'

As she turned away Rory grabbed hold of her wrist, circling the small bones, crushing them with his long fingers. 'Don't you bloody *dare*.'

Grace decided eventually to let Rory have what he wanted. He hadn't asked in so many words but in their silent grapplings on her single bed, his state of excitement left her in no doubt. At first Grace found this embarrassing, then she decided it was flattering. Eventually she decided it was – if she were honest – rather exciting.

Before Grace left home for music college her mother had been garrulously informative on the subject of teenage boys who apparently only wanted one thing. Grace had found this to be untrue. Rory wanted lots of different things, some of which she'd let him have and which they'd both enjoyed, but Grace knew there was more to give and more to be taken and that she needed to make up her mind what *she* wanted.

What she didn't want was to lose Rory and, despite his passion for her body and her cello-playing, she feared she might. He often had an abstracted air, as if his mind were on other things. Grace feared the other things might be other girls. Rory and Grace didn't talk a great deal, except about music. He wasn't good with words. She thought perhaps if they made love it would bring them closer together and dispel some of his febrile tension. Grace was disappointed in these expectations, but Rory's gratitude and energetic lovemaking almost compensated for the lack of conversation. Grace was satisfied and happy and, with her mother's warnings still ringing in her ears, she assumed Rory was too.

He wasn't. He was, however, exhausted much of the time, which at least allowed him to ignore the uncomfortable fact that, despite having almost everything he wanted in life, Rory was neither satisfied nor happy.

Hugh was a few minutes early for his appointment with Archie Dunbar so he lingered by the flowerbeds as he approached the front door of Orchard Farm. He admired the tapestry of plants Dora had woven, noted that much of their colourful effect was achieved by skilful juxtaposition of foliage, not flowers. A woman's touch. What was a home or indeed a garden without it?

Hugh looked at his watch again and strode up the path. Standing in the porch he checked his shoes for mud and removed a seed-head that had attached itself to the hem of his carefully pressed cassock. He rang the bell and said a rapid, entirely selfish prayer for his own deliverance. The sound of galloping feet on the stairs was followed by women's voices raised in altercation. Footsteps retreated, then the front door swung open revealing Dora, her welcoming smile already in place as if she'd known who would be on the other side of the door – which she had.

'Hugh! You *are* punctual! Do come in, it's lovely to see you. You must come and look at the roses. *Gloire de Dijon* is a picture! But maybe later,' she added tactfully, 'After you've seen Archie?' The question hovered anxiously, as did Dora, who looked as if she would have been glad of a coat, hat and umbrella to dispose of, but the fine summer's day had thwarted her.

Hugh glanced up and saw Flora standing at the top of the stairs, her face pale and anxious. He felt a familiar fullness in his heart at the sight of her, smiled broadly but decided against a wave. Flora greeted his smile with an answering flutter of her fingers. Dora indicated Archie's study and ushered Hugh through the open door.

The room was comfortable if shabby. Faded curtains of indeterminate hue and pattern hung at a window looking out on to the garden. Worn rugs were laid over dark varnished floorboards and the walls were decorated with a few aged botanical prints and an antique map of Scotland. Two walls were book-lined and a side table was heaped with scientific periodicals and newspapers.

Archie, seated at his desk as Hugh entered, rose immediately and walked round to greet him. Hugh noticed that Archie didn't seem a great deal taller standing than sitting. A short, burly man in his early seventies, bald, but with ears, nose and brows over-compensating, Archie showed no sign of feeling dwarfed by Hugh's height. A retired professor of botany, he was used to dealing with lanky Cambridge undergraduates who'd acknowledged him a tartar with an infectious enthusiasm for his subject.

Introductions were unnecessary. Hugh and Archie had met briefly at the village fête and discussed varieties of tomatoes, a conversation that had done little to pave the way for what was about to follow. Dora retreated to the door, muttering about something on the hob. Finding his mouth suddenly dry, Hugh was disappointed not to have been offered a cup of tea. As the door shut, Archie extended a plump, freckled hand to indicate an armchair in an advanced state of collapse. 'Will you take a drink, Reverend Wentworth? Whisky? Sherry?'

'No, thank you, Mr Dunbar, I won't.'

'You won't mind if I do?'

'Not at all,' Hugh said, sinking deep into upholstery. 'I'm an Anglican, not a Methodist.'

Archie shot him a look from beneath shaggy white brows. An alarming wheeze began to issue from the old man's throat. Hugh realised with relief that this was laughter. He watched as Archie poured whisky from a decanter, diluting it with a splash of water from a jug. His hands were steady; Hugh noted that his own were not.

'Before you say your piece, Reverend,' Archie said, waving his glass in Hugh's general direction, 'I'd like to say mine. Then you'll know how things stand between us.'

'Yes, sir. Thank you.'

'I don't want my daughter to marry and I certainly don't want her to marry a clergyman. She's not yet twenty! She may think she's old enough to know her own mind but her mother and I remain unconvinced. However,' Hugh detected a softening of the faded blue eyes. 'We *do* want her to be happy and she has made strong representations to us that her future happiness is entirely dependent on becoming Mrs Hugh Wentworth.' Archie sighed and drank deeply. 'In just over a year Flora will be able to marry whom she pleases, so when all's said and done, the most I can do is put the brakes on.'

'Sir, I had no intention of marrying Flora before she reaches her majority, even if you gave your permission. Believe me, I am as concerned as you about her ability to make the right decision about her future. I'm here to request your permission to ask Flora to marry me so that we may become officially engaged. That will regularise our position. I am aware that my friendship with Flora has caused a few eyebrows to be raised in the parish.'

Archie narrowed his rheumy eyes and looked at Hugh, trying to gauge his man. 'Do you love her?'

'Yes, sir, I do. Very much.'

'Aye, she's a pretty little thing. But hardly domesticated! Not what I'd call wife material – not yet, anyway. Both my children have their heads full of music, poetry, plays, what-have-you. Neither of them lives in the real world.'

'They're young, sir. And artistic. I'm sure as Flora grows older she will mature. Especially with guidance.'

'From you?' Archie asked, gruffly.

'And from God.'

Archie gave Hugh another long look but refrained from comment. He emptied his glass and said, 'You need to know the financial situation – which isn't good.'

'Sir, my stipend, though modest, is quite enough to support a wife.'

'And a family?'

'Yes. Not in the manner to which Flora is accustomed, it's true. Ours will of necessity be a simple life.'

'It is easier for a camel to go through the eye of a needle, than for a rich man to enter into the kingdom of God.'

Hugh nodded. 'You know your Bible, sir, even if you don't believe in it.'

'Oh, aye. Where I come from the Bible was rammed down our throats more regularly and with greater relish than food. I'm afraid my antipathy is born of long and harsh experience, Reverend.'

'I'm sorry to hear that. You're aware then that the Eye of the Needle was the name for a narrow gate in the wall round Jerusalem?'

'Is that so?'

'A camel could only pass through the gate if it was first relieved of its loaded saddlebags. I've often wished King James's translators had made that clear. I think all Our Lord meant was that it might be *easier* to lead a God-fearing life if one lived it unencumbered by material possessions. He wasn't saying it was impossible. Christ was a realist.'

'Flora tells me you used to be a monk.'

'Yes. For some years.'

'Why did you leave the monastery?'

Hugh had prepared answers to many different questions but this one took him by surprise. 'I wasn't suited. I'm too much a man of the world, I suppose. I missed my books. I missed music. I was happy in many ways but felt... incomplete. *"Monks live unloved and die unwept"*. Who was it said that? I found I yearned for a wife and family almost as much as I yearned to serve God. It was a rather painful process of self-discovery. Although my spirit was more than willing, my flesh was weak. I hadn't realised how weak.'

Hugh was conscious he'd said too much – none of it likely to strengthen his suit. Archie was watching him intently, his eyes sharp but not unkind. 'You're an interesting man, Reverend. I'm beginning to see why my daughter thinks you might be her salvation. Look, I'll be frank with you. I'm seventy-one. My wife is fifty-five. The house is Dora's until she dies and that's all there is. There's no money. Such savings as we had have been entirely consumed by Rory's musical training, then Flora's damn-fool drama school fees. There is nothing for the children to inherit but this house and another in Wester Ross which no one will take off our hands because it's falling down. Dora still has some jewellery. That will go to Flora and Rory will get the piano, of course. They'll have to squabble over the house after Dora has gone. But do you see what I'm saying? You must be able to support Flora. She has no money of her own and shows no inclination to earn a living – nor much talent for it. On the face of it, Reverend, you have to admit you're not a good catch.'

'No, sir, I quite agree.'

'How old are you?'

'Forty-one.'

Archie shook his head slowly as if this were yet another blow. 'You want children?'

'Of course. So does Flora.'

'Well, take my advice and have them soon. I'd hoped to provide better for mine but I was fifty-one when they were born. Dora had given up hoping and by then we'd ploughed a lot of money into the house and garden. The twins were a late and unexpected blessing, but an expensive one. For much of their lives we've lived on my pension and Dora's family money which is nearly all gone.'

'Believe me, sir, I had no financial expectations. But Flora is far from being a worldly creature. She's unlikely to hanker after luxuries, I think. Books do furnish a room, as the saying goes. I have plenty of those.'

'Aye, she loves books, always has. She lives in a world of make-believe. But books don't put bread on the table or shoes on bairns' feet.'

'No, sir, but you can rely on me for that.'

'Can I now?'

'I give you my word. The ministry is not a lucrative calling but the church provides an adequate roof over its servants' heads. That's one thing Flora will never have to worry about.'

'Well, Reverend—'

'Hugh. Please call me Hugh. As an atheist it must go against the grain for you to revere a minister of God.'

Archie wheezed again, his face crumpling into wrinkles. 'Aye, it sticks in ma craw, right enough! I thank you for your honesty, Hugh, and your generosity of spirit! Aye, I like you more and more. And if you're to become my son-in-law – God help you, laddie, if you do. She'll lead you a merry dance! – we'd best be on first-name terms.' Archie reached for the decanter. 'Will you not have a whisky now?'

Hugh, smiling with relief, said, 'No thank you, sir.'

'*Archie.*'

'Archie.'

'I wish you joy of my daughter, Hugh – but not yet. Wait a year and then...' Raising his glass the old man said, 'I wash my hands of the pair of ye!'

All things considered, Hugh thought the interview had gone well, much better than he might have hoped. As the front door closed he felt a weight lift from his heart and he thanked God for delivering him from this particular lion's den. The sun was shining and the air was full of rose scent and the humming of bees. He decided to circle the house and look for Dora who would no doubt be working in the

72

garden. *Gloire de Dijon* was indeed glorious as it rambled up and over the walls of the house.

There was no sign of Dora but Hugh stood on the bumpy croquet lawn for a while admiring the view. Through a gap in the beech hedge he caught sight of the scarlet flowers of a row of runner beans climbing up wigwams of canes. He remembered with a sudden pang long, hot days spent working in the kitchen garden at the monastery. Silent, repetitive and arduous labour had calmed his mind and body and nourished his soul. He'd been happy then, in his way.

The peace of the garden was broken by the sound of a piano. Hugh assumed someone was playing the gramophone or wireless very loud, then remembered Flora talking about her brother who was a music student. Hugh listened more attentively and recognised a Schubert sonata. The music was coming from the ground floor, through French doors that opened on to a small terrace where Dora had placed terracotta pots of cascading ivy-leafed geraniums. Hugh didn't want to disturb Rory but he did want to listen to the music and perhaps catch a glimpse of Flora's twin. He walked slowly across the lawn towards the open doors.

Hugh recognised the sonata now as Schubert's last. He would have known sooner but Rory's playing of the piece was unlike any performance he'd heard before. He was hearing things in the music he had never noticed, even though he knew it well. Rory eschewed sentiment, even beauty, in favour of stark intellectual clarity. Since the piece was composed by a young man two months before he died of tertiary syphilis, Hugh thought Rory's bleak interpretation as valid as any, but he did wonder what a nineteen-year-old boy could know of such loneliness and despair.

As he approached the music room Hugh saw that Rory had his back towards the windows. Stepping silently on to the terrace, he listened and looked. Flora's brother, dressed in jeans and T-shirt, was of slight build, although broad in the shoulder. His forearms were muscular, his skin pale like Flora's, but dusted with freckles. His hair was a darker, sandier shade of blond, thick and heavy, not flyaway like Flora's. It swung as he moved his head in time to the music, revealing damp tendrils plastered to the back of his neck. Rory swore suddenly but carried on playing. Hugh had detected no fault. As the music built to a loud climax, Rory's head bent lower in concentration, his hands moved faster. A line of sweat appeared between his shoulder blades, darkening his T-shirt. As the last chord reverberated, Rory was still, his hands resting in his lap. Without turning round he said, 'You must be Hugh.'

Hugh was too astonished to reply. He stepped backwards, bumping into an urn. Rory swivelled round on the piano stool to face Hugh. It was Flora's face, but harder, colder; Flora's bright blue eyes faded to a wintry grey; Flora's laughing, mobile mouth stilled into a long, sensuous curve – a curve suggesting that its owner relished Hugh's current embarrassment.

'I'm so sorry – did I disturb you? I tried not to move.'

'I saw you in the mirror.' Rory pointed to a mirror hanging over the mantelpiece. 'Ma placed it there so she can view the garden when she's playing. You've been there a while.'

'I was listening... I'm sorry if– Look, I'd better introduce myself properly.' Hugh entered through the French doors, his hand extended. 'Hugh Wentworth, vicar of St Edmund's.'

'And my prospective brother-in-law.' Unsmiling, Rory took the proffered hand without standing and shook it briefly.

Hugh noted the length of Rory's fingers, warm and damp from playing. 'Flora's told you then?'

'Not exactly. I know how she feels about you. But I don't know why,' he added.

Hugh laughed. 'No, neither do I!'

'Are you going to marry her?'

'I've just been to see your father. To ask for Flora's hand in marriage.'

'What did he say?'

'He wasn't happy about it. Which is understandable of course. But I think we came to an understanding.'

Rory said nothing. He looked up from his seat on the piano stool, tilting his head back to take in Hugh's full height. Scrutinised by this strange young man, Hugh once again felt at a loss.

'How old are you?' Rory asked.

'Forty-one.'

'You look younger.'

'Thank you.'

'It wasn't intended as a compliment. I meant my father must have got a hell of a shock when he found out. I presume you told him?'

'Of course.'

'So – are you marrying Flora?'

'We're to become engaged next week, on her birthday. Your birthday,' Hugh added with a warm smile which Rory did not return. 'The plan is that we'll marry when she comes of age.'

'Well, that gives her plenty of time to change her mind.'

'Yes... Which is what I want.'

'You want her to change her mind?'

'No, of course not! I meant I want her to be certain.'

'Are you?'

'Of course!' Hugh's mouth was suddenly dry. He wished someone would offer him a cup of tea. He wished he could see Flora or even her mother – a friendly face. He braced himself and tried again. 'Rory, I can see my relationship with Flora doesn't meet with your approval, but I do hope that, in time, we'll become friends.'

'Why? You're marrying Flora, not me. You and I have nothing in common apart from love for Flora – which is a fairly limited topic of conversation, if you ask me.'

'I'm sorry you feel that way. But I think I understand why.'

'I doubt it. Now would you mind leaving me in peace so I can get on with my practice?' Without waiting for an answer, Rory turned his back on Hugh and rearranged his music.

'Of course. I beg your pardon. I'm very sorry I disturbed you.' Hugh retreated to the French doors, then added tentatively, 'I'd just like to say... I enjoyed your playing of the Schubert. Very much indeed.' Rory raised his head and looked into the mirror. Hugh's eyes shifted to the reflection and met Rory's impenetrable gaze. 'That hardly seems adequate. It was... It was a revelation to me. I've never heard anything like it.'

'No, I don't suppose you have. But then you've led a rather sheltered life, haven't you?' Rory's unblinking gaze didn't waver. Hugh opened his mouth to reply, then turned and went out into the garden. He walked back to the vicarage with his head bowed, deep in thought.

Hugh knelt before the plain wooden crucifix in his bedroom and prayed for guidance. He'd expected the interview with Flora's father to be difficult – more difficult in fact than it had been – but despite

Flora's warnings, he hadn't reckoned with Rory. Hugh's confidence was shaken, his previously firm resolve weakened. He wanted to do what was right – most particularly what was right for Flora – but he no longer knew what would be right.

Hugh clasped his large hands together tightly so that his knucklebones shone. He asked God what he should do and waited for calm to settle on his mind, for certainty to emerge from his confused and contradictory thoughts. Hugh waited until his knees felt numb, until his joints locked with tension, until the light at the bedroom window failed.

For a second time, God did not speak to Hugh. In the yawning silence all Hugh could hear was a faint echo of Rory's sardonic voice saying, 'You've led a rather sheltered life, haven't you?'

Chapter 6

It was no whirlwind romance. Hugh and I took several years to come to the catastrophic conclusion that we should marry. It didn't occur to me for a long time that what I felt for Hugh might be love. How would I have known? All I knew was, what I felt for Hugh was quite different from what I felt for Rory, who up till then had been the most important person in my life apart from me, so I assumed what I felt must be love.

Hugh negotiated the Dunbar family obstacle race with ease, which was only to be expected. As a parish priest his social skills were honed and he was naturally warm, humorous, unthreatening. Dora grudgingly accepted my choice, knowing he would be a steadying influence on me; Ettie approved of Hugh, if not my marriage to him; my father didn't have a leg to stand on since Hugh was respectable, solvent and the age gap between us was not much more than the one between my parents. Archie would no doubt have liked to disapprove, but could find no real reason to do so apart from deploring Hugh's religious beliefs. So he compromised by withholding his blessing, which seemed to him the act of a reasonable man and Hugh – likewise a reasonable man – agreed.

Rory was the only difficulty. Rory would not be wooed. He made no attempt to get to know Hugh, but made it plain he didn't like him. I couldn't see why. Hugh was – is – a cultivated man and he was perfectly able to discuss music and musicians with Rory. Hugh made valiant attempts to befriend his future brother-in-law and appeared not to notice the snubs he received in return.

I was touched by Hugh's persistence and furious with Rory for being rude and unkind. I asked him why he was so vile to Hugh and he either couldn't or wouldn't explain. Once when he'd had too much to drink, Rory told me Hugh was 'a bloody hypocrite', which didn't make any sense to me since Hugh's religious beliefs were sincerely held and he always acted upon them. (I believed Hugh to be a truly good man. I still do, if one accepts that it's possible to be good without being honest; that in fact it's sometimes necessary to be dishonest in order to do good.)

Rory and I drifted apart once I got to know Hugh, but we drifted much further than we might have simply because Rory refused to accept Hugh as a member of the family. Privately, Rory prophesied doom and gloom for the marriage which drove a wedge between us and upset me more than I thought he realised. But he did realise. He knew exactly what he was doing. (Rory always knew what he was doing, but we all preferred to pretend that he didn't.)

Rory told me the marriage wouldn't work – couldn't work – and Rory was right.

It was a quiet wedding. My parents put on a brave face and made the best of it. I think Dora consoled herself with the notion that if I hadn't chosen Hugh I might have settled on an even less suitable candidate. (A fear I later confirmed for her – in spades.)

My brother behaved abominably. I assumed he was angry with me for hijacking his twenty-first birthday. He scowled throughout the reception, avoided Hugh and snogged Grace at every opportunity. He was barely civil to me, but since he'd already told me he thought I was making a big mistake, I wasn't surprised. I tried not to let his attitude spoil my big day, but of course it did.

Ettie wished us well and seemed genuinely pleased. Even though she clearly thought I was too young to be married (let alone to someone Hugh's age) she told me I was very lucky and that she hoped we'd make each other happy. There was something about her wan smile that said she knew we wouldn't.

Grace was thrilled. I think she hoped matrimony might be catching. She drank too much champagne, cried, hugged us both and said we were a beautiful couple. She giggled suggestively when we were in the Ladies' together, talked knowingly about the honeymoon and asked whether we'd already 'jumped the gun'. I didn't understand what she meant – I too had drunk a lot of champagne – and must have looked confused. She squeezed my hand. 'Don't worry about a thing, Flora,' she said in a patronising whisper. 'It really doesn't hurt that much and once you get used to it, it's lovely!'

Grace meant well and I was grateful for the reassurance, especially since my mother had been totally silent on the subject of my marital duties. But Grace was wrong, could hardly have been more wrong. It hurt like hell, I was never given the opportunity to get used to it and it was never lovely.

Not with Hugh.

Looking back, a few years later, I could see why things went wrong, or rather, I could find reasons why things had gone wrong. (They weren't the right ones but I wasn't to know that.) I was twenty-one, a virgin and thought myself very much in love with a man I scarcely knew. Hugh and I got off to a bad start and things went downhill from there.

My period started unexpectedly the day before the wedding. I was mortified and almost crippled with stomach cramps. Our wedding night saw me curled up with a hot water bottle while Hugh stroked my hair to soothe me. He didn't attempt to stroke anything else. I was very glad. Despite Grace's enthusiastic recommendation, I was frightened of what lay in store for me and was perfectly happy just to be held in this huge pyjama-clad man's arms. I could hardly believe that sexual intercourse itself could bring me any more pleasure or excitement than the sensation of being surrounded by so much moral and physical strength, such quantities of bone, flesh and muscle. I felt safe, I felt happy. If Hugh was disappointed, he was too kind or good-mannered to let it show.

I was still a virgin at the end of our very short honeymoon. When we arrived home at the vicarage I went down with a virus. As I was recovering, Hugh succumbed, so we'd shared the marital bed for more than three weeks before Hugh ventured to lay a proprietorial hand on me. We'd developed a way of being together that was affectionate but deferential. It was loving in its way, but that way wasn't sexual, wasn't even physical.

From the beginning I looked to Hugh for guidance in all matters, especially sexual. He was after all a widower. It dawned on me only gradually that things were not quite as they should be, but I wasn't about to break the habit of a lifetime. I assumed the fault was mine.

I was usually in bed when Hugh came upstairs and often asleep. He liked to read and write late at night. He said he found it easier to think when it was quiet. I think he meant when he was alone.

When we'd been married for about a month he surprised me by

closing his book when I said I was going up. He smiled and said he was ready for bed too. The ambiguity of that remark didn't strike me at the time, but as he followed me upstairs I began to feel a little flustered. I went into our bedroom to undress before going to the bathroom. Hugh followed. I had hoped he would go into the bathroom so that I could undress alone. I wasn't used to Hugh seeing me in my underwear and I still didn't feel comfortable undressing in front of him. When he started to undress in front of me I averted my eyes for reasons that I didn't understand, didn't even examine. I think I was afraid to look, even though I knew I wanted to. I suppose I was afraid of seeming brazen. I was unacquainted with my own body, which I never saw or felt naked except for the purpose of washing, so to look at a man in a state of undress seemed to me almost perverted. I couldn't think of any reason why I should want to do such a thing, yet I knew I did. I refrained, but felt guilty nevertheless. Guilty for wanting.

Hugh sat down on his side of the bed and started to unbutton his shirt. He cleared his throat and said softly, 'Flora... do you think we might—' I must have looked alarmed as he added immediately, 'Is it the wrong time of the month? I've lost track.' He walked round the bed, laid his hands on my shoulders, bent and kissed me on the forehead. 'We don't have to, if you don't want to. I don't want to impose.'

'It's not an imposition, Hugh. I love you! I want us to be man and wife... properly. I'm just a bit nervous, that's all. Especially after all this time.'

'Darling, don't be! I wouldn't hurt you for the world'. He kissed me again, this time on the mouth but his hands didn't move from my shoulders. 'Let's get ready for bed, shall we?'

We both undressed on our respective sides of the bed, I quickly, Hugh slowly, so that as I turned and drew back the sheets I saw him standing nonchalantly half-naked, his pyjama jacket in his hand, the trousers hanging loosely on his hips. Curling black hair sprouted from his chest. Straighter, silkier hair surrounded his navel and formed a sleek arrow pointing down below the waistband of his trousers. I stared at the shadowy valley between his belly and hipbone, following the miraculous curve, so beautiful I felt breath expelled from my body in shock.

I had no idea what men looked like. I'd never seen one. I had felt

Hugh in our chaste embraces but I had never really looked at him, never seen the magnificence of him. Tears pricked at my eyes and I didn't know if it was his beauty that moved me or relief that I felt what could only be desire. I was still terrified of lying beneath this great mountain of a man, but at least I knew it was what I wanted.

Hugh pulled on his jacket and looked across at me. 'Darling, are you all right?'

'Yes... I was just looking at you. Thinking how very splendid you are. In every way.'

He climbed on to the bed, crawled across the candlewick bedspread and took me in his arms. 'I do so want us to be happy.'

'We are happy!'

He laughed. 'Yes, we are, aren't we?'

I put my arms round his waist and slid my hands up inside his pyjama jacket, running them experimentally over his back which felt smooth and hard and quite unlike the yielding fleshiness of my own body. Hugh hugged me to him and through my thin nightdress I could feel the hardness in his groin. He kissed me again, this time with his mouth open. The bulge became harder and even more alarming.

Hugh reached for the switch on the bedside light. I was glad of the sudden darkness. I heard him pull back the covers, then he lifted me as if I were weightless and laid me on the bed. He lay down beside me and started to pull up my nightdress. Instinctively my hands pulled it down again and I felt him hesitate.

'Flora?'

'I'm sorry. I wasn't thinking.'

He pulled up my nightdress again, very slowly, in a way that I imagine was meant to be reassuring. Then I felt his warm hand between my legs and I cried out in alarm. 'Hugh! What are you doing?'

'I'm trying to make you ready for me. If I touch you… down there… it will be easier. If you aren't ready for me I might hurt you. And if I touch you, I will know when you are.'

'Can't I just tell you?'

'Well, yes, of course you can! But I meant when your body was ready.'

'How will you know that?'

'You'll feel moist, darling. It's something that happens when a woman becomes aroused.'

'Oh. I see… Don't worry about hurting me, Hugh. I expect it to hurt. I know it does the first time. I really don't mind,' I said bravely, glad that he couldn't see my face in the dark.

'It might not hurt all that much, if we take things slowly. Look, are you sure?'

'Of course I'm sure. Please—' I was going to say 'Let's get it over with,' but stopped myself just in time.

I'm sure Hugh was as gentle and considerate as it is possible to be and I know now that he was not so spectacularly well-endowed as to cause a woman discomfort, but at the time he seemed to me barbaric. I had never known such pain, such humiliating, animal pain and was not to know it again until I gave birth.

Hugh inched into me slowly and carefully but such consideration merely protracted the pain. I was rigid with tension, every muscle in my body braced to repel the invader. By the time he lay inside me I was weeping silently, my hand pressed to my mouth, hoping that he couldn't hear me.

The pain of Hugh entering me had been bad enough but it was nothing compared to the pain when he moved inside me. I felt as if I were being sawn in half, as if I were being violated with a carving knife. I couldn't prevent myself from crying out, clutching at Hugh, digging my nails into the flesh of his shoulders.

'Flora, my dear – shall I stop? I can't bear to hurt you like this.'

I took several deep breaths. 'No. I'm all right… Really. It's just… the shock.'

'It will be easier next time. I promise you, it will never hurt like this again.'

The pain seemed to ease off slightly as we talked but as soon as Hugh started to move again it returned. I threw my arms round his neck and pressed my lips together until I could bear it no longer, then gave way to sobs.

Suddenly Hugh was still, panting, his weight crushing the breath out of me. He rolled off me on to his back and the bed subsided with a creak of mattress springs. My insides seemed to be leaking out of me on to the sheet where I lay and I thought I must be bleeding to death. I sat up gingerly and switched on the bedside lamp. Hugh didn't stir. My thighs were wet and sticky but there was not a great deal of blood. I didn't know what to do to clean myself up and took a couple of handkerchiefs out of the bedside drawer. To my astonishment,

Hugh appeared to be already asleep, lying on his back, breathing deeply. I got out of bed stealthily, took a clean nightdress from another drawer and went to the bathroom.

I locked the door and gave way to tears. I couldn't stop myself crying – with pain, disappointment and something that felt like shame. I thought of what Grace had said and I hated her. I thought of Rory asking me if I'd already slept with Hugh and hated him. I sat down on the closed lavatory seat with my arms wrapped around my abdomen. My body felt battered, abused. I was appalled that such an event could occur, such an assault could be perpetrated in the name of love. I felt as if I'd been raped, but of course I knew I hadn't. I couldn't imagine feeling any worse if I had been raped, though of course I knew I would.

I rocked back and forth on the lavatory seat, staring into the abyss of my marriage.

The next time Hugh tried to make love to me, a fortnight later, he was impotent which didn't seem to surprise him very much. He was, however, quite upset, too upset to notice that I wasn't. I was relieved.

If we could have talked then, if we could have confided or even laughed, things might have improved, but silence congealed between us, a silence born of my ignorance and his guilt. We both refrained from discussing or even really acknowledging our problems because we loved each other too much to speak honestly.

As the weeks went by I felt more at home with Hugh physically, if not sexually and when we attempted to make love again I tried, in my very innocent way, to be loving and encouraging. This time when Hugh was impotent I wasn't relieved, I was disappointed. Without my knowing how or why, my body had tipped the scales for me. Something had changed. Now I wanted Hugh more than I feared him. It felt like a light dawning, a door opening. I began to have an inkling of what Grace might have meant when she spoke to me on my wedding day. I thought perhaps Hugh and I might have the power to make each other happy. But if the door had been unlocked by my curiosity and awakening desire, I couldn't pass through it without Hugh's help. Yet clearly he needed mine.

1963

Flora liked cleaning the church. It was boring work, cleaning things that weren't even dirty, but not difficult. Since she had to carry out the work in church she couldn't answer the vicarage telephone for the duration, which meant she didn't have to be polite to anyone, or helpful, or sympathetic. She could simply dust and polish, at liberty to think her own thoughts.

More often than not, Flora discovered that she had no thoughts; that when she stopped performing her rôle as clergy wife, it was as if she'd ceased to be. A blankness descended upon her. When people were no longer petitioning her as 'Mrs Wentworth', Flora began to wonder who she really was. She couldn't understand why Hugh had said, all those years ago when they'd first discussed her future in this very church, that whatever she decided to do with her life she'd always be Flora Dunbar. It simply wasn't true. She couldn't remember the last time she'd felt remotely like Flora Dunbar.

She thought hard and polished hard. The polishing seemed to help the thinking. (Or was it the thinking that helped the polishing? Flora wasn't sure. Flora wasn't sure of anything any more.) The last time she'd felt like herself – like Flora Dunbar – had been when she'd seen Rory. That was weeks ago. Months probably... The family had gone to a concert to hear Rory play and Flora had been able to wear something pretty for a change. In his off-hand way, Rory had seemed pleased to see her. They had laughed together until Flora's stomach muscles hurt. She couldn't remember now what was so hilarious. In fact, it can't have been all that funny because when she explained the joke to Hugh, he didn't laugh, he only smiled politely.

As she bent to tidy hassocks in the choir-stalls, Flora's back ached and a dragging sensation in her abdomen announced that her period would shortly begin. She hadn't really thought she could be pregnant, even though she was two days late. It wasn't very likely, but it was *possible*. Some progress had been made.

Flora decided she was relieved. The thought of cleaning the vicarage, shopping, cooking, washing and ironing Hugh's surplices, weeding the garden, mowing the lawn, delivering the parish magazine, baking for fêtes, running the Brownies and answering the telephone, all while pregnant, seemed to her an absolute impossibility. She didn't see how she would manage, so it really was a blessing she hadn't yet conceived.

But when Flora thought of a *baby,* that was different. Flora pictured herself as a Madonna cradling a black-haired, brown-eyed child, a son, a miniature Hugh. She saw herself sitting up in bed with the baby, surrounded by flowers, receiving visitors, opening presents, eating chocolates and not having to answer the telephone because she was too busy, busy looking after a baby, which seemed to Flora the most important job in the world.

She laid a hand where she thought her womb might be and wondered if, when she did conceive, she would bear twins? This thought had never occurred to her before. Did twins produce twins? Would there be two little Hughs? Flora tried to visualise a brace of dark babies but failed. The only picture that came to mind was a photograph of her and Rory, pale and flaxen-haired, sitting in their double pram, their chubby, inscrutable faces enveloped by white fur hoods, as cosy and identical as broad beans nestling inside their downy pod.

Flora couldn't help it. It was stupid to cry, she knew that. She wasn't even sure why she was crying because she knew she didn't want to be pregnant, but since there was no one in church to hear her cry she found she didn't care. Let God see how unhappy she was. What was the point of pretending since He knew everything anyway?

'Mrs Wentworth? Are you all right?'

Flora wheeled round and peered down the aisle. In the gloomy light she saw Miss Thompson standing in the doorway, removing her coat and headscarf. It was her day on the flower rota. She stood bright-eyed and vigilant, her head cocked on one side like a bird. 'Are you feeling unwell, Mrs Wentworth?'

Flora took out a hankie and wiped her nose. 'No, I'm fine thank you, Miss Thompson. Just a bit under the weather.'

'Would you like some help? We could do the silver together. I always think that's such a chore.'

'Oh, thank you, you're very kind. But I've almost finished now.'

'Well, if you're sure there's nothing I can do to help?'

'I'm sure. Thank you. I'm fine. Really.' Flora felt her womb protest again, mourning its emptiness. She thought again of the twin babies in their pram. Could she actually remember being in that pram with Rory? Or did she just remember the photograph? 'I'm just missing my brother, that's all.'

'Oh, I see,' Miss Thompson replied, uncomprehending. She'd

heard about the Dunbar boy. Talented apparently, but harum-scarum. Hadn't seen the inside of the church since he was held over the font.

'He's my twin. I don't see him very often nowadays. He's a music student and he lives in London,' Flora explained. 'He's performing in a concert tonight and I was thinking about him. Wishing I could be there to see him. Although I don't know why – his playing always used to make me cry!' Flora dabbed at her eyes with her hankie. 'I love to listen to him play but I can never really cope with seeing him do it. Sometimes it just leaves me feeling... *wrecked*.'

'How strange! Why should that be, I wonder?'

'I don't know. There's an odd quality about his playing. It's not just moving, sometimes it's... shattering. When I see Rory play – especially when he plays in public – it's as if I'm watching a man wrestle with his soul.'

'My *dear*!' Miss Thompson said, suppressing a shudder. 'How very unpleasant for you!'

Not long after I was married, Rory performed at the Jubilee Hall in Aldeburgh with Grace and one of their friends, Michael, a violinist. Since Aldeburgh was fairly local for us, a family outing was organised. The expedition was considered to be too much for Archie but Dora and Ettie were delighted to accompany Hugh and me.

As we took our seats for the concert the hall was welcoming, humming with anticipation. I scanned the programme, eyes blind with nervousness. I knew Rory and Grace were playing a Ravel piano trio with their college friend in the first half of the programme. I also knew I would take in nothing of the second half – a Haydn string quartet – having just watched Rory play.

Dora grumbled about the hard seats and hoped that the music wouldn't be 'too modern'. Hugh, who had obviously done his homework, reassured her that the piece was composed in 1914 and so we would probably be 'all right'. I turned my scattered attention to the audience which consisted largely – and I use the word advisedly – of elderly ladies in hideous frocks. There were only a few young people, some casually dressed, possibly music students.

Eventually the lights went down, the trio made their way to the front of the platform and my stomach turned over. I realised I hadn't seen Rory for weeks. After these gaps I always expected to see the brother I remembered – a boy. Rory the man, being taller and broader than I remembered, always came as something of a shock. Both he and Michael – the latter gangling and bespectacled – looked uncomfortable in their DJs, but Rory's at least fitted him well. It looked to me as if he'd forgotten to brush his hair and I wondered how Grace hadn't noticed. She looked stunning in a strapless burgundy velvet gown that made the most of her opulent figure. Her long dark hair was loose but drawn back on one side with a jewelled clip. She looked radiant as she acknowledged the audience's welcoming applause; both men looked bad-tempered with nerves – or in Rory's case concentration, since, as far as we knew, he didn't do nerves. His fingers flexed suddenly, hinting at energy waiting to be unleashed.

They took their places. Rory watched Grace arrange the copious folds of her dress around the cello and then he turned back to the piano. Neither Grace nor Michael lifted their bows to play and I wondered if something was wrong, then Rory started to play and I realised the trio began with solo piano – a simple, shimmering phrase of hopeless yearning.

I'm not sure I breathed during the first movement. When the music stopped there was a fusillade of coughing from the matrons, then the trio continued. Afterwards Hugh referred to it as 'a communion of souls' and he was right. Their eyes never met, but I watched them weave their hearts and minds together into one miraculous strand of music. At one point towards the end Grace tossed back her hair and closed her eyes, ecstatic. I felt a sudden, sharp pang of something that I suppose was envy.

During the interval Dora said she thought Rory's playing had been too ferocious in the final movement. 'I felt sorry for the poor piano. Why does that boy have to be so angry about everything?' Hugh disagreed and said he'd found Rory's passion very moving. Ettie asked me if I thought Rory was a chamber musician or whether he was really a soloist. I was still trying to compose myself and, without giving it much thought, I said the latter.

She sipped her lemonade and nodded. 'I'm inclined to agree. He's such a powerful personality on the platform, isn't he? He draws the eye – even away from Grace! She looked lovely, didn't she? And so happy.'

After the concert we trooped round to the artists' entrance and were shown to the dressing room. As I knocked on the door we heard shouts and a loud pop, followed by laughter. We found Rory pouring from a foaming bottle of champagne, filling glasses held by Grace. She shrieked as one overflowed and handed it quickly to Michael who passed her another. Rory appeared to be haranguing Michael about a tempo, an argument that resolved itself in sudden raucous laughter. Grace moved closer to Rory, slid a plump, bare arm round his waist, resting it on his hip. 'Rory, you might at least acknowledge your fan club.'

He raised his glass to us, his eyes shining and said, 'Cheers! Thanks for coming, folks.' Michael handed us glasses of champagne and we all drank to the trio. Grace arranged chairs for Dora and Ettie who thanked her and complimented her on her dress. She blushed and looked pleased. 'It's impossible to look elegant sitting there with your legs apart – you have to go for either dramatic or unobtrusive.'

'Remind me – which were you?' Rory said caustically.

'Dramatic, of course. I like to give you a run for your money.' She grinned at me and said, 'Flora, didn't you just adore that spooky bit in the Passacaglia, when Rory shuts up and let's Mike and me get on with it? It's the highlight of the trio, isn't it, Mike?'

'Oh – was Rory playing?' Michael asked vaguely, blinking behind his thick lenses. 'Can't say I really noticed.'

Rory lobbed a cork at him and muttered, 'Pearls before swine.' He grabbed another bottle of champagne and thrust it at Hugh without looking at him. 'Open that, Hugh, will you?' Rory grabbed my arm and pulled me towards him. 'Well – what did you think? I see I made you cry as usual.'

'Could you see?'

'No, of course not. But I can see you now.' He raised a hand and smeared his thumb under my eye. 'Your make-up's run.' He turned from me abruptly and sat down at an upright piano in a corner of the room and started to play Scott Joplin's Maple Leaf Rag impossibly fast, which made me laugh, as it always did. 'So – tell me what you thought of the Ravel.'

'It was brilliant. You were brilliant.'

'Is that all? Just "brilliant"?'

I walked over to the piano and flung my arms round his neck, bent my head to his ear and said in a husky, theatrical drawl, 'Dahling, you were marvellous!'

Rory continued to play with me draped round his neck. 'Oh, come on. You can do better than that.'

'You were magical! Stupendous! Coruscating!' Laughing, I released him, then covered his eyes with my hands and felt his lashes flutter for a moment like butterflies against my fingers. He carried on playing blind, not missing a beat or fluffing a note.

'So you liked it then?'

Still laughing, my hands still covering Rory's eyes, I glanced up at Hugh. He was watching the pair of us with an odd expression on his face, one I didn't think I'd ever seen before. There was admiration there, but also something else, something that looked to me suspiciously like jealousy.

1963

As they drove back to the vicarage after the concert Flora couldn't rid herself of an uneasy sense of guilt, as if she'd somehow excluded Hugh or hurt him in some way. He'd been unusually quiet during the journey but it was very late and he'd had a long and difficult day, hospital-visiting and administering last rites to a parishioner who'd died at home. Hugh was good at comforting the sick and bereaved and much loved for it, but Flora knew such things took their toll. She felt she'd somehow added to his burden, without knowing why. They sat silently side by side, staring through the windscreen into the darkness, each marooned by their own thoughts.

As they were getting ready for bed Hugh asked Flora if she thought Rory was pleased with how the concert went.

Stifling a yawn, Flora said, 'Yes, I think so. In so far as Rory is ever pleased with his own playing. He thinks he's good, but never good *enough*.'

Hugh smiled. 'Like someone else I know.'

'You mean me? Do you think we're alike?'

'Oh, yes, very much so. Only you're much prettier, darling.'

'I meant, do you think we're alike as people? I've always thought we were chalk and cheese.'

Hugh didn't answer immediately, folding his trousers carefully and smoothing them on the hanger. 'Yes, you are different as people, but... Well, there's something about twins, isn't there? Boundaries are a little blurred.'

'What do you mean?'

'Well, you and Rory are different. But I'm not sure you're *separate*.'

'I don't understand. You've lost me.'

'Oh, don't mind me, I'm just philosophising.' He smiled wearily. 'A secret vice of mine. I was thinking of a quotation from Aristotle. It came to me this evening when I saw you and Rory together in the dressing room. *"A single soul dwelling in two bodies."* Of course, Aristotle was actually defining friendship.'

'A single soul? Oh, that's lovely! Hugh, you are clever! I must remember to tell Rory about that.'

It didn't occur to Flora until much later, when she tried to recall the quotation, that if she shared a soul with her brother it meant they each possessed only half, which somehow didn't seem quite so lovely. Her thoughts then took a morbid turn and Flora wondered whether having half a soul reduced one's chances of eternal salvation. Was Heaven out of the question if you were an incomplete soul? Was Purgatory a more likely final resting-place, the eternal waiting-room where the spiritually incomplete were doomed to loiter, waiting impatiently for their other halves to join them? Feeling rather depressed, Flora decided not to mention the Aristotle quotation to Rory after all.

He would only have laughed at her anyway.

Chapter 7

If you wanted to point the finger of blame you might have said it was Rory who ruined my life, or Hugh with his well-meant lies, or even my poor son Theo (who, as he pointed out, never asked to be born and eventually wished he never had been). But actually blame must be laid at the door of the Bishop. It wasn't Rory or Hugh or Theo or Colin or any of the other men whose names and faces I've long since forgotten who ruined my life, but the demon drink. And it was the Bishop (God bless him) who drove me into that particular demon's wide and welcoming arms.

1964

Flora had never entertained a bishop before. She hadn't even spoken to one since she'd been confirmed. Hugh said she wasn't to worry, Peter was a jolly nice chap and that she shouldn't feel as if she were 'on show'. It hadn't occurred to Flora to think this until Hugh mentioned it as a possibility. Thereafter she felt sick with apprehension at the thought of the eminent man's visit and set about purging the vicarage with Dettol and Ajax. She also began to study cookery books, going so far as to ring Dora to ask for advice on recipes.

'Well, bishop or no bishop, darling, men always love puddings.'

'Steak and kidney?'

'No, Flora, I meant desserts. Apple pie. Trifle. That sort of thing.'

'Oh. Hugh and I usually eat fruit. He says it's good for you. Sometimes we have bananas and custard.'

Dora sounded doubtful. 'I don't think you could serve that to a bishop, darling.'

'No, I suppose not.'

'You can't go far wrong with a sherry trifle. Everyone loves trifle – especially if you're generous with the sherry! It needs to be a sweet sherry, though.'

'Do you have a recipe?' Flora asked, her pencil poised above her notebook.

Dora laughed. 'Don't be silly, you don't need a recipe! You just soak some boudoir biscuits in sherry – you could use a Swiss roll, but personally I don't like the jam – then you pile on the fruit. Fresh is always nicer, but you could use tinned at a pinch. But not fruit cocktail! That doesn't taste of anything at all. Then you cover it all with thick custard and when that's set, you decorate it with whipped cream. Nothing could be simpler.'

Looking at her hastily scribbled notes, Flora thought on the contrary, bananas and custard were *much* simpler, but she thanked her mother for her help and replaced the receiver.

There was a small selection of bottles in the sideboard where Flora kept alcohol. Most of these had been given to Hugh at Christmas by grateful parishioners. The bottles rarely emerged. Hugh occasionally offered sherry to couples during wedding interviews, believing that a small drink helped everyone relax. There was a whisky bottle, almost untouched. Hugh had made Flora a hot toddy when she'd had a bad cold, but she'd hated it and said it made her feel worse. The bottle of brandy was unopened but Flora felt comforted by its presence. She knew that in cases of shock, particularly bad news, brandy was administered and so the bottle made her feel prepared for emergencies.

Flora looked at the labels on three different bottles of sherry. None of them was described as 'sweet'. She wondered whether 'Amontillado' was Spanish for 'sweet'. She took the three bottles out of the cupboard and set them on the dining table. Withdrawing the cork from one, she sniffed experimentally. The aroma transported her immediately to Christmases past and vivid memories of the glass of sherry and mince pie she and Rory used to leave on the mantelpiece for Santa Claus. She remembered explaining to Rory that the disappearance of the mince pie and the presence of crumbs on the plate the following morning proved beyond all doubt that Santa did in fact exist. Rory had remained sceptical. His recent experiences at boarding school had modified his world-view. Rory's universe now encompassed the existence of unkind, deceitful grown-ups, the least of whose sins might be removing a mince pie with intent to mislead.

Flora poured a small amount of sherry into a glass, then raised it to her lips. It didn't taste particularly sweet, or indeed pleasant. She wondered whether sherry could go off. Pouring from a different bottle, she sipped again. This one tasted sweeter and more palatable. She took another mouthful to confirm her judgement, then set the glass down. Opening the third bottle, she sniffed, then poured, feeling as she did so quite proud of herself for dealing with the investigation in such a thorough and scientific way.

Having savoured the third sherry, Flora decided it was not as pleasant as the second, even though it was sweeter. Her preference was for Number Two, but Dora had said men had a sweet tooth, so perhaps the Bishop would prefer Number Three? Flora decided to sample Number Two again and gazed down at the glasses on the table. She couldn't remember which was which. Had she stood the glasses next to their respective bottles? She thought not and realised she hadn't been quite as scientific as she'd intended.

Picking up the glass containing sherry Number Two she took a mouthful and realised at once that this was in fact Number One. She pulled a face, swallowed, then set the glass carefully next to its bottle. Flora raised another glass which she thought was probably Number Two. She sniffed, then still uncertain, took a mouthful. It was getting rather difficult to tell now but she believed this was almost certainly Number Three which was really much too sweet, even for a bishop.

Feeling a little like Goldilocks, Flora raised the remaining glass to her lips and swallowed. Yes, this was just right! Pleased with her own decisiveness, encouraged by the warm feeling of her own certainty, Flora drained the glass for no better reason than that she wanted to. She set it down in triumph. She knew that her trifle would be a splendid confection, that the Bishop would shower her with compliments and that Hugh would be proud of her.

Really, it had been so *silly* of her to worry about the Bishop's visit! Hugh had said he was a jolly nice chap and although Flora had never met him, she felt sure the Bishop *must* be a jolly nice chap if he was a friend of Hugh's, who was himself a jolly nice chap.

All in all, Flora concluded, as she corked the bottles and replaced them haphazardly in the sideboard, it was a jolly nice world when you came to think about it. She simply couldn't imagine *what* she'd been worried about.

When Hugh appeared for supper Flora surprised him by suggesting a sherry before dinner. Without waiting for a reply she marched into the dining room to fetch the bottle from the sideboard. Examining the labels carefully she extracted Number Two and poured out two glasses.

The apéritif raised Hugh's hopes that dinner might for once be something substantial or at least unusual, so he was disappointed when Flora asked if rissoles and bananas and custard would be all right. He said, 'Yes, of course,' then put his unfinished sherry on the kitchen table. 'It's a bit sweet for me, darling. Not really a sherry man, to be honest. But it was a nice thought.' He smiled apologetically. 'I'd love a cup of tea.' Pleading paperwork, Hugh headed towards his study and Flora set the kettle on the hob.

When she turned round, Hugh's glass, hardly touched, caught her eye. Flora debated with herself for a moment. She decided that she would take Hugh his tea, wash up and peel some potatoes before she allowed herself to finish off his sherry. After all, it would be a pity to waste it.

It was the first of many such deals Flora made with herself.

It wasn't that drink made me feel happy. It made me feel myself. I remembered who I was, or rather who I'd been. Drink turned me back into the lively, funny, attractive girl I felt sure I used to be.

There were great gaping holes in my life and I papered over them with booze. I felt I'd been deprived of a proper marriage, babies and my family. All I had left was Hugh and God, both of whom were proving an inadequate substitute for the things I'd lost. Drink didn't give them back to me, but it made me mind less.

So to begin with I wasn't drinking to forget, I was drinking to remember. Drink heightened all my senses, made me feel alive. It dispelled the dismal fog of life at the vicarage and gave me access to sunny memories of my childhood at Orchard Farm.

I suppose drink made me miss Rory less.

1964

As Dora wrapped and labelled Christmas presents she thought how sad it was that this year neither of the twins would be present on Christmas Day. Rory was spending the day with Grace's family and this year as last, Flora and Hugh would be busy with a vicarage Christmas, beginning with a family carol service and then Midnight Mass on Christmas Eve, followed by Holy Communion and a sherry party for friends and lonely parishioners on Christmas Day itself.

Christmas was a busy and stressful time for a clergy wife and Dora had invited her daughter and son-in-law to stay for a couple of days afterwards so they could have a well-earned rest and celebrate the New Year at Orchard Farm. Rory and Grace had also been invited and Dora hoped that, with all her family assembled once again, it would seem quite like old times.

1952

'Rory, there's no such word as *mekon*.'

'There is.'

'No, there isn't. You made it up, just so you could get rid of one of your Ks.'

Rory stood abruptly and went over to a pile of opened presents spread under the Christmas tree. He picked up an *Eagle* annual and returned to the table. He opened the book at the contents page and ran his finger downwards. He cried 'Ha!' and thrust the book under Flora's nose. She took the book and read *Dan Dare and the Mekons*.

Flora looked up at Rory who was already placing his tiles on the Scrabble board. 'But it's not a *proper* word! It's just a made-up word for silly creatures from outer space,' she said scornfully.

'It's still a word.'

'But you won't find it in the dictionary, so it doesn't count.'

'Who says?'

'Everybody! In Scrabble you can only use words that are in the dictionary.'

'I bet it *is* in the dictionary,' Rory said, throwing down his pencil.

'Well, go and look then.'

Rory rose again and went to the other pile of presents under the tree. He returned with Flora's new dictionary and started to thumb the pages.

'Give it here! I shan't believe it unless I see it with my own eyes. You're quite capable of *lying*,' Flora said severely. She took the book from her brother and found the page. Her lips moved silently as her finger ran downwards. 'Mmm... As I thought. No Mekon.'

'Show me!'

Rory tried to grab the book but Flora held on tight and recited with some difficulty, '*Megrim... meiosis... Meissen... melancholy...* You see? No Mekons.' She handed the book to Rory.

'But it *is* a word.'

'Yes, but it isn't in the dictionary, so you can't have it.'

Rory was struck by a flash of inspiration. 'It doesn't *need* to be in the dictionary because everybody knows what it means!'

'I didn't.'

'That's because you're a girl and you don't read *The Eagle*.'

'Well, then – not everybody knows what it means, do they? And if it was a *real* word, it would be in the dictionary, wouldn't it?' Flora savoured her moment of triumph, but it was a Pyrrhic victory.

Rory pushed his tray of letter tiles away. 'This is a stupid game.'

'Just because you're losing!'

'Actually,' he said, pointing to the score pad, 'I'm *winning*, but I can't be bothered to play any more. Not till you get a better dictionary anyway.' He picked up his *Eagle* annual, hugged it to his chest and stalked out of the room.

Flora was livid. She knew she'd been right, but somehow Rory had still managed to win. Before packing the game away she took up her pencil and added a zero to the end of her score.

1964

Ettie and Flora cleared away the remains of the Stilton, port and mince pies while everyone else adjourned to the music room, leaving Archie to doze and digest in front of the fire. Dora set up the Scrabble board on a card table.

'Are you playing, Rory?'

He shook his head. 'I wouldn't want to humiliate you again, Ma, not after the ignominy of yesterday's defeat. But if you get stuck I'm happy to make a few suggestions.' He seated himself at the piano and started to sort through sheet music. Dora, Hugh and Grace sat round the table and began to help themselves to letter tiles from a cloth bag.

'You'll find the dictionary to your left, Grace, on the shelf,' Dora said. 'We keep it handy as Rory is inclined to be argumentative when he plays. He's been known to coin new words when in a tight spot.' She added in a stage whisper, 'Can't bear to lose, you see.'

'If you're not careful, Ma,' said Rory sounding dangerous, his hands poised above the keyboard, 'I shall play Bartók. *Fortissimo*.'

Dora's tiny hand fluttered and clutched at her throat. 'Good Heavens, anything but that! We shall be quiet as mice!' She turned and winked at Hugh who smiled indulgently.

Rory played Debussy instead, so beautifully that Hugh found it impossible to give the Scrabble game his full attention.

Later Rory brought everyone coffee and brandy, then hovered, looking over the shoulders of the Scrabble players.

'Go away, Rory,' said Dora. 'I'm planning something quite devastating and I don't want you spoiling my concentration.' Rory pulled a face behind Dora's back for Flora's benefit and moved away. He drew up a chair and sat down next to Hugh.

'I'll help poor old Hugh, then.'

'Poor old Hugh doesn't need any help, thanks very much,' Hugh said amiably.

'With three Os and an X? I admire your confidence.' Rory stabbed at the board with a long forefinger. 'You could make "moron".'

'Trust *you* to think of that,' Flora said as she helped herself to more brandy.

Rory looked up. 'Well, it would get him a double word score and it strikes me he needs all the help he can get.'

Ignoring him, Hugh leaned across the card table and placed several tiles on the board. Rory's mouth fell open.

'*Oxymoron*? What the hell is *that*?' He held out his hand. 'Dictionary please, Ma. The man's desperate.'

'It's a figure of speech,' Hugh said calmly. 'When you put two words of opposite meaning together for effect. "Organised chaos", that sort of thing. Look it up if you like.'

'Oh, well *done*, Hugh!' Dora exclaimed, clapping her hands together.

Hugh added up his score, which was impressive. 'But thanks anyway, Rory.'

'What for?'

'Your suggestion.'

Flora whooped with laughter and drank her brandy.

Dora sat in front of her dressing table, removing her earrings. Archie had already retired to one of the single beds that had seemed so much more sensible as husband and wife grew older. Archie was a light and restless sleeper, often up at dawn, pottering in the greenhouse in summer; in winter sitting by the Aga, wrestling with a crossword. Dora had suggested twin beds when symptoms of the menopause had left her drenched with sweat night after night. Since the marriage had long ago dwindled into a state of affectionate physical self-containment, she saw no reason why their double bed shouldn't be moved to the old nursery to make a guest room for the children and their future spouses.

Dora unscrewed the lid of a jar of cream and dipped her fingers in. She assumed Rory *would* one day acquire a spouse. She wouldn't have been disappointed if he eventually married Grace – a good-natured girl, steady, warm-hearted, if perhaps a little dull – but Dora suspected the love ran one way. Grace was clearly besotted. She touched Rory constantly, watched him when he moved or spoke. When Rory was out of the room Dora had a sense that Grace's life was in abeyance, waiting for him to return. But what did Rory think of Grace? Dora realised she hadn't the slightest idea. She couldn't recall Rory ever saying anything about Grace except in answer to a question. Choosing not to explore this surprising avenue of thought, Dora spread cold cream on her face, wondering as she did so whether, at fifty-seven, it was really worth all the effort, but the routine had become a soothing ritual and helped unravel her tangled thoughts before bed.

Grace would make a loyal, loving wife and doubtless a good mother. Childbirth would hold no fears for Grace with her wide accommodating hips. As she removed the last of the greasy cream Dora wondered whether Grace's hips were already accommodating Rory. She thought it likely given the length of time they'd been courting. The physical intimacy they shared suggested to Dora that certain boundaries had been crossed some time ago. She supposed too that if her son put his considerable mind to it, he'd be quite capable of seducing a young woman. Questions of moral rectitude had never troubled Rory (so different from his sister!) and he was a personable young man. Gazing at a favourite photo on her dressing table of the twins, aged ten, standing outside the house in Wester Ross, Dora tried to visualise Rory as Grace must see him.

A slim young man of medium height with a quantity of thick, fair hair – far too long and untidy, but a modern girl like Grace wouldn't mind that; a compact, athletic body with elongated, expressive hands; large eyes – so like Flora's, but a dark sea-grey. And about as warm, Dora thought. It had never been easy to guess what Rory was thinking and, faced with that unnerving stare, Dora hadn't always wanted to know.

There was sensuality in the wide mouth; the rare smile when it came lit up his face with a radiance that didn't quite reach his eyes, as if he were keeping some part of himself reserved, untouched. The suggestion of strength, even stubbornness in the jaw only served to remind Dora what a handful Rory had been as a child. A boy to be reckoned with and no doubt he'd become a man to be reckoned with, especially as far as women were concerned. Her son was attractive in his way, Dora concluded, but could never be thought of as – what was that peculiar word Grace and Flora used about men?... Dishy. Rory wasn't dishy. Certainly not compared to Hugh, who was everything a young woman of romantic disposition could wish for.

Yet there was no getting away from it – Flora was not happy. Her over-indulgence in drink at dinner had rendered her cheerful and talkative, but she wasn't content in her marriage, of that Dora was certain. Picking up a hairbrush, she dragged it through her fine white curls, trying to suppress her irritation with her daughter. Hugh was kind, attentive, affectionate in his undemonstrative way. He was a middle-aged man and a clergyman. What had Flora expected?

A baby possibly.

They had been married eighteen months now. It was early days. Flora was still very young... Setting down the brush with a sigh, Dora remembered all the encouraging things her own mother had said, year in year out, when her daughter failed to conceive. She removed her quilted dressing gown and turned back the sheets to reveal the hot water bottle Archie had placed in her bed before retiring to his own. Dora smiled. Such thoughtfulness... It was the little things that made a marriage last and it was the big things that destroyed it. Barrenness. Drink. Infidelity.

Try as she might, Dora couldn't ignore the fact that her daughter was thin, unhappy and drinking too much. She hoped that was *all* Flora was up to and switched out the light.

At New Year Rory and I slept in our old rooms at Orchard Farm but Dora had replaced my single bed with a double for Hugh and me. Grace was put into the spare bedroom which wasn't far from Rory's. Doubtless they made the most of that proximity. I don't suppose Dora and Archie minded, so long as the formalities were observed, but had I been single and in love I doubt they would have granted their daughter the same freedom as their son to wander round the house in search of nocturnal relief. (The Sixties swung, but only if you were male.)

I lay awake in the old nursery, staring up at the ceiling, my hands fingering the quilt Ettie had made before we were born. The patches were so worn and thin they felt like skin, a membrane wrinkled and scarred by the ridges of her tiny stitches. My finger found a patch of satin – Dora's old nightdress perhaps? – and came to rest. I stroked the fabric like a cat, enjoying the sensuous feel of the material.

Hugh lay snoring gently, his mountainous back turned towards me. I cast my eyes round the moonlit room searching for something to distract me, to quiet my mind. The room still teemed with things Rory and I had loved: a rocking horse, his trains and cars, my dolls, the wooden ark with its menagerie of painted animals. I remembered a hilarious wet afternoon when Rory had paired off all the animals, randomly. We nearly wet ourselves with delight at our subversion, convulsed with giggles at the thought of crocodiles mating with zebras, elephants with giraffes, and their subsequent monstrous progeny.

I drew my knees up and rolled on to my side. I felt an ache in my belly – not so much a pain, more a gnawing, gaping emptiness. I wondered if the ache could be assuaged by Ovaltine. I doubted it. Brandy might do the trick. I got out of bed, opened the nursery door carefully and went downstairs to the sitting room. I switched on the light and poured myself a generous measure. The spirit hit my stomach like a kick, but these days any kind of warmth, any sensation was welcome. It told me I was alive.

I heard a creak above me. Rory probably, on the prowl. I turned out the light and headed back upstairs with my glass, turning off towards the bathroom to drink in private. I thought I heard Dora moving about in her room and ducked quickly into the bathroom before she could surprise me in the corridor with a tumbler of brandy.

But the bathroom was already occupied. Rory was standing naked in a cloud of steam, rubbing his hair with a hand towel. The bath was full of soapy water and his clothes lay discarded in a heap on a battered Lloyd Loom chair. He didn't appear to have heard me come in and when his head emerged he started, then lowered the towel to cover his genitals. I tried to speak and couldn't. I tried to move and couldn't. I stood rooted to the spot, mesmerised like a frightened rabbit. He opened his mouth but no words came.

I was the first to recover. 'Hell's bells, Rory! Why didn't you lock the door?

'Sorry... I thought everyone was in bed. Chuck me that towel behind you.'

I threw a bath towel at him. 'Just as well it was only me.'

He caught the towel and slung it round his hips. 'Ma's seen it all before.'

'I was thinking of Grace, actually.'

He smiled slowly. 'So has she.'

'Oh... Yes. I was forgetting.' I took a mouthful of brandy and said, too loudly, 'Well, I haven't seen your willy for years. Not since you got it out to show Susan Taylor.'

He froze. 'Who?'

'Susan Taylor. You must remember her. That terribly common girl in Miss Brent's class. She had holes in her knickers and was always doing handstands.'

Rory watched me as I drank again. 'No, I don't remember.' He smiled, a little uncertainly, as if he wasn't sure yet what game we were playing. 'I can't have been very impressed by her gymnastics.'

'Well, you showed her your willy.'

He raised an eyebrow. 'Was she impressed?'

'I'll say. Talked about it for weeks. Probably still does. A girl that ugly must have led a very quiet life.'

Rory chuckled, a strange gurgling noise that came from the back of his throat. 'You're such a bitch, Flor.' He leaned over the bath and pulled out the plug and I watched his body twist, the muscles moving beneath his skin. He straightened up and rubbed his wet hand against a towelled thigh. 'Pass me my dressing gown. It's hanging on the door.'

As I turned and reached upwards I said, the brandy talking, 'D'you know, it never occurred to me you might have red pubic hair.'

'Flor!'

'Funny – your beard isn't red.'

'Give me my dressing gown, Flor.'

'Nor is your chest hair.'

'For God's sake, you're making me feel like some zoological specimen!' He held out his hand for the gown.

'Oh – am I embarrassing you?'

'Yes, if you must know, you are.'

'Gosh, that's a first! I didn't think it was possible to embarrass you. Anyway, you've nothing to be ashamed of. You appear to have a very nice body. Why do you want to cover it up?'

Rory looked down and dragged a hand through his tangled, wet hair. 'Because you staring at me is giving me an erection, that's why.' He glared at me, red-faced. 'Satisfied?'

I shrugged. 'Well, I haven't seen one of those in a long while either.'

He stared. I saw one emotion after another cross his face, like clouds scudding across the sky. 'Aren't you and Hugh – I mean, doesn't Hugh...?'

'I'm not sure if Hugh isn't interested or whether he just doesn't... function that way. Perhaps it's something to do with having been a monk. He's used to going without.' I drained my glass. 'And so am I.'

Rory looked uncomfortable. 'Maybe he's still grieving for Miriam. Have you ever – I mean has he—'

'Oh, yes. A few times. In the early days. Not lately.' Rory said nothing. 'You were right about it not working. Can't see how I'm ever going to get pregnant, short of divine intervention.'

'I'm sorry, Flor.'

'Oh, it can't be helped. He's very sweet in lots of other ways. Very kind. I suppose lots of women would be glad not to be bothered by their husbands... God, I should have brought the brandy bottle upstairs... You know, I wouldn't mind so much if he'd cuddle me in bed. Just hold me, stroke my hair or something. But there might as well be a bolster down the middle of the bed. We read our books, say "Night, night", turn out the lights and that's that.' I struggled to keep my voice level. 'I would just like to be held, Ror... Touched.'

To my utter astonishment I saw that my brother had tears in his eyes. He took the dressing gown and empty glass from my hands and set them down on a chair. He turned back, put his arms round me and pulled me gently towards him, saying, 'Poor Flor'. I laid my cheek against his neck, fitting my head under his chin. I felt the pressure of his mouth briefly on the top of my head.

We stood like that for a while, then I said, 'You're so much taller than me now. We used to be the same height for years, d'you remember? I hated it when you got taller.'

'I hated it when you grew breasts.'

I giggled. 'Why?'

'Don't know. It looked wrong somehow. Made us different. I always wanted everything to stay the same.'

'So did I... But everything changed.'

'Some things are the same.'

'No, Rory, nothing is the same. Everything's changed.'

'I still love you, Flor. And I always will.'

I started to cry. Hot tears trickled down my cheeks, over Rory's neck and on to his chest.

'Don't cry. It'll be all right!'

'Hugh doesn't love me!'

'I'm sure he does,' Rory said, sounding unconvinced. I lifted my head, looked up into his face and saw the lie. He put his hands on my shoulders and shook me gently. 'You've got me, Flor. You've always got me.'

'But I haven't, have I? I haven't got you – Grace has! I can't have you!'

There followed a silence in which my brother struggled to form words, his face contorted with anguish. He watched the tears run down my cheeks then cast his eyes downwards. I too looked down, saw his bare feet, his toes curling, burrowing into the thick pile of the rug as if he were struggling to stay upright. When he finally spoke his voice was low and hoarse, as if he were struggling with some constriction in his throat. 'You can have me, Flor... If you want.'

I stopped crying, stopped breathing and looked up. Two drops of water collided in the hollow at the base of his throat, united and rolled down over his chest. They swerved to one side following the bony outline of his ribcage, then slithered over the shadowy planes of his belly and disappeared into the towel. He started to tremble. 'I don't know how to help you, Flor... I don't know what you want.'

'What do you want, Rory?'

He threw his head up suddenly and appeared to look at the ceiling. He swallowed and I watched his Adam's apple rise and fall, then with a gulping sob he whispered, as if in disbelief, 'I want you.'

I took his face in my hands and pulled his head down to make him look at me, but he shut his eyes tight. 'Look at me, Rory.' He shook his head slowly, silently. 'Look at me! I want to see into your eyes.'

His eyelids flickered and then opened. His eyes darted round the room, avoiding mine, then settled on my face. 'What do you see, Flor?' he whispered.

'Me... I see me. I see a reflection of me. I look at you, Rory and I see me.' I stood on tiptoe and fastened my mouth on his. He recoiled for less than a second then his mouth was open, his tongue touching mine, live, moving, frantic, like an animal.

I whimpered, lay both hands on his chest and pushed him away. I shook my head, unable to speak.

'Flor?'

Still shaking my head, I stepped backwards, groping for the door-handle.

'Flor, I'm sorry! Please don't hate me – I thought it was what you wanted!'

'It is, Rory. It's what I've always wanted. I don't hate you. I hate myself.' I pulled the door open and fled.

I stood by the bed, staring at the figure of my sleeping husband, then turned away and climbed into a wing chair, shaking. I sat hugging my knees, shivering, listening to Hugh's heavy, regular breathing.

Some hours later, chilled and stiff, I unfolded myself from the chair and stumbled across the room to the bed. I slid between the sheets, careful not to touch Hugh with my icy limbs. As I lay still in the bed, I could feel warmth emanating from his body, like the glow from a stove. I turned to face him and in the grey moonlight discerned his *broad back, clad in striped pyjamas, turned towards me. I lifted a hand, intending to lay it on his arm, but instead my hand went to my mouth. My fingertips touched my lips, still bruised from Rory's kiss. My mouth remembered his tongue, my hands remembered his damp bare skin. The fingers of my other hand crept between my legs, moving urgently, instinctively.*

My body shuddered and my womb convulsed. I buried my face in the pillow to stifle my moans. Overwhelmed by a sudden wave of nausea, I got out of bed and rushed to the lavatory where I was violently sick.

1964

Dora, awake in the early hours of the morning and reading, heard the distant sound of someone vomiting. A woman. She smiled, then admonished herself for her selfishness. Poor Flora.

But *lucky* Flora. With a baby on the way...

Chapter 8

1965

Some weeks later Dora was astonished to find her daughter hadn't yet heard the glad tidings from her twin. 'I thought Rory would have told *you* first!' she said.

'Yes, so would I,' Flora answered, although she knew perfectly well why he hadn't.

That evening, when Hugh was out at a parish council meeting, Flora steeled herself and picked up the phone.

'Ror? It's me.'

'Hi... How's things?'

'I've just been speaking to Ma.'

'Oh.' Rory took a deep breath. 'She'll have told you our news, then? I was going to give you a ring.'

'Yes. I was very... *surprised*.'

He gripped the receiver tightly and turned his back towards Grace, seated on the sofa reading a book. 'Don't know why you should be surprised. Grace and I have been together for four years now. Thought it was time I made an honest woman of her.'

'Is it really that long? I suppose it must be.' Flora's voice was faint and she sounded confused. 'Well, I just wanted to say congratulations. To you both.'

'Thanks.'

'When... when is the wedding to be?'

'Soon as we can get it organised, really. We don't want a big do. Register office will be fine for us. Not much point *us* getting married in church.'

'No, I suppose not,' Flora said. Then, after a pause, 'Is Grace there?'

'Yes.'

'Oh.'

'She sends her love.'

'Does she?' Flora asked vaguely. 'Thanks. Give her mine.'

The conversation dangled. Without evincing much interest Rory asked, 'How's Hugh?'

'Oh, he's... fine. Busy. As ever. I don't see much of him, to tell you the truth. He's out most evenings. Meetings and so on. I'm busy too. I had no idea there was so much to do as a clergy wife. The phone never *stops*,' she said wearily, 'But it's never people you actually want to talk to... How are *you*, Rory?'

'I'm fine.'

'How's Grace?'

'She's fine too.'

'Oh. Good.'

'Flor, was there anything particular you wanted to talk about? Only Grace and I are going out to a concert later and—'

'Oh, I'm sorry. Don't let me hold you up.'

'I'll give you a ring later?'

'No, I'll have gone to bed. I get so tired these days. I was just ringing to say...'

Her voice tailed off. Rory heard a 'chink' at the other end of the phone that he recognised as the sound of a bottle neck hitting a glass. 'Flor, are you OK?'

'Yes, I'm fine. I'm absolutely fine.' Flora was silent for a few moments but he could hear her breathing heavily. 'Rory, don't do it. You'll be making a mistake – like I did! Please don't do it.'

He raised his voice. 'Look, I've really got to go. I'll give you a ring.'

'Ror, please, I need to talk to you—'

'Bye, Flora.' He replaced the receiver and sat back on the sofa, his eyes closed, the lines around his mouth etched deep.

Grace watched him, puzzled. 'Why did you tell her we were going out?'

'I wanted to get off the phone.'

'You sounded very odd.'

'*She* sounded very odd,' he said irritably. 'In fact, she sounded drunk.'

'Oh dear. Poor Flora. Whatever can be the matter, do you think?'

'No idea.' Rory sighed and closed his eyes again.

~

It soon became clear why Rory and Grace had decided to get married. Her figure grew more voluptuous, her long hair more luxuriant, her rosy complexion bloomed and it was obvious that a Dunbar scion was expected. Exactly when was not clear. Grace was cagey on the subject, in deference no doubt to Dora's and Ettie's finer feelings, although for the life of me I couldn't see how she was going to palm off what promised to be a strapping eight-pounder as premature.

In the event she didn't have to.

Rory seemed to show little interest in the pregnancy and I was the only one in whom Grace felt she could confide. I think she hoped I too would soon be pregnant so we could go shopping together for bibs and bootees. In that we were both disappointed.

Grace told me a date in September when, by her calculations, the baby would arrive. I felt both touched and burdened by the information. She was quite oblivious of my jealousy, of my impatience when she or any other member of the family chattered about the impending happy event. (To give him his due, Hugh was noticeably quiet on the subject – as well he might be.) I felt oppressed by the knowledge of when the baby was conceived. It was clear from what Grace said that the contraceptive failure – for that was how she referred to it, with a coy smile and a becoming blush – had taken place at Orchard Farm, at New Year. I couldn't prevent myself from wondering if, when I spurned my brother's advances, he just went back to bed and made love to his semi-comatose girlfriend and, if he did, was he thinking of me?

There were times when I felt sorry for Grace. I felt superior, older, deeply cynical. Sometimes I could even find it in my heart to pity her. But there were other times – usually after the second brandy – when I hated her with a passion, times when I could not stand being in the same room with her, could not bear to hear one more word on the subject of babies, as it seemed unlikely, given my husband's lack of interest, that I would ever bear one. When Grace sat smugly nursing her little bump, all smiles, I longed to tell her that her husband didn't love her, he merely screwed her. He loved me, had always loved me, would always love me.

But I never actually wished for her to lose the baby. I didn't have the guts.

~

In May 1965, Grace was five months pregnant. We were on our way out to a concert: Rory's first performance as a professional musician in a major concert hall. He was to play a Shostakovich piano concerto of fearsome difficulty and had left an hour earlier to go to the hall and fret about the height of his piano stool. Grace and I were sitting in the hotel bar having too many drinks on an empty stomach and Hugh was ordering our taxi. Grace went to the Ladies' and was gone a long time. I started to wonder if she was throwing up again. The pregnancy had been difficult from the start and she had been sick a lot. Eventually I went in to look for her. She was sitting on a chair, bent over, clutching her stomach.

'Grace, what's the matter? Are you all right?'

'I'm bleeding, Flora.'

'Oh, no!' I took her hand and looked at her white face. 'Very much?'

'No. Well, like a period.'

'Oh, God. You have to go to bed, Grace. You have to lie down. I'll get Hugh to ring a doctor.'

'Don't tell Rory.'

'We have to tell him, Grace! Don't be silly. He has to know. Anyway, when you don't turn up he'll worry.'

'If you tell him I'm bleeding he'll walk out! He'll walk out of his first major engagement and probably never get another. I forbid you to tell him, Flora! You and Hugh must go to the concert and tell him I'm ill. But don't say I'm bleeding. Say I'm being sick. Say anything you like.'

'You don't think I'm leaving you like this, do you? Hugh can go to the hall and deal with Rory. I'm staying with you till – till you feel better,' I said abruptly. We both knew I meant till it's all over. Grace looked up at me with tears in her eyes and mouthed a silent 'Thank you'.

I asked Reception to call a doctor, telling them it was an emergency. Then Hugh marched into the Ladies with me (which created a stir, especially as he was wearing his dog collar.) He picked Grace up as easily as if she were a child and carried her to her room. I helped her into her nightdress and put her to bed, then Hugh and I retreated to the corridor to discuss his script. I said he was to leave a message backstage saying that I – not Grace – had been taken ill and that Grace was staying with me to look after me. Hugh said that didn't sound very convincing. He would have been the one to stay to look after me, not Grace. What wife would desert a husband in his finest hour for the sake of a sister-in-law's migraine? We agreed that Hugh would have to tell Rory the truth, but I insisted he make light of it. 'Say she's been bleeding, but that it's stopped now.'

Hugh looked at me gravely. 'That's a lie, Flora.'

'Oh, for God's sake, Hugh – don't start preaching at me now!'

'I meant that if Rory is going to lose his child, and it looks as if he might, it doesn't seem right to raise false hopes.'

'If you tell him the truth the performance will be wrecked, then Rory will be wrecked and then Grace will be wrecked.' Hugh said nothing. 'There are such things as miracles! She may not lose the baby.' Hugh still looked uncomfortable. 'What else can we do?'

'We can pray.'

'Well, you can bloody pray if you like. I'm going back in there to look after Grace. Tell Rory she's going to be OK.'

There was a lot of blood. Like a Hammer horror movie. I was very calm and just said, 'Don't look. The ambulance is on its way,' which was meant to sound reassuring. I kept handing her wads of tissues to put between her legs and then when the box was empty I handed her a towel. As the pains got worse Grace started to cry. She clutched at my hand and yelled, 'Oh, God, no – the baby's coming!'

It was tiny and perfect and covered in blood. You could see it was a boy. Grace was sobbing, beside herself. I wrapped the baby in the bloodstained towel, carefully, so as not to cover its face. Its skin hung in wrinkles like a wizened old man's, but its forehead was smooth and its eyes were shut. It didn't look as if it had suffered.

I opened the door to the ambulance men who came thundering in with blankets and a sort of stretcher-chair. They handed me some thick, hospital-issue sanitary towels. I stared at them blankly till I realised they were for Grace. I handed them to her then picked up a carrier bag containing a box of new shoes and emptied its contents on to the floor. I put the baby and the towel into the shoebox, then realised it looked like a coffin. I set the gory package gently on the floor, helped Grace out of bed, pushed shoes on to her feet and kissed her on the cheek. The men helped her into the chair, wrapped her in a blanket and then strapped her in firmly, as if she were about to be executed. As they lifted her she shrieked, 'The baby! Give me the baby!' I handed the shoebox to her and she clutched it on her lap as they carried her out of the room.

Hugh and Rory found me in Casualty. I hadn't seen Grace for several hours. I'd been informed by a bad-tempered nurse that Grace had lost the baby – which we already knew – that she was in a gynae ward awaiting a D & C and no, I couldn't see her.

When he arrived Rory looked confused and physically exhausted. He was still wearing his DJ but his white bow-tie hung loose at his neck and his damp shirtfront stuck to his chest. Apart from his deathly expression he looked like a drunken reveller at a New Year's Eve party. He stared at me in horror. I realised then what a spectacle I must present in my blood-soaked cocktail dress, looking like Jackie Kennedy after the assassination. He searched my face for reassurance. 'She's going to be all right? The baby's OK?'

'Grace is fine... But she lost the baby. I'm really sorry.'

Hugh made the sign of the cross discreetly and bowed his head. Rory frowned. 'She lost it? But she wasn't bleeding much, was she? Why did she lose it?'

'I think she was bleeding because she was about to lose it. There must have been something wrong.'

Hugh put an arm round Rory's shoulders and said, 'It was probably for the best.' I could have killed him.

'She lost it?' Rory asked again, groping for meaning.

I nodded. There was a long silence. I took his hand. 'You had a son. I saw him. He was beautiful.'

Rory looked down at the floor, then his head jerked upwards and he stared up at the fluorescent lights, blinking.

Rory wanted to sit in Casualty all night waiting to see Grace, but I insisted there was no point. She would be having a general anaesthetic and no one would be allowed to see her until the morning. I suggested we go back to the hotel to get some sleep and then come back first thing in the morning. Rory still refused to leave, almost hysterical now with tiredness. I wondered when he'd last eaten. We'd planned a celebratory dinner after the concert and none of us had eaten since an early tea.

To pacify Rory, Hugh offered to stay at the hospital all night waiting for news of Grace and promised that he would ring the moment there was any. Rory went off to bully the ward nurses again, demanding to be allowed to see Grace. Hugh suggested I take Rory back to the hotel in a taxi. 'He may be in shock, Flora. Keep an eye on him and call a doctor if you're in any doubt.'

'Was he good?'

'I beg your pardon?'

'Rory. The concert. Did he play well?'

'Oh. Yes... Astonishing. Fiendish music, but somehow he managed to play it very simply. The audience gave him a wonderful reception. I wish you could have been there. He put me in mind of those lines at the end of Eliot's Little Gidding. You know, A condition of complete simplicity... costing not less than everything.'

I gazed up at him blankly.

When Rory and I got back to the hotel the girl at Reception handed me our keys and said in a low voice, 'Was everything all right?'

'Do you mean the concert or Mrs Dunbar?' I answered, too sharply.

The poor girl looked abashed. 'Both.'

'Mr Dunbar was a great success. Mrs Dunbar lost the baby.'

'Oh. I'm very sorry. We... sorted out the room,' she said, her eyes sliding sideways towards Rory who was reading telephone messages. 'We can't do the carpet until tomorrow,' she added. 'But we laid a rug over the worst.'

'Oh, bless you, thanks. Look, could you send us up some brandy? And some whisky and water, please. You couldn't rustle up a sandwich as well, could you? My brother hasn't eaten.'

'Of course. We'll send up a tray, Mrs Wentworth. In about ten minutes?'

'Thanks very much.'

I steered Rory towards the lift.

I opened Rory's door and went in, glancing round the room, relieved to see that the staff had removed all trace of the carnage apart from *a trail of red spots on the carpet leading from the bed to the bathroom. A rug had been laid on top of the worst bloodstains and I hoped Rory wouldn't notice them. The bed had been made up with fresh linen and there were flowers on the coffee table that hadn't been there when we left. Rory walked into the room, sank down in an armchair and closed his eyes.*

'They're sending up some food and some whisky,' I said.

'I'm not hungry,' he replied listlessly.

'I don't care. You're going to eat. You look awful.'

'Not as bad as you. Do you think you could go and change, Flor? You look as if you murdered my wife.'

I looked down at my stained dress. 'Yes, of course. I'm sorry.'

'That's OK.' He reached out, took hold of my hand and squeezed it. 'I'm very grateful. It must have been bloody awful.'

'It was certainly bloody.'

'Why didn't you phone me?'

'She wouldn't let us. You know what Grace is like.'

'Yes, I do... I wish you'd been there, Flor.'

'I wish I'd been there. Hugh said you were astonishing.'

'Did he?'

'Yes. He seemed very impressed.'

Rory laughed mirthlessly. 'I don't think it takes much to impress old Hugh.'

There was a knock at the door. I opened it and took charge of a loaded tray. I set it down in front of Rory and said, 'Pour some drinks while I go and get changed. Mine's a very large brandy.'

I returned wearing Hugh's pyjama jacket which came to my knees and his dressing gown which trailed on the floor. Rory burst out laughing when he saw me and I wondered how much whisky he'd already downed. 'What on earth are you wearing?'

'They're Hugh's.'

'Well, I didn't suppose they were yours!' he said, putting a brandy into my hand. 'You look as if you raided the dressing-up box.'

'I was cold. And all I had clean was a little summer frock. I wanted to be cosy.'

'Don't you have any pyjamas of your own?'

'Not with me. All I've got is the ridiculous negligée I bought for

my honeymoon...' My voice trailed off as I remembered why I'd packed it for this trip.

Rory swallowed a lot of whisky, then said, 'Things any better? Between you and Hugh, I mean.'

I sat down in the other armchair and curled my legs under me. 'It's none of your business, Rory.'

'No, you're right, it's not. Sorry.'

There was a long silence. Rory stared at the plate of sandwiches but didn't take one. I wrestled with my principles for about half a minute, then said, 'Things aren't any better, actually.'

'No, I didn't think so.'

'What do you mean?'

'I suppose I meant I could tell. You don't exactly radiate contentment, you two. You don't even touch each other. Well, Hugh doesn't touch you.'

'You noticed that?' I asked, surprised. Rory nodded and drank again. 'I'd hoped it wasn't that obvious.'

'It isn't.'

I swirled the brandy in my glass and took a mouthful, shivered and took another. 'Is it me, do you think?' Rory looked up and blinked at me, his eyes struggling to focus. 'Is there something wrong with me?'

He was silent for a moment and then said carefully, 'Not according to the prefects at St Columba's.'

'What?'

A muscle twitched at the corner of his mouth. 'They used to keep a list on the notice-board in the Common Room. Their Hit Parade. You were on it.' Rory refilled his glass. He was clearly enjoying himself at my expense.

'What on earth are you talking about? What sort of list?'

'A list of the women they'd most like to... sleep with. You came third after Marilyn Monroe and Ava Gardner.'

'What?'

'You heard. I think in terms of genuine aspiration, Flor, you can regard yourself as Number One. You probably never realised this, but what little popularity I enjoyed at school was largely thanks to being your brother. My friends were always on at me to get you to make up a four for mixed doubles.' He grinned. 'I think they were talking about tennis.'

114

'You're pulling my leg!'

'Nope… You were the subject of a hundred wet dreams. There's nothing wrong with you, my girl. Any man who doesn't want to screw you needs his head examining.' He buried his nose in his whisky glass. 'Or his cock examining.'

'Rory – please!' There was a tense silence, then I started to giggle. He looked up at me, then he too giggled. I heaved a cushion at him. 'Shut up, Ror!'

He ducked, spilling whisky. 'Shut up yourself!'

'You are insulting my husband,' I said, trying to sound offended.

'Husband in name only.'

'That isn't funny, Rory.'

'No,' he cackled, 'It's bloody tragic.'

'Please stop it!'

He clapped a hand over his mouth but then raised his eyebrows at me, snorting with laughter.

'You're so childish!' I sneered, then spoiled the effect with another fit of giggles. 'Anyway,' I said, composing myself, smoothing Hugh's dressing gown over my knees, 'it's all my fault.'

'Why?'

I emptied my glass with a flourish. 'I refused to have the operation.'

Rory sat bolt upright in his chair. 'What operation?'

'The one that all clergy wives have the night before their wedding.'

Rory smiled slowly. He stood up, sloshed more brandy into my glass, then flopped back into his armchair, his eyes bright now with anticipation. 'Tell me all.'

'Well, you see, what most people don't realise,' I said, lowering my voice, 'is that clergy wives have no private parts.'

'Really?'

'Really. You see, they're surgically removed before the wedding ceremony. Without anaesthetic.'

'Naturally. But what about babies? Clergy wives have traditionally shown a marked tendency to procreate.'

'Immaculate conception, of course! No need for all that nasty sexual intercourse! When it's your turn you get a visitation from the Angel Gabriel. No hanky-panky, it's all very business-like. Then nine months later – bingo! They unzip you like a banana and pull out the baby!'

One moment Rory was laughing, spilling whisky down his shirtfront, the next he was crying, sitting hunched in his chair. I launched myself across the room, knelt and put my arms round him, hugging him tight. 'Oh, God, Ror – I'm sorry! I'm such an idiot. I can't believe I was so tactless!'

He shook his head. 'It's not that... It's not the baby.'

'What is it then? What's the matter?'

He took a napkin from the tray and wiped his face. 'I'm... I'm just so bloody relieved! I'm glad the baby's dead. I didn't want it.' I stared at him, speechless. 'I'm a total bastard, aren't I? I'm actually glad Grace lost the baby! Our baby... And shall I tell you why?' He drained his glass. 'Because now I can leave her.'

'I don't understand. You mean – leave Grace?'

'Yes.'

'But – don't you love her?'

'I thought I did. But I find I don't,' he said simply. 'Grace loves me. A lot. But I knew almost straight away we'd made a mistake. She was already pregnant when we married, so I didn't feel I could say anything. Or do anything... I just kept hoping she'd lose it. So I could walk away.'

I stared at him, appalled. 'For God's sake, Rory – why on earth did you marry her?'

'Why on earth did you marry Hugh?' His level gaze, suddenly sober, defied me to look away, dared me to lie. I let go of him and sat back on my heels. After a while he said softly, 'That's why I married Grace. The same reason. To be free... Then I realised I couldn't be free, didn't even want to be free. Any more than you do, Flor.'

I stood up and cinched the belt of Hugh's dressing gown round my waist so tightly I could hardly breathe. 'I'm going to bed, Rory. I think you should do the same. Try and eat something,' I said mechanically, waving a hand in the direction of the sandwiches. 'Then get some sleep.'

As I headed for the door Rory hauled himself out of the armchair and followed me. I turned back to face him and, avoiding his eyes, said, 'I'm really sorry about the baby. I hope you and Grace manage to sort things out somehow.' He stood sullenly, watching me, saying nothing. 'Goodnight, Rory.'

I tried to kiss him on the cheek but he turned his head suddenly and kissed me on the mouth. I pulled away quickly and reached for the door-handle but he put his hands on my shoulders and pushed me against the door.

'You're hurting me! Let me go!'

'I'm not hurting you. I'm being very careful not to hurt you. I know exactly what I'm doing. And so do you.'

'Let me go!'

'You're sure that's what you want?'

My mouth worked. 'Yes... That's what I want.'

He let go of me, shaking his head. 'You paused too long, Flor! You're lying.'

'I do want to go, Rory.'

'So go.' He didn't touch me but he didn't move out of the way either. His grey, unblinking eyes didn't leave mine. 'Go, Flora.'

'Rory, I— '

Then his mouth was on mine again and this time his hands were purposeful. He tugged at Hugh's dressing gown, pulled it open and slid the pyjama jacket up over my naked thighs. He tugged at my pants and slid a hand between my legs.

'Rory, no!' I shouted in his ear. He flinched and looked at me, searching my eyes again. Then without looking away, his hands went to his fly which he unbuttoned with all the speed and dexterity you'd expect of a concert pianist. I started to laugh, hysterical. 'Dear God – are you going to rape your sister?'

'It isn't rape, Flora,' he said calmly. 'But if telling yourself it's rape helps you live with what we are, that's fine by me.'

I started to weep. 'Rory, no...'

I felt his hand between my legs again, then he pinned me with his body-weight against the door. He pushed into me, slowly, tenderly. 'For it to be rape you have to withhold your consent. You have to say no – and bloody mean it! Knee me in the groin, claw my face, gouge my eyes, draw blood!' He was inside me now but unmoving. We both leaned against the door, breathing heavily, joined at last. 'You have to hurt me, Flor. Do it! Hurt me, then I'll know you don't want this.'

'Rory—'

'Say no, Flora!'

I raised a hand to his face and saw blood. Grace's blood, on the inside of my wrist, where I hadn't washed.

'Say it!'

I shook my head from side to side, sobbing. Rory started to move, murmuring against my ear. 'You said it was what you'd always wanted, Flor... That's what you said. In the bathroom. You said you wanted me. Me... Always...'

My brother came inside me with a yelp like an animal in pain.

We were twenty-two.

Our lives were over. Or had just begun.

PART TWO

Chapter 9

1967

Breakfast was not a happy affair.

Theo woke at six o' clock to a wet mattress and cried pitifully. As Flora hauled herself out of bed to see to her son, Hugh's sleeping form did not stir, even when the bedroom door creaked loudly. Stumbling across the hall in worn carpet slippers, folding her dressing gown round her tightly, Flora shivered and cursed all the males in her family.

Theo stood up in his cot, his face puce and tear-stained, his chubby fingers clutching a rabbit that had seen better days and several careful owners. His condition was abject: cold, wet and, Flora could tell from halfway across the room, malodorous. Brushing springy blond curls back from his forehead, she wiped Theo's nose, changed his nappy and put him into clean pyjamas. Hugging the child for warmth and comfort, she went downstairs to the kitchen.

At twenty-five Flora had a husband, a son and a large house and garden, all of which were admired by visitors. As they departed they would cast an eye over vast expanses of dingy vicarage wallpaper, balding carpet and crumbling plaster mouldings and pronounce, 'It must be lovely to have so much *space*!' This was not the thought uppermost in Flora's mind when she swept and dusted, nor when she calculated just how much it would cost to replace the faded curtains in the enormous bay windows.

Flora placed Theo in his high chair with some cereal and switched on the kettle and transistor radio. Farmers were discussing the devastating effects of a fungal disease on sugar beet production. Theo smeared Weetabix around his face. Occasionally some found its way into his mouth and, surprised, he swallowed it. Flora preferred not to watch and sat by a window, staring into the garden, nursing a cup of tea. She was already bored and it was only half past six. By nine o'clock it would feel like lunchtime and by lunchtime she would be ready for bed, exhausted by boredom and the never-ending struggle to keep her temper with her child, her husband and his parishioners.

The farmers had finished their sugar beet post-mortem and turned their attention to the vexed question of agricultural subsidy. With a look of fierce concentration distorting his cherubic features, Theo filled his nappy again. Flora wondered if she dare leave it for Hugh to change when he got up. Chastising herself for this un-maternal thought, she lifted the child out of his highchair, kissed his encrusted face as an act of penitence and carried him back upstairs to the bathroom.

Amidst a flurry of cotton wool and baby lotion, trying to ignore the stench, Flora considered the heady cocktail of motherhood – the pee, the sick, the blood and the shit – and wondered why these ingredients were omitted from baby manuals and conversations about bringing up children. Sometimes at the end of the day she felt as if she wanted to fall into a hot bath and scrub her body with a Brillo pad.

When Theo was clean again Flora deposited him on the bathroom floor with a half-empty box of lavatory paper, calculating that the five minutes peace she would obtain by letting the child extract sheets one by one were well worth the two minutes it would take to clear up the mess afterwards. Life drove a hard bargain.

Feeling a headache coming on, Flora braced herself for the day and opened the medicine cabinet in search of aspirin. As her fingers closed around the glass bottle she noticed that her hand was trembling. She thought, quite involuntarily, of the brandy bottle in the sideboard downstairs, a thought which hovered at the back of her mind until nearly lunchtime when she allowed herself a small sherry.

If I drank enough and if I avoided actually looking at Theo, I could persuade myself that the child was Hugh's. It was what everyone believed, including Hugh. It should have been true, would have been true if Hugh had been a halfway decent husband to me. Nothing would ever change the way I felt about Rory, but if Hugh had allowed me the luxury of uncertainty, if there'd been the possibility of Theo being his child, I could perhaps have forgiven him, loved him more, loved poor Theo more. I could perhaps have forgiven myself for what

Rory and I had done, were it not that I was confronted with the evidence of my shame and sin every single day. And every single day I paid for that sin with the mortification of my flesh.

1969

Flora was locked in mortal combat with her child.

To an observer the scene presented a ludicrous if common spectacle – a mother struggling to dress an unwilling toddler in outdoor clothes – but Flora knew and Theo knew that it was a battle of wills no less fundamental because it was fought once or twice a day. At the moment Flora had the advantage. She had managed to push both wellingtons on to Theo's feet and was now wrestling with the reins, but Theo, with a superhuman effort, twisted out of his mother's arms, kicked off both boots and ran for the door. Flora lunged, caught him by the legs and brought him down on to the carpet. The child cried and began to kick his legs in the air. As Flora wrestled with the reins, one of Theo's heels caught her full on the nose and she reeled back, momentarily stunned. The boy stopped crying, rolled over, ran to the kitchen and hid under the table. Blood dripped from Flora's nose onto the threadbare hall carpet; she blotted it quickly with her handkerchief then held it to her nose.

She went into the kitchen, grabbed hold of Theo's feet and pulled him out from under the table, then dragged him through the hall, avoiding the litter of bricks and farmyard animals he'd scattered over the floor. Theo's cries were now hysterical and bubbles of green snot ballooned from his nose. Flora picked him up, wiped his nose with her bloody handkerchief and rammed him into the pushchair, feeling as she did so a muscle snap in the small of her back. Ignoring the pain she placed her knee squarely on Theo's chest and fastened the clips on the harness. She removed her knee and straightened up. With one last desperate jack-knife movement Theo managed to eject himself from the pushchair seat so that he dangled off the edge, suspended by his harness. Flora tried to lift him back in but the child arched his back, rigid and immovable.

Tears of pain and frustration mixed with a few drops of blood dripped down on to Theo's woollen coat as Flora undid the clips again, her fingers clumsy now with exhaustion. She lifted the child again and dropped him back into the seat, putting an arm across his chest and a knee between his legs to keep him in position. She quickly fastened the harness and then adjusted it so that Theo was held fast, pinned like a demented butterfly.

Flora stood up and looked at the screaming monster before her, his swollen face smeared with green slime and spotted with blood. She opened the front door of the vicarage, propelled the pushchair out into the garden and went back indoors, slamming the door behind her. She leaned against it and sank down on to the floor. Out of the corner of her eye she saw the discarded Wellingtons and thought of her small son sitting outside in his socks on a raw, wet November day.

'I hope an inspector from the NSPCC passes by,' prayed Flora, weeping, 'and I hope he takes him away...'

Grace was convinced we'd become good friends. Certainly I never disabused her of the idea. She seemed to think the bond had been forged the night we beheld her tiny dead baby together. Despite her dreadful loss she was grateful to me for the little I'd done. I too was in a kind of shock afterwards and couldn't stop crying for days. The family put it down to all the blood, my first encounter with death, the loss of a baby when I'd never even been pregnant myself. (By then of course I was, but not even I knew.)

When I finally told my family that Hugh and I were to become parents Grace stole my thunder by announcing that she too was pregnant again. It was then I realised that Rory was not going to leave her, that even if he did, it would be of no benefit to me. He was beyond my reach and always would be. Instead I tried to hate him for what he'd done, tried to feel repelled. I failed utterly.

Excitement about my impending happy event was eclipsed by family concern for Grace and Rory and whether they would be lucky this time. As my bump grew larger the family showed little interest (and Rory none at all), but Hugh was ridiculously pleased and proud. He was on his knees at every opportunity thanking God for His blessing on our marriage. There were times when I felt so ill and irritated by his piety that I was tempted to wipe the smile off his face and tell him exactly whom he should be thanking.

After the night Grace miscarried I couldn't bear for Hugh to come near me in bed, apart from one memorable and very necessary occasion. We never discussed our resumed celibacy. I suppose he thought it was something to do with the pregnancy. I managed to convey that I felt too ill to indulge in marital relations, which was in fact often the case. After Theo was born it would have been easy to plead healing stitches, sore nipples, general exhaustion as reasons to maintain our distance, but it was never actually necessary to discuss the matter.

Hugh eventually moved into the spare room to get a decent night's sleep. When Theo started sleeping through the night I knew Hugh expected me to invite him back and so I did, but new boundaries had been drawn up. Since Hugh continued to be affectionate and attentive – especially towards Theo – I assumed he was reasonably content.

My body was free of Hugh, free of Theo. Empty again, like my life. I filled my body and my life with booze and memories of Rory who'd been my seducer, but also my saviour.

1965

Six weeks after Grace's miscarriage the Dunbars assembled at Orchard Farm for a subdued Sunday lunch. In the middle of a July heat-wave, they gathered reluctantly round a huge joint of roast beef, cooked to perfection by Dora. Her head pounding with the heat, Flora felt her gorge rise as slices of the pinkish meat were put before her. She rose up out of her chair and the last thing she remembered before she fainted was the sound of Rory's voice shouting, 'Hugh! Catch her!'

Rory knocked softly and put his head round the bedroom door. Flora was lying dozing on the bed. The windows were thrown wide open but the curtains did not stir. 'You feeling any better now?'

'A bit. I just feel so tired...'

'I'll leave you to have a nap then.'

Flora propped herself up on an elbow. 'No. Rory, I need to talk to you. Come in. And close the door.' He froze in the doorway and Flora watched his face change. Brotherly concern vanished, to be replaced by something darker, something more opportunistic. Flora felt nauseous again.

Rory shut the door quietly and sat down on the edge of the bed. She hesitated before speaking. 'Where is everybody?'

'In the garden. Hugh's doing chores for Dora. Grace and Ettie are washing up.'

'Oh.' She hesitated again. 'Rory... I'm unwell.'

'The heat probably.'

'No. I'm unwell because... because I'm pregnant.'

He looked at a loss, then smiled and said, 'Congratulations!'

'No.'

His smile died. 'You think it's mine?'

'I know it's yours.'

'How can you know?'

'Because Hugh and I hadn't made love for weeks before – before Grace miscarried and we haven't made love since. It's yours. And I can't even pass it off as Hugh's.'

Rory threaded his fingers together and studied the pattern they made. Without looking up he said, 'Well, you can get rid of it. There are special clinics, aren't there? If it's a question of money, I'll get it somehow. You needn't say anything to Hugh.'

'Look, I don't really expect you to understand this, but I don't want to get rid of it. I know that's what I should do – especially in view of who the father is – but... I can't bring myself to do it.'

'You have to! What else can you do?'

She lay down again and put a hand over her eyes. 'You didn't see Grace's baby. Your baby. I did! I saw it and it was... *horrible*. Seeing something dead, a dead *baby*. I couldn't do that. Not to my child.' She opened her eyes and looked at him steadily. 'And it is mine, Rory. It's not just yours. It's *my* baby.' Her voice caught. 'It might be the only baby I ever have.'

'So, are you going to tell Hugh?' he asked sharply. 'Will you tell him it's mine? Flora, you can't! Supposing he tells Ma? It would kill her! You'll have to invent a lover.'

'Someone I manage to fit in between the Mothers' Union and the Brownies, you mean? Shall I tell Hugh it's one of his parishioners? For God's sake, be realistic! He'll want details. How do you think he'd feel about raising a child of unknown parentage?'

'Not quite as bad as raising a child of incest.' Rory's eyes were cold, his voice determined. 'You *have* to get rid of it, Flor.'

'I can't.'

He was silent a moment, deep in thought, then said, 'Perhaps you'll miscarry. Like Grace.'

Flora glared at him. 'Thanks. What a comfort you are.'

'Is it really too late to pass it off as Hugh's? I mean, if you and he...'

'No, I suppose it's not too late.' She groaned. 'Oh, it's so humiliating. If he would just make love to me – soon! – I *could* just about pass it off as his. I could lie about the dates, say it was premature. But how can I get him to do it? You're a man – tell me how I can make him want me!'

Rory laughed softly and shook his head. 'You're talking to the wrong man, Flor. How can he *not* want you?' He lay down next to her on the bed, placed his hand on the curve of her hip and slid it up over her waist. Flora felt the heat of his palm through her thin cotton dress. She didn't restrain him until he cupped her breast.

'Rory, no...'

'I'm not going to say I'm sorry, Flor, because I'm not. I'm not sorry about what we did. I'd do the same again tomorrow.' He lifted her hair and stroked her neck. 'I'd do it now.' Flora closed her eyes. 'I'm just sorry you're pregnant.' He kissed her mouth gently. In a travesty of protest she laid a hand on his chest at the opening of his shirt, sliding her fingers under the fabric to touch his skin. She sensed the tension in his body, taut, like a string about to break.

'I'm not sorry either,' she mumbled. 'I want the baby. I want *a* baby... I don't know how I'll survive the rest of my life without something to love. Someone to love me. I just wish it was *Hugh's* baby. Or that I could pretend it was.'

'Keep trying. You never know – maybe he'll respond. He's been working in the garden. Sun and exercise make some men feel randy.'

'Do they?'

He nodded slowly, considering. 'Wear something pretty for supper tonight. And perfume.' He lifted her hair again and held it close to her head. 'Put your hair up, make yourself look different. Surprise him!'

Flora looked at him and smiled uncertainly. 'I'll do my best.'

'That's my girl.' He stroked her cheek and traced the outline of her mouth with a finger. 'I expect you wear a nightdress in bed, don't you?'

'Yes, of course.'

'Don't. Let him see you naked. Let him feel your skin...' Rory swallowed and said faintly, 'You're so lovely...' He took Flora in his arms and folded her, unresisting, against his body. 'I wish it was me. I'd fuck you to kingdom come.'

She could feel him hard against her and pushed him away. 'Rory, no, please – you must go. Hugh might come in. Please go.'

He kissed her again and got off the bed, then stood looking down at her, his eyes dazed with lust. 'Forget you're a vicar's wife,' he whispered, then grinned. 'Seduce him. And if that doesn't work... Well, don't worry – I'll think of something.'

Rory went to his former bedroom and opened the bottom drawer of a chest where Dora kept some of his old clothes. He rifled through them until he found what he wanted. He pulled out a pair of faded jeans he hadn't worn for several years and a white T-shirt. He undressed and put on his old clothes, breathing in to button the shrunken Levis.

Rory stood in front of the wardrobe mirror and regarded his resurrected teenage self critically, then laughed out loud. He looked out of the bedroom window and surveyed the garden. Dora was dozing in a deckchair in the shade of a horse chestnut, a trug full of weeds at her side. Archie was in the greenhouse dealing death to invertebrates with a chemical spray. Rory could hear the sound of the lawnmower coming from the orchard, the rhythmic, back-breaking whirr of blades as Hugh toiled back and forth over the grass, then silence as he took the box of grass-cuttings down to the compost heap at the bottom of the vegetable garden.

Rory decided it was time to lift the potatoes. He turned his immaculate hands over and examined the soft skin of his palms. Blisters were inevitable of course, but he told himself it was all in a good cause. It was the least he could do for Flora, under the circumstances.

I would like to think that Rory didn't actually enjoy what he did for me, that he did it because he had to, because he had no choice. But knowing Rory as I do, I think he probably did enjoy it. Knowing Rory, he probably laughed about it afterwards.

Chapter 10

1966 was a productive year for Rory. In February I gave birth to his first son and three months later Grace gave birth to his second.

The babies could not have looked more different, which was a relief to two out of the three parents. Mine was named Theodore, which was Hugh's idea. It means 'Gift of God' apparently (which was perhaps more appropriate than it sounds since Theo's father behaved as if he was God's gift, both to music and to women). Theo was born with very little hair but his elfin features were said to be a carbon copy of mine – a resemblance Rory was the first to point out – and the white blond hair when it grew made him look even more like me. Colin arrived with a thick head of black curls, a pugilist's face and eyes that crossed slightly. (He improved considerably with age.)

In 1967 Grace suffered another miscarriage but in 1968 presented Rory with a daughter, Charlotte, another sturdy, dark baby and Colin was suddenly demoted to playing second fiddle to a more appealing sibling. Perhaps that was the beginning of my unholy alliance with Colin. At the age of twenty-six I was able to empathise with this poor toddler whom people largely ignored. I could see and understand the resentment, the desolation in his eyes as he gazed up at an assembly of hitherto devoted grown-ups, peering into a pram at a largely inanimate object, source of all manner of disgusting smells and noises.

I took a perverse delight in snubbing baby Charlotte and lavishing attention on my nephew. I would lift him on to my lap and read him stories (something I rarely did for Theo – Hugh did it so much better and more willingly). I applied salve to wounds inflicted by his unwitting, besotted relations. Colin and I conspired together. We were the rejects, a clique of two. Colin was a piece of Rory I could love freely, in a whole-hearted, uncomplicated way – when he was a child at least. Theo on the other hand was a piece of Rory I found myself unable to love, simply because he never should have been a piece of Rory.

I tried very hard to pretend the lies I lived were true. Drinking helped me ignore the facts; it also helped me ignore my husband and eventually my son. It helped me cope with the certain knowledge that Rory and Grace were now bound together by blood, deaths and births and that he would probably never leave her. For all I knew, he maybe even loved her by now.

But I thought not. I hoped not.

If I was going to spend the rest of my lifetime burning for Rory it seemed only right that he should do the same for me.

Spite was a source of cold comfort.

1969

Grace looked up from feeding Charlotte, the bottle poised. 'Something wrong?'

Rory was on his knees scooping up toys from under the baby grand piano and putting them into a cardboard box. 'No. Why?'

'Oh, nothing. You just seem a bit moody.'

He pushed the box into a corner of the room and sank down on to the piano stool which wheezed as his weight compressed the worn leather. 'I'm just tired.'

'Too tired to play to me?'

'I'm never too tired to play. I'm often too tired to play *well*.'

'Play us a lullaby. Something soothing,' Grace crooned. Rory spun round on the stool and started to rifle through sheet music. She leaned back on the sofa. 'So how were Ettie and the Outlaws?'

The ghost of a smile haunted Rory's tense face. 'You make your in-laws sound like a rock group... They were fine. But they're all getting old. And that makes *me* feel old.'

'Come off it! At twenty-seven?'

Rory started to play. 'Fatherhood makes you feel old. Having so many responsibilities.'

Grace listened to him for a while. 'What's this? I don't know it, do I?'

'No. I'm learning it – can't you tell? It's a Prelude by Shostakovich. There's twenty-four in all. They're bloody difficult and staggeringly beautiful. Like my daughter.'

'Who takes after her father.' Grace closed her eyes and listened, then murmured, 'It's *gorgeous*.'

Rory continued to play then glanced sideways at the sofa. 'Is she asleep yet?'

'No, but I am.'

'That wasn't the idea.'

There was a sudden cry from another room and Rory paused, his hands suspended above the keyboard. 'Young Master Dunbar is awake. I swear those two have an arrangement whereby they've agreed never to sleep simultaneously.'

'Dora said that's just how you two were. If you slept, Flora was awake. If Flora slept, you were awake. And sometimes you were both awake together. She says she didn't get any sleep for a year.' As Rory rose from the piano Grace said, 'Take him a glass of water, that usually settles him. But he might ask for a story.'

'He'll be lucky.'

Rory left the room quietly and reappeared a few moments later. 'Must have been a bad dream. He wasn't really awake. Seems OK now.' He sank on to the sofa beside Grace.

'You sounded worried.'

'About Colin?'

'No, earlier. When you were talking about responsibilities. Have you been worrying about money again?'

'No. Well, a bit.' He looked round the overcrowded room and raised his arms in the air. 'We need more space! How can I work like this?'

Grace surveyed the room. 'I suppose we could get rid of the dining table and eat off the piano.'

He gave her a bleak look. 'That isn't funny.'

She returned the look. 'You wanted kids too.'

'I wasn't complaining. It's just not easy. Music and kids don't mix.'

'Not while they're small, but that's not for ever. I do try to keep them out of your hair.'

'Yes, I know you do.' He leaned across and administered a perfunctory kiss on her cheek. Looking down at his infant daughter, he inserted his little finger into her fist and watched her tiny fingers curl round it automatically. 'She's almost asleep.'

'Thank God.'

'She's so like you.'

'Are you referring to the rolls of fat?'

'No. She's so dark. You're not fat anyway. You just haven't lost the weight you put on.'

'Or the weight I put on with Colin.'

'Well, it doesn't bother me.'

She glanced up at him quickly. 'Doesn't it?'

'Of course not. Why d'you ask?' Grace was silent and looked down again at Lottie, asleep in her arms. 'Oh... It's not *you*, Grace. I've got a lot on my mind. And I've been away a lot.'

'All the more reason for you to be pleased to see me when you get home.'

'I meant, it's tiring. All the travelling. Not to mention the playing. My schedule's been insane.'

'I know. I wish I could come with you. We need a holiday.'

'Fat chance.'

'We could go away for a weekend. Somewhere nice. Do something romantic.'

'We *could*,' Rory said without enthusiasm. 'A romantic idyll, complete with two children under three.'

'I'm sure Flora and Hugh would have Colin for a weekend. It would be nice for Theo to have someone to play with.' Lottie stirred and began to grizzle. Grace offered the bottle again. 'Did you go and see them today?'

'Yes. Well, I saw Flora. Hugh wasn't in.'

'How was Theo?' Rory didn't answer immediately and Grace continued, 'He's a dear little mite. Hugh just adores him. They should have another. And they should get a move on too – Hugh's no spring chicken.'

'I didn't see Theo. He was asleep. Shall I try and put Lottie down in her cot?'

'No, leave her, she's all right. I'm too tired to move anyway. How was Flora?'

'Oh... the usual. Tired. I think she finds Theo a handful.'

'She never seems very happy.'

'I don't think she is particularly.'

'What d'you think's the matter?'

'How should I know?' Rory shrugged. 'I don't think her life has turned out the way she expected. When she was a kid she had plans. Dreams. We both did. Hers don't seem to have amounted to much.'

'Oh, I don't know. She's got a lovely husband and son. And that great big house. I wish *we* had that much space! And the work she does in the parish is... very worthwhile.'

'Come off it, Grace. It's boring as hell and you know it! Brownies and baking and polishing pews? That was never Flora! She might not be Brain of Britain, but she was a lively kid. She had lots of energy and ideas. She was game for anything.'

'Yes, Dora told me. Wherever you led, Flora followed. And I expect you led her into all sorts of awful scrapes.'

'No, she was quite capable of getting into those on her own.'

'She told me about the time you cut off all her hair.'

'She asked me to! That was her St Joan phase. When she wanted to be a nun.' Rory chuckled softly. Grace thought how much she loved that sound, how rarely she heard it now.

'Didn't she have boyfriends?'

'No.'

'Never?'

'I don't think so. I don't remember any. I expect she did at drama school. *Must* have.'

'Strange. I mean, she's so pretty. I imagine men would find her very attractive, wouldn't you?'

'No idea. She's my sister. I can hardly be objective, can I?'

'She just strikes me as a certain type that men fall for – blonde, petite, very feminine... Like Marianne Faithfull. You know – fragile, but sexy. I always wanted to look like that. *Elfin*. When I first met Flora I felt like a shire horse in comparison. We couldn't be more different, could we? As women.'

'No, I suppose not.'

'Did you have girlfriends before college?'

'I played the piano. I did a lot of sport. There wasn't really time for much else. And all the girls I knew seemed pretty thick anyway. Their main interest in life seemed to be their hair. They knew nothing about music. It must have been much the same for you. What were your chances of meeting boys who shared your passion for the cello?'

'Practically nil. And the ones who did had spots. But it turned out all right in the end for me – for *us* – didn't it?' She laid her free hand on his thigh and smoothed the pile of the corduroy, registering the muscle beneath.

'Yes.' He laid a long, cool hand over hers. Grace wondered

fleetingly if she would be able to stay awake long enough for Rory to make love to her tonight; if he would even want to.

'It's such a shame Flora can't be happy. If only she'd try to make the best of things. There's no point in being bitter about missed opportunities, you've just got to get on with your life. Move on.'

'Maybe she can't.'

'Why not?'

'I don't know. I think she tries, but – it's all too much for her. She isn't… I don't think she was ever *strong*.   And she's not used to coping on her own.'

'How do you mean? She's got Hugh and he's ever so good with Theo. He helps around the house too. Not many men would do that.'

'No, I didn't mean that. Look, would *you* want Flora's life?'

'No, I wouldn't,' Grace said firmly.

'Why not?'

She tilted her head and laid it on his shoulder, nuzzling his neck. 'She hasn't got you.'

I showed quite a talent for secret drinking. What began as a sort of hobby, a small consolation for receiving the booby prize that was my life, quickly became a consuming passion, an addiction that went some way towards filling the voids – physical, mental and emotional – that Rory and Hugh had left. Secret drinking and its associated subterfuge were no particular challenge to me. My entire life was a sham. I was in love with my brother, I had borne his child and I was installed in my mausoleum of a vicarage as Mrs Holier-than-Thou, with a handsome husband who never laid a finger on me.

Pretence wasn't difficult. I had a natural flair for it, not to mention my training as an actress. No, my problem was bumping up against reality now and again, a hazard I mostly managed to avoid by numbing my brain with deadening domestic routine and equally deadening alcohol.

I was no longer drinking in order to remember – that was far too painful. I didn't want to know who I'd been, what Rory had been to me, what we'd lost. Now I drank to slake an unquenchable thirst. I drank to extinguish what remained of the fires that still smouldered in my mind and body.

1969

Flora sat slumped in front of the television, not drinking. Not drinking was how she spent a lot of her time. It was a conscious, virtuous act of self-denial and when she'd indulged in it for as long as possible, she rewarded herself with a drink. This was a way of eking out supplies at the same time as quieting her conscience. She told herself she didn't even *need* a drink this evening because she was going to watch Rory on television and that was treat enough. What she knew but didn't tell herself was that she would need a drink — possibly more than one — afterwards. Flora still believed drinking was a treat rather than a biological and psychological necessity and she told herself the same lie about seeing her brother.

Hugh had been called out by a parishioner and Flora hoped he wouldn't be home in time for the programme which she wanted to watch alone. She knew he would be very disappointed to miss it, but she didn't care. She saw her brother so rarely, she thought she deserved to have him all to herself now and again, even if it was only on a television screen.

She looked at the mantelpiece clock again and pulled the armchair closer to the television set. It suddenly occurred to her that the telephone might ring during the programme — some wretched parishioner calling her with a query or even asking her if she knew her brother was on television. Flora got up and hurried down the hall to the phone. She lifted the receiver and replaced it askew so that it was off the hook, but not obviously so. Hugh wouldn't approve, but if he noticed Flora would say Theo must have been playing with the phone. (This had actually happened once before, on a day Flora recalled as a sort of holiday: the phone had remained off the hook for many hours before Hugh had remarked how quiet things were, then gone to check whether it was working.)

Flora hurried back to the sitting room and switched on the television, even though the programme wasn't due to begin for several minutes. She plumped up a faded cushion, kicked off her slippers and curled up in the armchair. The programme was to feature several young musicians in their twenties who'd already made an impact in the world of classical music. Each was to be interviewed, then shown playing. Rory had said his section came at the end but Flora was determined to watch the whole programme in case somebody at the BBC had changed the running order at the last minute.

She sat impatiently through a pretty Japanese violinist whose English was laboured, but whose playing was remarkable. She was followed by a clarinettist. Flora thought he was American, but he might have been Canadian – she wasn't paying much attention. Then finally Rory's face came on to the screen, in close-up but much smaller than in life. Flora's fingers went to her mouth and she uttered a little cry of surprise and something like pain. Rory was in black and white.

Of course Rory was in black and white – how could she have been so silly as to think otherwise? What did it matter? It was Rory speaking, even *smiling* now and again, which Flora almost never saw these days. She tried to conquer her disappointment and concentrate on the programme. At least his grey eyes must be the right colour. Yet somehow they weren't. There wasn't that icy hint of green – or was it blue? It was so long since she'd seen him, she couldn't really remember. Then suddenly the camera was showing him seated at the piano playing some Schubert – Flora recognised it at once, Rory would have been pleased with her – and she was at leisure to study her brother's face without having to consider his words.

It wasn't Rory. It was a pale, colourless imitation, but it was better than nothing. There was the fragility in the pale skin around his eyes but it wasn't lightly veined with blue. You could see it was finely creased, like crushed tissue, but it wasn't creamy-gold and dusted with freckles. There were the dark lines at the corner of his mouth, deep straight furrows that ran from nostril to jaw and then disappeared as his face resolved itself into sculptured planes of repose, but the full, curved and perfectly symmetrical lips were grey, as was Rory's hair – grey and darker grey, instead of gold, ochre, honey, brown, copper... How many colours were there in Rory's hair, Flora wondered? How many pigments would an artist need to paint it? A whole palette-full...

The picture was blurred and she got up to thump the top of the set. It made no difference. She screwed up her face in anger and to her surprise, tears trickled down her cheeks. She gasped and rubbed quickly at her eyes with the hem of her apron. The picture became clear again. She knelt on the floor, her face inches from the set and watched Rory's monochrome hands moving across the keyboard, hands she would know anywhere. As they came to rest and the music died away, she raised her own hand to the screen and laid it on the grey image of his.

Flora stared at the credits as they rolled, then switched off the set and got to her feet. She stumbled over to the sideboard and withdrew a bottle.

Funding my habit was a problem. Hugh gave me money for housekeeping and never asked what it was spent on, but what he gave me barely covered what it actually cost to feed and clothe us. I made as many economies as possible and put by spare pennies and shillings in an envelope in my dressing table drawer. I used these to buy cheap sherry with which I topped up the bottles in the sideboard so that Hugh never realised they had long ago been emptied.

I bought loose broken biscuits, bruised fruit and vegetables, bacon pieces. Theo and I lunched on spam or haslet. I developed a real nose for a bargain. As chief organiser of church jumble sales I got first pick of children's clothing which I spirited away when no one was looking. My resourcefulness felt like some sort of achievement. Only occasionally did I feel downright deceitful. At Christmas Hugh gave me extra money to buy presents for Theo. So did Dora, who knew we were very hard up. I didn't tell Hugh. I spent his money on presents for Theo – really nice ones, all of them brand new – and I spent Dora's money on a bottle of brandy. I hid it at the back of the sideboard, where Hugh would never notice it. If he did, he would assume it was a Christmas present from a parishioner.

Eventually of course my consumption outstripped my income and my ingenuity.

In those days I never stole from shops, only from Orchard Farm and then only things my mother would never miss: tins of ham and corned beef, the odd packet of soup, jars of home-made preserves – little luxuries that Hugh and Theo would enjoy and which I could no longer afford to buy. Once, I caught sight of a ten-shilling note folded and placed under the clock on the kitchen mantelpiece. I palmed it when Dora's back was turned. I doubt she ever missed it.

I did feel bad going through the pockets of Hugh's clothes, looking for small change. He kept a small dish on his bedside table for keys, cuff links and coins. I never took all the money in case he noticed and I never took half crowns, but the small coins gradually accumulated and kept the sherry bottles topped up.

I was careful to make sure Hugh never smelled alcohol on my breath. He rarely came close to me anyway and I developed a trick of having my head bent over some task – mending or washing up – when he came home, so he just used to kiss the top of my head. I drank when Hugh was out at evensong, weddings and christenings, when I knew he wouldn't come home unexpectedly and surprise me. Sometimes I would get up at night when he was asleep and come downstairs to drink brandy. He was none the wiser.

In any case I always had my alibi ready: a large box of liqueur chocolates I'd won in the tombola at the vicarage garden fête. If Hugh were ever to mention a smell of alcohol on my breath I would confess I'd wickedly indulged in one of my precious chocolates. These were in fact all empty. I had long ago pierced them with a darning needle and drained off the cherry brandy contents, but the chocolate shells still sat in their be-ribboned box, meticulously rewrapped in their silver foil, ready to be called upon as evidence for the defence.

Such subterfuge became unnecessary after I saw a comedy programme on television in which a straight-laced spinster became tipsy because someone had laced her orange juice with vodka. Vodka, it appeared, had no smell.

The answer to a maiden's prayer.

Chapter 11

1969

When the doorbell rang Flora set down her glass on the kitchen windowsill behind the curtain. She then changed her mind, thinking a glass of orange squash left behind a curtain would be difficult to account for if found. She thought, very briefly, of tipping the vodka-laced squash down the sink but couldn't bring herself to do it. Supplies were low. The doorbell rang again. Flora set the glass down among a pile of dirty breakfast dishes on the draining board and then hurried to the front door, smoothing her hair and hoping that the bell hadn't woken Theo.

She opened the door to Rory.

'Hello, Flor.'

'*Rory*!'

'Well, don't look so surprised.'

'You *never* visit! I hardly ever see you—'

'So ask me in, then. I'm getting cold standing on your doorstep. And I can't stay long.'

Flora stood back and closed the door behind him. There was a hiatus in which she expected Rory to kiss her, at least on the cheek, but he didn't. She looked at him expectantly. He was dressed in dark corduroy trousers and a black polo-neck sweater. She thought he looked thinner than she remembered, but decided it was probably the dark clothes. He had the remains of a tan, a by-product of a southern European tour, but there were shadows under his eyes.

Removing her apron, Flora broke the silence. 'Have you come from Orchard Farm?'

'Yes. Thought I'd go and see everyone. Ettie's not been well. And Ma had a fall in the garden apparently.'

'Yes. I think she's been overdoing things. I expect they were all pleased to see you.'

'Seemed to be. Is Hugh in?'

'No. It's Saturday. He's marrying people. Theo's upstairs having a nap, I'm afraid.'

'I haven't come to see Theo.'

'No, I didn't suppose you had. Do you want a drink? Tea, I mean. Or coffee? Have you had lunch? I could make you a sandwich. Or there's some soup left over from—'

'Shut up, Flor. I'm not one of your parishioners. You can stop doing the vicar's wife routine.' He reached out and grasped her fingers, swinging them back and forth in a childlike gesture.

Flora smiled, felt the first intimation of tears and laughed to suppress them. 'Sorry! I was on automatic pilot. So used to feeding the five thousand, you see. The doorbell goes and I immediately start totting up loaves and fishes.' She laughed again. 'It's good to see you, Rory.'

'You too.' There was a long silence in which neither of them moved. Rory continued to hold three fingers of Flora's hand and she registered the cool softness of his skin, the familiar long bones of his fingers. He nodded his head. 'Perhaps I will have a cup of tea.'

'Yes, of course. Come and sit in the kitchen while I make it for you.'

Rory followed her into the kitchen and sat down at the table. Flora filled the kettle, checking as she did so that her glass was still where she'd left it, or rather, that she could remember where she'd left it. She was getting a little absent-minded these days, There were so many things to remember.

She turned back to Rory and sat at the table. 'You're looking very well.'

'You're not. Have you been crying?'

'No!' Flora couldn't actually remember if she'd been crying this morning, but she thought not.

'You've lost weight.'

'Oh, I was always thin.'

'Now you're even thinner. You don't look well, Flor.'

'I'm just worn out, that's all. Theo's had a cold and it went to his chest. I've been getting up at nights. He catches up on sleep during the day, I don't. You know how it is... How are the children?' she asked brightly.

'Fine. Charlotte had an ear infection recently but... They're fine.'

'Oh, good. It's hateful when they're ill, isn't it? So worrying. It's such a relief once they can talk and tell you where it hurts.'

'Why do you keep looking at the dishes?'

'I don't!'

'You do. Am I interrupting something? Do you need to get on with cooking?'

'No, of course not! You're imagining things. How's Grace?'

'Fine. Well, tired, I suppose.' He frowned and said, 'Flora, can we drop all this? It's just you and me. We don't have to pretend.'

The kettle came to the boil but Flora didn't rise from the table. 'What is it that you want, Rory?'

'I don't want anything. I just wanted to see you on your own for a little while. I never do.'

Her voice faltered. 'I'm not sure it's a terribly good idea.' There was another long silence. Flora felt an impulse to check the glass but kept her eyes firmly on Rory's hand, resting on the table, his fingers spread as if he were about to play a tune.

'Are things... any better?'

'Between me and Hugh? No. Worse, if anything.'

Rory was silent. Flora watched the hand clench then spread again. 'Have you ever thought of leaving him?'

She looked up, her eyes wide. 'For you?'

'No, of course not! Don't be stupid, Flora. Even if I didn't have a wife and kids we couldn't have any kind of a life together.'

'We could go abroad,' she said quickly. 'No-one would know us. We could start again. Hugh loves Theo, he would look after him, I know he would. And I could work! There must be *something* I could do... I can type! I could wait tables or work in a shop. My French is pretty good. You could send money home to Grace and the children. She'd manage. She's very capable.'

'Jesus, Flora! Are you out of your mind? Is this the little fantasy world you live in? What about my career? Do you expect me to turn my back on that?'

'People do.'

'Not me.'

Flora checked the glass again, folded and re-folded her hands carefully in her lap. 'I saw you on the telly last night. And we heard you on the radio. The concert from Madrid. Hugh and I listened together. You were very good.'

'Thank you.'

'Hugh said your great virtue as a pianist is that you manage to unite head and heart. He said he used to find your playing a bit intellectual but now he thinks you have the balance exactly right.'

'Does he? Well, bully for Hugh. And what did you think, Flor?'

'I didn't think anything. I just cried.'

'Well, thank God you weren't in the audience.' He screwed up his eyes suddenly as if in pain. 'I don't know why I said that. I *always* wish you were in the audience.' He watched her as she bowed her head and scraped long strands of untidy blonde hair behind her ears. It looked none too clean and she was wearing no make-up, not even a touch of lipstick. Her eyes swivelled up towards the draining board and then back again.

'Why have you come, Rory?'

'I wanted to say some things. Some difficult things.'

'Such as?'

'I think you should leave Hugh.'

Flora laughed then stood up and started to make a pot of tea. 'Now who's living in a fantasy world? How can I? Why should I?'

'You're not happy. You never will be happy with Hugh. You've tried. I think you should call it a day and try to start again. You might find love... with someone else.'

She looked at him over her shoulder. 'Are you trying to set me up as your mistress somewhere?'

'No, of course not! For God's sake, Flora, can you imagine what it would do to my career if it ever got out about us? I'd be finished! No performer could survive that sort of scandal.'

'Oh, I see! You're trying to match-make so I'm not such a threat to your *career*. Had you got anyone lined up for me? Have you been grooming anyone for the job? Who could possibly step into *your* shoes? Rather a tall order, I would have thought. Of course you could always try offering me money – I believe that's the standard procedure. You pay a regular amount into my bank account and I keep quiet about your incestuous bastard child. Will that help you to sleep at nights, Rory? Will that stop you worrying about your precious career?'

'I think I'd better leave.' He stood up then plunged his hands into his pockets. 'There's one more thing I wanted to say.'

'What?'

'I want you to stop drinking.'

'Don't be ridiculous! I don't drink.'

'I want you to stop drinking and if you can't, I want you to get help.'

'I don't know what you're talking about.'

Rory took a step towards the draining board, picked up Flora's glass and tossed the contents into the sink. She shrieked and watched appalled as the orange juice and vodka drained away down the sink.

Rory set the empty glass down. 'Get help, Flora.'

She lifted both fists and brought them down on his chest with a thud. 'You beast! I hate you! I *hate* you!'

He grasped both her wrists and shook her. 'Flor, d'you realise how dangerous this is? Disguising booze as orange squash? Supposing Theo drank it? It could kill him!'

'Why should *you* care? You've never shown the slightest interest in him!'

'No, I haven't and I think that's what's best for him and probably best for you. You know you only have to ask if you need money for him. I thought it would be easier for you and Hugh if I kept out of things. I thought maybe you could pretend—'

'*You* could pretend, you mean! Pretend Theo doesn't exist!'

He released her arms. 'The other thing I wanted to say was... I'm sorry.'

'*Sorry?* What for?'

He stared down at his feet and his heavy hair flopped forward over his brow. For a moment Flora saw her boy-brother, blinking back tears, standing in disgrace before Archie. 'I'm sorry I didn't stop you marrying Hugh... Sorry that I ever told you I loved you... Sorry that I got you pregnant... I'm sorry. For all of it.'

'You're sorry that you loved me?'

His head lifted suddenly. 'No. I'm sorry I told you.'

'So that's it, is it? Case closed, we all move on? I've heard your confession, you've repented, so now you can go back to your oh-so-important career and your devoted doormat wife and just get on with your very successful life.'

'Flor, please—'

'I'm going to make you suffer for what you've done to me, Rory.'

'You already have,' he said quietly. 'You exist. I can't have you. How could things be any worse?'

'I could ruin your career. All I have to do is say the word and you're finished.'

'You wouldn't do it. I can't believe you'd hurt innocent people. I can believe you'd want to hurt *me* that badly, but not Theo. Not Hugh.'

'Theo has a right to know who his parents are!'

'Oh, really? And a right to be unhappy and ashamed? Like *us*, you mean? Did *we* have rights, Flora? What happened to them? Did we deserve all this? Or were we damned even before we were born? Is this what your precious bloody God wanted for us? Was our misery part of the divine plan? Divine bloody lottery more like! An accident of birth means we can never be together, never admit what we feel for each other. Is that how you want things to be for Theo? Living every hour, every minute in silent shame, wishing he'd never been born? Is that what you want for our son?'

Flora started to shake. 'I – I shall tell Hugh!'

'You do that!' Rory yelled. 'Tell Hugh what you feel for me – maybe *he'll* understand! He might even find it in his big manly heart to forgive your sin. Tell Hugh, Flora, then tell Theo. Why not ruin *all* our lives while you're about it?'

Flora wrapped her arms around her body, bending over at the waist and groaning as if she were in agony. 'Oh, I am in *hell*!' Rory took a step towards her and she shouted, 'No! Don't touch me! If you touch me I shall die... Get out of this house, Rory. Leave us. Leave us in peace.' She reached up with a trembling hand and touched a wooden crucifix hanging on the wall. Her lips moved but at first there was no sound, then she began to recite in a high, sing-song voice.

'*And Jesus called a little child unto him and set him in the midst of them and said, Verily I say unto you, Except ye be converted, and become as little children, ye shall not enter into the kingdom of heaven.*'

Rory turned and left without saying another word. As he strode down the hall Flora called after him.

'*Woe unto the world because of offences! For it must needs be that offences come; but woe to that man by whom the offence cometh!*'

The front door slammed. As Flora walked into the sitting room, she heard Theo begin to whimper upstairs. She closed the door, went to the sideboard and withdrew an almost empty bottle of orange barley water in which she kept her vodka. Carefully unscrewing the top, she continued to recite, her voice becoming gradually steadier.

'*Wherefore if thy hand or thy foot offend thee, cut them off, and cast them from thee: it is better for thee to enter into life halt or maimed, rather than having two hands or two feet to be cast into everlasting fire.*'

Flora lifted the bottle to her lips and drank. As the spirit warmed her she closed her eyes and a beatific smile spread across her face. She sank to her knees, bowed her head and thanked God for vodka, for delivering her from sin and for giving her another chance.

I didn't curse Rory.
    I didn't.
    I didn't.
    I didn't.

1971

Theo was singing hymns. He sat at the kitchen table drawing chorus lines of angels. In the centre of the picture was an attenuated figure with a broad smile and a long pointed beard. One hand was raised in the air above the angels.

As she passed, Flora peered over his shoulder. 'Is God blessing them?' she asked, curious.

'No, He's waving,' Theo replied, without lifting his fair head.

His mother smiled. Given the choice of a blessing or a wave from the Almighty, Flora thought she might settle for a wave.

Theo surveyed his colouring pencils in their plastic wallet and selected three. 'Andrew Temple's got a new baby sister.'

'Has he? That's nice,' Flora said absently, tying on her apron.

Theo drew myriad stars in the firmament with different coloured pencils. 'Will *we* have any more babies?'

'No.' Flora was startled by the promptness of her reply. So certain? At only twenty-nine?

'Why not?' Theo asked.

'Because Daddy and I don't want any more babies.' And, Flora added mentally, another baby would require sexual congress to take place, a miracle of the first order. Flora doubted the Almighty thought she deserved any miracles.

Laying his head down on the table, Theo wrestled with the technical challenge of drawing circles for the Sun and Moon. 'Does God give you babies?'

'Yes, in a way. Some people think babies are the gift of God.'

'You mean, like a present?'

'Sort of.'

'For being good?'

'Well, no not really...' Sometimes for being *bad*, thought Flora, scraping the remains of breakfast into the bin under the sink. 'It's just a wonderful thing that happens when mummies and daddies love each other very much. They make a baby, a new person, someone they can both love together.'

'Do they love the baby for ever?'

'Yes, they do. The baby grows into a child, then into a man or woman, but the parents always love them.' Flora thought of her own mother and added, 'In their way.'

'And do the mummies and daddies always love each other?'

Theo, being only five, was not aware of the pause before Flora replied. He wasn't looking at his mother and even if he had been, he wouldn't have noticed her shoulders tense nor registered the change in her breathing, but he did hear her say, 'Would you like a sweet?'

He looked up, astonished. 'Yes... *Please*,' he added quickly.

Flora rummaged in the pantry, found a packet of dolly mixtures and tossed them on to the table. Theo tore open the packet and started to cram them into his mouth before his mother could change her mind.

'*Do* they?' he persisted, his cheeks bulging.

'Do they what?' Flora asked, playing for time, feeling the prickle of tears as they crept under her eyelids.

Theo swallowed and said patiently, 'Do mummies and daddies always love each other?'

Flora took a pile of dirty plates from the worktop and dumped them noisily in the sink. She turned the hot tap on full. 'No, not always. Sometimes mummies and daddies decide that they don't want to live together any more because – because they don't love each other... in the same way.'

The boy looked up and saw his mother silhouetted against the kitchen window, her head bowed, her arms plunged into the sink. 'But they still love their *children*?'

'Oh, yes. They do. They still love their children. They always love their children. Always...'

Theo hated it when his mother cried. He pushed the packet of sweets into his pocket, got down from the table and went out into the garden to play. The back door swung open and a gust of wind swept God and all his angels off the kitchen table, sending them hurtling through the air.

People said Theo was a little angel, a dear boy, no trouble, and with his bright blue eyes, blond curls and his pale, slightly anxious face, people said he looked like an angel too.

But not to me. I looked at Theo and all I ever saw was the personification of hideous, unnatural, unforgivable, irredeemable sin.

And I saw Rory.

Hugh was late home for supper and Flora put a plate in front of him that had sat in the oven for an hour. He ate the congealed food without complaint while Flora sat at the kitchen table with a cup of tea, turning the pages of *The Church Times*, wishing it were *Woman's Own*.

'I had a chat with Ettie after Evensong today.'

'Oh? What about?'

'Theo.'

Flora looked up. 'Has he been misbehaving at Orchard Farm?'

'No, of course not. He's always good as gold when he goes there. She asked whether we'd thought about Theo learning the piano.' Flora's back stiffened and she stared fixedly at the newsprint. 'Ettie said she'd be very happy to give him lessons. No charge of course. She realises we can't afford to pay.'

'I'm sure Ettie doesn't have time to give Theo piano lessons.'

'Apparently the bookshop's closing down so she's going to be out of a job. She says she'll be at a bit of a loose end. She seemed quite keen... I gather she was Rory's first teacher.'

'Well, she'd be wasting her time with Theo. He's such a clumsy child. He's like me, he's got no co-ordination. Ettie tried to teach me as well as Rory, but I was hopeless. No patience. Theo's just the same.'

'Actually,' Hugh said mildly, 'Ettie thinks he shows some promise. That's one of the reasons she suggested it. He's shown a lot of interest in the piano and she says he already has a well-developed sense of rhythm.'

'How on earth can she tell?'

'From playing with him, she says. And from his singing. You know what a lovely little voice he has. Ettie seems to think he's quite musical. She said he reminds her very much of Rory at the same age.'

Flora closed the newspaper, stood up and went to fill the kettle. 'Well, I don't want him to learn the piano. And I wish Ettie would mind her own business!'

'Flora!'

She banged the kettle down on the hob. The gas ignited with a roar. 'I want my son to grow up like a normal boy – playing football, climbing trees! I can't imagine anything *worse* for an only child than to spend hours every day cooped up indoors playing the piano. Look what it did to Rory!'

'What do you mean?'

'Well, he's hardly a well-adjusted member of the community, is he? He's not exactly what you'd call *normal*!'

'I think it's just that he's phenomenally talented and a price is paid for that. It's true Rory isn't like other people—'

'Rory is sick!'

Hugh sighed and shook his head. 'Sick at heart perhaps.'

'Well, do you want our son turning out like that?'

Hugh laid down his knife and fork, his appetite gone. 'I think you're over-reacting, Flora, but we can drop the subject if you wish. I just thought it was very kind of Ettie to offer. It would have been a wonderful opportunity for Theo.'

'Theo isn't musical! Believe me, Hugh – I can tell. Theo is *nothing* like Rory.'

At bedtime Theo clambered on to Hugh's lap and settled himself against the giant body as if into an armchair. He opened a battered book and laid it across his knees. Hugh peered over the top of Theo's head to see what he'd chosen for his story. The boy's soft curls tickled Hugh's chin and he brushed them aside affectionately, cupping the boy's head with his large hand.

'Daddy...'

'Yes?'

'D'you love me?'

'Of course, my dear! I love you very, *very* much.' He folded the boy in his arms and squeezed him, making the roaring bear noise that always made Theo laugh.

Theo turned the pages of his book, looking for the story he wanted. 'Daddy...'

'Mmm?'

'D'you love me more than God?'

Hugh was silent for only a moment as he deliberated, then decided to say what Theo wanted to hear. He quieted his conscience with the excuse that the boy couldn't understand an answer of any greater complexity. 'Yes, Theo,' Hugh said softly, 'I love you more than God.' He realised, with something of a shock, that what he'd said was true.

Theo settled back against Hugh's chest and put his thumb in his mouth. He removed it suddenly with a little popping sound. 'D'you love me more than Mummy?'

Above their heads, Hugh could hear Flora upstairs, her footsteps travelling back and forth, emptying Theo's bath, tidying toys, drawing curtains. 'No, Theo. I love Mummy just as much as I love you. I love you both the same.'

With another shock, Hugh realised he'd just lied.

After the bedtime story, Flora put Theo to bed and Hugh went to his study to pray. He intended to ask God to forgive him his lie, to forgive him the sin of loving his son more than anything in this world or the next. Instead, as he knelt, his defiant heart thanked God for the gift of his only son.

Hugh hoped that God, father of an only son, would understand.

Chapter 12

1974

To begin with Hugh thought God was simply putting him to the test. The difficulties of his first marriage followed by Miriam's sudden death had taken their toll, but he had rallied when he found new love with Flora. The birth of his son in 1966 had brought him more joy and pride than he had ever known and his love for the baby was uncomplicated, unconditional and overwhelming. But on the twenty-first of October in the same year an avalanche of mining waste slid down a Welsh mountainside and engulfed a primary school. One hundred and sixteen children died.

Hugh's faith had withstood the Allies' liberation of the concentration camps and he'd eventually come to terms with the iniquity and depravity of which human beings were capable. He hadn't known that his biggest battle – moral, intellectual and theological – would not be against evil, but against meaningless destruction, random tragedy, pointless waste – particularly of young lives. He realised that his new rôle as a father had sensitised him to the tragedy in Aberfan, but as he led prayers in the parish church facing a stunned congregation, Hugh realised he could find no meaning and therefore offer little comfort. His feelings were primitive and deep. He thanked God his own precious son was alive and was angry that many other sons weren't. Hugh didn't pray to be spared tragedy, he prayed simply to understand, but his prayers went unanswered.

And then Flora had started to drink.

It had been noted in the parish and the Bishop had had a quiet word with Hugh – had been very sympathetic in fact – but Hugh knew he was probably facing the failure of his second marriage.

The fabric of his faith was wearing thin. In places it had worn into holes through which a cold wind of doubt blew. He hunched his broad shoulders against the blast, tensed a body racked with headaches and sleepless nights. His smile was a rare event now, reserved for needy parishioners and his son, Theo, the only person with whom Hugh felt something like his old self. Theo allowed him to feel strong and certain because, for Theo, Hugh had to have answers, even if they were only lies. There were few certainties left in Hugh's life, but love – the possibility of loving and being loved in return – would be the last to be relinquished.

It was late when Hugh entered the sitting room and found Flora asleep in an armchair in front of the television. The large room (used so often for parish meetings that Flora joked it was little more than an extension of the church hall) was untidy with toys, newspapers and parish magazines. Hugh thought he could smell alcohol fumes and looked around for an empty glass. He could see none, which didn't surprise him. He knew Flora would have washed it up by now and replaced it in the cupboard, leaving no tell-tale sign on the draining board.

He looked down at his wife asleep in the chair. She was still wearing her apron and her hair was scraped back behind her ears revealing how thin her face had become. Even in sleep the tiny cleft of a frown between her brows was still visible. Gazing down at her, Hugh felt an uncomfortable mixture of tenderness and anger, although he thought the anger was directed mainly at himself. He thought of waking her with a kiss, like a fairytale prince, then thought better of the idea. Instead he bent down to switch off the television. The sudden silence woke Flora and she stirred in her armchair, sat up quickly and rubbed her eyes.

'I must have dropped off. What time is it?'

'Flora, can we have a talk? A serious talk. There's something I want to discuss with you.'

'It's getting a bit late for that, isn't it? What's the matter?'

Hugh sat down in the other armchair, facing her. 'I know this will come as something of a shock to you, but... I've decided I want to leave the ministry.'

Flora stared at him open-mouthed, then laughed. 'You're joking!'

'It's hardly a joking matter, my dear.'

'How can you even *think* about giving up the ministry? Where would we live? What would we live *on*?'

'I don't know yet. I've given it a lot of thought, but I haven't come up with any answers yet. No definite answers anyway. But I'm fit. I'm still only fifty-three. There must be plenty of work I could do. And with Theo at school now, perhaps you could brush up your typing and shorthand. Get a part-time job to help out. That would make a big difference. And it would get you out of the house. I think that might do you a lot of good,' he added, with an attempt at a smile.

'But... *why?* Why don't you want to be a minister any more? I don't understand.'

'I find I just don't believe any more.'

Flora stared at him. 'Don't believe in God?'

Hugh was silent for a moment. 'I think I still believe in God. Or something like God. I think I still believe in the value of Christianity, of Christ's teaching, certainly. But I'm not sure I believe any more in the *Church*.'

Flora threw up her hands. 'Oh, you've lost me now. If you believe in Christ's teachings, I don't see what the problem is! Aren't you just splitting hairs? In any case, why can't you just pretend?'

Hugh smiled. 'Yes, I could pretend. I've become rather good at pretending... But I don't *want* to pretend any more. It isn't fair on my congregation. They deserve better.'

'And what about Theo and me? We deserve a roof over our heads!'

'Yes, of course, and I'll make sure I continue to provide for you both. But... there may be difficult times ahead. While I try to find another job. I won't pretend things are going to be easy.'

'But where will we go? Where will we live? And what about Theo's school? You can't take him away. He loves it there and he's made lots of friends.'

'Yes, I know and that's why I think we should try to stay in this area – if we can.' Hugh shifted in his armchair and said carefully, 'I've had a word with Dora—'

'You've spoken to Ma? Before you spoke to *me*? Hugh, I'm your *wife*!'

'I'm sorry, but I needed to know whether – if the worst came to the worst, if we had to leave the vicarage and I hadn't found a job and somewhere for us to live – I had to know whether Dora and Archie would take us in. Temporarily, of course.'

Flora's face crumpled and she reached into a pocket for her

handkerchief. 'Oh, Hugh, that would be so humiliating!'

'It may not come to that. I'm sure it won't! But I needed to know. Just in case. Dora was very understanding.'

'But there isn't *room* for all of us at Orchard Farm!'

'It would only be a temporary measure. You and I could have the guest room and Theo would have Rory's old bedroom. He loves that little room. He likes playing with Rory's old toys.'

Flora wiped her eyes and sniffed. 'We could hardly live there for free. It wouldn't be right.'

'No, of course not. We'd have to pay our way somehow. It's a great pity we don't have any savings. But Dora said she'd be glad of extra help with the garden and around the house. Your parents are getting on now. Archie's eighty-five.'

'The garden's been too much for him for a long time. It's breaking his heart.'

'Dora said she and Ettie just about manage to keep the house ticking over but the garden has had to be neglected. So much so, she and Archie have been thinking of selling up.'

'Selling Orchard Farm?'

'Yes. Archie wants to apparently. Says it's too big and he's too old. But Dora thinks the upheaval would kill him. She wants to stay put until – well, until a move becomes... inevitable,' Hugh explained tactfully. 'So you see, your parents would be doing us an enormous favour, but we'd be able to return that favour in small ways.'

'But I can't go back and live there! It's my childhood home. There are too many memories. I was *happy* then,' she added wistfully and started to cry again.

Hugh got out of his chair and knelt beside her, taking her hand in his. 'Darling, I thought if you had your family around you, if you spent less time alone, things might be better for you. It might be easier for you to stop drinking.'

Flora snatched her hand away. 'What do you mean? I don't drink, Hugh! Whatever put that idea in your head? Just because I enjoy a sherry now and again... Have you been talking to Rory?'

'Does Rory know?'

'No, he doesn't,' Flora said hurriedly. 'I mean – there's nothing to know, so how *could* Rory know?... Oh, you're getting me all confused! Look, I think this is a crazy idea! Going back to live at Orchard Farm, surrounded by my geriatric relations – that would be enough to *drive* me to drink!'

Hugh sat back on his heels and sighed. 'Flora, I know you drink. You don't make a very good job of hiding it. It's even known in the parish. Word has got as far as the Bishop, I'm afraid.'

Flora's mouth worked but no words came. She screwed her handkerchief into a ball and sat looking down at her clenched fist. 'Are they kicking you out because of me?'

'No. I've told you my reason for leaving the ministry. I can't carry on as a parish priest. Too many things have happened… Too many things that I can't explain, that I can't live with. I can't face my parishioners, I can't face you. One day I might not be able to face Theo. I can't live with myself, not as a minister. And even if I could, I can't be a minister with a wife who drinks.'

'I don't drink!'

'Flora—'

'Just now and again! It's nothing serious. It's not a *problem*.'

'Flora, you don't cook any more, you hardly clean. Sometimes I don't even have a clean shirt to wear. You neglect your appearance. You neglect Theo.'

'I don't!'

'He asked me the other day why Mummy is always so cross with him. Was it because he was bad?'

'I don't know why he said that! I'm not always cross.'

'I asked him why he plays out in the garden all the time, even when it's cold and he said, "Mummy doesn't like it when I make a mess indoors. And she doesn't like the noise". '

'Oh, what rubbish! It's just that he gets on my nerves sometimes with all his singing and chattering away to himself.'

Hugh smiled but couldn't hide his exasperation. 'He has to play make-believe games! What else can he do? He's an only child.'

'And whose fault is that?' Flora snapped.

Hugh bowed his head, then hauled himself to his feet. He returned to his armchair and sat down again, clasping his hands in his lap. 'I haven't been a good husband to you, I don't deny it. I hope to be a better one in future. It's one of the reasons I want to leave the ministry. To give us more time together as a family. But I believe our son is being neglected and you cannot expect me to ignore that. I do try to understand your difficulties. I want to support you, but Theo comes first. Surely you must see that?'

'Oh, yes, I do! It's perfectly plain to me that he comes first! Your precious Theo, your little angel!' she sneered. 'You've no time for me, but you make time for *him*, don't you?'

'Flora, that's hardly fair. If I make a fuss of Theo it's partly because you don't.'

'You spoil him.'

'Good grief! Am I not allowed to express love for my son?'

'He's not your son.'

'He's as much my son as yours!'

'No, he isn't.'

'What?'

Flora's lip quivered and she said in a small voice, 'He's not your son.'

Hugh gazed at her, uncomprehending. 'What do you mean? Are you saying... I'm *not* Theo's father?'

'No, you're not.'

Hugh opened his mouth to speak, then closed it again. 'Are you *sure*?'

'Positive. Theo wasn't premature. I lied about the dates. I had to, owing to the infrequency of our lovemaking.'

Hugh stared into space, his face slack with shock. He took a deep breath and asked, 'Do I know the father?'

She hesitated. 'Yes.'

He spread his broad hands on his thighs, as if bracing himself. 'Will you tell me who he is?'

'No. I'm sorry, but I can't.'

'I see.' After a few moments Hugh said, 'I hope he was someone who loved you... I'd like to think that Theo was at least a love-child.'

'Yes, the father loved me. Loves me still,' Flora said with a hint of defiance.

'Married, I take it?'

'Yes.'

'And you loved him?'

'Yes.'

'Do you still?'

'Yes... Yes, I do.'

Hugh bowed his head. Eventually he said, 'I know I've been... *inadequate* in some respects. I want you to know that I won't put any obstacles in your way if you want to make a fresh start. That is,' he added, raising anxious eyes to her, 'If you'll allow me to continue as Theo's father. His nominal father at least.'

'You're not the obstacle, Hugh. You never have been. You were meant to be my salvation.'

'And I failed you.'

'Oh, I wouldn't lose any sleep over it. I think I was damned from birth,' Flora said, staring vacantly into space. 'Damned *by* my birth.'

'Has this man refused to divorce his wife?'

Her sudden laughter was harsh. 'I've never asked him to! There'd be no point. He can't live with me. He doesn't even want to acknowledge Theo as his.'

'Why not?'

'It would ruin his career. I think he'd really prefer to disown us both and just get on with his life.'

'You say I *know* this man?'

'Yes.'

'Will you please tell me who it is?' Flora didn't answer. 'If I'm to continue to be Theo's father in name and spirit, if I'm to be financially responsible for him, I think I probably have a right to know whose child he is.'

Flora tugged at her damp handkerchief. 'Yes... I suppose you do.'

'Flora, my dear, tell me – who is it that you love?'

'Oh, for God's sake, Hugh – just look at Theo's *face*! Who do you *think* is his father!'

'I've no idea! I've always thought Theo was the image of *you*!' Flora stared at Hugh, her eyes wide, imploring. Hugh swallowed, then whispered, 'Rory?'

She nodded.

'*Rory*?'

'Who else could it be? Who else have I ever loved? Who else has ever loved *me*?' She covered her face with her hands and began to sob.

Hugh repeated the name, as if in a trance. 'Rory...'

'Yes, *Rory*! I've loved him all my life and I always will! We made love just the once and I got pregnant. I didn't know what to *do*,' she whimpered. 'I couldn't pretend it was yours because we hadn't made love for months. I was going to get rid of it, then I thought, this might be the only child I ever have! In any case, I *couldn't* kill Rory's child, not after Grace lost theirs. I saw that dead creature, Hugh. I couldn't do that to my baby! Rory wanted me to have an abortion, but I refused. So he told me what to do... I got very drunk and just about raped you. Perhaps you remember! It was the day I fainted at Orchard Farm. You'd been working in the garden.'

'Yes, I remember... I remember it very well.'

'Seven months later, Theo was born.'

Hugh sat perfectly still as he digested this information, then asked, his voice unsteady now, 'Did you ever love me, Flora?'

'Yes. At least, I thought I did. I genuinely thought what I felt for you was love, but now I don't know. It felt so different from what I felt for Rory, so I thought it must be love. I was young, inexperienced... I'd had very few boyfriends and none of them meant anything to me. Not compared with my brother. As for sex – I hadn't a clue. I didn't know what I was supposed to feel, what I was supposed to do, or let men do. I had no idea that what I felt for Rory was... *sexual*. Not till after I married you. But even then I thought you would save me. You were so big and strong, so very handsome. So *good*. But...' She started to weep again. 'You weren't interested in me! Perhaps if we'd been physically close, Hugh, things might've been different, perhaps the marriage might have worked.'

'Yes... I'm sorry. I let you down.'

'Why on earth did you marry me if you felt no love for me, no *desire* for me?'

Hugh leaned back wearily in his armchair and closed his eyes. After a while he spoke. 'When I married Miriam I'd never been in love. I had no sexual experience other than what might be acquired at a boys' boarding school. I was a virgin as far as women were concerned. Miriam was also a virgin. I knew she loved me very much and I was convinced I loved her, but I didn't really know how to love her physically. What was worse, I found I didn't really *want* to. After she died I became depressed and lonely. My life seemed empty. Then I met you. Our friendship developed and... I found I was captivated by you, Flora. You were so full of life, yet so vulnerable, so trusting. I wanted to look after you. Protect you. I was convinced what I felt for you was love.'

'But it wasn't.'

'No, it wasn't. Not love in the sense you mean. Not the kind of love that makes a marriage work.'

'When did you realise you didn't love me, Hugh?'

He closed his eyes and didn't answer.

'Hugh? Answer me.'

'Oh, my dear... I never wanted you to know.'

'Tell me.'

'I realised I didn't love you when... when I finally fell in love. With someone else.'

Flora gasped as if she had been struck. 'When was that?'

Hugh gripped the arms of his chair with both hands and said softly, 'After we'd become engaged. Some time before we married.'

'*Before*? You... you bastard!'

Hugh closed his eyes. Steeling himself, he opened them again, looked at Flora and said, 'I went ahead with our marriage because... because I was *confused*. I thought I was probably imagining things, that maybe I was *ill*. Like you, I'd fallen in love with someone quite unsuitable. Unlike you, my love wasn't returned. I knew you needed me, I thought you loved me. In my naïvety, I believed that was enough. I thought we could make the marriage work somehow. I really *wanted* to make it work, Flora! But I knew very little about love. And nothing at all about desire.'

Hugh looked down at his hands, clasping the arms of the chair. Rope-like veins protruded from his skin, marked now with brown age-spots, tanned and dry from working in the garden. He thought suddenly how old his hands looked, how ugly and worn – the hands of an old man. Hugh smiled at the ridiculousness of it all: an old man, speaking of first love. He thought perhaps God did have a sense of humour after all.

He raised his head but looked away from Flora. 'If you'd asked me whether love at first sight was possible, I would have said, no. Categorically. How can such a thing exist? Can it be anything more than just a strong sexual attraction? But when it happened to me, it didn't feel like mere sexual attraction – although, God knows, the sexual undercurrent was there... like an electric shock... Waves coursing through my body. I felt ambushed. Completely taken by surprise. What is it the French say? *Bouleversé*. A marvellous word! I felt the impact in my groin but also in my chest. I couldn't *breathe*...' He frowned as if he didn't quite believe his own testimony. 'Couldn't tear my eyes away, even though I knew I was probably making a spectacle of myself. I thought if I could touch, if I could hold, *be* held, I would somehow be made whole. It was almost a religious experience. A revelation, a true epiphany.'

Hugh's enormous hands started to shake. He looked down and clasped them firmly in his lap, his knuckles whitening. 'I was forty-one. I'd never known love. Never allowed myself to feel desire. Then one day I walked into a room and... it was as if my world changed from black and white to colour.' He smiled. 'Like in *The Wizard of Oz*. It was as if my real life had begun. I'd finally found someone I *loved*. Someone I loved – dear God, forgive me – more than God.'

'Who was she Hugh?'

He passed a hand over his face, dragging at his jaw muscles, then sat with his hands folded again, quite still. His chest rose and fell as he steadied his breathing, then said abruptly, 'It wasn't a she...' Flora's hand went to her mouth and she stifled a sound. 'It was your brother. It was Rory.'

Flora shook her head from side to side. 'No... *No*...'

'I think I would rather have died than tell you,' he said solemnly. 'But since Rory is Theo's father you probably needed to know. So that you can understand how very... *difficult* all this is for me. More difficult than perhaps you'd imagined.' He looked into her eyes, his voice faint now, but level. 'And I wanted you to know that although I may never have loved you, I – of *all* people – will never judge you.'

They sat in silence while Flora wept. Hugh made no move to comfort her, knowing his touch would be the final insult. Flora looked up suddenly as a thought occurred to her, a thought that turned her tear-stained face ashen.

'Does Rory *know*?'

'Oh, yes.' Hugh smiled ruefully. 'Rory knows. Rory has always known.'

1965

Rory sauntered through the garden, past Dora who was still fast asleep in her deckchair. He put his head round the door of the greenhouse then reeled back from the wall of humid heat. 'Dad, I'm going to lift some potatoes. Will the border fork be in the shed?'

Archie was wrestling with a ball of twine and wayward tomato plants. 'Aye, behind the door. And be sure and put it back. Is Flora feeling any better now?'

'Yes, I think so. She's taking a nap.'

'Good, good,' Archie replied. 'You mind your hands now. Wear gloves.'

'I will.'

Rory collected a fork and a large bucket from the shed and set off for the vegetable garden.

The first time Hugh passed through the vegetable garden with the grass box Rory looked up, raised a hand in greeting but carried on digging. On his way back Hugh stopped to comment on the glorious weather. Rory leaned on his fork, removed a gardening glove and pushed hair wet with sweat out of his eyes. He said it looked as if there was going to be a good potato crop this year. Hugh looked pleased and strode up the path, swinging his empty grass box. Rory bent again to his task.

He'd intended to remove his T-shirt, so the fierce heat of the sun was welcome, but he hadn't realised how much he would sweat from the arduous labour of lifting potatoes. Despite the gloves, his palms stung, heralding blisters to come. Rory swore methodically under his breath.

When the lawnmower stopped again Rory thrust his fork into the ground and hung his T-shirt over it. He walked over to the garden bench on the path and sat down. Hugh appeared shortly with the full grass box and walked past Rory without comment. When he returned Rory had extended his legs across the path and was sitting with his face turned up towards the sun, his eyes closed, his arms extended along the back of the bench in a sedentary crucifixion pose. He felt a shadow fall across his body and his damp skin began to cool rapidly. Rory opened his eyes, looked up and beamed at Hugh.

'D'you want to sit down?' He slid along the bench.

Hugh hesitated a moment then said, 'Perhaps I will. That mowing has taken it out of me. Not as fit as I once was,' he laughed.

'You still look pretty fit to me.' As Hugh sat down Rory altered his position so that his bare forearm brushed Hugh's briefly. 'You play tennis, don't you?'

'Yes. Not very well, I'm afraid.'

'I'll give you a game some time.'

'I don't think I'm really in your league, to judge from what Flora says.'

'Oh, I don't know. A man your height must have a hell of a serve. But, yes, I'll probably beat you. I'm left-handed you see. It throws people.' Rory turned his head and stared at Hugh. 'They don't really know how to play me... But I expect you're a good loser, aren't you?' The two men were silent for a while, then Rory continued, 'I went to see Flora just now. She's feeling a lot better.'

'Is she? Jolly good. I've been worried about her. She's been a bit under the weather lately.'

'Has she?'

'Yes. Not her usual self. Tired all the time.'

Rory opened his eyes wide. 'Really? Now you come to mention it, she has seemed a bit... subdued.'

'Has she?'

'Oh yes. Compared to the *old* Flora.' Rory paused. 'She doesn't smile a lot these days, does she?'

'I'm sorry to hear you say that. I hadn't realised quite—'

'You might be forgiven for thinking she wasn't actually very happy.' Rory turned to face Hugh. 'Now why would that be, I wonder?'

Hugh returned Rory's level gaze but his voice was unsteady. 'What are you driving at?'

'Well, you see, Hugh, I know my sister *really* well. She doesn't need to tell me things, I just know. And I know she's not happy. In fact she's pretty much broken-hearted. And I know why.'

'I don't understand... What has Flora said?'

'Nothing. She doesn't need to. Because I already know. I know about you, Hugh.'

'What do you mean?'

As Rory stood up he glanced along the path, back towards the house. 'I know why you aren't making Flora happy.' He stood in front of Hugh and hooked his thumbs in the waistband of his jeans so that the weight of his arms pulled them lower, as he'd known they would. He watched Hugh's eyes move involuntarily as they travelled over his body. When they eventually found his face, Rory bent his head and pressed his parted lips to Hugh's.

He straightened up slowly. 'That's why my sister's not happy, Hugh. That's why *you're* not happy.'

Hugh sat motionless, staring at the ground. Then his broad shoulders sagged, he leaned forward on the bench and covered his face with grass-stained hands. Rory thought afterwards it was like watching a tree being felled.

'How long have you known?'

'Since we first met.'

From the top of an old apple tree a thrush launched into joyful song, piercing a long silence. Hugh looked up, his dark eyes stricken, his cheeks wet. 'What is it that you want from me, Rory? I know you don't want *me*.'

'I want you to make Flora feel loved.' He shifted his weight casually on to one leg, tilting his hips and folding his arms across his bare chest. 'How hard can it be, Hugh?' His smile was seraphic. 'To make her happy, I mean. Do it. For Flora's sake. Or mine. I'd appreciate it.'

'What's in all this for you?' Hugh asked wearily. 'Or were you the sort of boy who liked to pull the wings off butterflies to see if they could still fly?'

'I love my sister. I want to see her happy.'

'You believe *I* can make her happy?'

'No, I don't,' Rory said sharply. 'I've never thought that. But making her pregnant would be a step in the right direction. If she can't have a husband – a *proper* husband – you could at least give her a child.'

'Does Flora know... about me?'

'No. I don't think anyone knows apart from me. You disguise it very well. But then you must've had years of practice.'

'No, I haven't. I had no idea. It'd never occurred to me that I – it wasn't until I met you... that I realised. Things fell into place. And I understood myself.'

'You should have told Flora.'

'Yes, I should.'

'Or at least called off the engagement.'

'Yes. But I didn't really understand what was happening. Not then. I thought perhaps it was just something to do with you being twins. I still loved Flora, you see! I love you both. In different ways.'

'It isn't love.'

'It is. What I feel for Flora is love.'

'I meant what you feel for me.'

'What makes you think you know what I feel for you, Rory?'

He shrugged. 'The way you look at me.'

Hugh's mouth twisted in a wry smile. 'I can't deny that my feelings for you incorporate a degree of common or garden lust. But there's a lot more to it than that. I'm forty-four. I'm a priest. I was a monk. I feel other kinds of love for you. Pastoral. Fraternal. Perhaps I should say *paternal*. A small part, an ignoble part of me wants to possess you, Rory, but the better part of me wants much more than that.'

'What, exactly?'

Hugh looked up into fathomless grey eyes. 'I want to save you.'

'Save my soul?' Rory said with a derisive laugh. 'Not much chance of that. I'm damned. Double-damned now. I've got you on my conscience as well.'

'No, Rory. I want to save you from yourself.'

PART THREE

Chapter 13

1974

Strolling home from Evensong, where she'd formed a quarter of the congregation, Ettie was thoughtful. There was no use hurrying in this heat– one only arrived home all hot and bothered (although these days she became hot and bothered regardless of the weather as her hormonal thermostat went haywire.) Being female and middle-aged was such a trial. She shuddered to think where one would be without the consolations of religion and music.

No stranger to unhappiness herself, Ettie nevertheless found it hard to witness the unhappiness of others. She supposed it was the feeling of helplessness that was so painful, especially when it was loved ones who suffered. For herself, she was a great believer in work and prayer as both distraction and consolation, but it appeared neither was proving particularly effective for Hugh. Ettie hated to see him so miserable and smile as he might, she knew that he was. Flora made no secret of her discontent – or, to be fair, was it just that Ettie knew her better? – but Hugh did his best to convince family and parish that all was well, even though plainly it wasn't.

At least Hugh had the consolation of Theo who sadly seemed destined to be an only child. Theo evidently brought Hugh joy, but Flora seemed barely able to disguise her irritation with the boy. Ettie couldn't understand her attitude. The boy was intelligent, if shy, and showed an interest in everything, especially wildlife. He loved to walk round the garden with Dora, learning the names of plants. He insisted on learning the botanical Latin which he recited as other children chanted playground rhymes. Hugh had given him a plot to cultivate in the vicarage garden for which Archie had donated seedlings from the greenhouse. Theo himself had sown a handful of sunflower seeds in the vegetable garden at Orchard Farm and, to his delight, the plants had grown taller than he was. Ettie had taken a photograph of Theo standing proudly dwarfed by his flowers and given an enlargement to Hugh who had seemed much moved by the picture. He'd smiled and remarked that Theo was the image of Rory, which indeed he was, although as fair as Flora.

Theo it was who'd inherited the musical gene. Ettie could see no evidence of it in Colin, nor little Lottie, despite their mother's insistence that they learn instruments from an early age. 'You can take a horse to water,' thought Ettie with a smile. But Theo was a natural and she'd found it impossible to refuse his requests for piano instruction, even though Hugh had made it clear that, for some reason, Flora didn't want him to learn.

Ettie couldn't see the harm and simply encouraged Theo when she found him playing on the grand piano. She explained the musical stave to him and praised him when he mastered a simple tune, picked out by ear. She only instructed him in matters of technique if he asked questions, but she took care to leave suitable music on the piano where he was sure to find it. Her conscience was clear. She wasn't giving lessons; there were no appointments; she didn't suggest he practice. There was no need. Theo played whenever he couldn't get into the garden and whenever Flora was out of earshot. Sometimes he'd stop by the church on the way home from school to play on the vestry piano or to listen to Mrs Churchill practise the hymns on the organ.

Hugh's feelings about his son's musical talent were clearly mixed. It must, Ettie supposed, be the small element of deceit. Hugh knew that Flora disapproved although no one, Hugh included, seemed sure why. Flora's eccentricities were beginning to verge on the irrational. Ettie wondered whether the gossip she'd overheard on the bus about the minister's wife being a secret tippler might actually be *true?* It would account for a lot. She wouldn't put anything past Flora. That child had always met trouble halfway.

Ettie wished there were something she could do to help the unhappy couple. She couldn't imagine why Flora was so miserable with all her blessings. Ettie was sure if *she* were married to Hugh – but here her speculations came to an abrupt halt. She couldn't actually imagine what it would be like to be married, let alone married to Hugh. She found it hard to imagine even *touching* Hugh or being touched by him. (Although he did kiss her on the cheek on New Year's Eve, when Big Ben struck midnight.)

Ettie liked to think of Hugh as her nephew-in-law (*was* there such a relationship?) but she acknowledged reluctantly that her feelings towards Hugh were not very aunt-like. It was true she didn't think of him in a *physical* way – at least not very often and then with a vagueness based on complete ignorance of male anatomy – but she had to admit that her feelings were not in the least maternal. (What was the adjective to describe the feelings of an aunt? *Was* there one?) What feelings was an aunt supposed to have towards a nephew? It seemed rather a grey area.

Ettie admitted that, occasionally, when Hugh looked particularly tired or downcast, she would have liked to put her arm round his shoulders to comfort him, but despite her relative height, she thought she wouldn't be able to reach. In any case, she concluded, the gesture was *quite* inappropriate, however kindly meant.

Poor Ettie. I spent some of my teenage years and half my adult life thinking, 'Poor Ettie'. Poor old, plain, lonely, ridiculous Ettie. Beneath the constraints of her sensible liberty bodice, there beat a passionate, loyal and poetic heart. But that wasn't the half of it. Beneath her goodness lay shame.

She finally absolved us all from guilt by dying at the age of fifty-eight.

Even then she didn't take centre stage.

1974

Flora shivered in the unheated bedroom. They should have left this job until the spring. The wardrobe was almost empty now. As she sorted Ettie's clothes, she folded them into neat piles then put them into labelled cardboard boxes. She left the coat-hangers on the rail.

'You know, Hugh, this is a good coat. We can't put this in a jumble sale. Ma should keep it for herself.'

He looked up from the floor where he knelt in front of a bookcase, sorting through books. 'I don't think your mother would ever wear anything of Ettie's. Not now.'

'No. I suppose not. Jumble, then?'

'Yes. It will go to a good home, I'm sure.' He watched Flora fold the coat and then looked around the bedroom. 'It wasn't much of a room, was it? Reminds me of my monastic cell. So small.'

'Ettie led a small life. She had two rooms until Rory was kicked out of the nursery, when we were seven. Her study became Rory's bedroom. I don't suppose she really minded. Well, she was hardly in a position to mind.'

'No, I suppose not.' Hugh turned back to sorting the books.

'Ma said to keep as many as you want.'

'There's quite a few on music. I thought Rory might... ' Hugh's voice tailed off.

Flora sighed. 'Who knows what Rory wants? And it's high time we got rid of all this stuff. It's been *months*. You have them. It's what she would have wanted.'

Hugh set some books aside and put others into a box. He took the lid off a beribboned chocolate box and examined the contents. 'There're some photographs in here. Concert programmes, postcards. Do you want to sort through these?'

'No. Keep the photos and throw the rest away. What are the photos of?'

Hugh shuffled through them. 'The family, I think. Yes, they're all family snapshots. I expect Dora will want to keep them.'

'Show me.'

Hugh passed them up to Flora. As she glanced through them she smiled. 'These aren't family snapshots.'

'What do you mean? Of course they are.'

'I mean that isn't why Ettie kept them. These are all photos of you. You're in every single one.'

'Am I?'

'Yes. Look.' She handed them back and Hugh studied them.

'So I am. Well, what of it?'

'She kept them *because* they were photos of you. Look at that one.' Flora stabbed at one with a finger. 'You and a lovely view of the back of Theo's head! And that one: us on our wedding day – except you can't actually see *me* because my veil has blown right across my face! Why would she keep that? These are all photos of *you*, Hugh.'

'But – I don't understand. Why would she...?'

Flora stared at him. 'Did you never realise Ettie was in love with you?'

'*Ettie?*'

'Yes. You mean to say you didn't know?'

'If this is a joke, Flora, it's in pretty poor taste.'

'She always loved you. I think everyone knew, we just never

talked about it. No point really. You married me.' Flora tossed the photos on to the bed and turned away from Hugh.

'When did – I mean, do you know when Ettie realised she felt... that way about me?'

'Oh, right from the word go, I think. When you moved into the parish. She was suddenly awfully keen to go to church. We both were. She and I spent hours discussing the finer points of your sermons and what a nice man you were. I didn't realise then of course. What would I have been? Fifteen? It was only after we married that I began to notice.'

'What?'

'How she lit up when you came into the room. How she hung on your every word. Little things. But quite obvious. We all turned a blind eye, so's not to embarrass her.'

'But she was much older than me!'

'Only five years. But a middle-aged woman might as well be invisible as far as men are concerned,' Flora remarked bitterly.

'I'm sure I never gave her the slightest encouragement.'

'Oh, no, you treated her like the ageing spinster she was. No one could ever accuse *you* of being a flirt, Hugh.'

'I wish I'd known.'

'Why? What difference would it have made? Would you have kept your distance?'

'No, of course not.'

'So why shouldn't she have had the pleasure of worshipping from afar? You were probably the most excitement Ettie knew in what must have been a pretty dull life. She had no expectations of anything better.'

'But to have loved all those years. Without *hope*.'

'Oh, come off it, Hugh! Don't be so sentimental.' Flora dragged a cocktail dress, never worn, from the wardrobe and set the metal hangers jangling. 'There are worse things to endure than hopeless love.'

Hugh looked up at her from the floor, his eyes moist. 'Are there? Not many, surely?'

Flora gazed at him blankly for a moment. She heard her own words, then his and fled from the room.

~

Depending on how warped your sense of humour – and mine darkened considerably with advancing years – the web of tortured relationships in my family seemed Shakespearean in its ludicrous complexity. We were the stuff of farce, but when farce is actually happening to you it doesn't seem funny, it seems tragic.

That's because it is tragic.

1965

As Flora's knees buckled, Rory was already on his feet and moving round the dining table. He barked, 'Hugh, catch her!' As Hugh stood up he sent his dining chair toppling backwards and caught Flora neatly as she fainted.

Dora cried out in alarm but Ettie said calmly, 'She's fainted. It's all right, it must be the heat. She's just fainted.'

Grace poured a glass of water quickly and passed it across the table to Rory who dipped a napkin in it and dabbed at Flora's face. 'Take her to the music room,' Rory said, not taking his eyes off his sister. 'It's cooler in there. Lay her on the day-bed.'

Hugh scooped Flora up in his arms and strode towards the door with Rory following. As Ettie watched the men depart, she murmured, 'I'll put the kettle on,' and headed for the kitchen.

Grace turned to Dora, her face anxious. 'Should we ring for the doctor?'

'No, I don't think that'll be necessary, my dear. I'm sure Ettie's right. It's just this dreadful heat.' Dora thought there might be another reason why Flora had fainted, but she didn't like to mention it now. Hugh might not even know yet.

Hugh arranged Flora's limp form on the day-bed. Rory opened the French windows to let in a breeze, then sat down automatically on the piano stool. He watched as Flora's eyelids flickered and she returned to consciousness. A wave of relief flushed his face. Smiling, he glanced up and saw that Hugh had been watching him, not Flora.

Ettie entered the music room bearing a tea tray. 'Hot, sweet tea,' she announced. 'Just the thing!' She handed a cup to Hugh with an unguarded look of admiration.

As Flora regained consciousness she was aware of her brother's large grey eyes watching her intently. Hugh stood by his side, but appeared to be watching Rory. Ettie was handing her a cup of tea, but was gazing at Hugh. Flora sat up and tried to speak. Clapping a hand to her mouth, she pointed across the room. All eyes turned as Rory lunged, grabbed a waste paper basket and thrust it in front of Flora's face, just in time for her to vomit into it.

'Oh, well caught, sir!' said Ettie.

I wish I'd known about Ettie, all about Ettie. Not for her sake. Had I known the whole story I think I would have felt even more crippled by embarrassment than I already did. But if I'd known, I might have felt differently towards my mother. I might have respected her more, perhaps even liked her more.

At the very least I might have understood my mother's silence.

1974

Hugh was passing the telephone when it rang.

'Hugh, it's Dora. Am I disturbing you? I wonder if I could have a word.'

'Of course. How can I help?'

'I need your advice – as a minister but also as a member of the family. It's about the wording of the memorial stone. For Ettie.'

'Would you like me to call round so we can discuss it? I'm on my way out to Evensong now. Shall I drop in afterwards?'

'Yes, please, if you would. I promise not to keep you too long.'

'Not at all. I'm glad to be of service at this very difficult time.'

'You're a comfort to us all, Hugh. There's just one thing, though—'

'Yes?'

'I'd prefer you not to mention this to Flora. It's a rather delicate matter...'

When Hugh arrived at Orchard Farm Dora was in the front garden dead-heading roses. As she collected the faded blooms and placed them in her battered trug, petals fluttered to the ground around her feet. At the sound of the gate latch she looked up and smiled at

Hugh, raising her secateurs in salutation. Hugh strode up the path and bent to kiss her on the cheek.

'Now, Dora, you know I said if you want any garden chores done you only had to ask. You really mustn't overdo things, you know. You look quite worn out.'

'Oh, pooh! This isn't a chore. It's just an excuse to be in the garden on a glorious evening. There won't be many more this year.' Hugh took the trug and offered her his arm as they walked towards the house. 'Thank you for coming. I'm probably being a silly old woman and making a mountain out of a molehill, but it wasn't something I felt I could discuss on the phone. Let's go and sit on the terrace. We'll catch the last of the sun there. Shall we have a sherry? It's rather a long story, I'm afraid...'

1932

Dora stood outside Ettie's room and composed herself. Her words were well-rehearsed for she'd had many years to consider them. However much pain they caused, they must be said. Ettie had a right to know. She knocked gently.

'Come in.'

Dora entered the cheerful, tidy bedroom. Birthday cards were arranged on the mantelpiece and several new books were piled by Ettie's bedside. She sat on the bed with a writing pad on her knees. 'I'm on the very last thank-you letter.' She signed off with an adolescent flourish. 'I got *such* a lot of presents this year – and they were all splendid.'

'Well, it was a very important birthday.'

Ettie folded the sheet haphazardly and pushed it into an envelope. 'I suppose I'm meant to feel very grown-up now, aren't I? Shall I have to start behaving in a more lady-like manner?' She pulled a face. 'Fat chance!'

Dora bent and kissed the girl impulsively on her forehead. Although there were only nine years between them she looked upon Ettie as a child and her feelings towards her were maternal rather than sisterly. Dora had been married for four years and there had been no pregnancy, not even a miscarriage to give her hope. She wondered sometimes whether she and Archie would ever have another child, one of their own, to love.

Dora took Ettie's hand and squeezed it. 'My dear, I have some news for you. Well, information really. Now, I want you to brace yourself for a bit of a shock. This won't be easy for you to hear and it certainly won't be easy for me to tell you.'

Ettie looked alarmed. 'What's the matter? Is anything wrong? Are you ill?'

'No, nothing's wrong, darling. It's just that... things aren't quite as you think they are. And it's high time I explained.' Dora sat on the paisley eiderdown, perching nervously on the edge of the bed. She took a piece of paper out of her apron pocket. 'You've turned sixteen. You're almost an adult. You've a right to this now.' She held out the piece of paper.

Ettie stared at it. 'What is it?'

'Your birth certificate.'

Ettie looked a little relieved. 'Why are you giving it to me *now*?'

'Because I want you to read it, darling. I want you to know... who you are,' Dora said carefully.

Ettie took the certificate from Dora but didn't look at it. She laughed nervously. 'I'm your sister – aren't I?'

'No, darling, you're not. But you're no less loved for that! You're my *niece*. My brother's child. Henry's.'

'Henry?'

'Yes. You were named Henrietta after him. He never saw you. He was killed in 1915, before you were born. You were conceived before he went to the front and he died not knowing there was going to be a child... You've always thought Henry was an older brother you never knew. But in fact he was your father. So I,' Dora smiled gently. 'I am your *aunt*.'

Ettie struggled to assimilate her new identity. She studied the certificate, then looked up suddenly. 'So Mother and Pa...?'

'Were your grandparents. But they loved you as if you were their own child! They loved you because you were Henry's child and later they loved you for yourself. We all did. We all *do!* You have been a great blessing to us.' Dora threw her arms around the girl and hugged her. 'Oh, my poor girl – it's such a lot for you to take in, isn't it?'

Ettie nodded, her lip quivering. 'Who knows? Apart from you, I mean.'

'Only Archie. And there is no reason why anyone else should

ever know.'

'They weren't married, were they? My parents?'

'No, my dear. I'm afraid they weren't.'

'Would Henry have married my mother if he'd lived?'

It was now Dora's turn to brace herself, the easier part of her unpleasant task done. She released Ettie and smoothed her apron across her lap before looking up into the girl's tearful face. 'Your mother died shortly after you were born. She never really recovered from the shock of Henry's death and the birth had been very difficult. But no, Henry wouldn't have married her. It would not have been possible. But he *wanted* to, I'm sure. And if he'd lived he would have supported you and your mother, I'm sure of that too. That's why our parents – *my* parents, I should say – raised you as their own. They knew it was what your parents would have wanted.'

Ettie looked down at her birth certificate again. 'Who was Isobel Kerr?'

Dora turned away from Ettie's wide, enquiring eyes. 'She was Henry's aunt. My mother's youngest sister. She was only nine years older than Henry. She was very lovely,' Dora added, as if by way of explanation.

1974

'So you see, Hugh, I would have liked to refer to Ettie on the gravestone as "beloved sister". But I'm afraid she wasn't.'

'I see your difficulty.'

'Only Archie – and God, I suppose – know that she wasn't. And now you. But I don't feel I can put a lie on a *gravestone*, a lie for all time. It would seem like lying to God. But equally I don't want to betray Ettie, to betray her memory. We never discussed it but I believe she was deeply ashamed of her origins. I'm sure that's why she never married. I suppose I could just have a very simple inscription – her name and her dates – but that seems so formal, so *cold*. I'd like to convey that I loved Ettie as a sister, that as far as I was concerned we *were* sisters. Do you see my dilemma?'

'I do indeed. It's not at all clear what would be the best thing to do. But it's important to get it right, isn't it? For Ettie's sake as much as anybody else's.'

Not for the first time Hugh felt he was required to choose

between what would be the right thing to do and what would be the best. He often asked himself why people thought a priest would have any more idea about these things than a layman. He knew it wasn't his job to tell people what they wanted to hear, but surely it was his job to tell them what they *needed* to hear?

He plunged in. 'You know, the older I get, the more I realise that truth is not an absolute but a variable commodity. Our understanding of it – and use of it – may be limited by custom or language. But I don't think God's truth is limited in that way, do you? It transcends time. It transcends language.'

Dora wasn't sure she understood what Hugh was saying, but she had every confidence that he'd come up with a solution given time. She said nothing but watched his face expectantly.

'I think what we have here is actually a problem of semantics. In a religious context there is always some ambiguity in the use of the words "brother" and "sister". We are all brothers and sisters in Christ. That being the case, I see no real reason why the stone for Ettie shouldn't read "beloved sister". She was, in the widest and truest sense, your sister in Christ. I think her genetic relationship to you was... just a *detail*, don't you?'

Unable to speak or look at him, Dora reached out, placed her hand on Hugh's and squeezed it tightly.

Chapter 14

1974

Among the female members of the PTA it was generally agreed that Grace Dunbar was a stuck-up bitch. The lone male on the committee thought she was a handsome and intelligent woman, clearly wasted as a stay-at-home mother, but the other women (mostly stay-at-home mothers) thought she was a snob who traded on the celebrity of her musical husband, whom they conceded was a handsome and intelligent man.

Grace made few concessions to motherhood. She loved her children but loathed the rest of the package. Most of the conversations she had were with young children or the mothers of young children and she felt as if her brain were gradually turning to the consistency of the sago pudding she'd so hated at school. Grace and the other mothers discussed mixed feeding, toilet training and the shocking price of anoraks. They stood shivering in the rain at the school gates – why did it always start to rain at a quarter to three? – relating the minor catastrophes of their lives: a broken washing machine, an outbreak of measles, a surprise visitation from the in-laws. The women huddled together and, when they weren't discussing diets, talked about food: the price of food, the preparation of food, the consumption of food and the subsequent clearing up of food. They compared one product with another, making personal recommendations which were duly noted. Once three mothers with prams carried out an impromptu survey of fish fingers. Price, quality and nutritional value were compared until eventually they all agreed that one particular brand stood head and shoulders above the rest. Grace, who'd been listening in silence with mounting disbelief, was asked for her opinion but was saved by the bell – literally – as pupils suddenly poured through the doors into the playground.

After the fish finger debate, Grace abandoned her attempts to conform, standing apart from the other women and, when it wasn't raining, reading a book until Colin and Charlotte emerged. But she could still hear the women's chatter and felt mentally contaminated. She gathered that the price of anoraks just went up and up.

Rory was the only person with whom Grace had regular, adult, intelligent conversation and that was interrupted constantly by the demands of their children, but after years of practice Grace had developed the knack of conducting two conversations at once. She could lambast Tory policy on education, explaining in parentheses to Colin why toy guns were anti-social and unethical. Grace could sit and read George Eliot during *Playschool* and at the end of the programme she would still know how to make an elephant mask out of a cornflakes box and several toilet rolls. Living two lives simultaneously, Grace's mind would run along an adult track while dealing with the mental pap of day-to-day intercourse with her children. She squeezed every last ounce of time out of her day, carving out space for herself, claiming a piece of adult territory on which the children were not allowed to trespass. As soon as was practicable she started to give cello and piano lessons at home, although this meant yet more social intercourse with mothers and children, most of whom were not even particularly interested in music. But it was work, it was money (her own) and it stopped her feeling mentally, socially and economically obliterated by motherhood.

Colin and Charlotte had to fit in, as Grace had to fit in with the demands of Rory's musical life. Rory was the sun round which they all orbited and all of them knew their place in the galaxy – many light years away from Rory who lived his life, intensely and not very happily, in splendid isolation from the rest of his family.

Grace made allowances. She considered her husband a genius and didn't expect him to behave like other husbands and fathers. She knew she'd paid a price for her happiness, such as it was. Believing that the secret of life was low expectations, Grace tried hard to cultivate them, but despite her efforts she was finding it increasingly difficult to ignore the suspicion – never voiced and only rarely confronted – that Rory might be having an affair.

Rory had several reasons to remember 23rd August, 1974.

He was scheduled to play a programme of Bach in a concert at Snape Maltings and the day began with a phone-call from Ettie suggesting they meet up for tea in Aldeburgh before the concert.

As Rory replaced the phone it rang again. Picking up the receiver, he suddenly had a bad feeling, about the call, about the day. He knew before she spoke that it would be Flora.

'You knew, didn't you?'

'Flora?'

'You knew and you didn't tell me.'

'What are you talking about? Knew what?' Rory already knew what Flora was talking about. Playing for time, he closed the study door, shutting out the sound of Grace giving a cello lesson.

'You knew about Hugh. And you knew how he felt about you.'

Rory took a deep breath and said in a low voice, 'I didn't know. Not till after you were pregnant and asked for my help. I suspected. But I didn't *know*.'

'You're lying, Ror. Why would you suspect? And if you did suspect, why didn't you tell me?'

'How could I? Your marriage was in enough trouble without me telling you I thought your husband might be queer.'

'Don't use that word.'

'Well, that's what he is!'

'And you knew! In the bathroom at New Year... In the hotel... You *knew*.'

'I *didn't* know! How could I? He never touched me, never said anything. There was nothing I could confront him with. For all I knew he was bisexual! Hugh fancying me didn't necessarily mean your marriage was on the rocks. It wasn't till you told me he wasn't screwing you that I realised you were wasting your time. And *then* how could I tell you?' He lowered his voice. 'You'd turned me down as an alternative, so was it likely you'd believe me if I told you why your bloody husband wasn't interested?'

Flora was silent. Rory tempered his anger, trying to stem a rising tide of panic. 'After Grace's miscarriage... after that night in the hotel... you avoided me. Stopped speaking to me more or less. The next time you spoke to me for real, you needed a father for your child—'

'*Our* child!'

'Is *that* when I should have told you, Flor? Don't you think you had enough on your plate by then?'

Flora said nothing, then started to cry. Rory threaded his fingers

180

through the coiled telephone wire and clenched his fist. 'I admit I haven't been totally honest with you. But that's because – because I *love* you. Everything I did was because I loved you and wanted to prevent you from being hurt.'

'Does that include getting me pregnant?'

Exhaling, Rory glanced at his watch, then sat down at his desk, turning his back towards the study door. 'Look, it never occurred to me that if you got pregnant, you'd know it was mine. I didn't realise just how bad things were between you and Hugh! I wasn't thinking straight. I was pissed... Shattered... We both were! The baby had died and, as far as I was concerned, my marriage was over. I just – I just *wanted* you, Flor! More than I've ever wanted anything. I wanted to be inside you. And I thought – no, I *knew* – that's what you wanted too. I thought I was giving you what you wanted. It was meant to make you *happy*!'

As she hung up, Rory heard the sound of Flora sobbing. He placed the receiver back on its cradle and swore.

Later that morning Rory received yet another phone-call, this time from a callbox. Hugh announced that he was in London for the day and asked if he could see Rory briefly, at a time and place to suit. He said the matter was urgent and of a sensitive nature.

Rory closed his eyes and cursed silently. 'I haven't got time today, Hugh. Sorry. I've got a concert this evening and I've got several appointments before then. Can it wait?'

'No, I don't think it can. I think you'd better cancel something, Rory. It's time we talked.'

When Rory arrived at Charing Cross Station he didn't recognise Hugh at first. He was standing under the clock as arranged, holding a Foyles carrier bag bulging with books, dressed as Rory had rarely seen him before, in civvies: an open-necked checked shirt and corduroy trousers. Hugh's only concession to the August heat was a pair of leather sandals.

As Hugh watched Rory approach, he didn't smile. Even had his purpose been less grim, he was momentarily unmanned by the sight of Rory striding towards him, cool and tanned in a white linen suit, his hair streaked by summer sun.

The two men regarded each other. Rory was the first to speak. 'I didn't recognise you without the fancy dress.'

'Thank you for agreeing to meet me.'

'I got the impression I didn't have a lot of choice.'

'No. What I have to say is not the sort of thing one can say over the telephone and I didn't wish to put it in writing.'

'Well, can we get on with it? I'm meeting Ettie for tea in Aldeburgh and then I've got a concert tonight at Snape. I haven't got much time.'

'I won't keep you long. Shall we go and sit down somewhere?'

'I thought you'd never ask. Talking to you standing up always gives me a crick in the neck.'

Once again Hugh was disconcerted. He'd prepared himself for aggression, insolence, even ridicule. He hadn't bargained with self-deprecating humour. He wondered briefly how much Rory had changed since the last time they'd spoken frankly to each other, nine years ago, in the vegetable garden.

'Let's go to the buffet then. I could use a cup of tea. I came up to town early.'

Rory looked down at Hugh's carrier bag. 'More theological tomes?'

'No, actually. *Income Tax for the Self-Employed* and *Propagating Plants for Pleasure and Profit.*'

They sat at a corner table away from other customers. Hugh clasped his hands on the table and Rory wondered if he was about to say grace. He stirred his tea, suppressing an urge to laugh.

Hugh turned to face Rory and said, 'I'll come to the point straight away. Flora has told me about Theo's parentage. And I have told Flora that I am – have always been – homosexual.'

Rory dropped his spoon and it clattered into the cup, splashing his white suit. '*Jesus Christ.*'

'Yes, I wonder what He makes of it all?... There's more. I've told Flora that our marriage has never worked, not only because I am queer, as the popular parlance has it, but because I have always been in love with you.'

Rory stared. 'You bastard.'

'That's exactly what Flora said. But once she'd told me you were the father of my son I thought she needed to know just how *complicated* things actually were. I can't claim I gave it a great deal of thought. I was in shock, I suppose. I've been living a lie – a variety of lies – for many years now and I had a sudden longing, a *thirst* for truth. And I thought Flora might find it easier to forgive me – or at least understand me – if she knew you were the only man I've ever loved. That there had been no... infidelity.'

Rory retrieved his spoon and laid it carefully in the saucer. 'She wasn't unfaithful either. Not really. She turned me down.' He passed a hand over his face, damp with sweat. 'It was only the once. We were both very drunk. In shock, probably.'

'Yes. She explained that Theo's conception was... a one-off.'

'It never should have happened.'

'But it did. You loved each other. You love each other still.'

Rory bit his lip and nodded. Blinking, he stared down into his cooling cup of tea. 'Flora is eaten up with love for me... I mean, just *look* at her! I think she might actually be losing her mind. It's not so hard for me. I anaesthetise my brain with work. And sex.' He looked up, his eyes moist. 'Not much of it with my wife.'

Hugh hadn't expected tears, nor so much honesty. He cleared his throat. 'There was something else I told Flora. In fact, that was what started it all. I broke my news to her and – well, the walls of Jericho came tumbling down.'

Rory looked up listlessly. 'What news?'

'I told her I'd decided to give up the ministry.'

'You're joking!'

Hugh smiled. 'That's what *she* said. You really are astonishing, you two. You don't just look alike, you think alike – even speak alike!'

'Why are you quitting?'

'It's no concern of yours and I don't feel up to coping with your mockery – not today. I just wanted you to know that I believe Flora will leave me sooner or later and she will no doubt take Theo with her.' Hugh paused and took a mouthful of his tea. As he replaced the cup his trembling hand spilled tea into the saucer. 'I've said to her what I'll now say to you. If she tries to prevent my having access to Theo, if she does anything to undermine my standing as his nominal father, I will go to Dora and tell her who Theo's real father is. Then I will go to the newspapers.'

183

Rory leaned across the table. 'You can't prove anything.'

'Oh, I imagine I can prove fairly easily I'm *not* Theo's father. In any case, I don't think newspapers are all that concerned with truth. Rumours, accusations, scandal – that seems to be what sells papers these days. A few hints to an unscrupulous journalist would, I imagine, be enough to put the brakes on your meteoric career. But because Flora loves you more than me – more than Theo for that matter – she'll never risk it.'

'You're prepared to make Theo the centre of a scandal?'

'That's something you'll never know unless Flora tries to prevent me from seeing him. Are you a gambling man, Rory?'

'She'll have to divorce you now she knows you're queer. And she'd get custody.'

'Oh, yes, undoubtedly. Although as I'm about to become unemployed, suing me for divorce does beg the question of how Flora will support Theo and earn her own living. And if Flora is to hold down a job, *any* job, she'll need to stop drinking first.'

Rory winced. 'You know about that too?'

'Oh, yes. I've known for some time, but I always wondered *why*. Now everything's fallen into place... Flora can have her freedom, she can have you, I just want to be allowed to love my son, to visit him freely – preferably have him living with me. If I still believed in the efficacy of prayer I'd pray for Flora to leave me *and* Theo. She just might, you know. I don't think she feels much for the boy – something else I've never understood, but do now. So you see, it's in your interests to make sure your sister allows me to remain Theo's father.'

A slow, lopsided smile spread across Rory's face.

Hugh leaned back in his chair and folded his arms. 'You find all this amusing?'

'Not at all. But I do appreciate the splendid irony of being blackmailed by a priest.'

'Well, I shan't be one for much longer, so make the most of it.'

Rory looked at Hugh, his eyes calculating. 'If I exposed you as a homosexual you wouldn't get custody of Theo.'

'No, probably not,' Hugh said affably. 'Though if the mother is a drunk and sleeping with her brother, I think I might just have the advantage, don't you? But you *can't* expose me Rory, because I'm innocent. I've never laid a finger on anyone. Not even you.'

'I could say you had.'

Hugh pursed his lips. 'You could, but wouldn't that be shooting yourself in the foot? Bang goes your musical career. Homosexuals may no longer be criminals but, you know, we're not exactly *establishment* yet.'

Rory threw back his head and laughed. 'I've got to hand it to you, Hugh. I didn't have you down as such a fighter. I didn't think you were so damn clever either.'

'I'm not clever, Rory, I'm desperate and a man with nothing to lose is dangerous. I have nothing now, nothing at all, apart from Theo who, it turns out, isn't even mine. But that boy *is* my son and I *am* his father, regardless of blood. I want us all to be clear – for Theo's sake as much as anything – just how hard I'm prepared to fight to keep him and to prevent him from knowing who his real father is.'

Rory stared at Hugh. He thought he'd never really seen his face before, not even when he'd kissed him in the garden at Orchard Farm. It was a strong face, dark and gaunt now, the brown eyes dull with strain, the thick black hair brindled with grey. Rory felt a familiar pang of jealousy, though he didn't know to what he could ascribe it. He used to think he was jealous of Hugh because he possessed Flora, but he'd known for years that Hugh possessed Flora no more than he, Rory, did. Less in fact. Rory certainly wasn't jealous of Hugh's relationship with Theo – something he couldn't even comprehend. His eyes shifted to Hugh's large and capable hands, resting patiently on the table, his fingers longer even than Rory's own. He had a memory then, a fleeting memory of a tiny hand – it must have been his own – enveloped in his father's; his own small, cold fingers encircled by sudden warmth and strength, a sensuous mixture of softness and hardness, flesh and bone.

Rory was jealous of Theo.

It seemed perfectly clear now. He was jealous of his own son, of how much his son was loved by Hugh, jealous of how hard Hugh was prepared to fight for the boy, not even his own. He wondered if Archie would have gone to Hell and back for his son. Rory wondered whether, if he'd asked him, Hugh would have gone to Hell and back for *him*.

'You don't love me any more, do you, Hugh?' Rory hadn't meant to ask the question and covered his tracks immediately with sarcasm. 'Just out of interest, when did love turn to hate? When I betrayed you with a kiss?'

Hugh looked surprised, even shocked. 'I don't hate you. For reasons I don't quite understand, Rory, I think I still love you. In spite of everything. Certainly I pity you.'

'*Pity*? For Christ's sake, why?'

'I pity you because you've never really known Theo or been loved by him. I have, and neither you nor Flora can take that away from me. It's something I've learned since he was born, something fatherhood has taught me. Sexual love makes one vulnerable, weak – foolish sometimes. But paternal love – that makes one *unassailable*.'

Much to Hugh's surprise, Rory offered him a lift as far as Aldeburgh where he'd arranged to meet Ettie. Hugh declined, saying he felt he needed time for reflection and that he'd found a railway carriage was as good a place as any for that purpose.

Hugh was even more surprised when, as the two men parted, Rory offered him his hand. Hugh hesitated for a moment. As they shook, he remembered the last time he'd allowed himself to touch Rory, nine years ago, on the night Grace lost the baby, when he'd placed an arm round his shoulders to comfort him.

Dora was weeding in the garden behind the house when the car drew up. She heard the noisy rattle of the gate latch, the pained squeak of its hinges, all with what appeared at the time, but perhaps it was only with hindsight, to be a preternatural clarity. She heard footsteps on the gravel path, more than one pair. She struggled to her feet, wondering whether Ettie and Rory had returned early for some reason. The flutter of concern was there even before Dora rounded the corner of the house and saw the police constable remove his helmet before raising his hand to the doorbell. He was accompanied by a young WPC.

Dora knew at once.

She never forgave herself for the thought that entered her head then, a thought too sudden to suppress, too heartfelt to deny. Her mind was seared in that moment and she bore a guilty scar ever after.

'Take Ettie... Take Flora... Don't take Rory! Dear God in Heaven, please, *please*, don't take Rory.'

For once, Dora's prayers were answered.

Flora knew when it happened. She didn't know what had happened, but she knew precisely when. At ten to five, as she served up baked beans on toast for Theo's tea, she was suddenly overwhelmed with anxiety. She felt a shooting pain on her right side, her hand lost all sensation and she dropped the small saucepan and its contents on to the table.

Theo screamed as the hot beans splashed his hand and arm and he ran from the kitchen, shouting, 'Daddy! Daddy!' Flora bent over, clutching the table for support. She closed her eyes against the pain and nausea and everything was red.

Grace had no inkling until she received a phone call from Archie. She was on her way out with the children to a birthday barbecue party. She would much rather have got a babysitter and gone to Rory's concert at Snape, but the birthday boy was Colin's best friend and he (or the boy's mother) had been kind enough to invite Charlotte as well. Grace was looking forward to a quiet dinner on her own with perhaps a glass of wine when Archie rang.

He told her straight away that Rory wasn't dead but that she should prepare herself for bad news. Grace remembered afterwards feeling both terrified and irritated with Archie – how exactly did one prepare oneself for bad news?

She sat down because she knew that's what people did in films.

At ten minutes to five Rory was driving from Aldeburgh to Snape with Ettie sitting beside him in the passenger seat. It was a fine evening and they were enjoying the drive along dusty country lanes. Stationary at a T-junction, waiting for a stream of traffic to pass so that he could turn right, Rory had wound his window down and was resting his elbow on the car door. His shirtsleeve was rolled up and he could feel the late afternoon sun burning his forearm as his fingers drummed Bach impatiently on the hot metal roof of the car.

To her left, Ettie registered a lorry travelling at speed along the main carriageway. It veered suddenly into the middle of the road. Ettie said, 'Oh, my Lord', then the lorry came hurtling towards them. By the time Rory realised what was going to happen, the car had already been hit on Ettie's side and was turning over. He knew before the car hit the ground that his hand and arm would be crushed. He felt no pain but thought he sensed, even heard, bones snapping. The car landed on its side in a ditch with Rory's hand between the car and the ground. Ettie hung above him, trapped by her seat belt. Still conscious, Rory saw that his white shirt and trousers were gradually turning red. He still felt no pain and turned his head gingerly towards Ettie who was unconscious. Blood was spurting from her throat, slashed by flying glass and he realised the blood soaking into his clothes was mostly Ettie's. He thought she was probably dead or dying. Reaching with his good hand to take hold of hers, he prayed that he too would die soon.

Apparently there are twenty-seven bones in the hand. Rory broke or fractured fifteen.

They wanted to amputate, insisting that the hand was irreparable and that Rory would have a better quality of life and be able to do more for himself if he had a prosthetic hand. He refused. Or rather he said nothing, thereby withholding his consent to the amputation. They brought him a form to sign – he was left-handed so he could still write – but he just turned his face away.

The surgeon had to patch up the hand and told us that he thought he'd managed to do 'a pretty good job given the extent of the injuries'. We were suitably grateful. He told us that the hand would be effectively useless and would become riddled with arthritis, causing a lot of pain. He also told us that the blood circulation would be poor and Rory would feel the cold a lot. He didn't mention the piano and we didn't really need to ask, but I suppose Dora had to hear the words. She couldn't let go until she heard them and so she asked. The surgeon lowered his voice appropriately and told us Rory would never play with his right hand again. In the silence that ensued he informed us that he had two of Rory's recordings and that it was 'a terrible tragedy'.

Rory died in that crash. The man they cut out of the crushed and twisted metal wasn't my brother. My brother was a pianist and he lived for music. It was the only thing he really cared about. It meant more to him than his children, more even than me. The broken man they loaded on to a stretcher would never play the piano again and so he wasn't Rory.

I didn't know where that man had gone. Sometimes when I sat by Rory's bed and looked into his hopeless eyes and saw nothing but emptiness, heard nothing but his silence, I thought I knew where the real Rory, my Rory was.

In Hell.

Hell for Rory was silence.

Chapter 15

We couldn't take in what had happened. Even after the initial shock had passed we couldn't assimilate the information, get to grips with the facts of Ettie being dead and Rory being maimed. Because the two events happened simultaneously we were unable to prioritise them. It was impossible to say with any real conviction, 'Thank God Rory survived' (although Hugh did, of course, scraping the barrel for something his precious God had got right). We knew that Rory would much rather have died; that continuing to live without being able to play was a kind of living death, was perhaps for Rory worse than death. But we all said Rory had been lucky. We all knew that he hadn't.

Ettie's death should have put Rory's loss in some kind of perspective but somehow it didn't. It was a horrible way to die, but Ettie would have said she'd had a good life. She was spared long, lingering illness, the infirmity and indignities of old age. It sounds callous, but what happened to Rory seemed to me worse, much worse. He was thirty-two, the breadwinner, and his children were eight and five years old. He had no skills other than playing the piano and he was not insured against injury – a mixture of arrogance and economy.

I was angry, but I didn't really understand why. I was angry that the accident had happened, that it wasn't even Rory's fault, but I was also angry that I didn't know how to grieve. I felt Rory had somehow been cheated – of his life and career, but also of the family's grief. His loss was eclipsed by Ettie's gruesome death, by her funeral, by the empty chair at Orchard Farm.

But at the same time I felt poor Ettie had been cheated too – and not just by her premature death. Life had cheated Ettie. Even in death she had to share her tragedy with Rory.

Rory stopped talking and I stopped drinking. I did a deal with God.

I don't think it struck anyone immediately that Rory had stopped talking. Only Grace was allowed to visit to begin with and when the rest of us got to see him he was either unconscious or groggy after an operation on his hand. We all assumed he must be speaking to somebody else. Information about Rory's condition and his state of mind filtered back to us but it came via doctors, nurses and surgeons, not Rory.

He wouldn't speak, write notes or give any indication of comprehension, assent, anything that would have helped us to look after him or share the burden of his loss. He appeared to take painkillers but we discovered later when he overdosed that he'd merely pretended to swallow them, then hoarded them. (The willpower required to do that in a state of post-operative pain gives some indication of what we were up against.) He was prescribed anti-depressants but wouldn't take them. They were also prescribed for Grace, who did.

As soon as he was physically fit enough to be on his feet he was allowed some independence. Too much. He limped off in his dressing gown one morning and was found hanging from a high window in the Gents' toilet. He was discovered by a hospital porter, alive but unconscious. The man bore his weight and yelled until somebody came to cut Rory down.

Grace said it was just a cry for help, that Rory must have known he might be found before he was dead. She needed to believe that – we all did – and so no one contradicted her. No one mentioned Rory's frightening determination, his obsessive single-mindedness. No one told Grace (and we supposed she didn't know) that at the age of seven Rory had run away from school and lived rough, travelling across two counties before his pocket money ran out, he collapsed and was found. No one told her that Rory had played the silence card before, nor that he'd only spoken again when he'd got what he wanted.

I knew Rory had meant to die. It had probably taken him longer than expected to tie the knot in his dressing gown cord with only one working hand. He probably didn't know that when you're hanged it's usually the drop and the broken neck that kills you. He probably underestimated how long it would take him to asphyxiate. Who knows whether Rory was thinking straight? (Since he was trying to kill himself, I think we can assume he wasn't.) But how on earth can you gauge the state of mind of someone who never speaks or reacts, who doesn't even seem to hear?

After the botched hanging Archie was a broken man. A combination of grief, shock and old age banished my father to an incoherent twilight world of half-truths and memories. We told him Rory was on the mend; we even fabricated conversations with him. Archie meanwhile was adrift somewhere between the present and the past. He became confused and often called Theo, 'Rory', asking him to play the piano, a senile substitution that was understandable, but one which brought me out in a cold sweat every time. When Rory finally came home – still not speaking – his father didn't appear to recognise him. He asked Theo to tell him 'who the thin young man was'.

Archie wasn't the only one who wondered who the thin young man was.

Grace had a label for it: 'elective mutism'. She seemed to derive some comfort from talking about the condition. Perhaps she thought a diagnosis would speed recovery. Grace explained it could be a reaction to trauma and that recovery was therefore likely. It was simply a matter of time.

I think Grace probably understood what was really going on – she wasn't stupid – but she couldn't afford to confront too much reality. She was the one who had to tuck the kids up at night and tell them Daddy would get better one day. I think she probably knew that what we were fighting wasn't the destructive power of trauma but simply Rory's will.

He had lost the ability to play. For ever.

There was nothing more to say.

Rory had a limited number of ways in which he could try to despatch himself. After the hanging attempt he was sectioned and put on suicide watch. He was allowed nothing he could use to harm himself: no glass, knives or scissors, no razor blades. He was encouraged to walk in the grounds of the mental hospital with a carer, but once he realised he was too weak to run away he lost any interest in these excursions.

Eventually he refused all food and most liquid. He appeared to think he could gradually starve himself to death. Or maybe he just wanted to be in a coma and achieve oblivion. Who knows? He didn't say.

His psychiatrist, Dr Reilly, a warm, gentle woman to whom Rory never spoke, told him that he wouldn't succeed in killing himself this way. As soon as his condition became critical they would put him on a glucose drip that would save his life. When he was no longer in danger they would dismantle the drip and let him go back to starving himself. This was perhaps the first time Rory realised he was up against a will as formidable as his own. Dr Reilly pointed out that all he would achieve by playing this cat-and-mouse game was huge amounts of distress for his wife and children who had the job of visiting and seeing him in a state of semi-starvation.

Dr Reilly was a courageous and determined woman and also a music lover. She was of the 'tough love' school and she spared Rory nothing. Playing her trump card, she told him she'd overheard Colin say he didn't think Daddy would ever speak to them again, so what was the point of them visiting?

Rory said nothing.

She tried on one occasion to speak to Rory of music. His only reaction apparently was to shut his eyes. If Dr Reilly ever got any other reaction from him – a guilty look, an angry grunt, a mute appeal for mercy – she never mentioned it to us.

Nothing and nobody got through.

1974

Flora, Hugh and Theo were picking blackberries at Orchard Farm. There was a bumper crop and Dora had insisted they make jam 'as usual', as it was Archie's favourite. Jam-making had always been Ettie's job. Flora wondered if Dora thought they would all miss her less if jars of blackberry jam appeared on the table in September, as they had done for as long as anyone could remember.

Hugh handed a full china bowl to Theo and told him to carry it carefully indoors and place it on the kitchen table. The boy grasped the bowl with sticky, purple fingers and set off up the garden.

'I think he's eaten as many as he's picked,' Hugh said with a smile.

'Oh, no – he's eaten a *lot* more.'

Hugh smiled again and watched Theo plodding up the garden path. Flora watched Hugh watching and thought, if it weren't for the children, how rarely any of the adults would smile these days.

Hugh bent to his task again and after a moment said, 'I'd like to go and visit Rory in hospital.'

'Oh, don't be such a masochist! You're the last person in the world he'd want to see. He doesn't even acknowledge his children.'

'I know. But I'd like to go and see him just the same. He is my brother-in-law.'

'That's not why you want to see him.'

'No, I suppose not. But I *need* to see him. I don't think I'll be able to come to terms with... with what has happened to him until I do. In any case, it'll look a bit odd if I don't go and visit him soon. It's been nearly two weeks. And Dora thinks I'll be able to offer some spiritual comfort, talking man to man.'

'*Talking*? Rory doesn't speak! He'll just ignore you. Or worse – he'll think you've come to preach at him.'

'No, he won't think that. He knows I wouldn't have the nerve. I've been quite frank with him about my future.'

'You've told him you want to give up the ministry?'

'Yes. And I told him I know about Theo.'

'Good God! *When*?'

'The day of the accident. I met Rory in town. I'd asked to see him because there were things we needed to discuss.'

'What things?'

'Oh, it doesn't matter now. Events have rather overtaken us. We attempted to indulge in a little mutual blackmail but I think we actually parted on pretty good terms. We seemed to understand each other.'

'Wonders will never cease.'

'I'm not sure. It wasn't exactly a truce, more of a ceasefire.'

'He still won't want to see you. He doesn't want to see anyone.'

'I assure you, if he gives me the slightest indication that my presence is unwelcome, I'll leave immediately.'

Flora looked up and saw Theo running towards them, waving an empty bowl. 'If Rory gives you the slightest indication of *anything*, Hugh, you will have achieved more than all the rest of us put together.'

~

Hugh sat in silence, his hands folded in his lap, his head bowed. Occasionally he would look up and turn his head towards the bed where Rory lay quite still, facing the wall. Each time he did so, the sight of Rory's right arm in plaster, the hand completely obscured by bandages, caused Hugh's stomach to churn. Each time the sight came as a shock, as if he'd expected something to have changed, as if the shattered body might somehow have healed itself while he'd looked away. Each time, Hugh could not prevent himself from looking away again, his body and mind racked with the desire to take this man in his arms, hold him and comfort him, even though he knew no comfort was possible, no comfort from *him* was even acceptable. Hugh steeled himself to look back again.

He couldn't see much of Rory's face. His hair was untidy and unwashed, his face encrusted with several days' stubble and scabs of dried blood where his face had been cut by flying glass. One sleeve had been cut from his pyjama jacket to accommodate the plaster cast. Hugh noted that the plain white pyjamas looked expensive. Linen probably. Grace, ever thoughtful, would have brought him linen pyjamas to keep him cool in the overheated hospital. Rory's good left hand lay inert on the bedspread, as beautiful as a Michelangelo sculpture. And as lifeless, Hugh thought.

He wondered if Rory would prefer him to leave. He thought so, but Rory had made no move to indicate this. But then he barely reacted to anyone or anything. Grace had said he was refusing food and drink now. The poor girl was half out of her mind with worry. Hugh wondered how much more she would be able to take. He remembered the lie he used to tell sick and bereaved parishioners: that God never sends us more than we can bear. He'd believed it then.

Hugh started to speak before he'd even decided what he would say. 'Rory, if you want me to leave, I will. Raise your hand, give me some indication. I don't expect you to speak. Not to me. But if you don't tell me to go, I will speak to you. There's something I'd like to say.'

There was a noise of rattling trolleys in the corridor. Hugh waited but Rory said nothing and remained motionless.

'I imagine what you want most in the world at this moment is...

to be dead.' Hugh sensed rather than saw a tensing of the body. The slack jaw muscles at the side of Rory's expressionless face twitched briefly before relaxing again into their customary passivity. 'I imagine you're thinking, if only *I'd* died instead of Ettie.' Rory closed his eyes for a few seconds, then opened them again, still averting his gaze from Hugh who continued, his voice low. 'When I realised I was going to have to live without God... without love... from God, from any man – I thought *I* wanted to die. I thought there'd never been such a useless, sterile, *ridiculous* life as mine.' He smiled ruefully. 'Oh, I can see why you used to make fun of me. What a pathetic figure I must have seemed to you! Probably still do. Not just pathetic – hypocritical. Finding out that Theo wasn't even mine was the final blow. It seemed as if everything had been taken from me: my God, my wife, my son, my sense of myself as... a man. I think you must be able to understand some of this, Rory. I know you won't be able to respect my seemingly infinite capacity for self-delusion, but perhaps now you might pity me for it. Or maybe not. I took Flora away from you. I don't expect you ever to forgive me for that.'

Hugh paused and wiped his upper lip where sweat was collecting. Rory had given no indication he was listening. His chest rose and fell steadily and Hugh wondered if he was asleep. He looked away from the bed and clasped his hands together, staring down at his feet.

'I saw myself as a priest. And a family man. I never actually saw *me*. You were the only one who saw me for what I was. I was concerned only with the man I wanted to be, not the man I was. I thought I would be loved – by God, by my congregation, by both my wives – if I was a good priest and a good man. And I *was*. They did all love me. Except it wasn't me they loved, was it? It was a fake. A hollow man.' Hugh straightened up in his chair – like most chairs, slightly too small for him to be comfortable. Without looking at Rory, he continued. 'What I'm going to have to find out now is if anyone, anyone at all, will love me for myself. I think Theo does. But of course he's too young to understand who and what he loves. I wonder, will he love me when he discovers I'm not his father? I think he must be told one day. Even if he isn't told who his father is, he surely has a right to know I am *not*... And if he still manages to love me as his adoptive father – and I think he might – will he be able to love me knowing I am homosexual?' Hugh looked up towards the bed. There was no movement, no sound. 'Doesn't seem very likely, does it? So is that a reason to keep the truth from him? For his sake, if not mine? I don't think so. It's not as if I'm a criminal. Not any more... That's something you must be able to understand, Rory. Knowing that your love is unnatural. That it makes you a pariah. It's a strange and horrible feeling, isn't it? And so *unfair*. As if one could help one's feelings! Are our feelings sent to try us, do you think? Are they another test? Are we afflicted with these terrible loves just so we can spend our lives denying them? I don't know. I don't know anything any more.' Hugh put his head in his hands. 'I used to have an answer for everything, didn't I? I must have been insufferable.'

A nurse entered with a jug of fresh water. She removed an untouched jug from the bedside table and frowned. She poured a glass of water, then leaned over the bed and said, 'Please try to take some liquid, Mr Dunbar. You'll become very ill if you don't. And that won't help *anything*.' She didn't wait for a reply but nodded and smiled at Hugh, reassured by his dog collar. As the door closed behind her, Hugh resumed.

'I'm sure it's of no interest to you, Rory, but I'd like you to know how things are for me now. I think perhaps it might be relevant. To *you*.' He paused and waited for a reaction of some sort, of impatience perhaps, but none came. 'I stand to lose everything, absolutely everything I hold dear. The truer I am to myself, the more likely I am to lose. But,' Hugh smiled faintly. 'I don't know, there's a sort of recklessness got into me... I'm curious to know – *damn* curious – who I'm going to turn out to be! Who will want to befriend me, who might even love me? I've lost – or am about to lose – almost everything: my identity, my job, my home, my wife...' He swallowed. 'And my adored son. But... I'm now *myself*. And that feels good!'

Hugh's spine straightened and as his chin lifted he said, '*The people that walked in darkness have seen a great light; they that dwell in the land of the shadow of death, upon them hath the light shined.* You'll know that bit of Isaiah from Handel, I suppose... I still read my Bible, you know. So much beauty and wisdom! One can't give it all up, like... like tobacco. The words are still a comfort to me. But they're just words now. Poetry. Music. Beautiful sounds. But I find it no less a comfort, no less a wonder for all that. Does that make me a hypocrite too? I'm not sure. Maybe it does. But if anyone were to love me now it would be *me* they loved, not some deluded fool.' Hugh laughed silently, his broad shoulders shaking gently. 'You made an honest man of me, Rory! I'm no longer hiding behind the Word of God. Behind anyone else's words. I shall speak for myself in future. That's what I'm doing now. It's me who's speaking. Hugh Wentworth. Not God. Or a priest. Just a very ordinary man.'

From the corner of his eye Hugh saw Rory's fingers move slightly. An involuntary twitch perhaps. They moved again, then curled inwards slowly, forming a relaxed fist, then they spread again, splayed and extended to their full, remarkable length, then lay still on the bedspread. Hugh stared at the perfect hand, completely unmarked by the accident.

'You probably think you were just a pianist...' Hugh was silent for a moment, unable to continue. He gathered himself, then went on. 'That wasn't what we saw. Flora. Grace. Ettie. Your parents. Your children. We saw a husband, father, brother, son. We saw a brilliant mind. An incisive wit. A talent for explaining. A gift for interpreting. There were so many different Rorys. And we loved them all. Now one of them is no more – the one you valued most. But perhaps – who knows? – *that* Rory, the pianist, was holding back other Rorys. How much of a human being can one be, do you think, practising alone for five or six hours a day?' Hugh paused, then took a deep breath. 'The question you're going to have to ask yourself – unless you decide to die, of course – and I accept that probably seems like the obvious solution, the only way to deal with all this unbearable pain – the question is, do you have a connection with music in any way other than through your hands? Are you a *musician*, Rory, or were you simply a pianist?'

Rory's head turned slowly, rolling like a great stone across the pillow, until he faced Hugh. A lock of heavy hair fell back on to the pillow. Hugh forced himself not to look away, not to blink, but he'd found it easier to look into the eyes of the dead and the dying than to hold this man's tortured gaze.

Hugh's voice when he finally managed to speak again was no more than a whisper. 'You have a choice, Rory. You could choose to walk out of the darkness... and into the light. And you wouldn't be making that journey alone. We would be with you every step of the way.'

Eventually, without looking away from Hugh, Rory closed his eyes. He lay quite still, his long brown lashes resting in the dark hollows of his eye sockets. Hugh continued to watch as Rory's eyes shuttled rapidly back and forth, frantic, under pale, veined lids.

Chapter 16

The shock of discovering that my husband was gay had barely sunk in when the accident happened. One shock was superseded by another, then another. What with Ettie's death, Rory's injury, his suicide attempts, then Archie's decline, the unorthodox and unhappy state of my marriage seemed like the least of anyone's problems.

When I did have time to take stock I realised that, in a way, I was relieved about Hugh. Knowledge brought me relief. I knew the failure of the marriage wasn't my fault. How could I ever have made it work? I'd had no idea how comforting it would be to have someone else to blame for my misery. That in itself made it easier to bear.

Once I'd got over my initial feelings of shock and revulsion, Hugh's homosexuality conferred a strange kind of freedom on me, a freedom to love with a whole heart. My feelings towards Rory were unnatural and adulterous, but they didn't appear to hurt my husband so I felt I was no longer betraying him. I would never love my brother without guilt, but now I could love him with less.

I suppose Hugh must have been relieved to find he hadn't driven me to drink. It was one less thing for him to atone for. I believe he told me about his feelings for Rory partly so that I shouldn't feel so guilty or, rather, so alone in my guilt. He knew, had known for all the years we'd been married, what it was like to feel ashamed, to feel outcast. (It was only after he'd told me about his true nature that I realised Hugh did in fact love me, he just didn't love me sexually.)

We achieved a kind of uneasy equilibrium. We knew each other's secrets and had to keep them, but we could speak freely to each other, almost like the old days when we were just friends and I was too young and he too old to be regarded as a potential partner. Hugh now understood my ambivalence towards Theo and could forgive it; I understood Hugh's lack of interest in sex and forgave that. It was a relief to have things out in the open and life became much simpler in a way, especially after I'd stopped drinking.

Simpler that is, if you set aside the fact that the man we both loved was suicidally depressed and seemed unlikely to survive.

Everyone applied themselves to helping Grace cope, taking Colin and Lottie off her hands as much as possible so she could deal with Rory and make decisions about their future. There was nothing any of us could do for Rory so we focused on Grace and the children. The survivors.

Buoyed up by drugs, Grace was full of plans. She got Rory's agent to cancel two years' worth of musical engagements and his lucrative recording contract, then she made arrangements for a future that none but she could envisage, a time when Rory would be physically and mentally well – and talking – but simply not playing the piano.

It was impossible not to admire Grace. She refused to give up. With their income wiped out overnight, no insurance, no savings to speak of and a husband incapable of speech, let alone earning a living, she had little time to grieve and none at all for self-pity.

Once it was clear that Rory was beyond caring about the family's future she made all the decisions alone, asking Hugh's advice or occasionally mine. My mother was useless, preoccupied as she was with Rory's condition and Archie's decline.

I rarely saw Grace cry in the months following the accident but on one occasion when we were out shopping together she burst into tears and sobbed, 'How am I going to afford Christmas presents for the kids? They both want bikes, for God's sake!' So she sold the baby grand without consulting Rory. That secured their rented London flat for a few more months, paid for a second-hand car and gave Colin and Charlotte the best Christmas they'd ever had, despite the fact that their father, when he was allowed home for the festivities, seemed disorientated and more depressed than ever.

Grace also sold her family heirloom cello and bought an inferior specimen, arguing that since she was going to have to teach cello for a living now, her old one would be casting pearls before swine. What it must have cost her to part with it, I can only imagine.

It was Hugh who pointed out that there really wasn't a lot of point in maintaining, at huge expense, the flat in London. He suggested Grace move to somewhere cheaper, possibly somewhere closer to the family who could help share the burden of virtual single parenthood. It was then that Dora (prompted by Hugh, I suspect) roused herself from her stupor of grief and announced, 'You could come and live here. Why not? There's plenty of room and the children love it here. They'd have a big garden to play in, a bedroom each and they could go to school with Theo.'

Since Grace had complained, pre-accident, about the kids having to share a bedroom and bemoaned the lack of even a balcony for them to play on, the only resistance she could offer was on financial grounds. She thanked Dora, then pointed out that her only source of income was giving cello lessons in London.

Dora was undeterred. 'Give cello lessons here. Use the music room. You could advertise in the local paper. Ring the music department at the high school. It might take a little while to build up again, but word would soon get round. Especially when people knew... the circumstances.'

Grace insisted that she would have to pay Dora the going rate for rent but Dora simply waved an autocratic hand. I suspected she was beginning to enjoy herself. 'Oh, pooh! Don't bother about that. Payment in kind, my dear. We'll work you to death in the kitchen and garden, not to mention looking after Archie. How on earth do you suppose I am going to manage here without Ettie? I'm sixty-seven. If you don't move in to Orchard Farm we shall be obliged to sell up anyway because I simply cannot manage it on my own – even with help from Hugh and Flora. Give up the flat, get yourself settled in with the children and we'll talk about the future when – well, when Rory comes home.'

So Grace moved in. Colin had Rory's old bedroom and Lottie had Ettie's. She was thrilled to have a bedroom of her own, especially one with a washbasin (which she used mainly for washing dolls' clothes). Grace took my old room, the nursery, which Dora had long ago furnished as a double guest bedroom. Grace and I cleared out a box-room, Hugh gave it a coat of paint and it became a sort of den for all three children to play in on wet days. They formed a secret society with badges and membership cards. Its purpose was unclear but it seemed to entail looking (with the aid of torches) for secret passages, underground tunnels and spies, none of which they ever found, but this didn't seem to mar their enjoyment.

The two Dunbar children settled in easily at the village school. Colin was put into Theo's class and Theo took it upon himself to broker friendships for both his cousins. Colin and Lottie found the

Suffolk pupils friendlier and less sophisticated than their London counterparts and they received invitations to tea and birthday parties, invitations issued by mothers who were doubtless keen to hear the latest developments in the Dunbar family saga.

By the beginning of November, the London Dunbars were settled in at Orchard Farm. Rory was stable, but clinically depressed and still hospitalised. Grace was working part-time as a peripatetic cello teacher for the Suffolk LEA. The children were flourishing at school and – as far as one could tell – were happy, although Colin seemed prone to sudden bouts of tearfulness. Archie was deteriorating but Dora was bearing up. Hugh had been a wonderful support to just about everybody and – much to my surprise – Grace and I had become friends of sorts.

Hugh and the children built a huge bonfire in the vegetable garden. Grace spent a small fortune on fireworks and we had a party with baked potatoes and sausages to celebrate the fact that we appeared to have come through the worst; that maybe better times lay ahead.

It was a fiction we were able to maintain until it was time to visit Rory.

We all found our own ways of coping, all of them a mixture of faith, blind hope and denial. Rory's visitors sat by his bedside, or eventually in a day room, delivering monologues about the weather, the news, the NHS. Dora talked about the garden; Grace talked about the children, all three of them, and how well they got on, now they saw a lot more of each other. She didn't mention the cancellation of Rory's engagements, but told him of the benefit concert to be organised by his friends in the music business and how they hoped to raise £3000 which, she said, 'would help'.

Apart from that, nobody talked about money, nobody talked about the future and nobody ever talked about music – to Rory or among ourselves. The accident plunged us all into a world in which only the present moment existed, a nightmare world where the only bulwark against horror and uncertainty was a kind of heartfelt, superstitious gratitude. We were grateful that Rory was – despite his best efforts – still alive. We prayed our gratitude would keep him that way.

1974

Ankle-deep in fallen leaves, two boys in school blazers and shorts searched for the last of the conkers beneath the spreading branches of a horse chestnut. Their bare knees, purple with cold, were encrusted with scabs and dried mud. The smaller boy, dark and shorter by a head, though not much younger, sniffed occasionally and wiped his nose with the back of his hand. His companion looked up and watched him, his bright blue eyes concerned.

Theo hoped Colin wasn't crying again. It wasn't really that he minded Colin crying. Theo was used now to members of his family crying. They all seemed to do it at one time or another – even his father, which had surprised Theo. It was just that he felt sorry for his cousin and didn't know what he could do to cheer him up, so he preferred him not to cry.

Colin pounced on an outsize conker and, his face shining with triumph and smeared snot, held the specimen up for Theo to admire. 'What a whopper, eh?'

Theo smiled with relief, nodded and bent again to his task. Colin polished the already gleaming conker on the sleeve of his blazer and dropped it into his satchel, saying, 'I'm going to show that one to Dad. It's even bigger than his.'

Theo knew Colin was referring to a conker on a piece of filthy string they'd found in a drawer in Colin's bedroom, Rory's old room, at Orchard Farm. Rory hadn't explained its presence – Rory never spoke – but Flora had realised what it was as soon as Colin had shown her. She'd explained that Rory's monster conker had been retired, undefeated champion and veteran of a hundred or more encounters in which it had literally smashed the opposition. Colin had held the aged conker, dull now but still intact, weighed it in his palm and replaced it reverently at the back of the drawer where he'd found it.

Theo knew his uncle would say nothing about Colin's conker, would probably barely glance at it. 'You could show it to my mum, too,' he said gently. 'She might be interested.' Theo didn't really think his mother would be, but he'd noticed that she was often kind to Colin. He thought it was worth a try.

Dropping his modest haul into his blazer pockets Theo hoisted his satchel on to his shoulder. 'It's getting dark. We'd better go. Gran'll be worried about you.'

'D'you want to come round and play?'

'I'd have to ask my mum.'

'C'mon then.'

The boys set off in the direction of the vicarage, kicking piles of leaves into the air as they walked. Theo loved to be outdoors. There was so much to see, hear and smell. He lifted his head and inhaled the mixture of damp, decay, bonfire- and chimney-smoke that signalled autumn. Plunging his hands into his pockets, he fondled the cool, smooth conkers, listening for the gentle knocking sound as they tumbled over one another.

Theo wrapped his fingers round a conker and thought of his Uncle Rory and the hand that seemed perpetually encased in plaster as operation succeeded operation. The fingertips protruded beyond the plaster but they didn't move. They were pale and soft, somehow dead-looking, like the baby bird Theo had found on the garden path at the vicarage last spring. His father had said the mother bird had thrown the baby out of the nest because there was something wrong with it and it was too weak to survive. The dead bird had lain on the path, an object of Theo's pity and fascination, until Hugh had cleared it away with a shovel.

When Theo looked at his uncle's fingers peeping out from their plaster casing he felt the same confused mixture of feelings, but didn't understand why. The baby bird was dead. Uncle Rory wasn't dead, it had been Great Aunt Ettie who'd died. Thinking of Ettie and the funeral brought tears to Theo's eyes. To distract himself he broke a long but companionable silence with an abrupt question. 'Why d'you think your dad doesn't talk any more?'

'Dunno...' Colin looked down at his feet as they tossed leaves into the air.

' 'Cos he's sad, I suppose.'

'You'd think,' said Theo, frowning, 'if he was sad, he'd cry.'

'He did. Mum said he cried a lot. When it first happened.'

'Oh. My dad cried too.'

'*Your* dad?'

'I only heard him, I didn't see him. He was in his study. He'd been to visit your dad at the hospital, I think... I didn't know men cried.'

'Oh, yeah, sometimes. But things have to be pretty bad.'

'Well, they were, weren't they?'

They walked on in silence until Colin said, his voice leaden with disappointment, 'I don't think I'm going to get a bike for Christmas.'

Theo hesitated. He wasn't sure whether Colin, being slightly younger, had yet discovered that Father Christmas wasn't real and he certainly didn't want to add to his cousin's troubles. 'Why's that?' he asked tentatively.

'Mum said we can't afford it. She says we've all got to get used to going without. But it won't be for ever,' Colin added cheerfully. 'She's going to get a proper job and she says when Dad is better he'll get some work too. But there won't be any bike for Christmas.'

Theo was silent and felt once again the ache somewhere in his chest that he thought might go away if only he could think of a way to help Colin. 'I've asked for roller skates,' he said helpfully.

Colin's face brightened. 'Yeah, skates would be good.'

'I expect you could have those. Ask your mum. Or Gran. *She'd* get them for you. Maybe you could have a bike for your birthday.'

'Maybe,' Colin said doubtfully.

'I haven't got a bike either.'

Colin felt cheered by this admission and wondered whether Theo would like to be his special friend. Colin hadn't acquired a special friend since moving to Theo's school and he wasn't sure if cousins qualified.

'Actually,' Theo continued, 'I'd *rather* have skates than a bike.'

'Yeah, so would I.' Colin hoped this expression of solidarity, though insincere, would somehow cement relations. He liked Theo, who wasn't like the other boys. He seemed not to notice how often Colin cried. Theo didn't say much, but what he said was always kind and often interesting. Colin remembered that was how it used to be with his dad, before the accident. Mum talked a lot and you didn't really need to listen because it was usually the same old stuff about clean hands or dirty shoes or tidying your room, but whenever his Dad used to talk to him Colin always wished he'd say more. Now of course he didn't say anything at all. Ever.

As if reading his cousin's mind, Theo asked, 'D'you think he'll ever talk again? Your dad, I mean.'

'Oh, yeah,' Colin said, with a nonchalance he didn't feel. 'Mum said so. But she didn't say when.'

'Don't suppose she knows,' Theo said reasonably.

Colin felt depressed again and wondered how they could get the conversation back on to skates. He was about to ask Theo if he would like to be his special friend when his cousin said, 'D'you know what my dad said about your dad?'

'What?'

'My dad said he can't speak because he can't find the words.'

'What words?'

'Words to say how sad he feels. My dad says your dad feels *so* bad, it isn't possible for him to describe it.'

Colin digested this, then said, 'He could talk about something else.'

'How d'you mean?'

'Well, he could say *Hello*. Or *Goodnight*. He could say *Please* and *Thank you*. He doesn't have to talk about... the accident. We don't.'

'Do you talk to him?'

'Mum does. I don't.'

'Why not?'

' 'Cos I feel stupid! I *know* he's not going to answer, so I don't bother any more.'

'What about Lottie?'

Colin shrugged, embarrassed. 'She sings.'

'*Sings*?'

'Yeah. She sits on his lap or she lies on the bed and sings to him.'

'What does she sing?'

'I dunno. Hymns. Skipping rhymes. Girls' stuff,' he added, pulling a face.

'*Skipping* rhymes? Why?'

' 'Cos she doesn't know what to say, I s'pose.'

Theo smiled at the thought of little Lottie bouncing on the bed singing rhymes. His heart felt suddenly lighter. 'Perhaps Uncle Rory will sing.' Colin stopped rooting among the fallen leaves and stared up at Theo. 'Perhaps he'll sing one day. Instead of talking. If he doesn't know how to say how bad he feels, perhaps he'll *sing* it. Like Lottie.'

Colin looked doubtful as he tried to grasp this new and unexpected idea. 'Dad never used to sing. Except when he was shaving. He used to hum a bit. And sometimes when we were in traffic jams—' He flinched as he remembered the story of the accident, the explanations, all the tears, the fear that his father might die.

'I think he'll sing one day,' Theo said, confident now. 'I think one day he'll just open his mouth and start singing. Then he'll probably start talking. Gran said that's what happened when he was little.'

Colin frowned. 'What – my dad?'

'Yes. Gran said when he was really little he didn't talk and everybody worried about him. Then one day he started singing to people and then everything was all right! I think that's what'll happen. But maybe not yet. Maybe when he isn't so sad.'

'D'you think it would help if we sang to him?'

'It might. Does he like Lottie singing to him?'

'Dunno. He doesn't say anything, does he?'

'My dad says the important thing is that we all tell Uncle Rory how much we love him and that we want him to get better.'

'Why?'

'Don't know, But my dad said it was really important.'

'Theo?' Colin swallowed and squeezed the conker he was holding very tight. 'D'you think my dad'll die?'

'No, of course not! Not if we all believe he's going to get better. I mean, if we all *believe* it, he'll *have* to get better, won't he? Like Tinkerbell in *Peter Pan*.'

'She was a fairy.'

'Yes... But she didn't die,' Theo said desperately.

Colin could see Theo was now close to tears and tried to change the subject. 'D'you believe in fairies?'

'No,' Theo said firmly. 'But I believe in your dad.'

Although she felt it was akin to an act of vandalism, Dora eventually locked the piano at Orchard Farm after she found Theo in there one day, playing very quietly. She barely coped. It was the first time the keys had been touched since the accident, but she managed to maintain her usual composure, even when Theo explained he'd wanted to play the piano because he thought it was sad it was never touched now by Aunt Ettie or Uncle Rory. He'd wondered if it was possible for a piano to feel lonely.

When Dora told me, I badly wanted to tell Rory what his son had said, but I didn't. It couldn't possibly have helped. In fact I said very little to Rory. I told him I'd stopped drinking but not why. (He would have known why.) Eventually I said nothing at all. I sat in silence with him. He allowed me to hold his good hand which, when we were alone, I carried to my mouth and kissed. Otherwise I sat still and silent. When I could bear it no longer I held him, unresisting, unresponsive, in my arms.

I knew nothing in this world or the next could compensate for the loss he'd sustained. By sharing his silence, I hoped to convey to him that I knew there was nothing that would help, that I accepted there was nothing. I thought in some strange way it might spare Rory some pain if I at least didn't contaminate his room with hopes and lies, the need for him to be well, for him to speak.

I didn't need Rory to speak. We were beyond speech – always had been, always would be. What was silence to us? I just needed Rory to exist. Death was the only thing that could ever come between us.

And death was the only thing that ever did come between us.

Chapter 17

It wasn't until after the accident that we realised the high regard in which Rory was held by the musical world. He was headline news in the music press and journalists requested interviews even while he was still in shock. When their calls weren't returned they door-stepped Grace and pestered her for an interview. She declined but some of the more unscrupulous hacks pointed out that personal interest stories about Rory – particularly those with a tragic angle – would keep his back catalogue selling nicely and that in turn would keep money trickling into the fast-emptying Dunbar coffers. Grace told the journalists to 'Bugger off and leave us alone!'

Rory's agent was inundated with cards and letters of condolence from all over the world. Some were from music-lovers, many were from students and musicians. Some enclosed cheques and Grace agonised over what to do with them. At first she wanted to return them, but Hugh said it would be a shame to deprive the donors of the feeling they'd helped in some small way. Then Grace thought of donating them to the Musicians' Benevolent Fund, but in the end we persuaded her to keep them.

Hugh gave Colin and Theo a map of the world and they drew crosses on it marking every place from which Rory received a letter. Grace and I answered every letter and card between us, explaining Rory wasn't well enough to write himself. We refrained from mentioning he hadn't even looked at them. When, seated at his bedside, Grace ran out of things to say, she'd remove a sheaf of letters from her handbag and read excerpts to him, but Rory showed no interest.

Some people sent gifts with their letters: books, poems, paintings, good luck charms, religious icons, photographs of themselves. (Rory's admirers appeared to include a disproportionate number of middle-aged men and I began to suspect Hugh's feelings for my brother weren't quite as extraordinary as I'd thought.) A woman in Tokyo sent a white silk kimono ablaze with gold chrysanthemums. It looked like an antique. The sender was an elderly piano teacher who'd been to all of Rory's concerts in Japan. Grace was so overcome by both the present and the letter she sent the woman a large photograph of Rory and his family. She inscribed the photo, faking his signature, arguing that the woman would never know the difference.

Many people wrote about – some even sent – music to be played by the left hand only. It turned out that there was a substantial repertoire of pieces written by, among others, Strauss, Ravel and Britten. A famous pianist, Paul Wittgenstein, had lost his right arm in World War I and he'd commissioned composers to write pieces for him so that he could continue to play. Grace already knew the Ravel piano concerto for left hand and said it was a very demanding piece, a great concerto in its own right.

Grace and Hugh fell upon these pieces of music, overjoyed to think that Rory would still be able to play, but I took it upon myself to suggest to Grace that she shouldn't show these particular letters and gifts to Rory yet – maybe not for a long time. If I knew my brother (and I did, in every sense, including the carnal) Rory would be incensed by the music. He wouldn't even consider some cut-down version of what he used to be able to play. If I knew Rory, he would cut music out of his life altogether before he'd settle for second best, before he'd accept any kind of limitations or make any concession to his disability.

So Grace filed the music and letters away carefully in what she called, with conscious irony, her Hope Chest, a wooden box in which she stored all the things she hoped Rory would one day look at and appreciate: the letters and cards, the presents, the retrospective articles from music journals, advertisements for his records (which enjoyed a macabre popularity after the accident), family photographs taken at Christmas and New Year, school photos of the children, photos of friends' weddings and babies, programmes for concerts which Grace attended on her own, including a precious sheet of mimeographed coloured paper issued by the children's school, recording the musical contributions of Colin, Lottie and Theo to the Christmas concert of 1974.

These were souvenirs of life as it was lived in the year that Rory left us, the year he was absent as well as silent. Grace couldn't bear to shut the kimono away, so she put it on one of Ettie's old padded coat-hangers and hung it on the door of the nursery, the bedroom she would share with Rory when he eventually came home. The golden chrysanthemums glowed and the white silk rippled as she passed, but the garment hung there, empty, like her life, waiting for Rory to fill it.

In an attempt to cheer ourselves up, Grace and I celebrated her thirty-second birthday with a modest girls' night out in Ipswich. We saw Shampoo at the cinema and enjoyed ogling Warren Beatty, then we went for a pizza and drank far too much chianti. By the time we'd broached the second bottle, the conversation was loud, racy and utterly hilarious. Well, we thought so.

Too much was drunk and too much was said. Companions in booze, misery and sexual frustration, Grace and I found we liked each other and had a lot more in common than love for Rory.

1975

'Darling!' Grace was aghast. 'I can't believe *you're* not getting laid either! Gosh, what a coincidence!'

'Keep your voice down! We're getting some very funny looks. If you carry on like that, we might get some very funny offers.'

'Sorry! But how *awful* for you. Is Hugh just not interested?'

'No, not really. I don't know that *I* am now, Not any more, so it really doesn't matter. Grace, do stop pouring. The glass is full.'

'Oops! Oh, bugger. Now I've made a mess of the cloth.'

'And what is worse,' Flora said sternly, 'you've wasted some of our precious wine.'

'Oh, let's order another bottle. Damn the expense! We haven't had pudding yet. Tell me about Hugh. I'm curious.'

Flora picked up her menu and appeared to study it. 'It seems rather disloyal to talk about it.'

'Rubbish! You and I are practically sisters. And I told you speaking's not the only thing Rory's given up.'

'I realise things must be rather strained. As he's so depressed, I mean.'

Grace leaned forward, shielding her face with her menu and said in a stage whisper, 'Hasn't laid a finger on me since *long* before the accident. It'd already crossed my mind he might be having an affair.'

'Oh, no – surely not?'

212

'You think you'd know? The famous twin telepathy?'

'I don't know. I never used to see him much. But, no, I don't think I'd have known.'

Grace opened her menu and scanned the pages. 'I nearly had an affair.'

'*Did* you? Who with?'

'One of Rory's friends. A chap who used to hang around a lot when Rory was away. Michael. Do you remember him? You met him at Snape. Sweet man. Wonderful musician. I was flattered, a bit tempted even. But I didn't actually fancy him. I mean, he wasn't exactly Warren Beatty, was he?' The two women giggled. 'Have you ever had an affair?'

'*Me?* Of course not! When would I have had the time or the opportunity?'

'Hugh was your first then?'

'Yes, of course he was.'

'Your one and only, in fact.'

'Yes... My one and only.'

'God, it's really tragic a man that handsome isn't interested in sex. What a waste! I suppose it's all the God stuff. Dampens the libido.'

'I suppose so.'

'I don't know what happened to Rory's. *He* certainly wasn't nobbled by God. You know, once upon a time we were always at it.'

Flora bent her head over the menu. 'So – are we having pudding or not?'

'I'm going to have another glass of wine. Several. Come on, drink up, girl! You're letting the side down.' Grace upended the bottle clumsily into Flora's glass, then caught the eye of a waiter, a well-groomed young man with a discreet earring. Grace waved the bottle at him. He smiled pleasantly and went to fetch another.

Grace studied her menu. 'Nice bum, but obviously queer.' Flora choked on a mouthful of wine but stole a glance at the retreating posterior. 'You know, it's one of life's tragedies,' Grace said expansively. 'All the attractive men are married or queer. Or both.'

'Look, I really think we should order pudding if we're going to have it. Time's getting on and we mustn't miss our train. I'm going to have cassata.'

'We should have birthday cake!'

'Cake's not on the menu.'

'Oh, I'm sure they can stick a candle in something!' Grace snorted with laughter and spilt more wine on the cloth. 'When he comes back with my bottle I'm going to smile sweetly at that young man and tell him it's my birthday. What's the Italian for cake?'

'Haven't a clue.'

'Well, I shall do my best with sign language. If he remains impervious to my charms it will be proof categorical that he's queer.'

'I should have made you a cake. I don't know why I didn't think of it. I'm always baking for bazaars.'

'Don't worry, darling – I can't afford the calories and Colin and Lottie would have scoffed it anyway. Home baking's a treat for them. I only ever give them shop cake. My cooking skills are very limited. Maternal skills generally, in fact. I'm the world's worst mother.'

'No, that's definitely me... Motherhood isn't all it's cracked up to be, is it? I mean, it's nothing like the Mothercare catalogue.'

Grace laughed, then said, 'We're over-qualified for the job, that's our trouble. To be a mother you need half a brain and the constitution of an ox.'

'I know what you mean. A day spent in the company of a two year-old whose entire vocabulary consists of "juice", "bicky" and "No!" is not a life-enhancing experience.'

'And you can't even read a book or daydream on the job because that's when the little sods decide to throw themselves downstairs or drink Domestos.'

'But some women do actually *enjoy* motherhood. Well, so I've heard.'

Grace shook her head vehemently. 'Propaganda put out by male supremacists who want to keep us in our place. How can any woman with an ounce of intelligence or spirit enjoy looking after small children? OK, it calls upon reserves of patience and diplomacy and an ability to negotiate that most men can only dream about, but if a woman *has* those skills she should be working for the bloody UN, not pushing a supermarket trolley.'

'I've *tried* to be a good mother... But I've failed.'

'Don't be daft. Theo is gorgeous, I love him dearly. I'd swap him for Colin any day. My son is such a thug. No chance of *him* becoming a musician.'

Flora picked up her napkin and began to fold it carefully. 'I think I was miscast. In the theatre of life, I mean... Motherhood was a rôle I took on, at short notice, with no rehearsal. It never really suited me. But the show has run and run and now I find I'm... typecast.'

She looked up to find Grace wasn't listening. Craning to see past Flora, she muttered, 'D'you think that wretched poof is *ever* going to bring us more wine?'

At Easter Hugh was too busy with church services to help put in the potatoes – traditionally a Good Friday job – and Dora announced that it just wasn't possible to keep the vegetable garden going without Ettie's and Archie's help. The family – minus Archie and Rory who'd stayed indoors – were gathered after lunch on the sheltered terrace, drinking coffee and watching Grace allow herself to be beaten at croquet by both Colin and Charlotte, a feat which took considerable skill.

'Grace and the children have done their best to help with the spring clear-up of the garden, but I suppose we must be realistic,' Dora said gloomily. 'So I've decided to focus on the borders, especially those near the house. The lawn and the other beds can just go hang,' she said with a dismissive wave of her hand.

Hugh said gently, 'Wildlife will thrive on your neglect, you know. What you lose in tidiness you'll gain in an increase of species.' He looked down at Theo, seated at his side and explained, 'Visitors to the garden.'

'Animals you mean?'

'Yes, and birds and insects. They love a wild habitat. Perhaps we should start a notebook for sightings of anything new.'

Rory had wandered on to the terrace and sat down on a low wall. The family had learned to make no fuss when he appeared, to accept his comings and goings without comment as this seemed the best way to induce him to stay. He looked unkempt, his hair longer now, stubble disguising hollow cheeks. Flora sensed Hugh had seen Rory arrive and was talking partly for his benefit. 'You and your cousins could make a note of anything you saw, Theo. It would make a very interesting record.'

'You mean like a sort of diary? With dates?'

Flora was already watching Rory so when he caught her eye and nodded towards Theo, she understood. Without taking her eyes from

Rory's, she said, 'Your uncle used to keep a notebook like that when he was a boy. He kept it for years. I think it was a red exercise book?' Rory nodded. 'He made a note of all sorts of exciting things he'd seen.'

'Do you know,' said Dora, 'I think we might still have it! I seem to remember Ettie refused to throw it away.'

'One winter he saw a fox walking across the lawn,' Flora continued. 'And there were dragonflies and damselflies in summer.'

'*Damson*flies?'

'*Damsel*flies. And a hideous toad! He tried to catch it and put it down my neck!'

Rory lifted a hand and, looking at Flora, pointed towards the dense yew hedge.

'Oh, yes! Once we saw a sparrow-hawk.'

'Did you?' Theo turned, his eyes wide and gaped at Rory. 'Here?'

Rory nodded and smiled faintly.

'It was lurking in that hedge, waiting to pounce on unsuspecting small birds. It flew out of the hedge and swooped over our heads. I was terrified.' Flora laughed as she remembered. 'I suppose we must have been quite young. I thought it was an *eagle* at the very least, but Rory knew what it was straight away. He'd never seen one before but he recognised it from his bird book.'

Hugh put his coffee cup down and leaned forward. 'It might be interesting, Theo, for *you* to keep a nature notebook and compare notes with Rory's if we can find it. See what has changed in twenty years.'

'Uncle Rory would have to help. I'm not here all that often.' The boy looked up at Rory who was staring down at the terrace paving.

Without glancing at Rory, Hugh deflected Theo's attention from him. 'Oh, I think we should *all* keep the nature notebook. Colin and Lottie will want to, I'm sure, and I'm bound to spot things when I'm gardening. I think we should call it the *Orchard Farm Nature Notebook* and *everyone* can contribute.'

'All right. But I bet Uncle Rory sees the most things – *and* the most interesting.'

Flora turned to Theo and asked, 'Why do you say that?'

'Because he spends the most time sitting looking out the window. And because he's very good at being still.' Rory lifted his head fractionally to look at the boy. 'He won't frighten things away.

Lottie will *never* spot anything. She's too loud. And she fidgets.'

Hugh laid his hand on Theo's shoulders and laughed. 'It's natural for children to be impatient! And don't forget Lottie's younger than you.'

'Yes, I know. But you have to keep still and wait, don't you, for wild creatures to come to you. They're small and frightened of humans. I bet even that sparrow-hawk would've been frightened of a big human being! You've got to wait... Wait until they just don't *see* you. Or until they trust you. Isn't that right, Uncle Rory?'

Without looking up, Rory nodded.

Dora coped by living in and for her beloved garden. Increasingly unable to sleep as she got older, she rose early and was out in all weathers. When it was too wet to weed or prune, she patrolled the beds in galoshes with a notebook and pencil, planning the renovation of borders. I'm sure she wanted to get away from her menfolk indoors: Archie who rarely emerged from his study and Rory who, when he did finally come home, rarely emerged from his bedroom. I called in most days with shopping for her, occasionally some home baking. Hugh dropped in several times a week to do heavy chores and, when the weather allowed, some gardening. He always went in to see Archie but his father-in-law seemed not to know who he was. He no longer recognised Hugh as a family member and spoke to him as if he were collecting money for charity. The children also baffled Archie. He was fond of Theo (whom he believed to be Rory) and would ask him in a plaintive refrain, 'Where's Flora?' Theo told him of course, or would point me out, but this only distressed Archie further, as did the rare sight of Rory. If he saw Theo and Rory standing side by side, the one a miniature of the other, he became confused and irritable, as if he were contemplating some biological impossibility. When I looked at them I felt much the same.

Strangely enough, Rory allowed Hugh to sit with him. Hugh must have talked about books, poetry, plans for his own future. He got no response of course, but Rory never actually threw him out which always surprised me. I thought Hugh was the last person Rory would have wanted anywhere near him, but his animosity seemed to have vanished, along with every other emotion.

It was no wonder that my poor mother sought refuge in the

garden. Without the buffer of Ettie between her and her family, Dora was at a loss to know how to cope, so she retreated, like her husband and son, into a world of her own.

Dora's spring project was a white border. She condemned the wide herbaceous border that ran in front of an old red-brick wall and said it needed complete renovation. Hugh agreed and suggested they import the contents of the compost heap to enrich the soil before re-planting.

On a sunny day in late April, Dora, wielding clipboard and sheets of squared paper, supervised and encouraged Hugh as he dug out every plant from the border that wasn't white, silver, grey or the palest of blues and lilacs. Theo, in attendance as gardener's boy, couldn't understand why anyone would remove all the colourful plants from a flowerbed and leave in all the dreary ones, but Dora captured his interest by adopting a mysterious voice and saying they were in the process of creating a 'ghost' border.

'It will look nothing special during the daytime, Theo – except on a hot summer's day when it will dazzle your eyes – but it will come into its own in the evenings, you wait and see. As the light fades, the white and silver flowers will sparkle and shimmer. It will be quite, quite magical, I promise.'

Impressed, Theo barrowed compost from the vegetable garden, tipped it on to the flowerbed and took away barrows full of weeds and discarded plants that Hugh and Dora had removed from the border. Rory and I sat on the terrace watching the activity. I didn't speak to him but sensed that he wanted me there to keep him company. Watching the others work soothed him I think, as if he were somehow able to feed off their energy and industry. And Hugh's was prodigious. I rarely saw my husband out of his cassock and just as rarely did I ever look at him as a man, but seated at a distance, seeing him dressed in old cords and a work shirt, the sleeves rolled back over muscular arms shadowed with dark curling hairs, watching him dig, hack, chop, rake and plant, with a word of encouragement for Theo or a joke for Dora, I remembered why I had fallen in love with him, asked myself if I didn't in a way love him still.

My husband's strength and energy moved me, aroused me and I felt the familiar cold anger that only his love and was available to me, not his body. The bitterness and resentment resolved themselves into a hunger, then a thirst. I realised I wanted a drink.

I remembered Rory and looked up to find him watching me. He knew what I was thinking, what I wanted, what I needed. A man. A drink. Either. Both. I looked into his dull grey eyes and saw nothing there, except perhaps pity. No hunger, no desire, not even companionship, just an empty sadness. He stretched out the long fingers of his good hand towards me and laid them on my bare forearm. Perhaps he was testing himself, to see if he felt anything, or he may have been trying to comfort me, I don't know. He curled his fingers round the narrow bones of my wrist and I wondered if he could feel my pulse, feel it racing.

Without letting go of me, Rory looked towards the border where Hugh was leaning on his fork, watching us seated on the terrace. Rory turned back to me, a question in his eyes.

'Yes... Yes, I do,' I said softly. 'I love you both. I love you more, but I love you both. And I know that both of you, in your different ways, love me. But as luck would have it, I can't have either of you. I wonder if – as some small compensation – I could possibly have a drink? Would that be too much to ask, do you think?'

Rory turned my hand over and looked at it as if he were telling my fortune, then he pressed the palm briefly to his lips. In the warm spring sunshine his skin was moist and stubble grazed my fingers.

I rose abruptly from my garden chair and went indoors to the kitchen where I filled the kettle. I stood and waited for the water to boil, staring at my distorted reflection in the gleaming metal. While I tried to calculate how long it was since either man had touched me with any tenderness or desire, I found my eyes scanning the kitchen shelves and cupboards, wondering if Dora still kept cooking brandy and sherry in the kitchen, or if she'd never bothered to replace the bottles I'd emptied.

By the time I took a tea tray out on to the lawn, Rory had gone.

Chapter 18

Hugh provided Theo with a leather-bound notebook which he kept in the summerhouse at Orchard Farm. This little hut was covered in honeysuckle and Virginia creeper and blended so well with its surroundings we tended to forget it was there and rarely used it. It became a sort of hide and Theo would wrap himself in an old rug on cool evenings and peep over the windowsill, pencil poised, hoping to spot something interesting.

Theo told Rory about the book and invited him to record any of his own sightings. He issued the same invitation to the rest of the family but warned Lottie she should try to do her best writing. Colin announced he would help Lottie with her spelling (which was pretty much a case of the blind leading the blind.)

Over the years that notebook took on the significance of a family Bible, the sort in which births, deaths and marriages were recorded. It included not only what was seen at Orchard Farm but who lived there and who visited – animals as well as humans. It even revealed something of how the human inhabitants felt about all the others, both animal and human.

I don't know at what point Rory turned a corner, began to invest something of himself in his family again, in his home, his surroundings. But when, to please Theo, he decided to scrawl in that nature notebook, using what Theo called his 'special pencil', given to him by Rory, a long, slow and painful process had begun.

Theo treasured that notebook for years. Perhaps he still does. But I think it far more likely he destroyed it – probably when he decided he wanted nothing more to do with Rory, the year it was Theo's turn for the world to fall apart.

1987

Hugh had given a great deal of thought to how and where he would break the news to Theo. In the end, for reasons that were not at all clear to him, he'd chosen the Church of the Holy Trinity, Blythburgh, 'the Cathedral of the Marshes'.

Hugh kept his own counsel, made sandwiches, and lured Theo away from greenhouse propagation with the suggestion of a visit to a local nursery in search of new stock, followed by a picnic. As he filled a Thermos Hugh prattled away to Theo, attempting to drive from his mind visions of Abraham about to sacrifice his son Isaac to the greater glory of God.

'No, not the Earl Grey. Pass me the PG Tips. Altogether more robust and better suited to storage in a Thermos, I find. I've started taking a flask of tea up to bed with the *Telegraph* crossword. Gets me through the long watches of the night. I lie awake and contemplate the wickedness of the world and the deviousness of men – especially those who compile the *Telegraph* crossword.'

Theo drove and, as the church came into view, rising above the surrounding marshes and dominating the Suffolk landscape for miles around, Hugh exclaimed, with carefully rehearsed spontaneity, 'Let's do a detour to Blythburgh! It must be ten years since we've been inside the church. Don't suppose you even remember it. You must have been – what? – eleven when we were last there?... Good Lord, where *do* the years go?'

But as soon as they stepped inside the church, Theo remembered.

It was as if God had just popped out for a minute. The church waited breathless and still, expecting His return at any moment. Absence was the word that reverberated in Theo's mind. An absence of people, of sound, of colour. What remained was a mournful and monumental simplicity. Here was a church that had once been great. Now it had a forgotten, almost neglected air, a dim glory, as faded as the bleached paintwork of the angel roof where the gaudy hues of medieval artists had been scoured away by the sands of time, leaving only traces of pigment here and there on the great wooden rafters and central bosses. The twelve pairs of wooden angels, with their disproportionately large carved wings were pale, anaemic creatures whose beauty was enhanced rather than diminished by their absence of colour. Theo gazed up at the roof, his shaggy golden head thrown back at a dizzying angle and regarded them. It seemed for a moment as if their ashen wings were about to flutter. He wondered if the angelic host beat their wings when the church was empty, like toys coming to life at night in the nursery. He thought it possible. In this place anything was possible.

Theo became aware of a shuffling noise behind him and looked round to see Hugh easing himself into a pew right at the back of the church. Once seated, he stared at the altar fixedly, as if waiting for something or someone. Theo smiled to himself. Hugh had the resigned and dispirited look of one who had been stood up before and knows he will be again.

Theo sauntered up the aisle, listening to the echo of his own footsteps and sat down beside Hugh, both men so tall their legs touched the pew in front. They sat in companionable silence for a while until Hugh began to declaim in a rumbling baritone: *'I wait for the Lord, my soul doth wait, and in his word do I hope. My soul waiteth for the Lord more than they that watch for the morning: I say, more than they that watch for the morning...'*

Theo turned his head and arched a brow. 'A psalm?'

'One hundred and thirty. The words are a comfort. A consolation in times of sorrow, but...' Hugh shrugged. 'They're just words now. Beautiful sounds. Echoes. Ghosts from the past... Your mother told me she'd marry me here. I'd brought her here to see the angel roof. She'd kept me on tenterhooks for a few weeks. She wasn't sure, you see. She was so very young. Younger than you are now. But we thought ourselves very much in love.' Hugh turned to face the young man he'd raised as his own, whom he loved more than Flora, more even than Rory, more than life itself. 'My dear boy... There's something I hoped I'd never have to say to you. But I find I must.'

Theo frowned, his bright blue eyes clouded with concern. He laid a hand on Hugh's arm. 'Dad?'

'No... That's just it, you see. I'm not.'

1975

When Grace woke she was alone. There was enough moonlight to see that Rory was gone. She sat up in bed, her heart racing, then told herself not to panic. He was probably restless, perhaps in pain. His hand bothered him more at night. He would be downstairs reading.

Before she'd arrived at any of these sensible conclusions however, Grace was out of bed and pulling on a thin dressing gown, resenting the extra layer in the sultry midsummer heat. The nursery window was wide open and the curtains drawn back but there was no breeze; the air was like syrup and the heady scents of jasmine and lilies wafted up from the garden below. As she passed the window Grace looked out at the garden, grey and unearthly under a full moon. The white border where Hugh had worked with Theo gleamed in the moonlight. Grace smiled to think that Dora's beloved garden looked beautiful even in the dark.

She was about to turn away from the window when she saw a ghost. A figure in a long white robe drifted across the lawn and stood in front of the white border, ashen head bowed. It was Rory. Sleepwalking? Or sleepless? He stood for a long time, quite still, then looked up at the sky. He bowed his head again and covered his eyes with his good hand. Grace was halfway down the stairs before it struck her that Rory might prefer to be alone. She hesitated, was about to turn back, then realised *she* didn't want to be alone.

The front door was ajar. She walked across the lawn barefoot, the dry grass springy under her step. When she was within a few feet of Rory, he spun round. His shoulders dropped and an expression passed across his face that might have been relief or perhaps disappointment. Grace couldn't tell in the half-light. Rory rubbed at his eyes with the fingers of his good hand. He was a pale, spectral figure, naked beneath his white kimono. The gold chrysanthemums had turned, like the gold of his hair, to silver in the moonlight.

She took a step towards him, wanting but fearing to touch him. 'I couldn't sleep either. It's so hot... Would you rather I left you on your own?'

He considered, then shook his head. Grace took another step towards him but Rory turned away and gestured towards the white border, shaking his head slowly and smiling.

'Yes, it's beautiful, isn't it? Especially in this light. Dora says this border looks its best at dusk. I wonder if she's ever seen it by moonlight?'

Rory shrugged. The kimono shivered, iridescent in the moonlight.

'Dora's so clever with her plants. She and Hugh worked so hard.'

Rory put his two index fingers together to form a letter T.

'Theo? Yes, of course. Theo too! He moved barrow-loads of weeds, didn't he? And watered all the bedding plants. He's such a lovely boy. So eager to please. Flora and Hugh must be so proud of him.'

Rory nodded and looked away. He turned his back on the border, walked over to a garden bench and sat down. Grace followed and sat beside him. A white form swept down across the lawn in eerie, silent flight and Grace cried out in alarm. Rory chuckled softly.

'What was that? An owl?'

He nodded.

'A tawny owl?'

He shook his head.

'Barn owl?'

He nodded again.

'I don't know how you can tell the difference – especially in this light.'

He looked directly at her then, his face grey and gaunt with shadow, his eyes dark in their sockets. Grace thought he looked as if he wanted to speak, as if he longed to tell her how he could tell the difference between barn owls and tawny owls. His lips twitched, then were still. He sat motionless, his face impassive, his breathing heavy. Grace watched his chest rise and fall, the V of tanned skin dark against the white silk. She lifted her fingers to his mouth and laid them on his lips. 'One day... One day it will come back to you, my love, I *know* it will. We'll talk again. You wait and see.'

He nodded slowly, then offered Grace his good hand. She took it, then reached for his right hand. She held them both – one warm, one cool – and pressed the damaged hand to her cheek.

A breeze like a sigh shifted in the trees. Rory cocked his head on one side, hearing before Grace the distant rumble of thunder. Rain began to drop out of the sky, landing with a splash on the wooden bench, on Grace's nightdress, on Rory's bare feet. They watched the big drops fall, trickle and spread. Grace laughed as Rory turned his face up to the rain then licked the moisture from his lips. His hair, cobwebby with damp, fell back from his face and the rain ran like tears over the planes of his face, down over his chin, his throat and chest. She shivered, partly with cold, partly with desire, long unsatisfied.

'I love you, Rory Dunbar. I love you so much. Do you have any *idea* how much?'

He looked at her for a long moment, then withdrawing his useless hand from her grasp, he nodded. Standing, he pulled her to her feet so that their faces almost touched. His lips moved again but this time she prevented his failure by kissing them. His mouth was cold and wet, unresponsive. Grace withdrew and stared at him, pleading. Shocked by the need in her eyes, Rory studied her face, stroked her long dark hair, then bent his head and returned the kiss, tentatively at first, then purposefully. Grace shivered again and he folded her in his arms.

1987

Theo had been silent a long time, his head in his hands. He sat up slowly, straightening his back, then lifted his head to look at the angels in the roof. Their pale, grey faces stared back, impassive, indifferent. He turned to Hugh, his face as ashen as the angels'. 'And you expect me to *forgive* them?'

'It may not be possible to forgive your parents, but it surely shouldn't be necessary to condemn them?'

'I don't condemn them... But I don't know that I'll ever be able to forgive them.'

'It's quite possible that you won't. There is after all a great deal to forgive. But you are hardly in a position to judge. You may remember the woman taken in adultery? *He that is without sin among you, let him first cast a stone at her.* Very sound, you have to admit.'

'But they *knew* what they were doing!'

'Yes, they did. I've often thought that must have made it harder to bear. The guilt must have been all the greater.'

Theo rose suddenly from the pew and strode towards the altar. He stopped in front of an arrangement of cream and white flowers and stood with his arms folded, his back to Hugh. Naming the flowers mentally, one by one, Theo tried to impose order on the tumult of his thoughts. *Gypsophila. Nicotiana. Lilium regale. Campanula. Phlox...*

Hugh was standing beside him and speaking in a low voice. 'Your conception wasn't planned, therefore it wasn't prevented. Nor was your birth. Flora went ahead with the pregnancy because she very much wanted a child... and I hadn't provided her with one. In any case, when she found herself pregnant she didn't have any legal alternative. You must realise, things were very different twenty years ago. I presume you wouldn't have wanted your mother to resort to a back-street abortionist?'

'No, of course not.'

'So what choice did the poor girl have? She was twenty-two. And a rather naïve twenty-two at that. In whom could she have confided? Your grandmother? Me?... No, she did what she'd always done. She told Rory. And Rory told her to say the baby was mine. I've had many years to think about it and I believe if I'd been in Rory's place I might have given Flora the same advice. It seemed the best thing at the time. The *only* thing. We weren't to know...'

Theo closed his eyes and Hugh watched as tears seeped out from beneath the long lashes. He laid a trembling hand on the young man's shoulder and said, 'I'd hoped you might take some sort of comfort from the fact that you are – in *every* sense – a love child. I've never known anything like Flora's love for Rory, or his for her.' Hugh allowed himself a wry smile. 'It's like the peace of God. It passeth all understanding. I hope one day you'll find it in your heart to forgive Flora at least.'

Theo wiped a hand across his eyes quickly and said, 'You don't understand, Dad! You don't know what you're asking!'

'Oh, I do. I know perfectly well.' Hugh turned to face the altar and fixed a baleful eye on the crucified Christ. 'You forget. I am still trying to forgive *God*.'

1975

Leaning against the door of the summerhouse, mesmerised by the dance of butterflies on a white buddleia, settling like confetti on a bride, Rory believed at first that he'd imagined the piano. He'd spent all of the last year trying not to remember what a piano sounded like, trying not to recall the sound of his own playing, but he sometimes wondered whether it had been counter-productive, whether in fact he heard piano music as a continual counterpoint to all other sounds. The notes came again, very softly. He knew at once it was his own piano, not a distant radio. He stood rooted to the spot, trembling in the sunshine.

When he felt able to move he turned to face the house and looked towards the music room. The French doors were slightly ajar. Whoever was playing probably didn't know they could be heard in the garden. But who was playing? Hugh was in the vegetable garden and in any case couldn't play. Grace and Dora were both out of the house with Colin and Lottie. Flora couldn't play. That left Theo who'd stayed behind with Hugh. Could Theo play the piano? If so, who had taught him? Ettie?

Rory approached the French doors and stood on the terrace, looking into the music room. Theo sat at the piano, curly fair head bent in concentration. He was practising a Grade One piece, a German dance by Beethoven. His playing was accurate but hesitant. Rory observed at a glance that his posture was awkward and the piano stool was the wrong height. The boy persevered calmly with the piece and Rory remembered his own youthful impatience and thunderous moods.

Theo reached up to turn a page and the music slipped off the stand, the loose sheets fluttering to the ground around the piano. He got down from the stool to gather them up and, as he did so, caught sight of Rory on the terrace. The boy's face was suffused with horror and he clapped his hand to his mouth. Rory watched as Theo's large blue eyes filled with tears. Lifting his hand to the door, Rory pulled it open and stepped into the room.

'I'm sorry, Uncle Rory, I'm really sorry! I didn't know you were there. I didn't know the door was open. I thought you were in the summerhouse. I'm really sorry—'

Rory raised his good hand, palm facing Theo, and shook his head a little, indicating that there was no problem. He bent down and gathered up the sheets of music, set them on the music stand, then looked down at the music stool briefly. At the sight of the old cracked leather he found he had to suppress an urge to sit at the piano. Instead he gestured to Theo to resume his seat. Theo looked horror-struck again. Rory raised his left hand and wiggled his fingers in the air, then pointed at the keyboard.

'You *want* me to play?'

Rory nodded.

'Are you sure?'

He nodded again.

'I'm not very good. I haven't played in *ages*.'

Rory frowned and shook his head quickly to indicate this was of no importance.

Theo sat down at the piano and played again. Rory was impressed that the boy didn't go to pieces under scrutiny. When he played several wrong notes he made a good recovery and continued unperturbed. As soon as the piece was over Theo turned to face him and Rory noticed the boy looked happier, that he'd evidently enjoyed playing to an audience.

Rory turned away and rifled through a drawer until he found a book of manuscript paper and a pencil. He opened the book, leaned on the piano and started to write. When he'd finished he passed it over to Theo who read: *I didn't know you were having lessons.*

Theo looked up and said, 'I'm not.'

Rory scribbled again. *Who taught you?*

'Aunt Ettie,' Theo said softly. 'But please don't tell Mum.'

Rory looked puzzled, then wrote: *You had lessons in secret?*

The boy wrinkled his nose. 'Sort of. Not *proper* lessons. Dad said Mum didn't want me to learn. But Aunt Ettie just let me play on the piano and I kind of picked it up... Then she started teaching me a few things. And she gave me all your old grade music. I just watched her play and she watched me play. And we talked about it. She never told me to practise. But I did – at church! There's a piano there. Not as nice as this one, though.' Theo stroked his fingers across the keys at the upper end of the keyboard, making a high tinkling sound. 'But I'm stuck now, now Aunt Ettie's... gone. And the piano's always locked anyway.' He looked up anxiously. 'You won't tell Gran I unlocked it, will you?'

Rory shook his head, then wrote: *How did you find the key?*

'I just looked. It was in that Chinese pot on the mantelpiece. I knew it would be in here somewhere.'

Rory gazed at the boy for a moment, then wrote again: *Why won't Flora let you have lessons?*

'Don't know. 'Cos it's too much money, I expect. And because we don't have a piano at the vicarage. I said I could come and practise here, but Mum said it would upset everybody. I think she meant you.'

Rory considered this, then bent down to the piano stool. He adjusted the height, looked up at Theo, then adjusted it again. He straightened up and gestured towards the keyboard. The boy played a scale with both hands, looked up and grinned. 'That's much better!' Rory ignored him and looked round the room as if searching for something. He reached under a table and drew out a battered footstool. He carried it over to the piano and placed it over the pedals, beneath Theo's feet, so they were now supported instead of dangling in mid-air. Rory gestured once again, inviting him to play. The boy began his piece again. Rory listened for a while, then picked up the manuscript book and wrote. He thrust the book in front of the boy's face.

Would you like to have lessons?

Theo stopped playing. He turned and stared. 'Yes! I mean, yes, *please*!'

Rory regarded the boy. After what seemed to Theo an age, Rory wrote something else in the book and handed it back to him.

I could teach you.

Theo's head shot up. He was speechless, his eyes bright with excitement, his face glowing. Rory looked away quickly, reaching for the book. He wrote, *Probably not a good teacher – very bad temper.*

Theo read the words, then watched as Rory added: *Won't say much.*

The boy laughed, then shot a guilty look at Rory. Reassured by a semblance of a smile hovering at the corners of Rory's mouth, Theo threw his arms round the man he believed to be his uncle and squeezed as hard as his thin arms would permit. '*Thank* you!' Rory didn't respond to the embrace but allowed himself to be held. When Theo released him he picked up the book again and wrote: *You'll have to ask your parents. Flora might not agree.*

'I'll ask them. But if *you* don't mind...' Theo grinned up at Rory who stretched his mouth in an awkward attempt to smile back. He pointed at the keyboard and raised his eyebrows at Theo. The boy resumed his piece, then stopped suddenly.

'Was Aunt Ettie a good pianist?'

Rory hesitated, then shook his head, slowly.

'She must have been a good *teacher,* though.' Rory put his head on one side and looked a query. Embarrassed, Theo said, 'Oh, I didn't mean me – I meant *you*. You were the best! That's what my dad said. And he *loves* music.'

Rory looked away. Theo thought he noticed a tremor in the scarred hand that held the manuscript book. Concerned, he looked up at Rory's face and saw his lips part slightly. The tip of his tongue appeared between his teeth. A low buzzing sound seemed to issue from his mouth. Theo thought it sounded like the noise a trapped bumblebee makes as it beats against a window-pane. As the boy watched, Rory's lips moved almost imperceptibly as he uttered two barely recognisable words.

'Thank... you.'

Theo sat completely still. The tremor was now quite marked and had spread to both of Rory's hands. Staring at them, Theo said softly, 'Perhaps you can't be both... I mean, perhaps if you were a really good pianist you wouldn't be a good teacher. Imagine having to listen to all those boring scales and wrong notes. It'd drive you crazy, wouldn't it? But Aunt Ettie, she *never* lost her temper with me. Not once.'

In the silence that followed, Theo heard the low sound again, this time like a hum.

'N-nor me...'

The pencil and manuscript book fell to the floor and Rory swayed. Theo grabbed hold of both his father's hands and cried, 'Uncle Rory – you're *talking*!'

Rory's left hand clutched at Theo's; his right lay motionless, crushed in his son's grip.

'Y-yes... I... *am*...'

1955

When he'd finished playing, Rory turned to Ettie, his face flushed with awkward pride. She regarded her former pupil, no longer a boy, not yet a man. Ettie wondered whether the time was ripe to say what she wanted to say, what Rory needed to hear. There was no doubt that his current teacher had brought out the best in him, had taken him to levels of technical proficiency quite beyond the scope of Ettie's own teaching skills, but something was missing. Or rather, something was there that shouldn't be.

'That was excellent playing, Rory. Quite brilliant.'

His smile faded. 'But...?'

'There's always a "but", isn't there? My dear, you must bear in mind I wouldn't say what I'm about to say if I didn't believe you were a fine pianist. A *very* fine pianist. This might be rather difficult for you to understand at the moment, but I'd like you to try to remember it. You will understand one day.'

Rory nodded, his expression serious and a little apprehensive.

'You must always remember that *you* aren't important. The

music is what matters. You are simply the channel through which the music flows. If the audience is thinking what a wonderful player you are, then you have failed. They should be thinking about the *music,* what a genius Beethoven was, or Mozart, or whoever it is you are playing. Does that make any sense?'

Rory nodded his head slowly but couldn't disguise a look of disappointment.

'It's very hard, I know, especially for a boy with your talent. But I'm afraid the music doesn't need you, it's *you* who need the music. Never forget what you owe the music and always treat it with respect. It has been *lent* to you for a while. For your lifetime. You don't own it, so don't play as if you do. Do you understand?'

'I think so.'

'Good! I thought you probably would. Remember: the music is much bigger than you, Rory. However good you get, it always will be.'

1975

When Hugh looked up from hoeing between the lettuces he saw Theo and Rory walking towards him along the path. He was astonished to see they were holding hands. Hugh didn't recall ever seeing Rory touch Theo before. Indeed, he'd observed him go to considerable lengths to avoid physical contact with the boy, who was by nature tactile and affectionate.

Theo seemed to be leading Rory down the garden, tugging at his good hand. The boy suddenly let go and ran towards Hugh, waving and shouting.

'Daddy! Uncle Rory's started talking! He spoke to *me*!' Theo launched himself at Hugh who dropped his hoe, caught him and lifted him easily into the air, settling him on one hip. Theo put his arms round Hugh's neck, squeezed till he gasped, then exclaimed. 'It's a miracle! God sent us a miracle!'

Hugh loosened Theo's grip round his neck and turned his head towards Rory who stood on the path, a few feet away.

'Is this true?'

Rory looked at Hugh. His lips parted, then he nodded.

'Speak! Speak!' Theo shouted, bouncing up and down in Hugh's arms. Rory raised his good hand towards Theo, gesturing silence. He bowed his head and appeared to be studying the cracks in the paving stones. His shoulders heaved and without looking up he murmured, 'I'd... like... t-to teach... your son...' His hands began to tremble again. 'P-piano.'

Hugh was bereft of words. Unnerved by the long silence, Rory lifted his head slowly and saw Theo wiping tears from Hugh's eyes. In a voice somewhere between a laugh and a sob Hugh said, 'Welcome back, Rory!'

Tired now and unsteady on his feet, Rory stepped forward, raising both his arms. He put one round Theo's neck, one round Hugh's and, closing his eyes, laid his head on Hugh's chest.

PART FOUR

Chapter 19

I never really forgave Rory for speaking to Theo and not me. I'd assumed if he ever spoke again it would be to me. I found it just as hard to forgive his enthusiastic resumption of marital relations. Tension fell away from Grace almost visibly and she regained the beatific smile that sometimes made me want to slap her. Once Rory started talking, Grace never confided in me again, except once to say that her period was late and she dreaded she might be pregnant, with another mouth to feed. Her fears were unfounded, but mine were confirmed. Rory was lost to me.

So at the age of thirty-three I decided I would make a new start.

I told Hugh, who'd resigned from the ministry and was working his notice, that I was leaving him and taking Theo. I said I intended to work to support myself but asked if he would send me money to help support Theo as I didn't wish to be beholden to Rory, who in any case hadn't two ha'pennies to rub together. Hugh threw me by saying that he wanted Theo to continue to live with him and that he'd already spoken to Dora about possible living arrangements. (By now Grace had moved her family to a rented house near the girls' public school where she taught music and Dora was faced once again with selling up.) Hugh said Dora had invited us to move in to Orchard Farm and to my astonishment I found he had tentative plans for a business venture there.

I told him there was no way I could face living at Orchard Farm, nor could I cope any longer with having a homosexual husband, let alone one who was in love with my brother. I told him he was welcome to raise Theo if that was what Theo himself wanted. The truth was I'd never known how I was going to start a new life as a single working mother, nor had I relished the thought of raising a son on my own – a son who was, in addition, the living image of Rory.

So Theo was allowed to choose. To give the poor boy his due, he had the grace to pretend to deliberate. Should he move to Orchard Farm with his indulgent Granny and his devoted 'father', where he'd have a large garden full of wildlife, familiar school friends and piano lessons with his hero-'uncle'? Or should he move with his emotionally remote mother to a tiny flat in London, become a latch-key kid at a city school where his quiet, sensitive nature, angelic looks and Suffolk accent would single him out for the special attention of playground bullies?

Theo chose to stay with Hugh.

I didn't even pretend to be hurt. I loved and respected Theo enough to be honest with him. (Well, partially honest. I never found 'the truth, the whole truth and nothing but the truth' a very manageable concept.) Hugh, Theo and I were all satisfied with the arrangement, but my mother told me if I deserted my husband and son, she'd never speak to me again. To be fair to her, I don't think she thought it was a threat she'd ever have to carry out. She underestimated me, or rather my desperation.

I was sorely tempted to tell her the truth about her son-in-law, her son and her favourite grandson, but Dora was sixty-eight. Archie was sinking, Rory had moved away again and she was facing a lonely and painfully arthritic old age. There was no point in a truth-telling session. The truth wouldn't benefit anyone – least of all me – and it would cause any amount of pain to every family member, most of whom were innocent. Refusing to tell Dora some home truths about her family was one of my few unselfish acts. Hugh gave me his blessing and said he'd send me money whenever he could. Quite where he thought he was going to get it, I didn't like to ask. As a fifty-four-year-old ex-priest, his employment options were limited.

I packed up my few personal possessions into cardboard boxes and my clothes into a large suitcase. I went to London because it was the only city I knew. I thought I'd be able to find work, possibly even friends, in a city. I was confident I'd never bump into Rory who I knew would avoid all his old haunts: concert halls and music studios, the pubs and wine bars where he used to meet his musician friends. I knew London was the last place I'd ever see Rory.

And so I escaped. Temporarily.

1984

'Aunt Flora?'

Flora raised her eyes from her typing and peered over the top of her reading glasses at the young man standing in the doorway.

'Sorry? Did you say something? I can't hear a damn thing with this on.' She removed an ear-piece and set it down on the desk beside her typewriter. 'Can I help you? If you're here to audition, you need to tick your name off the list and take a seat.' She rose and handed him a clipboard and pen. 'They'll call you when they're ready.'

The young man beamed at her, his large brown eyes crinkling with suppressed laughter. 'You don't recognise me, do you?'

Flora removed her glasses and studied his face. 'Should I? Are you famous?'

'No, not yet! I'm not really surprised you don't recognise me. I must have been nine the last time we met.'

Flora stared at him, frowning, then her mouth fell open. 'Oh, my God – *Colin*?' He laughed and nodded. 'Colin! I don't believe it. But – you're *huge*!'

'Well, not exactly. Bit of a short-arse in fact, but I suppose I was in short trousers the last time you saw me.'

'With perpetually scabby knees, I seem to remember.'

'That's because I picked them.'

'Spare me the details, *please*! Well, who would have thought such an objectionable little boy would have turned out so well? Just *look* at you...'

Colin laughed and pushed his heavy dark hair away from his eyes and off his forehead. It fell forward again immediately and it wasn't until then that Flora noticed the resemblance between father and son. The same large eyes, but Colin's were a lustrous brown; the same slim build and breadth of shoulder, but his hands, Flora noticed as she glanced downwards, were nothing like Rory's. These hands were workmanlike, the fingernails clean but chewed. There was strength in these hands, but no poetry. She felt something like relief.

'But – what on earth are you doing *here*?'

'I'm auditioning.'

'For the acting course?'

He pointed to the clipboard. '12.30. Colin Dunbar. That's me.'

'You want to *act*?'

'Yes.'

Flora's smile was mischievous. 'Your parents must be absolutely livid.'

Colin laughed again and nodded. 'Dead right. Mum's not really speaking to me. Says I'm throwing away my education.'

'I bet Rory tried to talk you out of it too.'

'Yeah. How did you know?'

'Oh, I know my brother. He doesn't approve of drama. Never has. Thinks it's a vastly inferior art to music. It was the great debate when we were teenagers: Music vs. Drama. Rory always won, of course, despite the fact that he doesn't really believe in words. Doesn't trust them. Sometimes I think I decided to become an actress just to spite him.'

'Yeah, that's what *he* said. And you were held up as a shining example of how spectacularly unsuccessful I was likely to be—' Colin's face fell and he reddened. 'Oh, hell! That wasn't very tactful, was it? Sorry.'

'My dear, don't apologise! It's all water under the bridge. I don't care what anyone thinks about me now, least of all Rory. Life's too short. But tell me – how on earth have you avoided becoming a musician with Grace and Rory for parents? That seems like quite an achievement.'

'It wasn't easy. Non-co-operation, basically. I refused to have any more piano lessons after Dad's accident. I kept up the violin for another year or so but I hated it and I never practised. In the end they gave in and bought me a guitar as a sort of compromise and I taught myself. I'm pretty good! I write my own stuff and sing a bit.'

'*Do* you? How wonderful! Well, don't lose any sleep over disappointing your parents. They would never have been satisfied unless you'd gone to the Guildhall or the Royal Academy – neither place suitable for normal, healthy, young people if you ask me. But when did you decide you wanted to act?'

'When I was thirteen. Uncle Hugh took Lottie, me and Theo to the theatre to see *Romeo and Juliet*.' Colin spread his hands. 'That was it. I thought, "That's me. That's what I want to do".'

'Good for you! And good for Hugh. Now there's a man who knows the value of words.'

Colin glanced at his watch. 'Look, Aunt Flora, would you mind if I sat down and looked through my speeches? It's nearly time for my audition.'

'Oh, yes, of course, you must. And I must do some work! Sit down and get yourself organised. They're running late but the next person hasn't turned up so you might be seen on time. Are you heading straight home afterwards?'

'No, I was going to have some lunch, wander round a few record shops, then get the train home. Though I had wondered whether to get a ticket for a show tonight and catch a late train.'

'McKellen's playing *Coriolanus* at the National. It's worth selling your *soul* to get a ticket.'

'You've seen it?'

'Yes. But I'd go again like a shot.'

Colin's eyes brightened. 'Shall we? I don't know the play – but you could tell me all about it. Oh, but I wasn't thinking – you've probably got plans for the evening.'

'My plans, such as they are, involve a tin of tomato soup, an early night and a good book. I think they could *possibly* be set aside for Mr McKellen and an evening with my nephew.'

'Well, don't feel you've got to do the long-lost aunt thing—'

'I've no intention of doing the long-lost aunt thing,' Flora snorted. 'In fact, I think we should drop the whole auntie business. It makes me feel a hundred. Just call me Flo. All the students do.' She took his arm and propelled him out of the office. 'Now, go and prepare to meet thy doom. What are you giving them?'

'Henry V and Alfred Dolittle.'

'Splendid! Which Henry?'

'*Upon the King.*'

'Oh, excellent! They usually do *Once more unto the* bloody *breach*. Or sometimes that nasty speech before the gates of Harfleur. God knows why. It's just a rant. Not much scope to show your range. But *Upon the King* is good. Subtle. An intelligent choice, they'll like that. I hope you play it as an ordinary man, not a king. That's the whole point. You mustn't try to be *regal*. Henry's just a normal human being under terrible stress... Oh, hark at me giving notes! Sorry, I do go on. Just ignore me.'

'No, that's really useful stuff! Thanks a lot. Do you actually teach here?'

Flora laughed. 'No, I'm just the secretary and general dogsbody. I'm a sort of librarian-cum-curator for the archive. We have our own book and picture collection here and people come to do historical research. Go and sit down, we'll talk later. Over lunch maybe. You'll be needing a pint by then, I should think – oh, are you old enough to drink? You look it.'

'I'm seventeen. A few months younger than Theo, remember?'

Her smile wavered. 'Oh yes, of course. How silly of me. I was forgetting... How *is* Theo? Do you ever see him?' Without waiting for an answer Flora continued hurriedly. 'I've lost touch. With all of them really. I'm the Black Sheep. You've probably heard all sorts of horror stories about me.' Colin looked away, nonplussed. 'Ah, I see you have! Don't worry. Some of them are quite untrue. You're perfectly safe with me. I don't visit opium dens in my lunch hour. Well, only on Fridays.'

Colin was that rare and wonderful thing in a man – straight men, anyway – a good listener. As an actor I suppose he was happy to be a student of human nature. Sometimes when he was listening to me prattle on, I got the impression he wasn't just listening but watching, taking notes, filing away my verbal and physical mannerisms for future use. He was a superb mimic, a result no doubt of his eye and ear for detail.

Colin was only ever moderately successful as an actor and in his "resting" periods he filled the time by writing plays and film scripts. After I finished with him, he became depressed and started drinking, but out of all the mess he managed to salvage a novel, the protagonist a thinly-disguised version of me. He found a publisher, the book was successful and was eventually made into a film.

I didn't hear any of all this first-hand. By then I'd lost touch with everybody – our friends, my family. I was in the wilderness. But I saw the occasional snippet about Colin in the newspapers I used to pick up. I once saw a photo of him on the gossip page of the Daily Mail. *He looked very handsome in a DJ, escorting a glamorous older woman to a film première. I thought she looked a bit like me.*

I tore the photo out and kept it. For old times' sake.

1999

'Dad – I've seen her.'

'Flora?'

'Yes. Look, can you ring me back? My phone's died. I'm in a callbox.'

'Where are you?'

'Waterloo. I'm meant to be at a script conference at the National.'

'Is that where you saw her? The theatre?'

'No. On Waterloo Bridge. Well, on the steps. As you go down to the National. I didn't recognise her and just walked straight past, I was in a hurry. Then I realised and went back, but she was gone. I think she must have recognised me.'

'You're sure it was Flora?'

'No, I'm not sure, but I *think* it was. She looked at me, as if she knew me. I just didn't register. She looked *terrible*.'

'Never mind. At least she's alive. We'll find her now. Colin, I'm coming up to town. Can I stay with you?'

'Dad... Look, I don't know how to tell you this, but – I don't think Flora wants to be found...'

In the year after the accident Rory hadn't been able to drive nor had he wanted to. He had very little mobility in his wrecked hand, although it gradually improved with physio. He could pick up a tennis ball but nothing smaller. Fine motor control was completely gone. His fingers couldn't move individually and he used his right hand only as a sort of scoop or claw.

But it was possible for him to drive – once he'd persuaded himself to get back inside a car, which took many months. Grace made it easier for him by adapting a driving glove, sewing on velcro so that Rory could fasten his index finger and thumb together and encircle the wheel. This meant he could relax his hand periodically and let it just rest on the wheel.

When he suggested we go to Aldeburgh for the day, on our own, I thought he must have taken leave of his senses. The trip would entail following the same route he'd taken with Ettie a year ago. He would have to revisit the scene of the accident. I assumed he was laying some sort of ghost to rest, so I agreed to go with him.

It was the end of the summer. I left Hugh and Theo a cold supper in the fridge in case I was late back and I made up a picnic for Rory and me. I assembled shrimp paste sandwiches (with cress), a packet of the biscuits we'd always known as 'jammy dodgers' and a bottle of ginger beer. It was meant to be a joke.

When we got to the junction where the accident happened we had to pull up and wait to turn right, as Rory and Ettie had waited. There was a long, uncomfortable silence. Rory broke it suddenly by asking what was for lunch. I told him. He said nothing but after we'd turned onto the main road he pulled the car over into a lay-by and sat with his head in his hands, shaking.

It would have been the memories.

All of them...

I didn't need to ask.

1952

The twins had finished the shrimp paste sandwiches and were now engaged in the Jammy Dodger Contest: the ritual of licking out the red jam from the hole in the middle of the biscuits. Rory found this much easier than Flora and always won. Rory tended not to compete in anything unless he knew he would win.

'It's not fair!' Flora whined. 'Your tongue's all hard and pointy.' Rory stuck his tongue out at her as if to demonstrate. 'Mine won't do that. It won't go into the hole. It's too big and floppy.'

'All gone!' Rory held his empty biscuit aloft, then tossed the sodden remains to a gull that had taken up a position on a nearby rock, eyeing the children and weighing up the likelihood of scraps. Rory pulled up his jersey and withdrew a box of matches from the pocket of his shorts.

Flora gasped and pointed in horror. 'Where did you get those?'

'From the scullery.'

'That's stealing.'

'No, it isn't. I shall put them back when I've finished. It's not stealing if you put things back.'

Flora changed tack. 'We're not allowed matches.'

'That's what they said *last* year. We're a year older now. Ten-year-olds can have matches,' Rory said with authority.

'What are you going to do?'

'Make a fire.'

'There's nothing to burn.'

'We can burn our rubbish.' He screwed up the grease-proof paper the sandwiches had been wrapped in and put it inside a brown paper bag. Flora watched as he crushed it, moulding the paper into a ball with his strong brown hands. 'Right, let's collect some driftwood.'

She looked down to the shoreline. 'The tide's going out. Everything'll be wet.'

'We'll look higher up then.'

They ran up the shingle slope and started to kick over the piles of seaweed and rubbish, searching for anything that would burn. Rory took off his jersey and used it to collect what they found, tying the sleeves together to make a bundle.

'You look like Dick Whittington,' Flora said.

He grinned, his teeth a sudden white flash against his brown skin. 'A long way from London!'

'How far?'

'Don't know. Hundreds of miles. Ask Uncle Hamish. He'll know.'

'D'you think we'll come here every year?'

'We always have.'

'D'you think we'll come here even when we're grown up?'

'*I* will.'

'Ma and Dad will be dead by then.'

'Maybe not.'

'Dad will be. He's *old*.'

Rory pounced on a piece of wood, a branch stripped of its bark by the sea. 'This'll burn well.'

'I wonder which of us will die first?'

'You. You're the oldest.'

'Only forty-five minutes older. Anyway, it isn't always old people who die. Mrs McNab said Peggy's baby died in January. Of whooping cough.'

'Maybe we'll both die at *exactly* the same moment.'

'That's not possible!'

'If they dropped a bomb on us, we would.'

'Why would anyone drop bombs on us?'

Rory shrugged. 'Another war?'

'Oh.' Flora knelt down and began to disentangle a branch from a heap of seaweed. 'If I die first, I shall wait for you in Heaven.'

'What makes you think they'll let *you* in?'

'That's where you go if you've been good. And I'm going to be good.'

'Well, *I'm* going to be bad.'

'You'll be punished if you are. You'll go to Hell.'

'Don't care. It'll be worth it.'

'Nothing's worth going to Hell for, Rory. You'll burn for ever and ever and *ever*.'

'That's rubbish.'

'That's what Mrs McNab said. The Minister told her. And he should know!'

'Nobody knows! Nobody's ever been and come back have they? Nobody's ever sent a postcard! *Dear Flora, here I am in Hell. Having a lovely time but it's a bit hot. Missing you. Love from Rory.*'

Flora laughed and fell backwards as she tugged the branch free. Rory offered her his hand and yanked her to her feet. She stared at her brother's face, close to her own, his nose pink and peeling, his cheeks bronzed with freckles. '*Would* you miss me?'

Grey eyes stared candidly back into blue. ' '*Course* I would.'

Flora's heart leaped. 'Shall we live together when we're grown up? Shall we live here, by the sea? At *Tigh na Mara*, with the pine marten? For ever and ever and *ever*?'

'Yes, let's.'

'And you can have a boat and a piano and I can have a pony and a dog and it will be like the holidays all the time!' Rory shivered as the breeze stiffened and Flora put an arm round his thin, bare shoulders. 'But I do wish you would be *good*, Ror. Then we could both go to Heaven when we die.'

'I'll try... But I think it'll be very boring.' He sighed. 'And difficult.'

'Well, if *you* can't be good, *I'll* be bad,' said Flora cheerfully. 'And we'll go to Hell together.' She took his hand and squeezed it. 'I wouldn't mind if I was with you. I wouldn't mind *anything* if I was with you.'

1975

Aldeburgh was small and getting smaller. The sixteenth-century Moot Hall, a half-timbered building filled in with herringbone brickwork, stood originally in the centre of the town. Now it perched improbably on the shore, looking for all the world like an Elizabethan beach hut. The North Sea gnawed at the town's side, reclaiming its own, tearing constantly at the shingle, churning up mud and sand into a murky soup shunned by all but the most intrepid bathers.

Rory and Flora sat on the steeply sloping shingle beach, the remains of their picnic spread on a rug. Neither had spoken for a while. Flora gazed torpidly out to sea, watching the waves hurl themselves at the shore. Without looking at Rory she said, 'I think I'm going to leave Hugh.'

'Good. You should have done it years ago.'

'Theo wants to stay with him.'

'Oh.' Rory sounded surprised. 'Well, that's better for you, isn't it? Probably better for Theo in the long run. And Hugh. It means you're a free agent. You can start again.'

'Yes, I can. Or rather, I could if I weren't still a little in love with Hugh. And completely in love with you.'

'Still?'

Flora turned to face him as he lay stretched out on the rug, propped up on one elbow, his eyes narrowed against the sunlight. 'You didn't really need to ask that, did you? You know. The same way I know how you feel about me.' She looked away again, out to sea. 'Although I don't know if what you feel is love. I've never really known... Sometimes I think you don't actually like me very much, you just want to go to bed with me.'

He rolled on to his back and lay staring up at the sky. 'I wonder what we'd feel for each other, Flor, if we stopped being angry?'

'Angry?'

'Yes. Angry with each other. Angry with Grace and Hugh. Angry with God. Do you still manage to believe in Him these days?'

'I don't know... No, I don't think so. I think the only way I can believe in God now is by seeing Him as a divine practical joker. One with a particularly sick sense of humour.'

Rory smiled. 'Now He sounds like *my* sort of god... I wish we could stop being angry – at least with each other. Even if it was just for a day. A few hours.'

'I'm not angry with you now.'

He squinted up at her. 'Are you sure?'

Flora thought for a moment. 'Well, maybe I am in a way. But only angry that you're *you*. That I can't help myself, can't stop feeling what I feel. But I know that's not your fault.'

He stretched out his left hand towards her and ran a finger down the length of her bare arm. She shivered.

'Are you cold?'

'No. That's you.'

'Shall I stop?'

'Yes... No.'

'You look like the Little Mermaid. Sitting on her rock.'

He circled her bare ankle with his long fingers, gently squeezing the bones, then loosened his grip and slid his curved palm over her calf, up under the skirt of her dress.

'Rory, stop. People will see.'

'Nobody knows who we are! We could be a married couple. Lovers. I could kiss you now and no one would turn a hair. Can I?' Flora was silent. '*Please*, Flor.'

She turned and looked down at him lying on his back. The wind lifted his thick fair hair from his forehead, revealing furrows that Flora didn't remember ever seeing before. She traced them with her fingertips, then bent and placed her mouth on his. As Rory's lips parted she pulled away, then drawing her knees up to her chest, she hugged them. Watching the waves, she murmured, '*The wicked are like the troubled sea, when it cannot rest, whose waters cast up mire and dirt.*'

Rory lay quite still, then said, 'If I weren't your brother—'

'Don't, I can't bear it. I can't bear to think about... alternatives.'

'If I weren't your brother... I'd still be a selfish bastard.'

She laughed and tossed wind-blown hair out of her eyes. 'A *miserable,* selfish bastard.'

'Yes.'

'But you'd be *my* miserable, selfish bastard.'

'I am anyway.'

'Don't.'

They sat, not touching, not moving for several minutes, then Rory breathed, 'Flora, I used to come here. Before the accident. I used to meet a woman here. Someone I knew in London.'

She turned and stared down at him. 'A *mistress*?'

'Yes. I suppose you'd call her that.'

'Did Grace know?'

'Of course not.'

'You used to meet this woman here? For sex?'

'Yes.'

'In a hotel?'

'No... She has a holiday flat here. She doesn't use it much. She works in London. It's empty most of the time.'

'Why are you telling me all this? Is this your confession? I didn't think you did remorse.'

He didn't answer immediately, but closed his eyes, then said softly, 'I still have a key. To the flat. She's never asked for it back.'

Flora turned away quickly and looked up at the sky where gulls wheeled and screamed hysterically at the approach of a fishing boat. 'Is that why you brought me here?'

Rory sat up. 'No. I was just going to tell you about it. As a possibility. I didn't expect... I mean, I just wanted you to think about it, that's all. And I thought I needed to get you away from the family so that you *could* think about it.' Flora lowered her head and rested it on her knees. 'I know it wouldn't be real, Flor, but it would be *something*. And it's all we're going to get in this world.'

'Please. Don't ask me.'

'You're leaving Hugh anyway. He'd never know. And why should he care? Why should *you*, after the way he treated you?'

'I thought you and Grace were happy!'

'We're as happy as we can be, given the circumstances. But... it doesn't stop the pain. It doesn't fill the... *void*.'

'And you think I would?'

'No, I don't, but given what I've lost already, I don't see why I should have to lose you too. And if you go away I will lose you, won't I? You'll make a new start, new friends. Meet other men. Believe me, you'll get offers, Flor. Plenty of them.'

'Oh, but who could possibly step into *your* shoes, Rory?'

He ignored the sarcasm. 'You've loved two men. Maybe you'll love others.'

'But Grace... She thinks of me as her *friend*! I couldn't do that to her!'

'I think you probably could.' He slid a hand around the back of her neck, gathering up the long, fine hair in his hand, tugging gently downwards until she raised her head. He turned her round to face him and kissed her slowly. Releasing her, he watched the pale, silky hair tumble on to her shoulders, framing her face, suffused now with a mixture of horror, guilt and lust. He turned away and rolled on to his front, pillowing his head on his arms.

Eventually Flora said, her voice unsteady, 'How could we possibly meet here? What reason would I have to come?'

'You don't need a reason. You're forgetting. If you leave Hugh there's no one to account to. You could come whenever you wanted. Whenever I could get away. Which wouldn't be often. And I don't think it could ever be overnight. Grace would get suspicious.'

'So it would just be for sex. Sex in the afternoons. Tell me – would I get lunch thrown in? Or dinner perhaps? Or would it just be a picnic on the beach? Shrimp paste sandwiches and ginger beer?'

He groaned. 'Forget I mentioned it. I just wanted you to know there was... the possibility. Clearly you don't want me as much as I want you!'

'I don't think you understand, Rory. You've never really understood, have you? I don't want just a little bit of you – Grace's leftovers! I want *all* of you. All of you, all of the time. And if I can't have that, I–' Her voice faltered. 'I don't want anything to do with you. It's just too painful! I can't bear it any more – what you do to my head. To my body. You *possess* me! But I don't possess you. And I never will.'

He propped himself up on his elbows. 'It doesn't have to be like that—'

'For me it does. All or nothing. Now and for ever.'

He shook his head. 'Never in this world, Flor.'

'No, maybe not. So I'll wait. As long as it takes...'

1987

They sat in silence, side by side on the back doorstep, quite still, staring into the pinewoods.

Rory sighed. 'It isn't coming.'

'Ssh... It will. Be patient.'

As the light faded gradually, there was a movement in the woods and the pine marten loped down, dodging between the trees. Flora sensed rather than heard Rory's breath expelled from his body. She laid her hand on his and squeezed it. The marten stopped, hesitating at the edge of the wood, surveying the distance between its cover and the bird-table, then it bounded forward: dark-brown, cream-throated, the size of a cat, but longer. It shinned up the bird-table and grabbed a marmalade sandwich with delicate hand-like paws. It ate casually, looking about, its large eyes expressive, while the twins watched, scarcely breathing. The marten rolled the hard-boiled egg across the bird-table as if in play, then took it gently in its jaws. Slithering to the ground, like liquid poured from a jug, it trotted back into the woods.

They sat for a long while, not moving, not speaking. Eventually Rory said, 'Show's over.'

She didn't reply.

He extracted his hand from Flora's grasp and said, 'I have to go back, Flor,' then stood and went indoors.

Flora sat staring into the pinewoods as darkness fell.

Chapter 20

1976

It was with great sadness but little surprise that Father Hugh's flock received the news that he was to resign as their parish priest. If ever a man had been beset by grief and trouble, it was he. It had become impossible for any but the visually or mentally impaired to ignore the fact that Mrs Wentworth had a drink problem. This odd little woman had been a poor support to him even when sober. When she disappeared from the vicarage it was assumed at first that she'd gone to a rehabilitation clinic and would return, refreshed and reformed, to fight the good fight. When Father Hugh informed his flock that Mrs Wentworth had in fact left permanently, that it had been an amicable arrangement and that he was quite happy to bring up their son single-handed, shock waves reverberated around the parish, but these barely registered on the gossip Richter scale compared with the seismic reaction to his announcement that he was giving up the ministry altogether.

It was assumed that the poor man was on the verge of breakdown. Heaven knows, he'd had a year of tribulations. There'd been the terrible car accident in which his good friend Miss Sinclair had died and his brother-in-law had been so tragically disabled; then his father-in-law had sickened and died; now his wife had upped and left him with that poor mite of a boy. If Father Hugh was cracking up, it was no wonder. Those broad shoulders had had much to bear and, there was no denying, he was no longer a young man.

His mother-in-law had opened her heart and home to Father Hugh and her grandson. The musical branch of the family had moved to a house in the next village and poor old Mrs Dunbar had been left alone with her grief in that big old house and garden, which were nothing but a burden to her in her seventieth year. She would surely have to sell up. What else could she do, with her arthritis getting worse every year and her only daughter gallivanting round London without a thought for her family?

Parishioners kept a watchful eye open for an estate agent's board but none appeared. Builders did, however. Builders arrived and converted disused outbuildings into a self-contained unit, complete with shower and kitchenette. Plumbers installed showers and washbasins in the bedrooms and converted the scullery into another bathroom. The grand piano was taken away by a firm of specialist removers. Some said it was being moved to the other Dunbar household for young Mrs Dunbar's use, but others pointed out that there was no room in that modest little house for a grand piano. When an upright was delivered a week later, it was assumed the grand had been sold.

While builders worked, Father Hugh (it was a long time before people in the village could bring themselves to address him simply as 'Hugh') renovated and repaired the greenhouses and cold-frames. He hired a rotavator and ploughed up the croquet lawn. (Some wondered whether poor Dora Dunbar would survive the shock.) Trees were lopped or felled, moribund shrubs and fruit bushes were grubbed up, manure and compost dug in. The old garden sat for the winter like a blank canvas, waiting for spring to sketch in the outline of a new scene. At Easter a large sign was erected at the front gate announcing *Orchard Farm Garden & Nursery.* There was another, smaller sign indicating that bed and breakfast (en suite) was also available.

Father Hugh's erstwhile flock was pleased. They did their best to support the new venture, buying plants, donating propagating stock, telling friends and relatives about the guest-house and – with relish – the various sad stories attached to it. The renovated garden was featured in a gardening magazine, then as an item on local television. Hugh and Theo made a telegenic pair and the producer of the programme didn't miss the opportunity to mention (against Hugh's advice) that this was where the famous pianist Rory Dunbar had grown up.

Orchard Farm Nursery was not an immediate commercial success and wouldn't be for some years yet, but Hugh's bank manager was no longer sceptical. Gardening seemed to be enjoying a huge revival of interest, thanks to television programmes and a back-to-the-land move towards self-sufficiency and organic gardening. The business looked set to make a profit and everyone agreed it was a blessing that old Mrs Dunbar would now be able to stay in her home, to which end the dining room had been converted to create a downstairs bedroom for her, with a good view of the rose garden and the white border.

The old lady could be seen travelling round the village and patrolling her garden in her battery-driven cart. She offered advice to plant buyers and even learned how to operate the till. Widowed and estranged from her daughter, Dora Dunbar remained doggedly cheerful. She cherished her three grandchildren – especially poor motherless Theo – and told anyone who would listen that her son-in-law was nothing short of a marvel.

No one was inclined to disagree.

1977

'Theo, hold that flashlight steady.'

'I'm *trying*.'

'Yes, I know you are. You're doing very well. Goodness knows what I'd do without you – my right-hand man.' Hugh bent over the greenhouse bench and sprinkled the contents of a packet of seed into a tray of compost. He flicked the seed into position, spacing them carefully, then scattered more compost on top.

'What are they?'

'Nasturtiums.'

'They're orange and red, aren't they?'

'That's right. And these have variegated leaves. That means mottled. Patterned with cream and green. They're very pretty. That is if the blackfly don't get them.'

'Have we nearly finished?'

'Nearly. Are you getting cold?'

No,' Theo replied, shivering.

'One more packet, then we really must call it a day. And *you* must get to bed.'

'But there's no school in the morning,' Theo said, his fair brows raised, pleading.

'No, I know, but a growing lad needs his sleep.' Hugh looked down at Theo's spindly legs, brown and colt-like in grubby shorts. 'I swear you're an inch taller this week than you were last.'

'I'm going to be tall, aren't I? Like you.'

'Yes, I think you *will* be tall.' Hugh smiled and in the dim light

Theo couldn't be sure of his expression. He thought he looked proud but somehow he also looked sad; except that Theo couldn't see how a happy thing like a smile could look sad, But he'd noticed it was sometimes like that with grown-ups. They'd *say* one thing and *look* another. Uncle Rory would crack jokes about sad things like his hands, or Granny having to travel around in her cart, or even about Theo's mother having gone off to London, 'like Dick Whittington'. You couldn't help but laugh at Uncle Rory's jokes, even though he never did. Theo had asked him why and Rory had laid his hand on the boy's shoulder and said, 'I suppose it's because all my jokes are serious.' Theo thought about this for a long time afterwards. He wasn't sure, but he *thought* he knew what Rory meant.

Hugh took a block of wood, shaped something like a rubber stamp, handed it to Theo and said, 'There – tamp those down gently, like I showed you. Pass me the torch. Gentle but firm, that's right. Do you want to sow this last packet?' He handed it to Theo, then straightened up, his back aching from several hours spent bending over seed trays. They'd sown fifty today – annual bedding plants to sell in early summer. Nothing unusual or exotic, but the profit margin on such plants was large if you ignored the cost of labour, which Hugh did, the work being done entirely by him and Theo, with Dora and occasionally Rory lending a hand. Hugh shone the flashlight steadily at Theo, gilding his curly hair which, he noted, could do with a cut. He must remember to ask Grace if she'd oblige. He didn't trust himself near the boy's ears with a pair of sharp scissors and Dora's hands were not very steady now. 'We're all getting older,' thought Hugh, not unhappily.

Stupefied with tiredness, he stared vacantly at Theo's hands as they worked. The nails were too long and very dirty – Hugh made another addition to his mental list of jobs – but Theo's fingers were long and capable as they tore open the seed packet and moved across the tray, scattering seeds with the same confidence and precision Hugh so loved to observe when the boy played the piano.

Hugh thought of Rory briefly, then pushed the thought away, as he almost always did. 'Give the trays a good watering. But keep the can moving so you don't drown them.' He laid his large hand over Theo's, completely enclosing it, directing the can as it swayed over the seed trays. '*That's* the idea. Good lad!'

Hugh's mind was too tired to exercise his usual self-discipline and the thought of Rory returned. Their relationship had changed over the last few years. Hostility had gradually been replaced by warmth, even a reserved form of friendship. That friendship met most of Hugh's needs for Rory's conversation, his companionship, his physical presence. He knew he'd earned the younger man's respect, possibly even his affection.

It was very nearly enough.

Just occasionally – it was happening less and less often now, Hugh observed – he yearned for more. He never stopped to ask himself what precisely it was he wanted. His years as a monk had taught him that the clamorous demands of the body for food, comfort, sleep or the touch of another body would, if ignored, eventually fade away, like the cries of a hungry infant, fallen asleep in despair.

At the age of fifty-six, Hugh's mind was far from despairing – he considered his life showered with blessings – but he took care to keep his body exhausted. His heart was full of love and a profound desire to serve the Dunbar family, especially Rory and Rory's son. To wish for more would be quite unreasonable. But Hugh, being a reasonable man, knew it was also only human.

1980

Theo hadn't been playing for more than a few minutes before Rory interrupted. 'You're playing beautifully.'

'Thanks.'

Leaning forwards in his chair, his eyes and body alert, Rory said, 'No, that's bad. You're doing what I used to do. Stop!' Theo swivelled round on the piano stool, his expression puzzled. 'You've got a big neon sign lit up above your head saying, *Listen to me! I'm playing beautifully!*' Theo laughed at Rory's smug expression. 'Don't tell me about you, tell me about the music. That's much more interesting than *you*.'

'Thanks.'

'You're welcome,' Rory said sweetly. 'So – what's it about? The music?'

Theo thought for a moment. 'It's about—'

'I don't want to know,' Rory said abruptly, holding up his hand. 'Not in words anyway. Tell me what it's about with your playing.'

'That's what I've been trying to do.'

'Yes, I know, but you're working too hard. Look, imagine this Beethoven chap just barged into the room and thrust a piece of music under your nose – he'd do that, he was a grumpy old sod by all accounts – and said, "Here, what do you think of this?" What would you do? You'd play it through, think about it, think about what he was trying to say. You'd enter into a kind of dialogue with him, with him and the music, wouldn't you? Well, that's what I want to hear. That dialogue. I don't want to hear you play *beautifully*. Anyone can do that – it's just a matter of killing yourself with practice. Save beautiful for Granny. She'll swoon. Women do. I want to hear what old Ludwig is *saying* to you... and what you are saying to *him*. But not in words.'

Theo looked up at Rory from under his fringe, his wide blue eyes ironic. 'Oh – is that all?'

'Yes. That's all.'

'Thank goodness for that,' he replied with exaggerated relief. 'I thought for a minute you were going to ask me to do something *difficult*.'

Suppressing a smile, Rory sat back and listened to Theo play – quite differently. He wondered whether Ettie had ever had to tolerate such heavy sarcasm delivered so charmingly. He thought she probably had, but never from Theo.

When he'd finished playing, Theo turned to Rory. 'Was that better?'

Rory spread his hands. 'The neon light went out. Beethoven spoke.'

'Thanks.'

'No, thank *you*. And thank Beethoven.'

When Rory arrived home he heard the sound of a piano as he approached the front door. This in itself was unusual. No one in his family played recorded piano music or played the piano for pleasure. Grace gave cello lessons but not piano. In any case, what Rory heard was someone who could play well. And yet... The sound was limping, odd, incomplete. He felt sure he knew the piece but couldn't identify it. He turned the key, still listening to the music, closed the door quietly and approached the dining room. He stood by the open door

255

watching Grace.

Even before he saw her he'd worked out what she was doing and why. He stood quite still, trying to control his anger. Grace sat at the piano, not in the centre but slightly to the right. Her left hand rested by her side but fidgeted occasionally, rising towards the keyboard, as if instinctively. Eventually she sat on her left hand and continued to play with her right.

Grace was playing the right hand part of a Chopin *étude*, the so-called *Revolutionary*. Rory realised with grim satisfaction that, to sugar the pill, she'd had the decency to choose a piece with a taxing left-hand part. Clever Grace! He leaned against the door-frame and folded his arms.

'And what the hell do you think you're doing?'

Grace swivelled round on the piano stool. 'Oh, God, Rory – you made me jump! I didn't hear you come in.'

'You were engrossed in your new piece. Or is it *our* new piece? What's the plan, Grace? One-handed duets, sitting side by side on the piano stool like Siamese twins, joined at the bloody hip?'

Grace was silent, defeated before she'd even begun. She said carefully, 'If you can't live without the music – and I don't think you can – then play! Play it piecemeal, play it badly – but *play*, Rory!'

His soft laughter was mirthless. *'The music doesn't need you,'* he muttered. *'It's you who need the music.'*

'What?'

'Something Ettie once said.'

'It's *killing* you not playing. And it's killing me to watch you,' she added quietly. He said nothing and she looked up at him, her dark eyes beseeching. 'People are more important than music!'

He arched his brows. 'Really? Yes, I suppose that *is* what the rest of the world thinks.'

He turned away and went upstairs. Grace heard a door slam.

Charlotte put her book down and lay on the bed, listening to the silence. Her mother had stopped practising the piano because her father had come home and shouted, as he so often did. Charlotte was fairly certain that if she went downstairs now she'd find Grace crying. She picked up *The Wind in the Willows* again and stared at the pages, but the mood was broken. How could you read a story about talking animals when your family was always yelling? Why couldn't people just be *nice* to each other, like Ratty and Mole?

She got off the bed, went to the door, opened it quietly and listened.

Nothing. Sometimes, Charlotte thought, the silence was worse than the shouting.

She went and stood at the top of the stairs, keeping an eye on her parents' bedroom door, but she knew Rory wouldn't emerge for some time, possibly not for the rest of the day. Door-slamming like that meant he would be lying curled on the bed, staring out the window at the sky for the rest of the day, like some hunted animal gone to earth.

Overcome by sudden anger Charlotte stomped off down the stairs and went into the kitchen. She filled the kettle noisily, comforting herself with familiar, domestic sounds. Bracing herself, she put her head round the dining-room door.

'Want a coffee?'

Grace looked up, red-eyed, and smiled. 'Thanks, love. That'd be nice.'

Charlotte took a deep breath and said, 'Don't let him get you down. He's not the only person in the world with problems.'

'No, I know, but other people are able to handle theirs. Your dad doesn't know how. Life hasn't really equipped him to deal with… setbacks.'

'Well, I don't see how being nasty helps anything.'

'It doesn't. And he knows it doesn't. And that makes everything worse, don't you see? He ends up hating himself. Feeling useless. And *pointless*. I don't think we have any idea how hard it is for him, even after all these years.'

'And *I* don't think,' said Charlotte sternly, 'that he has any idea how hard it is for *us*.'

1985

'Anybody home?'

Charlotte stood in the cool, flag-stoned hall of Orchard Farm, her eyes adjusting gradually to the dim light. She closed the back door, walked into the scullery and called again. There was still no response so she wandered out into the garden. The sunlight dazzled after the gloom of the old house and she raised a hand to shade her eyes as she looked out across the lawn.

Dora was in her cart patrolling the flowerbeds, poking at the soil with a long-handled hoe, awkward but absorbed. Theo was working some way off at the back of the white border, his lanky figure half obscured by lush undergrowth. He was wearing a frayed straw hat and dungarees. He wore no shirt and his brown skin gleamed with sweat. Bending, he caught a bare arm on a rose bush and swore; Dora looked up and laughed; Theo glared at her, said something and Dora laughed again. Charlotte found she was smiling even though she hadn't heard the exchange that had passed between her relatives. Just the sight of Theo and her grandmother together made her feel better.

Being at Orchard Farm made Charlotte happy – irrationally happy. She supposed it was to do with all the memories, memories of her extended family rallying round to look after them at a critical time, a sense that there was always someone you could turn to: Gran or Uncle Hugh, or even just Theo. There was always someone around to make you feel better, whatever was wrong. Very often in those dark days after her father's accident, Charlotte hadn't known what was wrong, just that the music had stopped and so had her father's speech. She'd been glad to hear voices, any voices. Dunbar conversation, then as now, had been reassuring.

Theo leaned on his fork, looked up and saw Charlotte. His face was shaded by his hat and she couldn't read his expression. He thrust his fork into the ground and picked his way through the flowerbed. He walked across the lawn towards her and called out, 'Good morning.'

'Good morning. You look like Huckleberry Finn.'

'You say the sweetest things.'

'What are you actually doing in that border? It looks like hard work.'

'Clearing weeds. Gran's instructions. *Ours not to reason why...* I'm just the rather inadequate brawn round here.'

Charlotte looked down at his slim brown arms and pointed. 'You're bleeding.'

'*Ours but to do or die...* Her bloody roses. Why can't they breed them without thorns?'

'I think there *is* a thornless variety.'

'Really?' Theo's face brightened. 'Could you tell Gran about it, please? Would it look OK massed in beds? That would make my life a whole lot easier.' He rubbed at the scratches on his arm and Charlotte cried out in alarm.

'Don't do that. Your hands are filthy!'

Theo ignored her and turned back to look at the flowerbed. 'She should have permanent planting under those roses. Perennials. Ground cover to keep down the weeds. It would save a lot of work and it would make the border more interesting.'

'Why don't you suggest it?'

'She wouldn't listen to me, I'm only the gardener's boy.' He grinned. 'I'll get Dad to suggest it.'

Charlotte glanced round the garden. 'Where is Hugh? He surely can't be indoors on a day like today?'

'He's in the orchard, braving the wasps, picking plums. Rather him than me.'

'Coward.'

'Dead right.'

'Your love of wildlife doesn't extend to wasps then?'

'Only as architects. Have you ever seen a wasps' nest? A work of art.' Taking off his hat, he ran a hand through his hair, darkened now with sweat. The damp and dusty curls clung to his neck and forehead. 'Be a darling and get me a drink, would you?'

'Coffee? Tea?'

'No, something cold. Water'll do. "Adam's ale", as Dad would say. But Gran might like some tea.' He turned and surveyed the border again while Charlotte fetched a glass and filled the kettle. 'What she needs are some hardy geraniums and some low-growing shrubs. Grey foliage perhaps. That would make a good foil for the roses.'

'If you say so.' Charlotte handed him a glass of water and watched as he downed it in one. 'Kettle's on. Look, will you let me put a plaster on that cut?'

He shook his head and handed back the glass. 'That's better, thanks. You staying for lunch?'

'Am I invited?'

'Of course. There's a standing invitation. But you might have to prepare it.' Theo smiled his light-bulb smile and Charlotte found herself smiling back, even though she'd planned a sharp retort.

Before she could stop herself she said, 'Shall I make a cake?'

Theo's face lit up. He treated her to the smile again and she wondered if that was why she'd made the rash offer. His face fell suddenly and he assumed a grave expression. 'Hang about – this is all getting a bit gender-stereotyped, isn't it? Surely *baking* goes against your politico-feminist principles?'

'Not at weekends.'

Theo grinned at her again and Charlotte giggled for no reason – no reason at all that she could see.

After she'd put her cake into the Aga, Charlotte spent the afternoon working with Theo in the garden while Dora dozed in the shade. The young people said very little to each other. Occasionally Charlotte would ask Theo to identify which were weeds and which were plants in an overgrown patch, then he would fork over the border while she cleared away the rubbish and hand-weeded.

At four o'clock they all took a break and Charlotte served tea, a dish of plums and cake on the lawn. Dora was ecstatic at the sight of tidy borders and Hugh was ecstatic at the sight of ginger cake. Theo ate three slices.

As she cleared away Charlotte laid a hand on her grandmother's shoulder. 'Shall I give you a hand with dead-heading the roses?'

'Oh, *would* you, my dear? That would be such a help. I find the secateurs so awkward – it's infuriating! Just collect the flower heads in a bucket and we'll burn them later... Or—' She looked up at Hugh. 'Perhaps we should compost them?'

'Ah, that reminds me,' Hugh said, setting down his plate, cleared even of crumbs. 'I've been meaning to talk to you about the compost heap.'

'Yes, I know, it's a disgrace, and situated in quite the wrong place.'

'Well, it is a bit conspicuous, I suppose. But I had an idea when I was washing up this morning and looking out of the window. Why don't we turn that patch into a herb garden? It would be ideal. The soil's really poor and the bed's south-facing. Perfect for herbs. If you put some taller things at the back, such as – oh, I don't know – what would do well there, Theo?'

'Bronze fennel. Angelica. Borage,' Theo mumbled, his mouth full of cake.

'Yes, just the job! They'd screen the compost heap. It could make quite a pretty feature. Positively Mediterranean, with the scents of sage and thyme and bees humming.'

Silence fell as they contemplated Hugh's vision of a transformed compost heap. Charlotte's mouth twitched and she caught Theo's eye. 'That would be a good name for a lady gardener, wouldn't it? One of those county types in green wellies and a waxed jacket.'

Theo frowned. '*What* would?'

'Angelica Borage.'

Theo looked away, selected a discarded plum stone and, with casual but deadly accuracy, lobbed it into Charlotte's teacup.

Smiling, she basked in his disapproval.

1975

Theo rounded the corner on his roller skates just in time to see Colin shove his sister in the chest, pushing her over backwards on to the path. Charlotte began to wail like a siren, even before she hit the gravel. Colin stared down at her for a moment, shocked by his own violence, then turned and ran.

Theo unbuckled his skates and hurried across the grass to Charlotte. He grabbed her hand to pull her to her feet but she shrieked. He let go and she spread her palms wordlessly, revealing tiny stones embedded in her skin. Theo bent and put his arms around her ribcage and lifted her, still crying, on to her feet. He took one of her hands and gently brushed away the stones, carefully picking out those that remained embedded. As he started on the other hand, Charlotte composed herself, then yelled, at no great distance from Theo's ear, 'I *hate* him!'

He flinched and asked, 'Why did he do it?'

'Don't know.' She sniffed. 'Because he's a pig.'

'He probably didn't mean to hurt you.'

'Yes, he did! He's *always* hurting me!'

'Well, you're not bleeding very much. That's something.' Charlotte started to wriggle, hopping from one foot to another. 'What's the matter?'

'I think I've got stones in my knickers.'

Theo, ever practical, said, 'Jump up and down. They'll fall out.'

Charlotte did a little war-dance on the path, shedding gravel, while Theo looked away tactfully. 'All right now?' She nodded, blushing. 'You'd better go and wash your hands.'

'But they hurt.'

'Gran's got some magic cream. Ask her to put some on. It stops the sting.'

'I *hate* Colin,' she said rubbing her sore palms. Theo was silent, his loyalties divided. 'I wish *you* were my brother.'

'Well, I'm your cousin. That's almost as good. *And* I'm your friend.'

'Will you always be my friend?' Charlotte asked, brightening. At seven, she was much preoccupied with the impermanence of playground alliances.

'Oh, yes,' said Theo. 'And friends are better than brothers anyway. My dad says friends are God's apology.'

'What for?'

'For your relations.'

My son grew into a fine young man. Apparently. I wasn't there to witness it. He appeared to inherit the best from both his fathers: a sensitive intelligence and caustic wit from Rory and an all-embracing generosity of spirit from Hugh. From both men he inherited a love and respect for all living things. 'One is nearer God's heart in a garden.' Apparently.

And what did I throw into that murky gene pool?

Looks. Theo was striking even as a boy. I thought when he grew up he would probably take after Rory. I hadn't reckoned on the height he would finally attain or how his refinement of feature would make him so much more handsome than Rory, handsome almost to the point of beauty.

I never saw Theo in his prime. I saw him once or twice as a spotty, awkward youth after I'd left the vicarage, when we were all still going through the motions of keeping in touch and Hugh insisted on sending me the occasional photograph. Then I saw Theo at my funeral, aged thirty-four, dressed, very becomingly, in black. He was tall, thin, detached, sardonic, his face finely lined by the rigours of an outdoor life and a broken heart. There was no mistaking whose son he was at my funeral, but by then everyone knew who Theo was.

Except perhaps Theo. Theo didn't appear to know who or what he was, any more than I ever had. All he knew was whose child he was, which wasn't quite the same thing.

When I saw Theo at my funeral – I sensed he was still angry with me even then – I saw Rory's son, Hugh's son, but not mine. (Had Theo ever been mine? Had I ever allowed him to be?) He had good reason to hate me and he tried very hard to hate Rory too. I'm quite sure Hugh did everything in his power to persuade Theo to forgive us, or at least understand. But Theo couldn't. Or wouldn't. In that at least he was not Hugh's son. In every other respect, the impossibly tall, impossibly handsome young man casting a professional eye over the crematorium flowerbeds might have been – and in a way was – Hugh's son.

My legacy to Theo Wentworth was a passionate, unchanging heart, a talent for loneliness and a capacity for guilt.

Poor Theo.

My poor son Theodore, gift of God.

We should have loved each other. Or at least understood each other. Then perhaps we might have been able to forgive each other.

Chapter 21

The drama students adopted me as a sort of mascot. They saw me as something between a big sister and a counsellor and they'd perch on my desk, drinking execrable coffee from plastic cups while they confided in me, detailing their torments and triumphs. I did my best to listen sympathetically and offered the wisdom of maturity, or if not maturity, the experience of a woman who had, by then, been around the block a few times. I didn't have a lot of natural sympathy with all their frustrated ambition, but I seem to remember I was pretty sound on unrequited love and hangover cures.

They called me Flo and bought me doughnuts and occasionally drinks in the pub on Friday. They rehearsed speeches in front of my desk, bitched about each other and slandered the teaching staff. I saw the students as my charges, but they paid me the enormous compliment of treating me as if I were their friend. I wasn't, of course. I was old enough to be their mother, but we had a satisfactory arrangement based on mutual respect and affection.

I thought I had it all under control.

Perhaps I might have made some real friends if it hadn't been for the students. Perhaps if I'd had real friends I might not have got involved with Colin, but Colin moved the goalposts by becoming a real friend. We were so comfortable and easy together, he was such good company, that I didn't really notice what was happening. Then he moved the goalposts again – right off the pitch this time – by treating me not as a secretary, aunt or even friend, but as a desirable woman.

I was forty-three, living alone in relative poverty, separated from a husband and son I never saw and lonely to the very marrow of my bones. You think I was going to look the other way?...

1985

Flora tidied her desk, tucked her Thermos into her shopping bag, closed the office door and locked it. As she passed the rehearsal room she heard sounds of a struggle and a woman shouting, as if in fear for her life. Flora knew it must be students rehearsing but decided to check anyway. She knocked gently and opened the door. Colin was standing over a female student who lay on the floor cowering as he spoke – Stephanie, a tall girl with a strong clear voice, whose height tended to land her mature roles. Unnoticed by the students, Flora recognised at once the closet scene from *Hamlet*. She watched for a few moments and was about to withdraw when Colin straightened up suddenly, put his hands on his hips and said 'Bugger'. The girl prompted him quickly but he waved an impatient hand at her.

'No, I know what comes next! Look, this just isn't working. I'm delivering all my lines to the floor. The audience can't see me, they can't see you. It's just... *boring*.'

'It's certainly not that,' Flora said from the doorway. Two heads shot up and looked towards her. 'But there's more mileage to be got out of placing her on the bed.'

A grin replaced Colin's scowl. 'Flo, come on in! Come and help us out here. We're floundering.'

Flora noticed that Stephanie's smile wasn't quite so welcoming and wondered if she'd interrupted more than just a rehearsal.

'Oh, you don't want me butting in. Believe me, once I get started on *Hamlet* I could bore for England. I'm sure you can sort it out yourselves. Just get her up on the bed.' Flora attempted to withdraw but Colin came bounding over and pulled her into the room.

'No, honestly. We really need an audience. Please – spare us a few minutes. Our blocking's all wrong, I know it is. I feel a complete prat. Can you just watch for a bit?'

Flora turned to Stephanie who was watching them, fiddling with her hair, her body language eloquent. 'Is that OK with you, Stephanie?'

'Fine... We've only just come off the book, so it's a bit rough.'

'That's good, that's just how the scene should look. Hamlet's terrorising his mother, he's out of control. You don't want it looking choreographed.'

Colin beamed at Flora then at Stephanie. 'You see? I knew she'd say something helpful. The fact that we're under-rehearsed and peeing ourselves with fright is an *asset*.' Colin yanked a chair off a stack and placed it with a flourish in the middle of the room. 'Take a seat, madam.' Flora removed her coat and sat obediently. 'Can we go from after I've killed Polonius? Robbie's buggered off early as usual.'

'Start where you like. I know the scene pretty well.'

'Did you ever play it?' Stephanie asked pointedly.

'Good lord, no. I was an Ophelia, not a Gertrude. Being so small I used to get the fey, fairy parts. Very tedious.'

Colin gave her an appraising look and Flora felt momentarily uncomfortable. 'You, tedious? *Never!* I can imagine you as Ophelia. I bet your mad scene was good.'

Stephanie cleared her throat loudly. 'Shall we get started?'

'Yeah, OK. Flo, will you read the Ghost? It's only one speech.' He tossed her a battered copy of the text. 'Act Three, scene four. Let's go from *"Now mother, what's the matter?"* '

As the students took up their positions, Flora called out, 'Play the scene without stopping if you can. Just keep going, whatever happens. If you can get that *drive*, it's hair-raising. The audience should be as scared as Gertrude.'

They played the scene and the problems soon became apparent. Flora wondered how to address them tactfully. Both actors were miscast. Stephanie was twenty years too young for her rôle; worse, she evidently saw herself as a leading lady and was trying to dominate the scene, maintaining her regal composure as if she were still in control, not in mortal fear. Colin, relaxed and amiable as ever, seemed reluctant to manhandle Stephanie for fear of hurting her. His angry tirades were almost respectful.

Flora stood up at the end of the scene and walked towards them applauding. 'Well done, both of you! You've got the scene basically, but there's so much *more* in it. Are you sure you want me to tell you where I think you're going wrong? I mean, it's only my opinion, after all. I'm no director.'

'No, go ahead. We want feedback. Don't we, Steph?'

'Yes, of course,' she answered doubtfully.

'Right, then.' Flora took a deep breath. As she thought, she placed her palms together in front of her lips and stared down at the floor. She'd first read *Hamlet* when she was fourteen. She hadn't really understood the play but she'd grasped enough to feel moved, excited, disturbed. She'd discussed it with Rory when he studied it for A-level and her reading had subsequently been coloured by his morbid but simple view of the play: *It's all about sex and death, isn't it? God knows why they think school kids should study it.* Flora pushed the thought of Rory to the back of her mind and turned to face Colin. 'This scene isn't just an argument about Gertrude's sex life, which is how you're playing it. It's about sexual *disgust*. Hamlet is revolted by the idea of his mum and Claudius in bed together. He thinks she should have given all that up when Daddy died. At her age it's just obscene. So, Colin, you're not just angry with her, you're outraged, OK? Now, Stephanie... How old do you think Gertrude is?'

The girl looked blank. 'I don't know exactly. Middle-aged, I suppose. Hamlet's meant to be thirty, isn't he?'

'Well, yes, that's one reading. If Gertrude had him when she was sixteen that would make her forty-six. Three years older than me.'

'Not exactly drawing her pension, then,' Colin added.

Flora shot Colin a look. 'Quite. And if you play Hamlet *younger* – after all, he's a student, home for his father's funeral – Gertrude could be under forty. Decide how old she is and play that age. Don't be vague.' Flora turned back to her nephew. 'It's good, Colin, surprisingly assured considering you've only just come off the book. But you're being far too nice. Too polite. Find your mean streak.' Flora wondered briefly if Colin had one and decided it was unlikely. 'You're absolutely *livid* with this woman. What she's done, what she is, repels you. But I think at the same time, it also quite excites you. It's a bugger of a scene to play because you've got to get both those aspects and they're contradictory.'

Colin nodded and looked at Flora, his frank brown eyes enquiring. 'Do you think there's an incest thing going on here?'

Flora faltered for a moment. 'Between Hamlet and his mother?'

'Yes. Or d'you think that's reading too much into it?'

'No... No, I don't. This is centuries before Freud but I think Hamlet gets worked up about her nocturnal activities because he's *jealous*. Maybe he was even jealous of Hamlet Senior when he was alive. Who knows? Shakespeare set this scene in Gertrude's closet, in her *bedroom*. It couldn't have a more intimate or suggestive setting, could it? And as you've already discovered, unless Hamlet throws her on the bed for all the wrestling, you end up playing the scene to the floor. So go for the sex. Be an *animal*, Colin, don't be nice. Scare the wits out of her. Lose control. I know you can't do that in performance, but this is only a rehearsal, so see how far you can push it.' Flora turned to Stephanie and asked belatedly, 'OK, Stephanie?'

'Yes, fine.' She smiled coyly at Colin, as if the prospect of a certain amount of rough handling would not be entirely unwelcome. Flora felt a flare of irritation. 'You think this man is mad. He's just killed an elder statesman before your very eyes. He's threatening to kill your husband and you think he might even kill *you*. Hamlet might get turned on by all this, but Gertrude definitely doesn't. She's a gibbering wreck. You must *both* of you blow a fuse.'

'Right.' Colin grinned and clapped his hands together. 'Let's have a bash, then.'

They took their positions for the scene and as Flora walked back to her chair she called out over her shoulder, 'Play the scene fast. Take a running jump at it. And Colin?'

'Yeah?'

Flora fixed him with a look. 'Don't be you.'

'Right.' He dragged a hand through his thick dark hair, pushing it back from his forehead – the same futile gesture his father had always made. The hair sprang back immediately and memory twisted Flora's innards.

She sat down and thumbed blindly through Colin's copy of the play. 'Think of your dad, Colin. Think of Rory in one of his flaming, unreasonable rages. Being obsessive. And *nasty*.'

'Got you.' He raised his thumb towards Flora and turned away to prepare for his entrance.

'And, Stephanie—'

'Yes?'

'Try not to be so middle-class. You're the Queen of Denmark. You don't need to impress anybody.'

Stephanie gazed at Flora, mystified.

The huddle of figures fell silent. 'Don't know about anyone else,' Colin said, his voice ragged now, 'but I need a beer.'

'Yes, we'd better stop. It's getting late. Off you go, you two. You've certainly earned a drink.'

'Come with us, Flo. We can carry on talking in the pub.'

Flora caught a disappointed look from Stephanie. 'No, you've done enough for one day. And I need to be getting home. I've... I've got a lot to do.' She contemplated the desert of her evening, the highlight of which would be beans on toast and a concert on Radio Three.

Colin put an arm round her shoulders. 'One drink. Come on. We owe you. That was a really useful session. I feel as if we've finally cracked it!'

'Do you? Oh, I *am* pleased! I think it's going to be really good. You've both worked so hard.'

'So have you. Come on. The pub. We're celebrating. And the first round's on me.'

They occupied a small table in a pub not far from the school. Flora had bought a second round soon after Colin's and no one seemed anxious to break up the evening, even for food. Flora wasn't sure if the young people were enjoying her company or were simply too tired to move. They all helped themselves to crisps from a packet in the middle of the table.

'I know it's Hamlet's scene,' Stephanie said, 'but I still don't see why Gertrude has to be such a wimp. She's a feminist ahead of her time, demanding sexual equality with men. I definitely see her as a strong woman.'

'*Do* you?' Flora sounded surprised. 'But she's not very bright, is she? She doesn't see what's going on between Hamlet and Ophelia. Expects them to get married even when they're barely speaking. And she thinks Hamlet should be getting drunk at her wedding even though he's still mourning Daddy. Then at the end she goes and drinks the poisoned wine, even though Claudius warns her not to! I don't see her as strong, I see her as, well, *stupid*, actually.' Seeing Stephanie's crestfallen face Flora added quickly, 'And that's very difficult to portray. Acting stupid when you're not is one of the hardest things to do convincingly.'

Sulking now, Stephanie said, 'I don't see how you can make a *stupid* character interesting.'

Flora hesitated and Colin chipped in. 'Maybe she isn't meant to be that interesting. She's on stage a lot but she's actually got very few lines. It's more what happens *to* her. And *around* her.'

'Exactly. Gertrude's really just a pawn in a political game.'

'Mmm...' Colin agreed, his mouth full of crisps.

'But in the closet scene,' Stephanie persisted, 'She shows what she's made of. I mean, I don't think I can just hand the whole scene over to Hamlet! She's got to fight back.'

Flora was feeling tired and her patience was wearing thin. 'Well, you can, I suppose, but there's not a lot of point, either for the character or for you the actress. You haven't got a hope in hell. He throws you on the bed and verbally rapes you, then just when you think it might be your big moment, you get upstaged by the entry of the Ghost!' Flora emptied her glass. 'All you're really required to do in that scene is portray witless terror and blank incomprehension. You can't go playing it like Lady Macbeth.'

Colin laughed. Stephanie glared at him, then stood abruptly. 'I'm going home. I want to do some more work on my lines before tomorrow.'

'Oh, Stephanie, I didn't mean to hurt your feelings. I really don't know why Colin laughed. I wasn't trying to be funny.'

'I think we see the character very differently, Flora, which is hardly surprising. As you said earlier, you've never actually played the part.' Stephanie gathered up her coat and bag. 'But I did find your comments on the sexual frustrations of middle-age very helpful. I'll bear them in mind. Bye, Colin. See you tomorrow.' She lifted her head and swept out of the pub, every inch the leading lady.

Flora set down her empty glass. 'The bitch.'

'Er, I think maybe that was my fault.'

'Yes, it was, but not in the way you think.'

'How d'you mean?'

'First of all I spoilt her big scene for her, then I ruined her evening. She wanted to spend it with you, then boring Auntie Flo muscled in. She fancies you rotten, my lad.'

'Get away!'

' 'Course she does. God, why are men so blind? She's very pretty. Don't you fancy her?'

'No, not particularly.' Colin looked puzzled. 'I've been trying to think of her as my *mother*.'

'Well, take it from me, darling, she is *not* thinking about you as her son. Be an angel and get me another drink. Here, let me give you some money.' Flora reached down for her handbag.

'No, it's my round.'

'Don't be daft. You can't afford it.'

'Yes, I can! I think...' He sprang up and patted his back pocket in an exploratory way.

Flora grabbed his hand, pressed a five-pound note into his palm and wrapped his fingers round it. 'Don't argue with your elders and betters. Mine's a vodka and tonic. When you come back I'll tell you all about overwhelming passion.'

Colin raised a dark eyebrow. 'Yours?'

'No, cheeky. Gertrude's. I'd need a few more vodkas before I told you about mine.'

'Well, the night is young,' he replied with a wink.

'Colin Dunbar, are you flirting with your aged aunt?'

'No.' His expression was wide-eyed but far from innocent. 'With an attractive, intelligent woman in her prime.'

'I have a son your age.'

'Older, in fact.'

Flora winced. 'That was uncalled for.'

'Sorry.'

'Are you *ever* going to get me that drink?'

'Sorry.'

'For God's sake, Colin, stop apologising!'

'Sor—' He nodded. 'I'll be right back.'

Through a vodka haze, Flora watched Colin as he shouldered his way through the crowded pub and leaned casually on the bar waiting to be served. Her thoughts came randomly, wantonly and she relished them in the privacy of her lonely, aching mind.

Nice arse. Broad shoulders. Like Rory's.

Don't go there...

Bambi brown eyes. Crinkly. Kind... Not like Rory's.

Don't...

He's so young... Nineteen.

Old enough.

His body must be taut and firm. Fit. Like Rory...

He's nothing like Rory.

Like enough...

Flora stood up unsteadily and headed for the Ladies. As she passed Colin at the bar he looked up anxiously and said, 'You're not running out on me, are you?'

'No, darling. Just off to repair the ravages of time. I may be some time...'

'Overwhelming passion, then.' Colin nudged the vodka towards her.

'I beg your pardon?'

'You said you were going to tell me about overwhelming passion.'

'Oh, yes! Gertrude's... It disgusts Hamlet. He can't handle the sexuality of a middle-aged woman.'

'What's his problem with it?'

'It upsets the established order. It's threatening. It's unnatural. Women are just goods and chattels, for bearing children and offering comfort to men. They aren't supposed to have libidos. In Hamlet's book, passion makes women mad, bad or sad.'

'Or all three?'

'Quite possibly. Look at what Ophelia talks about when she goes mad: sex. Once insanity removes her inhibitions she reveals that her love for Hamlet – and probably her relationship with him – was sexual. And Hamlet thinks she's conspiring against him with the others, so there you are. Mad, bad and sad.'

'How did you play it?'

'Ophelia? Oh, I just did as I was told. I was seventeen. What did I know about sex? As I recall, I played it festooned with daisy chains. Terribly picturesque. Like a Flower Fairy.'

Colin laughed and said, 'I wish I'd been there to see it.'

'My dear, you weren't even a twinkle in your father's eye.'

'Did my dad ever twinkle?'

'Oh, yes!' Flora swirled the contents of her glass. 'When he was young, Rory... *glittered.*'

'You amaze me. So what about Hamlet and passion, then? He's a passionate guy, isn't he?'

'No, he's a bloody intellectual! *He's* never known overwhelming passion. I don't think he really loves Ophelia. He's vile to her! Oh, once she's safely dead he says, *"I loved Ophelia"* and jumps into her grave – big romantic gesture! – but when she was alive, it was probably just a quick fumble behind the arras. Out of sight, out of mind.'

'Yeah, I know what you mean. He doesn't exactly treat her like the future Queen of Denmark, does he?' Colin raised his glass and drank. 'You know, I've always thought Hamlet seemed fonder of

Horatio than Ophelia.'

'Oh, God, Colin, you're not going to play it *gay*, are you?'

'No!' He looked alarmed and Flora thought she detected a faint blush. 'It was just a thought.' He stared down into his pint.

'So how *are* you going to play it?'

'The scene?'

'No, Hamlet.'

'Fuck knows,' he said gloomily.

Delighted, Flora took his face in both her hands and kissed him on the cheek. Colin blinked in astonishment. 'What's that for?'

She shrugged. 'Fuck knows.'

He continued to stare at her, then tilting his head to one side, he leaned forward and kissed her on the mouth.

Flora said nothing. Colin leaned forward again, intent on repeating the exercise. 'I think I'd better be going,' Flora said hurriedly, grasping her handbag. 'It's getting late and I should probably eat something.'

'May I join you?' Colin asked in a small, polite voice.

She looked at him. His dark eyes were sleepy with drink, exhaustion and something she thought was probably an advanced state of sexual arousal. 'Something tells me you're not talking about food.'

'No, I wasn't.'

'Aren't you hungry?'

'Ye-es...'

'You're still not taking about food, are you?'

He shook his head. Flora reached for her glass, then realised it was empty. She opened her purse and found only small change. Exasperated, she snapped it shut and turned to face him. 'It would be wrong, Colin.'

'Mad, bad or sad?'

'All three. I'm your *aunt,* for God's sake!'

'So?'

'It's also unprofessional! I'm an employee at an institute where you are a student. It would be an abuse of trust.'

'Bollocks.'

'You know, for a Shakespearean actor, your vocabulary is surprisingly limited.'

'OK, I get the message. But if you don't take me home I've got a very long walk back to Paddington. I've got no money for the tube.' He tapped her purse. 'Nor have you. Let me walk you home. I'll sleep on your sofa.'

Disappointment made Flora angry. 'Is that what all this is about? A bed for the night and saving the tube fare home? You've got a nerve!'

His eyes flared for a moment, then he took her hand and, sliding it under the table, pressed it against his crotch. '*That's* what all this is about. And that, Auntie dearest, can't be faked.'

We didn't get much sleep. The recovery period for a nineteen year old appeared to be about fifteen minutes. Colin made love to me five times during the night and once on waking, which was almost more sex than I'd had in all the years of my marriage. He was enthusiastic, clumsy, talkative, hilarious, very sexy and very sweet. I had a wonderful time and in the morning I could hardly walk.

Having disposed of the erection he woke up with, Colin bounced out of bed and brought me a pot of tea and biscuits on a tray, with milk in a jug and sugar in a bowl. Grace had trained him well. I was so touched, I cried. He devoured the meagre contents of my fridge, showered and set off for his nine o'clock fencing class ten minutes before me so we didn't arrive together. He was thoughtful like that. Old beyond his years.

As I sat, gingerly, at my typewriter that morning I took stock. Overnight I had acquired an almighty hangover and a teenage lover who just happened to be my brother's son. Plus ça change... Or, as Colin had put it the night before when I'd made a last feeble attempt to occupy the moral high ground, 'Vice is nice, but incest is best.'

Chapter 22

It couldn't last, of course. My being happy. Colin and I got careless eventually and students talked. Toby Tavistock, now the school's Principal, had to take a stand against my moral turpitude. Colin thought this was a bit thick since Toby had made several overtures of a horizontal variety towards him. We wondered whether spite had motivated him to deliver the ultimatum that deprived me of a job I'd really loved and done rather well.

I was given a choice: I could resign and depart with a neutral reference or I could refuse and be sacked in disgrace. I was tempted to call Toby's bluff. I knew I was popular with staff and pupils and Colin (bless him) wasn't averse to the idea of a spot of retaliatory blackmail, but I went quietly in the end, mainly because I was sick of all the subterfuge, but also because my relationship with Colin, far from being a quick fling, looked likely to continue.

I tramped round the agencies looking for work but it soon became apparent that I'd reached the end of my shelf-life. My skills were outdated, my references indifferent, my working career chequered and I was a lot older than the younger, prettier girls with whom I had to compete. When one of his housemates moved out Colin suggested I move in with him, as an economy measure as much as anything.

I was terribly grateful. I was already living on an overdraft and the rent for the room was less than I was paying for my shabby bed-sit. I got to live in a house again, the first house I'd lived in since the vicarage. We moved all my stuff into the empty room but I shared a bedroom with Colin. It was furnished with a double bed – with which I was already familiar – and so we were soon established in our love-nest, a happy couple, despite my lack of job and a worrying tendency to kill the time that hung heavy on my hands by indulging in booze and memories.

1986

Flora sat in an armchair leafing blindly through a magazine. Colin was upstairs learning lines. She'd listened to his footsteps pacing back and forth all evening. It occurred to her she could go upstairs and ask if he wanted a drink. Or she could continue to sit and hope that he would come down soon. She wondered, if she denied herself the self-indulgence of a trip upstairs, would God reward her with Colin's company downstairs? Would God even notice her self-sacrifice? Probably not.

Closing her eyes, she leaned back in her chair. If she could sit and not think of him for ten whole minutes, he might come into the room...

Step on the cracks and the bears will get you...

Who'd said that? Rory? No, Theo. He'd said it to Lottie when they were young, walking to school. Ever after, Lottie had repeated it half in fun, half in fear. The trip to school had become even more slow and tortuous as she avoided stepping on cracked paving stones. Flora had pointed out that, as far as she knew, there were no bears in England and even if there were, they had better things to do with their time than chase little girls who accidentally trod on broken paving stones. But none of this made any impression on Lottie. *'Theo said...'* and for some reason, Theo's sayings – particularly those involving animals – were regarded by Lottie as little short of oracular.

Flora smiled at the memory. She wondered where Lottie was now and what she was doing. She tried to remember how old she would be. Two years younger than Colin. Eighteen? Perhaps nineteen by now. Flora couldn't remember birthdays. There were lots of things she couldn't remember nowadays. Or wouldn't remember. Then some things just jumped out at her – vivid, real, as if they'd happened yesterday.

She tossed the magazine aside and sat, waiting, hoping that a young – *very* young – man would walk into the room, smile at her, perhaps put his arms around her. She felt a churning mixture of humiliation and excitement. Her fingertips tingled at the thought of touching Colin's flesh.

Unbidden, a memory of his mother sprang into her mind: Grace, in the bistro, years ago, after the accident, drunk and tossing her long, dark hair. What was it she'd said then? It had made Flora blush...

Have you ever noticed how much firmer young men's bodies are? I mean, their flesh doesn't wobble like ours. It's sort of taut – d'you know what I mean?

Flora hadn't known then. She knew now.

Grace had given up trying to hoover round Charlotte's discarded underwear and abandoned homework and she sat on the edge of her daughter's unmade bed, leafing through *Cosmopolitan*. According to the results of a quiz, 'How compatible are you?', Charlotte appeared to be enamoured of someone scoring an improbable 17/20. *Cosmo* advised her to hang on to this paragon, while warning her that in all probability he was already married. Picking up a chewed pencil from the floor, Grace decided to answer the quiz herself.

She was dismayed to find that Rory scored only 6/20 even though she'd been careful to give him the benefit of the doubt and in one instance had lied. She was not at all surprised to find that *Cosmo* advised her to 'Dump this one and move on. He's not for you unless your speciality is ego massage.'

Grace scanned the floor for a rubber, found one and carefully erased her ticks.

'My brother says he's sleeping with your mum.'

Theo snorted with laughter. 'Oh, yeah?'

'No, seriously.'

He laughed again, then examined Charlotte's face. 'You *are* kidding?'

'Nope.'

'My mother and *Colin*?'

'Apparently.'

'He's having you on.'

'Look, if you don't want to know what your mum gets up to in London, that's fine by me, but shocked disbelief is getting a bit boring.'

'Sorry. It's just that it's... it's *incredible*.'

'I know. Believe me, I find it hard to imagine *anyone* fancying Colin, even a desperate middle-aged woman, but I suppose that's just because he's my brother.'

'But she's twice his age! Colin's younger than *me*!'

'Well, some women like younger men. And I suppose some men like older women.'

'How do you know all this?'

'Colin blabbed. Accidentally. But I think he wanted to tell someone. It's been going on for months apparently. He says they're very happy, but he doesn't want anyone to know yet. I think he means Mum and Dad.'

'But – it's *incest*.'

'Oh, come off it!'

'No, technically, it is. You can't marry your aunt. Or your nephew. It's to do with something called consanguinity. The rules are all laid out in Leviticus.'

'What's Leviticus?'

'A book of the Old Testament, you heathen child. When Dad was a vicar he sometimes had to deal with some dodgy situations when couples wanted to marry. It's a nightmare these days. So many broken marriages, step-relations, adoptions, IVF. He says, "It's a wise father who knows his own child". '

'Meaning?'

'You just don't know these days who you might be related to. It's one big melting pot.'

'Well, obviously Colin and Flora aren't bothered.'

'No... Well, good luck to them,' Theo said doubtfully. 'If they make each other happy, that's all that matters, I suppose.'

Charlotte sighed and said, 'I'd better get going.'

'Already?'

'It's late. Mum thinks I'm at a party and I promised I'd be home by two.' She got out of bed and pulled on a T-shirt over her slim naked body. Theo propped himself up on one elbow, smiling.

'What are you laughing at? Do I look funny or something?'

'No, you look gorgeous.' He stared at the dark triangle of hair below her T-shirt. 'I was just looking at you and thinking, you're so dark... and I'm so fair. We couldn't be more different, could we?'

'Opposites attract.'

'I'll say. Come here.' He grabbed her hand and pulled her back towards the bed. 'It's not *that* late...'

~

When Colin and I had been together for over a year I received a carefully worded invitation from my mother to take tea at Orchard Farm. (Note the prodigal was offered tea, not even lunch.) I declined by return of post and awaited developments. After an interval I received another invitation – more of a summons really – to tea at the Ritz. Ma was clearly determined to say her piece in style. I was intrigued. I said nothing at all about the meeting to Colin. I had my hair done; I dressed up to the nines; I was practically sober. I hit the town and did battle with my redoubtable mother.

Perhaps if she hadn't looked quite so old, so frail, so pathetically small, I might have been kinder to her. She sat hunched in her chair, her clothes (at least twenty years out of date) hanging in folds on her wasted frame. Something seemed to be missing apart from flesh. I couldn't place it to begin with, then realised it was her gardening hat. I'd rarely seen her without it. I checked her feet for galoshes but she'd shoe-horned them into boat-like brogues that made her pale stockinged legs resemble pipe-cleaners. She was visibly in pain and I felt guilty for dragging her up to London. I couldn't forgive her for that either.

It was a shock seeing Ma. I'd always thought of her as old, even when she wasn't. Now she was, which meant I was no longer young myself (a fact I'd managed to ignore by surrounding myself with young people and avoiding mirrors). I'd spent ten years trying to forgive Dora for being the sort of mother one couldn't turn to in a crisis, the sort that didn't deal in truth or unconditional love and I thought I'd made some headway. Could any mother have heard the truths I needed to tell with any kind of equanimity? 'Ma, my husband's gay and he's in love with my brother. Oh, by the way, so am I. And there's something I've been meaning to tell you about Theo...' I hardly think so.

I forgave my mother for imposing silence on me, but for some reason I couldn't forgive her for being old. The sight terrified me and I remembered the words of the pop song: 'Hope I die before I get old.'

As things turned out, I needn't have worried.

1987

'How dare you judge me!'

Dora fixed her daughter with faded blue eyes, still astute, still

279

steely. 'I may be very old, but I am not yet a fool. Colin is twenty-one and you are forty-four. At best it's mutual infatuation. Put an end to it now before Colin is hurt.'

'Why should I? It's not as if he's a child. Or particularly immature. He wasn't even a virgin, actually.'

Dora winced and held up her hands in protest. 'Please! I don't wish to hear details of Colin's private life. Or yours for that matter.'

'So why is it wrong? Tell me. He says he loves me. And I – I'm terribly fond of him...' Her voice faltered. 'We have a lot of interests in common,' she added quickly. 'And we enjoy sleeping together. Why is that wrong?'

Dora looked down at her hands, registering the throb of pain in her arthritic knuckles. The ugliness of her once beautiful hands never failed to repel her. She looked up into Flora's still lovely face and, against her better judgement, relented. 'I don't know if it's wrong, but I do know that one day you'll regret it. I think you will feel...' Dora cast around for a word and seemed almost surprised by her choice. 'I think you'll feel ashamed.'

Flora laughed, a high, barking sound that had nothing to do with mirth. 'Oh no, Ma! That's one thing I won't feel. I was inoculated against shame a long time ago.' She stood up and brushed crumbs from her skirt. 'Well, thanks for tea. Tea at the Ritz... What a way to celebrate our reunion! I suppose you thought if we had it within these hallowed walls I wouldn't make a fuss or turn up drunk. We should do this more often,' Flora said brightly. 'Shall we meet up again in another ten years? But I might have given up sleeping with young men by then, so we'd have to find something else to talk about.'

'Flora, please. Don't leave. I didn't want it to be like this. I really—'

'Did Rory put you up to this?'

'No, of course not. But he's very unhappy about what's going on.'

'*Is* he? Well, poor Rory. My heart bleeds for him. Goodbye, Ma. I'll give your love to Colin.'

Clutching helplessly at her napkin, Dora watched her daughter's retreating figure. She'd hoped to spare Flora a visit from Rory but it seemed that was unavoidable now. Her attempt to intercede had failed. Dora leaned back in her chair, closed her eyes and tried to think. It was so difficult to know what to do for the best.

It always had been.

1958

Dora lifted the lid of the shoebox and gazed in dismay at the hank of blonde hair coiled inside. 'Oh, Rory! How *could* you?'

'She asked me to!' His voice cracked comically, something that happened now only when he was agitated. Dora told herself she was arguing with a boy, but now that the maturity of his body almost matched that of his intellect, she felt as if she were confronting a man.

'If Flora asked you to commit a crime, would you do that too?'

'Cutting hair isn't a crime.'

'But it was wrong. You *know* it was wrong!'

'No, I don't!' he said indignantly. 'It's her hair! It's up to her what she does with it. It's nothing to do with you! I was just... *helping*. Anyway, I think it looks a lot better.'

'That's hardly the point, Rory.'

'Yes it is, it's the whole point! She doesn't like what she looks like. She wanted to look different. *Be* different!' Dora stared at her son, uncomprehending. He shrugged wide, bony shoulders and plunged over-large hands into his pockets. 'If you ask me, I think Flor *hates* herself.' He seemed shocked by his words and looked at his mother, his grey eyes wide, not with anger now, but guilt. 'Oh, you wouldn't understand!'

'And I suppose you *do*?' Dora replied with heavy sarcasm.

'Yes, of course I do,' he said simply. 'She's my sister.'

1987

Flora ignored the door-bell and turned over in bed. The bell rang again, more persistently. Colin had not long since left the house and she wondered if he'd forgotten his key and come back for it.

The bell pusher was now pressing continuously and Flora decided it must be Colin. Cursing her lover and her hangover in equal measure she hauled herself out of bed and reached for the nearest garment – a crumpled shirt of Colin's, discarded on a chair, the buttons still fastened. She swore again, pulled it on over her head and hurried downstairs.

From the silhouette on the frosted glass panel Flora could see that it was Colin, his arm extended, leaning on the bell. As she turned the handle she yelled, 'All right, all right! Stop ringing the sodding bell!' She yanked the door open and stood face to face with Rory.

He was thinner than she remembered. His sandy hair, dusted with grey, was paler now, almost ashen. Lines ran from the sides of his nose to his jaw, hard lines that drew attention to his mouth, set in a line, unsmiling. He appeared composed, almost stony, apart from his eyes which seemed to have grown larger, staring out at her from bony cavities. She saw shock and confusion in their grey-green depths, then a flicker of something familiar as his eyes travelled, taking in her dishevelled appearance: her hair unkempt, her legs bare, her small body swamped by Colin's shirt.

Flora shivered and folded her arms across her breasts, hugging her ribcage for warmth. Rory opened his mouth to speak but made no sound. She was ambushed by an old sensation of panic, but then he opened his mouth again and said, 'Is Colin in?'

'No, he's—'

'It doesn't matter. I've come to see you.'

She hesitated, then said, 'You'd better come in.'

Rory stepped across the threshold and she shut the door behind him. They stood facing each other in the cramped hallway.

Flora scraped her hair back behind her ears, then tugged nervously at the hem of Colin's shirt, as if it might stretch and cover more of her thighs. 'I'll go and get dressed.'

'Don't bother. I mean, this isn't a social call. I won't stay long.'

'It's been three years, Ror,' she murmured.

'Three and a half.'

'You know, there was a time when I believed I would actually die if I was separated from you for three months, let alone three years.'

'Flora—'

'I know why you've come,' she said briskly. 'You want me to give him up.'

'Yes.'

'Why?'

'I would have thought that was bloody obvious.'

'Not to me. Or Colin.'

'You're living off him. He's in debt. And you're older than his

282

mother. Get out of his life and get your own.'

'He says he loves me.'

'He's twenty-one! What does he know about love?'

She shrugged. 'What does anybody?'

Rory didn't answer, then said scornfully, 'You think you *love* him?'

'I don't think that's any of your business.'

'So you don't. I didn't think it very likely. So what is it – just sex?'

Flora turned away and grasped the door-handle. 'I'd like you to leave, Rory. I refuse to be bullied by you. I know what I'm doing.'

'No, you don't! You never have. Your life is a complete bloody mess!'

'And whose fault is that?' she cried.

'Well, it certainly isn't Colin's! If you want revenge, hurt me! Hurt Hugh! We deserve it. But Colin doesn't! Can you really not think of a better way of getting back at me? Is screwing my son supposed to keep me awake at nights thinking about you? About what I'm missing?'

'*Does* it?'

He turned away and sat down on the stairs. 'You're pathetic!'

Flora leaned against the front door and looked down at him. 'Let me get this straight. Do you want me to stop sleeping with your son? Or do you want your son to stop sleeping with *me*?'

'Finish with Colin,' he said wearily. 'Get a job. Get your own place. Your own man. You still could. You're only forty-four. If you bothered to make an effort, you'd still be attractive.'

'Colin thinks I *am*. But then love is blind, isn't it? Obviously Colin sees me through more forgiving eyes than yours.'

'Colin's just a boy.'

'Oh, I think I should be the judge of that, don't you?'

Rory stood up. 'This is pointless. Goodbye, Flora.'

She didn't move away from the door. 'Do you think about me and Colin in bed, Ror? Is that why you're here? You couldn't stand it any longer? If you can't have me, nobody else will – is that why you've come?'

'Don't be ridiculous. All that was over years ago.'

Flora narrowed her eyes. 'Was it?'·

They stood facing each other and neither spoke for a moment, then Rory said, 'And you – do you think about *me*? When you're in bed with Colin, do you think about me? Is that why you want him? Because he reminds you of me? Oh, Jesus, Flora, you are *sick*.'

'Your son is kind, affectionate, unselfish. He's all the things you're not!'

'Which is why you don't actually *love* him.'

She stared at him for a long moment, then said, 'It started off as friendship. We just enjoyed each other's company. Then it was friendship plus sex... And that was *him*, not me! The thought would never have crossed my mind. Well, it *did*, but I would never have done anything about it. Now it's – well, I don't know what it is. I don't *think* he wants me to go. He's never said so. Anyway, there's nowhere I *can* go. I haven't got a job. I don't seem to be able to keep a job these days. And I haven't got very good references.'

'What do you expect if you sleep with your students? You're a fool, Flora.'

She wasn't listening. 'I can see I'm going to have to lower my sights. Do some waitressing, bar work, that sort of thing,' she said vaguely. 'Just to tide me over. I'm going to pay Colin back. I'm making a note of all that I owe him. He'll get it back eventually. Every penny.'

Rory took out his wallet and withdrew five £20 notes. He handed them to Flora.

'I don't want your money.'

'It's not for you, it's for Colin. I want you to give it to him. Don't say you got it from me. Say Hugh sent you some money. Or Dora. Make it look as if *you* are paying him back.'

Flora took the notes, folded them and put them in the breast pocket of Colin's shirt. 'I realise you're doing this to help Colin, not me. But thanks anyway.'

'If you leave him I'll pay off whatever you owe him.'

Her mouth fell open. 'You think I can be *bought* off?'

'No. I just hope so. Because I can't see any other way of helping Colin. Or helping you.'

Her expression softened. 'Are you happy, Rory?'

'It's not a question I ever ask myself.'

'I mean, are you and Grace happy?'

'I'm financially dependent on her. I can't afford to ask if we're happy. She provides me with a home, food, clothes and a modicum of self-respect. By giving up a promising musical career she's allowed me, and our children, to lead a comfortable life. She's given me the luxury of pursuing my own musical projects – such as they are,' he added bitterly. 'Teaching, composing, charity work... All of that is subsidised by Grace. I don't ask if we're happy, I just keep a tally of how much I owe her.'

'Does she still love you?'

'Yes.'

'Do you still love—'

'Flor, what is the *point* of all this? Why do we have to torture ourselves? Why do you have to make everything more painful than it needs to be?'

'Do you still love me?'

He hesitated, unable to mouth the lie. His answer when it came was just a breath. 'Yes...'

'Do you still want me?'

He was silent.

'*Do* you?'

'You know I do.'

'Then leave Grace.'

'I can't!'

'Come away with me.'

'Don't be ridiculous! You've got no money, nowhere to live.' He shook his head. 'You're not living in the real world, Flor.'

'If you come away with me I'll leave Colin.'

'*What*? You're *bribing* me to leave my wife? You are priceless!'

'You want Colin to be free and you want me. It's simple.'

'You're out of your mind. Where are we supposed to go? What am I supposed to say to Grace? "There's good news and there's bad news. The good news is Flora's dumped Colin. The bad news is I'm leaving you".'

Flora ignored him. 'We could go to *Tigh na Mara*. No one would ever think of looking for us there.'

'It'll be uninhabitable by now. It's been on the market for years.'

'We'd manage. It can't be *that* bad. And if the roof's blown away, we'll camp out. Like we used to.'

'You're mad.'

'We can live there to begin with. None of the family need know we're there. It will give us time to think. To plan. It will be like it used to be. Just us. And we'll be happy.'

'It's just a fantasy! You're living in the past.'

'*I was happy in the past!*' she said fiercely. 'So were you! Why shouldn't we live there? Why shouldn't we be happy again?'

'Flora, I have a *life*. Family. Friends. Commitments. I give piano lessons. Lectures. I'm trying to write a book. I have commissions for articles. I have a diary and it's full.'

'But your life is empty.'

'If I gave it all up, what... who—' His voice gave out. His head shot up and, blinking rapidly, he appeared to study the patterns on the artexed ceiling. Flora stared at his exposed throat, the protruding Adam's apple rising and falling as he swallowed. Rory lowered his gaze but didn't meet her eyes. 'If I gave all that up, who would I be? The other half of *you*? I can't just... *walk away* from everything.'

'Like I did.'

'I can't. I won't.'

'Not even to save your son from my corrupting influence?'

'It will end one day, with or without my intervention.'

'You're very confident of that, aren't you? You think he'll dump me.'

His smile was bleak. 'No, I don't. That's why I'm here. Don't undersell yourself, Flor. Colin is bewitched. Like his father before him. Like Hugh.'

'So you think I'll dump him?'

'I know you will. When they try to help heroin addicts kick their habit, they put them on something called methadone. It's a heroin substitute. Not so dangerous. And it reduces the physical cravings.' Rory paused to allow his words to sink in. Flora stared at him, appalled. 'You'll finish with Colin. Eventually. You won't be able to pretend any more. Not now you've seen the real thing again.'

She lifted her hand, drew it back and slapped him hard across the face. Rory saw the blow coming but made no move to avoid it. His head yielded slightly as her palm connected with his face and his eyes closed involuntarily. As his cheek reddened he opened his eyes and stared into Flora's. His lips moved in an abortive attempt at a smile. 'And you thought you could get through all this without touching me, didn't you?' He turned away, opened the front door and, without looking back said, 'You won't be able to pretend any more now, Flor. And, if it's any consolation, neither will I.'

~

When Colin returned from his rehearsal some hours later he was surprised to find Flora exactly as he'd left her: asleep in bed, apparently dead drunk, but unaccountably, she was now wearing one of his shirts and the bed was strewn with damp and crumpled tissues.

Rory was right, of course. (When was the bastard ever wrong?) Things were never the same after that visit. I don't think I had ever thought about Rory when making love with Colin, but after I'd seen him, after he'd put the idea in my mind, things were different.

I was furious. And very sad. Rory destroyed what I had and I didn't have all that much. He'd known exactly how to break up my relationship with Colin, but he'd given little thought to the consequences for me. I had nowhere to go. I still had no money. I got the odd interview, but somehow I always seemed to blow it. Actually, if I'm honest, I have to admit I didn't always make it to interviews if they were early in the morning. Hangovers were becoming more of a problem, so much so that even Colin got irritated enough to complain about my drinking. But he didn't understand why *I was drinking. Why I had* to.

I suppose I was falling apart even before I ran away to Scotland. And I was pretty damn sure Rory was too. Music had always been his defence against me, against people, everything. Without that, how did he bear the emptiness of his life? The wonder was that he'd lasted as long as he had.

I knew it was only a matter of time and time was one thing I did have. So when he rang me two weeks after his visit, I wasn't surprised. Relieved, that the waiting was over, but not surprised.

1987

Rory lay awake, staring at the window, waiting for the first grey light, listening for the first birdcall. In the silence he was aware of sounds in his own ears, of his own breathing, even of his digestion. It was 4.00am and he was hungry, but lacked the energy to get out of bed. Grace lay beside him, her back towards him, her breathing soft and steady. He lay on his back with his arms on top of the duvet, aware, as he always was, that one hand was warm and the other cold. He rubbed the cold hand with the warm to stimulate the circulation, listened to the whisper of skin brushing skin, then spread his hands and stretched his fingers, letting them sink into the soft depths of the duvet.

He no longer woke expecting his hand to be restored, expecting to find it had all been a bad dream. That shattering daily disappointment had lasted for some years, but nowadays he woke in the full knowledge of what had been lost. He awoke every day with the sensation of a weight on his chest, as if he were being pressed to death.

His left hand was moving, fingering something absently on the surface of the duvet – the tune in his head, but only the left hand moved. He could feel muscle impulses in his right hand as he thought the music through, but apart from his thumb and little finger, there was no response, no movement he could control. He could feel the music in his right hand, but couldn't finger it.

He tried to remember what his hands looked like when he used to play. He'd spent nearly thirty years watching his hands move up and down keyboards, so it wasn't difficult to remember. What was difficult was coping with the memory. Watching his hands move in his mind's eye, Rory heard what they were playing. The *Waldstein*. The *adagio molto* in the second movement. He'd recorded the sonata in 1973. It had been well-received, selected as a *Gramophone* Record of the Month. It had sold well and there were plans to record more Beethoven – there had been talk of the *Hammerklavier* – when the accident happened.

Rory ran through the list once again of great piano pieces he'd never played, would never play now. He'd become an expert in masochism, but he still wasn't sure which was more painful: to list the pieces he'd never played, or the pieces he would never play again. He tortured himself in this way, probing wounds to see if they were healing and as he probed, he opened them up again. Then, once his soul's blood was running freely and nothing could staunch the flow, he'd list the pieces of music he would learn to play if ever his hand were restored to him. Sometimes he'd take down the dusty scores and study them, as a kind of mental preparation for a miracle.

The dawn chorus began. A robin solo as usual. Then a blackbird. Then an answering blackbird. Rory tried to notate the trio in his head, incorporating a ground bass of distant lorries as they rumbled along the main road. In the dim light he could see his hands more clearly now. Scars were visible, pale raised lines that caught the light and gleamed as he turned his right hand over, noting how muscle had wasted. His left arm and hand looked bigger than the right.

Grace had said his hands were beautiful. Beautiful in repose; even more beautiful when they played. She would gather up one or both of his hands and press them to her mouth, or cheek, sometimes her breasts. He felt a stirring in his groin at the memory of Grace's hands on his body, of his hands on Grace. He watched his hands, the memory of his hands, removing Grace's clothes, languorously, to an accompaniment of soft laughter, but when in his imaginings she was naked, he saw it wasn't Grace, but Flora. Except that it wasn't really Flora, whom he'd never seen naked except as a child. The woman of his imaginings was a Flora he'd never seen, never held, but one he thought about – not often, but often enough to know that the thought was to be avoided, like his musical lists; that thought, if pursued, would lead to more self-lacerating pain.

Was there a limit to all the pain? If he suffered enough, punished himself enough, would he finally reach saturation point? And would it then stop? Would he eventually feel no more pain, no more desire? Would he pass through some sort of barrier, descend to a hellish underworld where his senses were cauterised, where there was no more longing and therefore no more suffering? Rory wondered how much more he would have to go through before he reached that point. There must surely be a limit, a pain threshold at which the mind either disintegrates or numbness sets in. A death of the spirit and the senses.

He thought of Flora, anaesthetised by vodka and sex. He'd tried both. He couldn't drink enough to dull his mind. He threw up before he achieved oblivion. Sex, with Grace and others, tired his body but left his mind untouched, craving something – he'd no idea what – that he believed only Flora could supply.

What was the ultimate pain? What refinements were there that he hadn't yet experienced? What could he do to push himself through that barrier, so that, if he survived, he would suffer no more?

The cacophony of the dawn chorus reached an ecstatic fortissimo. It was obvious really. And quite simple. Amazing how his mind had baulked at it for so long. Grace had known for years and taken steps to ensure neither he nor the children could ever inflict this particular pain.

With something like a feeling of exaltation, Rory got out of bed, stealthily, so as not to wake Grace. Closing the bedroom door behind him, he went downstairs to the sitting room.

Grace was woken by music. Music she knew well, yet it was somehow unfamiliar, as if she hadn't heard it in a long while. As she struggled to surface from sleep she became aware of a piano playing. Beethoven. A sonata. But it wasn't just the music that was familiar... She sat bolt upright in bed, fully awake now and listened intently.

It was Rory.

She stifled a cry, pressing a hand to her mouth so hard that her lips hurt, crushed against her teeth. Her mind flooded with joy. She was scrambling out of bed, stumbling towards the door before she realised that this was no miracle. With a dawning sense of horror she realised Rory had found his own recordings and was playing one of them.

Grace ran downstairs, calling out his name.

He was sitting on the floor in the middle of the room with his back towards her, his pyjama-clad legs crossed, his naked torso hunched over a group of records spread out on the carpet in front of him. He was rocking back and forth like a small child, listening to his own recording of the *Waldstein* sonata, a recording that used to make Grace cry even before the accident.

She didn't speak but approached slowly and knelt down beside him. His face was wet with tears and his eyes were closed. His hands were spread out in front of him, pressing down into the carpet as if supporting him, preventing his collapse, his fall into the abyss.

Grace was afraid to touch him, afraid to speak. She didn't think he knew she was there and she feared to disturb his agony, as one might fear to wake a sleepwalker. Nor did she want to speak over the music, interrupting whatever it was Rory had decided to put himself through. She simply wanted to be present, to endure it with him. So she sat on the floor facing him, in case he should open his eyes. She watched him weep, listened to him play, letting her own silent tears flow as Rory's hands thundered out the final joyous chords of the *Waldstein.*

Chapter 23

1987

Rory wandered through the garden at Orchard Farm and found Hugh in the greenhouse, potting on seedlings. He was engrossed in his work and didn't notice Rory arrive. Standing in the doorway, watching Hugh's big hands manipulate the fragile seedlings so lovingly, Rory felt soothed. He remembered watching Archie perform the same task, explaining that young seedlings can recover from a damaged leaf, but not a damaged stem, so they should always be handled by their leaves. Rory had helped his father on many an occasion. His long, supple fingers, exquisitely sensitive, were ideally suited to the delicate tasks of sowing seed, pricking out and potting on. He thought how familiar and reassuring it might feel, to plunge his fingers now into the warm, damp compost, to handle something small and beautiful, so full of potential life.

Hugh had straightened up and was looking at him expectantly.

'You've come to talk about Flora.'

'Yes.'

'You've seen her?'

'Yes. At Colin's place. She's living there.'

'So I gathered.'

'We had a God-almighty row.'

'I can imagine. You know, it's really nothing to do with you,' Hugh said gently, brushing compost from his hands. 'With any of us. Colin's twenty-one. It's his life.'

'She's not paying him any rent. She hasn't even got a job. And she looked bloody awful.'

'You haven't seen her in a long time.'

'She's drinking again. You can tell. She looks... puffy.'

Hugh looked at Rory and thought he too looked awful – thin, red-eyed, as if he weren't sleeping. Turning back to his workbench, Hugh said, 'If only she'd let us *help*.' He resumed his task, but Rory knew he was still thinking about Flora. He didn't feel he'd been dismissed, nor did he feel the need to talk. He knew Hugh was comfortable having silent company in the humid, fragrant heat of the greenhouse. The warmth and Hugh's repetitive movements with trowel and dibber made Rory feel tired.

'Are you sleeping?'

Hugh's gentle enquiry jerked him out of his reverie. 'What? Oh... No, not very well.'

'You should talk to the doc about that. I'm sure he could give you something.'

'No. Grace would do her nut. We don't have pills of any kind in the house. She still worries about me.'

'We all do. It's because we love you.'

Rory smiled awkwardly. Hugh had never lost his clerical way of talking easily about love. It embarrassed Rory, yet he could never quite bring himself to deride it. He admired Hugh's honesty, his refusal to simplify, to judge. Hugh's love encompassed and nourished them all. Rory didn't ask himself if Hugh's love for him was still partly sexual. He didn't really care any more, he simply thought of Hugh as a friend. A good friend. Someone he could talk to. The only one, in fact.

'You'd do anything for Theo, wouldn't you?'

Hugh looked up, surprised. He considered a moment. 'Yes, I suppose I would.'

'Commit a crime?'

'No, I don't think I'd do that. Not unless it were to save his life.'

'Would you do something wrong? Something that would harm other people? To help Theo, I mean?'

'I suppose I might. It's hard to say. Look, what's the matter?'

Rory raised his head to look Hugh full in the face, searching his eyes for a lie. 'Do you think I'm bad?'

'*Bad?*'

'Yes.'

Hugh stared at him for a moment, then said, 'No. Not *bad*. Selfish. I think you're utterly selfish.' He smiled gently. 'But I don't think that makes you bad. Do *you* think you're bad?'

'No.' Rory lowered his eyes and Hugh knew he was looking down at his own hands. 'But I sometimes wonder if I've been punished.'

'For something you've done?'

'No. For what I'm going to do.'

When Grace came home and found Rory gone she wasn't unduly concerned until she saw the sealed envelope propped up on her desk. Her first thought was that he'd left a suicide note, so when she read the few lines that informed her he'd walked away from the marriage leaving no forwarding address, she was at first relieved.

Rory was alive and planning a future.

It just didn't include her.

What Rory and I did was bad. Unequivocally bad. We hurt people, lots of people, people who didn't deserve to be hurt, people who, on the contrary, deserved to be loved and protected.

No one knew exactly what had happened. No one was able to put all the pieces together, apart from Hugh who must have guessed straight away. I walked out on Colin, but he didn't tell anyone, afraid his parents might gloat, I suppose, or appear inordinately pleased. Then Rory left Grace. It wouldn't have occurred to Colin to burden his mother with his own problems, so Grace assumed I was still living with Colin.

Poor Colin coped on his own. He believed I'd left him for someone else, but he didn't know who. I hoped he'd never know and I could see no reason why he ever should. I wanted him to believe ours had been a good relationship, that I'd genuinely liked him, really wanted him, because it was true, I had. I wanted Colin to feel good about our affair because my brother was wrong. Colin wasn't a substitute for Rory. (If Colin had come anywhere near being a substitute for Rory, I would never have left him. It was uncharacteristically modest of Rory to think that anyone could replace him in my life.)

But Colin didn't feel good of course. He felt rejected. Who wouldn't? He refused to accept my money (Rory's money) and I had to hide it in the pockets of his trousers and tuck it into corners of drawers before I left.

I tried to soften the blow but I failed dismally. It might even have been less painful for him if I'd just packed my bags and buggered off with no explanation, as Rory did. But instead I tried to explain (without actually telling the truth). I tried to thank him for what we'd had. But he just glowered at me – looking remarkably like his father –

and said, 'There's someone else, isn't there?' And, without thinking, I said, 'There always was.'

It wasn't a good thing to say. As soon as I'd said the words, seen the look of shock on his face, of incomprehension, I remembered the night Hugh told me he'd always loved Rory. I understood Colin's anger.

He wasn't just angry, he was incandescent. (The thing about rowing with an actor is that it goes on and on. They don't get tired of shouting, their voice never gives out and they have no concept of over-reaction.) It was horrible and noisy. Eventually the neighbours banged on the wall. Colin stormed out of the house and I packed a large suitcase with most of my clothes and a few of my possessions. With disturbing prescience, I left him a note telling him to donate the rest of my stuff to the Salvation Army. I took a taxi to Euston where I caught the sleeper to Inverness.

I never saw Colin again, except once, very briefly, on Waterloo Bridge. I don't think he recognised me. I hope he didn't, for his sake.

I wish he could have known that we'd never stood a chance; that Rory had always been there, would always be there; that I simply didn't exist independently, I came as part of a package.

Buy one, get one free.

2000

Flora leaned against the wall of the telephone kiosk. Trying to steady her shaking hands she unfolded a dirty scrap of paper. It had been folded and re-folded so many times, it tore as she opened it. She keyed a number and waited. When a voice finally answered she was so startled she dropped one of the coins she was holding. Pressing the receiver hard against one ear, she put a hand over the other in an attempt to shut out traffic noise.

The voice spoke again. Flora's throat tightened at the sound. She opened her mouth but no words came.

'Hello?' The voice sounded irritated now. 'Is anyone there?'

Flora's knees gave way and she slid slowly down the wall of the kiosk until she was sitting on the floor amidst litter and cigarette stubs, her knees under her chin.

'Who *is* this?'

She clapped her hand to her mouth and began to sob, still

holding the receiver to her ear.

'Flora.' It wasn't a question. 'Flora – is that you?'

She nodded, her throat constricted, her eyes blind.

'Flora – answer me! Tell me where you are!' Rory paused but there was no reply. 'Flor, speak to me! Tell me where you are, just speak, say anything, tell me it's you! Flora, *please*. Come home!' As his voice began to break, Flora buried the receiver in her lap, swaddled it in the many layers of her filthy clothing and howled like a stricken animal.

I woke up in the far north of Scotland, to the sound of a stranger snoring in the berth above me. I went out into the sleeper corridor and watched the desolate moorland speeding by. Torrential rain did nothing to dampen my spirits. The sky and light were unmistakably Highland; my lungs were already expanding at the prospect of clean, delicious air. And Rory and I would soon be together again. Like it used to be.

At Tigh na Mara.

The house by the sea.

1952

'Are we nearly there?'

'No, darling.' Dora tidied her daughter's flyaway hair absently. 'There's still a long way to go, I'm afraid.'

'Will there be snow?'

'In August?' Rory scoffed.

'No, there won't be any snow. Not on the ground anyway.'

'I can see the sea!' Flora pressed her nose against the window of the railway carriage.

'Aye, that's the Moray Firth,' said Archie, with a hint of pride.

Rory looked up at his father. 'Where the dolphins live?'

'Aye. Inverness is a good place to watch for dolphins. The tail-end of the Gulf Stream brings them in.'

'Can *we* go and look for dolphins?'

Archie laid a hand on his son's shoulder. 'No, we haven't time. We're going to have breakfast in the station hotel.'

'Porridge!' Flora exclaimed.

'Aye, if you wish,' Archie laughed. 'It's breakfast with Uncle Hamish, then he'll drive us up to *Tigh na Mara*. We'll be there by lunchtime.'

'And then can we go and play on the beach?' Flora asked. 'Can we take a picnic?'

'Of course you can. If it's not raining,' Dora added.

Flora grasped her mother's hand and shook it impatiently. 'Can we play even if it *is* raining?'

'We'll see.'

Rory looked at his sister. 'That means no.'

'Look! We're stopping!' Flora shrieked.

'Aye, this is Inverness. Look out now for Hamish on the platform.'

Flora began to wave indiscriminately at people on the platform as the train came to a standstill. Giggling, she threw her arms round her brother and squeezed him. He tolerated the crushing embrace but turned his head away and looked out of the window at the gulls wheeling above the platform. 'Herring gulls,' he remarked to no one in particular.

Releasing him, Flora announced, 'The first thing *I'm* going to do when we get there is run down to the sea! Will you come with me, Ror?'

He considered. 'After I've put some food out for the pine marten.'

'D'you think he'll still come?'

'He always comes. Uncle Hamish feeds him every day. But we won't see him until dusk.'

'When's that?'

'When it isn't quite light and it isn't quite dark. When it's half-and-half. That's when lots of creatures come out. That's when some birds perch and sing.'

'Why do they do it then?'

'Because they feel safe. Predators can't see to hunt because their eyes don't work properly in the funny light.'

'What's a predator?'

Rory closed his eyes, summoning patience, then opened them again. 'Flor,' he said, not unkindly, 'You're an ignoramus!'

'What's an ignoramus?'

~

297

I caught the bus to Gairloch on the north-west coast. From there I'd have to take a taxi to Badachro. Rory had sent me the house keys, which he'd taken from Orchard Farm without telling Dora. He found them where they'd always been kept, in a drawer in Archie's bureau.

In Gairloch I shopped for groceries, paraffin and some whisky for Rory. I didn't know exactly when he was arriving but I hoped he'd bring a car-load of food and fuel, or at least some cash. After some deliberation I picked up a bottle of vodka. I thought I'd be able to manage a long wait without food, but not vodka.

I took a taxi to the house. The driver looked surprised when I gave the name and queried it, but being a Highlander he didn't ask questions except to remark by way of cautious conversational opener, 'You'll be on your holidays then?'

I stared fixedly out of the window, my eyes swimming and replied, 'No. As a matter of fact, I've come home.'

The keys were hardly necessary. A tree had fallen – blown down in a gale probably – and a branch had shattered a downstairs window, leaving what had once been the dining room open to the elements and wildlife.

The house which had belonged to my Uncle Hamish originally, then to my father, was a traditional croft house, over a hundred years old, not modernised since the sixties. We'd taken long family holidays there every summer for years until Rory went away to music college. The house had once been painted the traditional white but years of neglect and Highland weather had scoured away any protective coating so that it now looked flayed, its faded paintwork peeling from doors and window-frames, its rendering exposed, grey and porous, like sick, elderly skin.

The path had completely disappeared and I ploughed through knee-high thistles, wild flowers and coarse grass to get to the front door where a rowan tree leaned, performing its traditional task of keeping evil spirits from the door. I was undeterred. I passed a For Sale board lying face-down in the grass and wondered how many years it had lain there.

Archie once told me that the house was mine. When we were children he said that the grand piano was Rory's and Tigh na Mara was mine. As a child I thought I'd got the best of the bargain which compensated a little for Rory's autocratic dictates about the use of the music room and the piano. The music room was his kingdom; I pretended Tigh na Mara was mine. The difference was that Rory didn't want to share his kingdom with me, but mine was of little interest to me without him.

Dora had put Tigh na Mara on the market when Rory had the accident. She was hoping to raise some cash – I suppose she'd have given it to Rory and Grace, even though the house was meant to be mine – but offers were few and risible and somehow it had never been sold. Probably its only value now was as a secluded building plot with a sea-view.

The land at the back of the house shelved gently down to a stony shore that revealed sand only when the tide was out. The large, spherical, many-coloured pebbles shone like jewels when they were wet, so that the beach was actually more colourful in the rain than in sunshine.

Rain or shine, Rory and I virtually lived on the beach as children, climbing rocks, skimming stones, exploring rock pools, beachcombing. Our feet were rough with weeks of going barefoot, our hands and knees scarred with climbing and tumbling off rocks and out of trees. We were permanently wet and frequently half-naked – brown-skinned, straw-haired sea creatures, mer-children who lived half on land, half in water.

I turned the key, pushed the door hard and walked into the hall. There was a convulsive flapping of wings and several birds fluttered away upstairs. I stood at the foot of the staircase and looked up. There was a hole in the landing ceiling which had clearly been caused by water cascading through a hole in the roof. A grey tongue of floral wallpaper hung curling down the brown-stained wall and the air stank of mildew and rot.

I turned away, dispirited, and entered the primitive kitchen. It wasn't too bad if you ignored the mouse droppings. I flicked a switch and a light came on but the bulb went immediately. There were still a few pots and pans in a cupboard, some crockery and cutlery, a can opener, even a corkscrew. I began to feel a little more optimistic, as if I might get by until Rory arrived. And after Rory arrived, nothing else would matter.

Whatever the difficulties – cold, wet, rot, holes in the roof, mice, rats, bats, owls, feral cats – none of it would matter because Rory

and I would be together.
My brother would look after me.

1953

'We're lost.'

'No, we're not.'

'Yes, we are.'

'We're not *lost*, we just don't know where we are on the map.'

'Same thing.'

'No, it's not! You can't be lost if you've got a map.'

'You can if you can't *read* the map!'

'Shut up, Flor – I'm trying to concentrate.' Rory turned the map round again, studied it, then looked up into the distance, searching for landmarks.

Flora sank down on to the heather and lay on her back, staring up at the sky, counting the colours: pink, orange, lavender, and a little bit of blue, the colour of a blackbird's egg. 'We're lost and we're going to go round and round in circles for ever. And *then* we'll starve to death,' she added cheerfully.

Unconcerned, Rory stared at the map again. 'You'd die of thirst long before you starved to death. But not here - there's plenty of water.'

'I'm hungry!' Flora whined.

'You only just finished the biscuits!'

'I was hungry *before* we finished the biscuits. And I'm *still* hungry.'

'Well, there's nothing left to eat, so just belt up and let me think. We need to go south. If we keep going south we'll be bound to hit the road and then we can hitch a lift.'

'What if there are no cars?'

'If we don't get a lift, we'll just follow the road. A road has to lead *somewhere.* As soon as we find a telephone box we'll dial 999 and get them to tell Ma and Dad.'

'They'll have given us up for dead by now,' Flora said with gloomy satisfaction.

'No, they won't. We've been out all day before. They won't be worried. Not yet. We just need to head south.'

'Why don't you use the compass?'

Rory hesitated. 'I've lost it.'

'*Lost* it?'

'It must have fallen out of the knapsack when we had lunch.'

'Oh, so now we're *completely* doomed! They'll send out a search party and find nothing but *skeletons*. We'll have been eaten up by buzzards and eagles and... and *vultures*!'

'There aren't any vultures in Scotland,' Rory said calmly. 'Now, will you just put a sock in it and let me think? There has to be a way of doing this without a compass.'

'Well, hurry up. The sun's going down and it'll soon be dark.'

Rory's eyes widened and he turned to look at Flora, sprawled on the ground, squinting up at the sky. 'That's it!'

'What?'

'The sun! The sun's going down *in the west*! If we keep the sun on our right, we'll be walking *south*! Come on!'

Dazed, Flora got to her feet again. 'Did I say something clever?'

Resuming his usual cool authority, Rory said, 'No, not really. You just jogged my memory.'

'So – are we going to be all right then?'

' 'Course we are! Have I *ever* let you down?'

Flora thought for a moment. 'No.'

'Well, there you are then.'

As they set off in the failing light Flora took Rory's hand. For once he didn't snatch it away.

There were some blankets and some old darned sheets in a rusting tin trunk in one of the bedrooms. I unpacked the clothes I'd brought with me into a chest of drawers: jumpers, cord trousers, thick woollen socks. This far north it was only ever summer during the day. The nights would be chilly, especially in an unheated house.

The nights...

I turned and looked at the bare mattress on the old brass bedstead my parents had shared. I laid my hands on the ticking, registered the damp, told myself it didn't matter. Nothing mattered. Not any more.

I made up the bed and lit a fire in the bedroom grate using lumps of coal I found at the bottom of the bunker. The heavy paraffin stove could stay in the kitchen until Rory arrived. I was prepared to sleep wearing all the clothes I'd brought with me if necessary.

I gave the kitchen and its rodent population a wide berth. Instead I emptied a tin of ravioli into a saucepan and set it on the coal fire, feeling like a Girl Guide. I sat down in the old rocking chair with its reassuring creak and polished off the pasta with a spoon, straight from the pan. For pudding I heated up some long-life milk in another pan and melted a bar of chocolate in it. It tasted wonderful.

Standing in front of the fire, I changed into an old pair of winceyette pyjamas, then, shivering, donned my raincoat again. I pulled back the blankets, got into bed and looked across at the space where Rory would lie. A shudder racked my body – whether of fear, desire or just cold, I couldn't tell. I sat up, got out of bed and went downstairs to the kitchen, making lots of noise to disperse nocturnal wildlife. As soon as my hand clasped the vodka bottle I felt better, safer. I found a dusty tumbler, rinsed it under the tap and ran upstairs again. I poured myself a generous measure, pulled the rocking chair up to the dying fire and sat staring into it.

Waiting.

1949

'Flora, what are you doing, sitting on the stairs? Get back into bed at once!'

'I'm waiting for Rory to come home.'

Dora sat down beside her daughter and put an arm round her shoulders. 'Darling, he isn't coming home! He's gone away to school. We won't see him until half-term.'

Flora screwed up her face as she made her calculations. 'But that's not for weeks!'

'No, I know. He's gone away to school to be a boarder. He'll live at school and we'll see him during the holidays.'

'But he told me he'd be back soon.'

'Did he? Well, that was very naughty, because he won't. Perhaps he was just trying to be kind.'

'It isn't kind to tell *lies*.'

'No, you're right, it isn't,' Dora said vaguely. She was brought up short – not for the first time – by her daughter's stark moral code which admitted only black and white, good and evil; which acknowledged no nuance of behaviour, no grey area where one might stand comfortably and prevaricate, evading or simply ignoring all that was difficult about human nature.

'It isn't kind to tell lies,' Dora conceded. 'But sometimes it's kinder to tell lies than to tell the truth. Truth can hurt just as much as lies, you know.' Dora was of the opinion that truth, by its very nature, had a far greater capacity to hurt. Lies at least had the virtue of being untrue and, once identified as such, could be dismissed. Truth, Dora had found, was rather more persistent.

'You'll see,' she said briskly. 'The weeks will soon pass. And Rory will send us letters. You can write to him! You'll enjoy that. You can tell him all your news. In a proper letter with a stamp!'

Refusing to be seduced by stationery, Flora said solemnly, her voice tolling like a bell, 'He *said* he'd be back *soon*.'

'Well, he was mistaken. He won't. Now come along, it's time for bed. Would you like me to read you a story?'

'No, thank you. I'm waiting for Rory. He said he'd be back. He promised.'

'Flora, you can't spend the night sitting on the stairs!'

'Yes, I can. I'm not tired. It's all right, you can go to bed and leave me, I shan't be frightened. But I'm not sure if I shall be able to open the front door when Rory comes. The handle is hard for me to turn.'

'Darling, he's fast asleep in a dormitory, miles away. He won't come!'

Flora bunched her fists and brought them down like hammers on her knees. 'He will! He *said*! If I wait, if I stay awake, he'll come back, I know he will. He *has* to...' she added, choking on a sob.

1987

Rory stood on the threshold, his hair and clothes unkempt, his face drawn, his features blurred by a two-day growth of beard.

'Hello, Ror...'

'Hello.'

'You look as if you've been sleeping in ditches.'

'No... In the car. I didn't want to stop.'

'You've driven straight here? From *Suffolk*?'

'Yes.'

'Jesus! Have you eaten?'

'I had something...' He cast his eyes upwards as if trying to remember. 'Yesterday.'

'Well, there's not much here. Only tins.'

'I'm not hungry.'

'Did you bring booze by any chance?'

'No.'

'Pity... There's no kindling left either. It's bloody cold. How did we use to bear it here?'

He shrugged, his shoulders tense. 'We were kids.'

'Yes, I suppose so.'

'Flora...'

'Yes?'

Rory's gaze was level but his chest rose and fell as he tried to control his breathing. 'You know I will never forgive you for this.'

'Yes, I know,' Flora said mildly. 'But you see, Ror, I'm past caring if anyone forgives me. Even you. The only thing that matters to me now is that you're here. Come in and shut the door. Mind that hole in the floorboards – the dry rot's got a lot worse.'

Chapter 24

1987

Grace parked her car outside Orchard Farm, switched off the ignition and sat staring through the dirty windscreen. Fighting an impulse to cry, followed by an impulse to turn the ignition back on and drive home again, she took her powder compact out of her handbag and studied the damage. Her eyes were bloodshot and swollen and an attempt to disguise this with eye-shadow had made her look bruised. Which was exactly how she felt. She also felt like a cliché: a forty-four year-old-woman with greying hair who needed to lose a bit of weight, whose husband had walked out after a mid-life crisis.

That wasn't really fair on Rory. His mid-life crisis had started when he was thirty-two and would probably persist until he died. Tears began to well as Grace wondered yet again whether Rory was already dead. She told herself it was far more likely he was screwing some skinny blonde in a hotel room – a thought which, oddly enough, she found comforting. Men tended to come back. That's what the magazines said. That's what her women friends would say, if only she could summon the courage and energy to tell anyone that Rory had gone.

But the family had to be told. She couldn't put it off any longer. He'd been gone a week. Charlotte already knew and it was only a matter of time before she told Theo and Colin. It would be better if Dora heard the news from the horse's mouth. Or perhaps from Hugh.

And then there was Charlotte's own news. Clouds with silver linings... 'Bloody hell,' thought Grace. 'I *am* a cliché and now I'm thinking in clichés.' Furious with herself, she got out of the car, slammed the door and started to stride up the path towards the house. Her nerve failed and she veered across the lawn, heading for the nursery area where she was certain she'd find Hugh – she hoped alone. She was simply playing for time and she knew it, but she'd decided to be kind to herself. Well, somebody had to.

Hugh was bent over strawberry plants, wrestling with netting and straw, picking berries and placing them carefully, almost lovingly, in small punnets. He looked up as Grace approached.

'Can I interest you in some freshly picked strawberries, madam?'

'You certainly can. But I insist on paying for them. I'll have none of your charity hand-outs.'

'In that case, try before you buy.' He selected a strawberry and handed it to her. 'You can eat them straight from the garden. We don't use any chemicals – as the depredations of our slugs testify.'

Grace smiled and bit into the strawberry. 'There's nothing quite like English strawberries, is there?'

'*Doubtless God could have made a better berry, but doubtless God never did.* William Butler in the seventeenth century, when I expect they tasted even better.'

'Why are the seeds on the outside?'

'Couldn't tell you. Ask Theo. What that boy doesn't know about plants isn't worth knowing.'

'Are you ever going to retire and let him run this place?'

'I suppose I should, shouldn't I? The trouble is, I'm having too much fun. And Theo's still quite young to run a business. I think I'll soldier on for a few more years yet. But he's taking on more and more responsibility. He's the business brain. I'm just the old family retainer. Kept on purely for sentiment's sake. And decoration.'

'Rubbish. I've seen you flirting outrageously with old ladies, foisting plants on them they'd never have dreamed of buying.'

Hugh pursed his lips. 'People need guidance. They're overwhelmed by too much choice. I just try to share my enthusiasms.'

'Well, you don't fool me, you old rogue. You're a ruthless charmer, but I can see it makes for very good business. I've got a lot of orders for you, by the way. Bedding plants mainly. I put your notice up in the staff-room and they liked your prices. Which probably means you should have charged more.'

'I'd rather have satisfied customers spreading the word.'

'Where's your killer instinct?'

'Sadly under-developed, I'm afraid. But don't be deceived – you should see me jostling for position at Chelsea. There are times when I'm prepared to use my height and bulk to my advantage, as well as my supposed charm. Have another strawberry. How's the family? Rory seemed rather low the other day when I spoke to him.'

Grace's face fell. She realised she'd forgotten the purpose of her visit. 'I don't actually know how Rory is. He—'

There was a fluttering noise behind Hugh. He turned and bent down to the netted strawberries where a blackbird was ensnared. Donning gardening gloves, he grasped the bird and netting, then with painstaking care, tried to disentangle it. After several moments of fruitless struggle he withdrew a penknife from his pocket, cut the bird free, then cast it up into the air where it flew off squawking into the treetops. As he watched it go he laughed and said, 'Blackbirds like strawberries just as much as slugs and humans.' He turned back to Grace and, noting her expression said, 'Shall we have a cup of tea? I could do with a sit-down.'

She looked up at him quickly. 'I don't actually want to see Dora at the moment. There is a reason...'

Unperturbed, Hugh nodded and said, 'Let's go and sit in the orchard. There's a pleasantly secluded bench.'

'What about your customers?'

'There's a bell by the shed. An old-fashioned school bell. Theo's idea. People love to ring it. Especially the old ladies. Follow me.'

'Something's up with Rory.'

Grace nodded.

'Is he depressed again?'

'I don't know. I sometimes wonder if I know anything at all about my husband. Do you think that's possible? To live with someone, be married to them for years, yet not really know them?'

'Yes, I think it perfectly possible. Quite common, in fact.'

'Did you feel you knew Flora?'

'Yes.' He spread his big hands in a helpless gesture. 'But I didn't.'

'Do you think you need to know someone well in order to love them?'

'I know that you *don't*. I suspect it might even be easier to love someone you know very little. Love is not only blind, it comes more easily to the partially sighted,' he said gently.

'You loved Flora.'

'Yes.'

'Do you still?'

'In a way, yes, I do. I miss her still, after all these years. I worry about her. I wish she'd stayed in touch. Not just for Theo's sake, for mine. But that's a rather selfish wish.'

'Oh, Hugh! You're so hard on yourself! What you describe as selfish is just being human.'

His face clouded. 'I told Rory I thought he was selfish.'

'He bloody well is.'

'Yes, but I wish I hadn't said it. At the time it seemed like the lesser of two evils.'

'It's hard knowing what to say to Rory. God knows, he was never an easy person even before the accident, but what he went through – *still* goes through... I don't think we have any idea.'

'No. We don't.'

'And I know he misses Flora. He never mentions her, but I know he does.'

'I think we all do,' Hugh said quickly.

'She was too young to marry, wasn't she?'

'Yes, I think so.'

'I know I wasn't much older, but Rory and I had been living together. I knew what I was taking on.'

Hugh avoided her eye. 'You were certainly more mature than Flora.'

'Living with Rory would put years on anybody.'

Hugh's smile was wry. 'Yes, I suppose so.'

'If two people thought they loved each other, but were too young to really know each other, how would you rate their chances? In marriage, I mean? Is there a magic formula? Why do some marriages last and others don't?'

Hugh thought for a moment. 'I think the only reason any marriage lasts is because one or both partners refuse to give up on it. A marriage isn't only sustained by love. And it isn't always destroyed,' Hugh said carefully, 'by infidelity.'

'No, it isn't destroyed. But it takes some pretty hard knocks.'

'That's what I meant about not giving up. Forgiveness is as important as love. It's essential, in fact. And a lot harder to do than love.'

Grace turned to face him on the bench. 'Can I ask you something? You don't have to answer if you don't want to. Did Flora tell you why she was leaving you? I presume it was you she was leaving? Not Theo. Or the Church.'

'No, it was me. But I think the Church played its part in driving her away. Having to be a clergy wife. She hated all that. But it was mainly me. I was the problem.'

'I'm not asking why she left, I'm just asking if you understood, if you were able to see why she went.'

'Oh, yes, I understood. Perfectly. That's why I did nothing to persuade her to stay. I thought she was doing the right thing.'

Grace was thrown by his frank reply. Without thinking she asked, 'Was there someone else?' Hugh hesitated. 'Oh, I'm sorry, I shouldn't—'

'No, it's quite all right. It was all a long time ago. But I'm not sure there's a simple answer to your question. There was someone else. But she didn't leave me for him. I think it was probably all over by the time she left me, but she realised we had no future together. And she was right. But why are you asking these questions now, so long after the event? Flora left ten – no, eleven years ago.'

'Oh, I've been thinking a lot about marriage. Relationships. For better, for worse. You know the script.'

'Is something wrong? Between you and Rory? Something you want to talk about?'

'I suppose I am going to have to tell people, so I might as well start with you. Perhaps you could break the news to Dora? I don't think I can face it.'

'Grace, my dear, what is it?'

She opened her handbag and took out a tissue which she proceeded to screw in to a ball. 'Well, as Rory would say, there's good news and there's bad news. Which do you want first?'

'The bad.'

Grace looked away from Hugh's kind but searching eyes and stared into the distance. 'Rory's left me. And I don't have the foggiest idea why, or where he's gone. I don't even know if there's another woman. I suppose there must be! There usually is, isn't there?'

'Grace, I'm so sorry.'

'Now for the good news. Shame Rory's not here to help us celebrate! I wonder if he'd have been pleased... The good news is that our daughter has announced she's engaged to be married.'

'Lottie? Engaged?'

Grace laughed, her eyes beginning to fill. 'I know – isn't it ridiculous? She's only eighteen! But wait, it gets better. Who is to be the lucky man?' Grace clutched at Hugh's hand. 'Your son. She's going to marry Theo! Isn't that wonderful? Congratulations, Hugh! I think we should get roaring drunk together. For entirely different reasons, of course.'

And with that Grace burst into noisy tears and cast herself into Hugh's arms, affording him the luxury of several moments' privacy during which he struggled to school his features and assimilate the information that Theo – like his father before him – was in love with his sister.

It was not in Hugh's nature to judge, nor to panic. As Grace sobbed out her misery on to the bulwark of his broad chest, his mind was already grappling with urgent questions of who needed to be told, how much and by whom?

And where – in the name of God – was Rory?

Rory put his suitcase down in the hall and, flexing his hand, looked around him. 'The house seems smaller than I remember.'

'We were smaller.'

'Yes, I suppose so.'

They stood awkwardly, each waiting for the other to speak.

'Do you want something to eat?'

'No. Just a bath. I'm aching all over.' He looked doubtful suddenly. '*Is* there hot water?'

'Hot-ish. But I think the thermostat is on its last legs. You'll need to boil a kettle or two. How did Grace—'

'I didn't see her,' he said quickly. 'I left a letter.'

'Oh. You didn't tell her where—'

'No. Just that I was leaving. She'll think I've had a nervous breakdown or something. Maybe I have.' Flora's answering smile was wan, uncertain. 'How did Colin take it?'

'Badly. He was very angry.'

'You didn't tell him why?'

'No, of course not. But he guessed I was leaving him for someone else. I was sorry to do that to him, sorry he was so hurt. But I was bad for him, wasn't I?'

'You're bad for all of us, Flor.'

'I've done him a big favour, getting out of his life.'

'He won't see it like that. But I do.'

'Grace will be pleased.'

'I hardly think so. Under the circumstances.'

'She doesn't know. No one knows. Do they?'

'I think Hugh might guess.'

'If he does, he won't say anything.'

'No, maybe not. He's a good man, your husband.'

'I suppose he *is* still my husband. I never give him a thought these days. Is he still in love with you?'

'Don't know. He's getting on now. And I'm practically middle-aged. Not the gilded youth I once was.'

'I suspect that wouldn't make the slightest difference to Hugh. I don't think it was ever really about… *sex*. He was just captivated by you. First by me, then by you. The whole package. I expect he does still love you. He's terribly loyal. And forgiving.'

'It doesn't matter anyway. Not to me. Not any more. Hugh's been a good friend. He lets me be.'

Flora thought this was an odd thing to say but she nodded, adding, 'I'm glad you two have… settled your differences. Hugh was a good friend to me too. Before we married,' she added. 'We should have stayed like that. Just friends.'

Rory shook his head. 'Men and women can't be friends.'

'*We* are.'

'No, we aren't. We're brother and sister.'

'We're still friends.'

'Are we?'

'Yes,' she answered, less certain now.

'And will we stay friends? Afterwards, I mean?'

'I don't see why not.'

'I do. We haven't been friends since… since that night in the hotel. When we haven't been trying to get each other into bed, we've been at each other's throats. Something died that night… I killed it, didn't I?'

'Maybe this will bring it back to life.'

Rory said nothing. She felt the prickle of tears and said brightly, 'Shall I run you a bath? Get you a drink? I bought you some whisky.'

'Yes. Whisky would be good. Flora, we—'

'Oh, don't let's talk any more! I don't want us to talk, I want us to just *be*, be *here*, be together! Just us!' She clapped her hands like an excited child.

He gave her a long look. 'How drunk *are* you?'

'Fairly. The waiting's been awful. But never mind, you're here now!' Her smile was dazzling but unfocused and her eyes glittered. He wanted to touch her but she was out of reach and he thought if he moved he would probably fall down. She prattled on, not looking at him. 'The sheets were a bit mouldy but the blankets were OK. I've lit a fire in the big bedroom. It smoked like hell. Birds' nests, I suppose. I opened the window to let the smoke out and the draught just about set the chimney on fire.'

'You want to be careful. God knows where the nearest fire engine is.'

'Oh, Ullapool, I should think. The house would be burned to the ground before they were halfway here.'

She watched him, waiting for his eyes to meet hers again. When eventually they did, she saw only weariness. 'Flor, I want to sleep in my old room.' He paused. 'I need to *sleep*.'

'Yes, of course. You must be shattered. I'm afraid I didn't make up the bed. Your old bed, I mean.'

'I brought a sleeping bag.'

She couldn't hide her disappointment. 'Couldn't we just be together, Ror? I'm not expecting anything. I mean, I don't want—'

'I need to sleep. In my own room.'

'Yes, of course.'

'And I need a bath.' He rubbed the stubble on his chin. 'And a shave. Then I'm going to sleep. I hope for a long time. Good night.'

'Night, night, Ror.' She kissed his cheek, close to his mouth. He appeared to sway a little and she laid a hand on his arm to steady him. 'Sleep tight.'

'Don't let the bed bugs bite.' His smile was strained and turned into a yawn.

Flora lay awake under the coarse blankets, watching the dying embers of her fire. The coals shifted, then collapsed and one toppled into the hearth. She got out of bed, replaced it with the tongs and rearranged the fireguard carefully. She stood for a moment staring into the fire, then went to the open door and listened. Rory had shut his door, so there was nothing to hear apart from a rattling window-frame and the wind in the trees outside. She padded over to his door, remembering to avoid a loose floorboard that creaked. She listened for a few moments but could hear nothing.

She wondered if he were dead. Had he brought pills with him, intending to overdose? Is that why he he'd wanted to sleep alone? Or was he hanging from the open window? Flora grasped the door handle then told herself Rory was simply tired out, sleeping soundly. She shouldn't disturb him. Raising her arms, she placed her palms on the door and pressed her body against the wooden panels, turning her cheek and flattening her ear against the chipped paintwork. She breathed his name but there was no answer.

Unpeeling herself from the door, she shuffled back to her own room. She tugged a couple of blankets off the bed and dragged them across the hall. Turning the door-handle slowly, almost silently, she pushed open the whining door, took a moment to get her bearings, then headed towards the uncurtained window above Rory's bed. Her eyes were adjusting to the darkness now and she could see his pale face, waxen in the moonlight, expressionless, like an effigy on a tomb. His hair, silvered by the moon, had fallen across his forehead. Flora thought he looked young again. Almost a boy.

As she stood by the bed, the blankets bunched in her arms, watching him, he opened his eyes and blinked.

'That you, Flor?'

'Yes.'

'Was that you crying?'

'Crying?'

'Outside the door.'

Had she cried? She didn't remember crying. Maybe she had.

'Suppose so. Sorry. Did I wake you?'

'I think I was awake anyway.' He rubbed his eyes.

She bent and stroked his hair back from his forehead. 'Go back to sleep.' She dropped the blankets on to the floor and started to arrange them on the bedside rug.

'Are you staying?'

'Yes.'

'Oh...' He rolled over in his sleeping bag and was asleep.

Flora wound herself in the blankets and lay down on the rug. She listened to Rory's steady breathing, synchronised hers with his and was asleep.

~

When I woke, stiff and cold, Rory was gone. I went back to my bedroom and pulled on a jumper over my pyjamas and pushed my feet into some shoes. I knew where he would be but I went to the kitchen first, filled the kettle and switched it on, then grabbed a coat and went outside.

He was standing down by the water's edge, his back towards me, his hands in his pockets, staring out to sea. He didn't turn as I picked my way across the rocks and pebbles, so I stood behind him, slipped my arms under his and round his waist, linking my hands. I lay my head in the hollow between his shoulder-blades and listened to his heart.

Eventually he said, so softly that I didn't hear, I only felt it. 'You missed the seal show.'

'Seen it before. Did they sing to you?'

'No, I sang to them.'

'Were you good?'

'I was rubbish.'

'Well, that's modern music for you. Have you had breakfast?'

'Not hungry.'

'There's bacon and eggs. Or I can make you some porridge. The kettle's on – shall we have some tea?'

'In a while, maybe.'

'Did you sleep?'

'Some... It never really gets dark here, does it? You forget the northern summer. The nights are never black, just grey... Dusk for hour after hour. And then it's dawn. A different grey.' He paused. 'Then it starts all over again.'

'What does?'

'The day. Bloody life.'

I felt the hard ridge of his ribcage rise and fall as he sighed. I squeezed him round the waist and said, 'It's all right now – you've got me. We've got each other. The nights won't be so bad for you. Not now.'

As he turned in my arms I let go and stepped back. I saw the tense set of his head, slightly bowed; the taut tendons in his neck that I longed to touch; the hollow at the base of his throat that I wanted to kiss.

314

An oystercatcher flew overhead, squealing, and Rory looked up, a sudden darting movement, like an animal startled. He looked back at me and his wide mouth stretched, his face creased into deep pleats, but his eyes stared, uncomforted. He looked away again, out to sea.

'You never realised, did you, Flor? You didn't know till you kissed me. In the bathroom. At Orchard Farm.'

'No. I didn't. Not consciously. I knew I loved you, but I didn't realise how much. I didn't know I wanted you. Not till I... I saw you then. It was like looking at a different person. Not my brother at all, just... a man. In all your maleness. You didn't seem like the other half of me any more. You seemed... complete. Completely yourself. Then I realised I loved you in every way it's possible to love somebody. I think it was the most terrible moment of my life... And the most wonderful.'

He nodded, then placed his left palm under my right. He twisted his hand, lacing his fingers with mine so you could hardly tell which were his and which were mine. He opened his mouth to speak but words wouldn't come. Staring at his face, stark with pain, with longing, I wanted to hold him, to trace the contours of his face and body with my hands, my mouth, to prove he was there, he existed, that he was mine, he was me.

But instead I said, 'When did you realise?'

'Know for sure, you mean?'

'Yes.'

Not looking at me, his eyes far away, he lifted his other hand, the dead hand. With a long, crooked forefinger he felt the golden stubble on his upper lip. 'You touched my mouth. When I was cutting your hair. We were sixteen.'

I shook my head. 'I don't remember.'

His voice was faint. 'I do.'

Twining his fingers with mine he smiled at me then, a luminous, blinding smile. Our fingers still locked, he raised his hand and pressed them to his lips, his eyelids closing slowly. His eyes remained shut and I watched as his lashes darkened and the pale skin in the hollows under his eyes became wet.

'Ror... How can loving someone be wrong?'

His eyelids flickered, then opened. 'It's not the love that's wrong.' He smiled again. 'It's what love makes us do.'

Tugging at my hand, he pulled me up the beach, towards the

315

house. He pushed the door open, slammed it behind us, then led me upstairs to the chilly bedroom. There we undressed each other, crying, laughing, like children unwrapping presents on Christmas morning.

1987

Hugh loaned Grace a clean handkerchief and escorted her to the gate. She stood on tip-toe to kiss his cheek, then got into her car and drove away. He returned to the garden bench and sat for some time, his head bowed, his hands clasped, as if praying. Eventually he stood, straightened his shoulders and set off towards the house.

He found Dora in the music room, sitting in front of the open French windows, her eyes closed, her mouth sagging open. A light breeze lifted silky white curls from her forehead but otherwise she sat motionless. There was something about the awkward way in which she sat slumped in her chair that made Hugh's heart miss a beat. Was Dora to be spared?... He bent and gently touched her mottled hand, the joints grotesquely swollen.

She woke with a start, her wasted limbs jolting like a marionette's. Composing herself neatly in her chair, she smiled up at him. 'Ah, Hugh! I was just having one of my catnaps. I had another bad night... Pull up a chair and tell me what's new in the garden. I haven't been out yet today.'

'Grace just called in. She sent her love. She had to rush off for an appointment. But she had some news.'

'Did she? Not good news by the sound of it.' Dora paused, fixing Hugh with her sharp blue eyes that missed nothing. 'Let me guess – Rory?'

'Yes. She says he's left her.'

'*Left* her?'

'Yes, I'm afraid so.'

'For somebody else?'

'She doesn't know. He's just disappeared.'

'Good grief! That *wretched* boy. Do you know, sometimes I think that family would be better off without him. He spreads misery like a disease. I'm sure Lottie comes here just to avoid her father.'

'There's more to it than that,' Hugh said carefully.

'Oh?' Dora looked at him, her head on one side, her eyes bird-bright. 'Don't be mysterious, Hugh. What's up?'

'Grace had some other news. Happier news.'

'Really? Well, *you* don't look too happy about it!'

'I'm still rather surprised. It's all come as a bit of a shock.'

'Come on, spill the beans. You know I hate surprises.'

'Theo and Charlotte are engaged. It would appear they are... in love.'

Dora said nothing, her face a blank. Eventually, shrinking back into her chair, she said, 'Theo and Lottie? Good God, are you *sure*?'

'Yes. It's come as a surprise to everyone, I think. Even Grace had no idea. I knew they were very fond of each other of course, but I thought it was more of a brother-sister relationship—' Hugh heard himself and looked away quickly, into the garden. 'I mean, I had no idea they felt that way about each other.'

'And they're engaged, you say? Well, well, well... They've caught us on the hop, haven't they?' She smiled, but Hugh could see it cost her an effort. 'Well, I suppose they're old enough to know their own minds.'

'Theo's twenty-one. Lottie must be... eighteen?' Dora nodded. 'Flora was only nineteen when I proposed to her.'

'Yes, but I'm not sure it could be said that Flora knew her own mind.'

'Or even that *I* did,' Hugh murmured.

They sat in silence for a while until Dora announced, 'They could change their minds. They're still very young. Are they sleeping together?'

Hugh was surprised by the frankness of the question. 'I've no idea! I wouldn't know what Theo gets up to over in the annexe. Once he turned eighteen I thought it best to turn a blind eye. But Lottie can't have been staying overnight. Grace would know.'

'Did Rory know about Lottie and Theo?'

'No. He's been gone a week and Lottie only told Grace yesterday. I think she was trying to cheer her up.'

'Bless the child! She has such a kind heart. So Rory doesn't know... Does Flora?'

'No.'

'Will you tell her?'

'I can't. Nobody actually knows where she is. She's left Colin apparently.'

Dora's fingers clutched at the arm of her chair as she struggled for words. 'She's *left* him?'

'Yes, according to Lottie. She rang Colin to tell him her news and he said Flora was no longer living with him. He doesn't know where she's gone. It's all rather worrying.'

Dora leaned back in her chair and closed her eyes. For a moment her lined face was contorted with pain, or perhaps anger, then in a thin voice like crackling parchment, she said, 'Flora will be with Rory.'

Hugh didn't reply. Instead he studied the intricate pattern of the faded carpet beneath his feet. Dora opened her eyes and regarded him. 'You know, don't you, Hugh? About my children?'

He lifted his head and said, 'Do *you*?'

'Oh, yes. I'm their mother after all.'

Hugh was silent for a long time, then said, 'How long have you known?'

'Oh, I suspect I knew before they did,' Dora said, her voice matter-of-fact. 'I always knew something wasn't right. But they were both such strange children... And being twins, one made allowances for their closeness. It's not as if I had any other children with whom I could make comparisons. But I can't say I ever actually *knew* because I never had any proof, but I always felt as if I knew in my heart... what they felt for each other. I watched them both make unhappy marriages as a substitute for being together. Oh, I was hugely relieved at first! I thought music would bind Grace and Rory together, music and... a physical relationship. But in that respect I underestimated Rory. And the depth of his feelings.' She shook her head and smiled. 'I wonder – in what respect did I *not* underestimate Rory?'

'Did Archie know too?'

'Oh, no, I don't think so! Well, if he did, he never said anything. Archie knew a great deal about sexual propagation in plants, but human beings were pretty much a closed book to him. Thank goodness,' she added. 'I'd hoped you'd be the salvation of my daughter, Hugh – you and babies. But I was wrong there as well. Flora didn't love Theo and I could see only one reason for that. Rory avoided the boy too. They both shunned him, didn't they, when he was small? It used to make me so angry. It still does... I did my best to compensate. I know you did too. But I was never sure whether that was because you were just a wonderful, natural father or because you knew. Knew Theo might not be yours. Is Theo your son?'

'No.'

'He's Rory's?'

'Yes.'

'I see.' Dora folded her hands in her lap, then said, 'I'm very sorry to hear it, for your sake, Hugh, but my respect for you – as a father, as a man – is possibly even greater now. Have you always known about Theo?'

'No. I believed him to be my son for the first eight years of his life. Then Flora told me he wasn't and eventually, because I pressed her, she told me whose child he was. It didn't make any difference to how I felt about him. It never has. I think of Theo as my own son. I think even Rory sees Theo as my son.'

'Does Rory know Flora told you?'

'Oh, yes. My relationship with Rory is... Well, let's say it's on a very frank footing. I don't think we have any secrets. We're friends of sorts. Despite everything. And if he has to hear this news about his children, I think it best he hears it from me. That's why I have to find him. He has to tell Theo.'

'You could tell him yourself.'

'I don't think I have the right. I'd rather it came from Rory.'

'It would be kinder to Theo to hear it from you.'

'You're probably right, but I'd still want Rory's permission. Or Flora's.'

'She wouldn't give it. I doubt she could bear the shame.'

'Then I have to find Rory.'

'Yes, I suppose you do.'

'And you think he'll be with Flora?'

'Yes, I'm afraid so.'

'Do you have any idea where they might have gone?'

Dora turned towards a side table and, lifting a heavy hand, reached for a black-and-white photograph in a silver frame. The Dunbar twins - kilted, blond, almost identical - stood side by side on a front door step, their arms linked. The head of one twin was turned towards the other and appeared to be speaking. The other twin, head thrown back, was laughing.

Dora stared at the photograph, her eyes moist. 'If I know my children – and I'm very much afraid I *do* – I think you'll find them both in Wester Ross. At *Tigh na Mara*. The house by the sea...'

~

There was no telephone at *Tigh na Mara* and never had been. Hugh decided against sending a letter because he didn't even know if Rory was there and time was of the essence. In view of Rory's possibly fragile mental state, Hugh thought it best to break the news personally but his journey to the north of Scotland had to be postponed for a couple of days to allow Theo and Charlotte to throw a family party to celebrate their engagement. Grace, still tearful, looked proud and happy and flirted outrageously with Theo. Charlotte hugged Hugh repeatedly. Dora sipped sherry, her smile fixed, her hands shaking slightly. Colin sent his apologies.

Hugh asked Theo to mind the nursery for a few days while he went to visit an elderly colleague who had been taken ill and was unlikely to recover. He was vague about when he might return.

Dora insisted on paying for a first-class sleeper and so Hugh travelled in relative comfort. 'Sleeper' was something of a misnomer, however. At no point on the long journey north was Hugh able to sleep.

As the taxi dropped him outside *Tigh na Mara*, Hugh recognised Rory's car. It wasn't until then that he realised he'd been praying Dora was wrong, that Rory and Flora would not be here, that they wouldn't be together.

The taxi driver helped Hugh with his case and wondered privately why an elderly man should be coming to such a god-forsaken spot to stay in a house that was thought locally to be little more than a ruin. It was on the tip of his tongue to recommend his sister's comfortable guest-house in Gairloch, but he thought better of it. The old gentleman seemed distracted and struggled to find the correct change.

Hugh stood in front of the house and listened as the taxi drove away. When he could no longer hear its engine he registered other sounds: the wind hissing in the pine trees; the cheerful slap of waves on the shore behind the house; the bubbling song of a curlew. An earthly paradise. Hugh raised his eyes to Heaven and was astonished to see a pair of heron flying overhead, their ungainly legs dangling like streamers on kites. He hoped it was a sign, a *good* sign.

He knocked on the door and waited, then turned the handle. Walking into the hallway, he cleared his throat of some obstruction and called Rory's name. There was no answer. He set down his case. They couldn't be far away, not without the car.

Perhaps they were upstairs.

Hugh felt an urgent need to announce his presence, to let them know they were no longer alone. He called out again, then, his heart beating too fast, he mounted the stairs.

He knew what he would find. During his sleepless night on the train he'd tried to prepare himself, to put away judgement, anger, sadness, even envy. He was here as a harbinger of bad news, not Flora's husband or Rory's would-be lover. Even so, it came as a shock and he grasped the banister for support as he reached the landing.

The bedroom door was open. They lay sleeping in a tangle of sheets and limbs, their naked bodies entwined. Rory lay on his side, his head resting on Flora's shoulder, his face pressed against the curve of her neck. Locks of her pale blonde hair had drifted across his face and stirred gently as he breathed out. A thin, pale arm curved round his shoulder and a small hand rested, its delicate fingers splayed, on the freckled ridge of Rory's shoulder-blade. His left arm, so much thicker and darker than Flora's, lay across her breasts, bent upwards at the elbow so that his fingertips – the ones that could still move, that still had sensation – touched the line of her jaw. Flora's right arm was thrown back on her pillow, circling her head in a gesture of abandon, her hand cupped like a flower opening. Her lips were parted slightly, her brow smooth. Studying her face, Hugh realised he'd rarely, if ever, seen Flora at peace. He'd seen her happy; never at peace.

Standing on the threshold, still grasping the door-handle, Hugh was gazing at Rory's sleeping face when he opened his eyes. He blinked several times, the long lashes brushing Flora's neck, then lifted his head slightly and looked towards the foot of the bed. He stared at Hugh and blinked again. Hugh held his gaze for as long as he could bear it, then looked down.

Rory began to extricate himself from the constraints of Flora's inert body. As he moved she rolled away from him, taking the sheets with her. He made a move to grab them, then thought better of it.

He watched Flora as she settled again with a sigh, still fast asleep. Drawing up his knees, Rory circled them with his arms and said, 'How did you find us?'

Hugh's voice was a whisper. 'Dora.'

Rory looked up, his face drained of all colour. 'She knows?'

'She guessed. A long time ago, apparently.'

'Jesus...' Rory covered his eyes with his good hand and began to shiver. Hugh wondered whether it was shock or if he was just cold in the unheated room.

'She thought you'd be with Flora. And she thought you might be here. I took a chance.'

'You've come to take me back.'

'Yes.'

'Why?'

Hugh suddenly felt like a very old man. He hesitated, then said, 'You're needed.'

Rory registered his grave expression and, not breathing, waited while Hugh struggled to compose himself. At length, wiping a hand across his mouth, Hugh said, 'Your daughter is in love with your son. They intend to marry... I think you'd better come home, Rory.'

PART FIVE

Chapter 25

1987

With Hugh seated beside him, Rory drove south, so fast that Hugh wondered if he'd decided once again that suicide would provide a solution to all his problems.

When they'd been driving in silence for half an hour, Rory suddenly pulled the car over to the side of the road. He reached across his body to open the car door with his left hand and got out. Without closing the door behind him he made straight for a ditch. Hugh watched as Rory's body suddenly jack-knifed and he vomited copiously into the ditch. He vomited again, sinking to his knees. Hugh got out of the car and hurried to his side. Laying his hands on Rory's shoulders he attempted to support him but Rory jerked forward again involuntarily as his already empty stomach attempted to void itself again.

Finally, when Rory was still, Hugh took a handkerchief from his pocket and handed it to him. Rory spat into the ditch several times, then wiped his face. Hugh helped him to his feet and guided him, stumbling, towards the passenger door. Rory climbed into the car and sat staring through the windscreen, white-faced. Hugh watched him for a moment, then got in behind the wheel and started the car.

Neither man had spoken.

Rory and Hugh went home and wrecked lives. Three of them, one after the other. It should have been four, but apparently Dora already knew. (I'd underestimated my mother's capacity for suffering in silence, just as she'd underestimated mine.)

After they'd gone and I'd finished sobbing, I packed up a picnic: the remains of the vodka, a bottle of tonic and an apple. I walked down to the shore and sat cradling the vodka, reading the label now and again, postponing the ecstatic moment. The beach was empty as usual, a desert of stones. I started to count them.

In the distance I could see toy fishing boats, cheerful splashes of blue and red. Huddled against the rocks, I drew my raincoat over my knees. Staring out over the greasy, grey sea, I unscrewed the vodka bottle and put it to my mouth.

1952

Rory scrambled up the rocks, his strong hands gripping and pulling, until he stood upright, hands on hips, precariously balanced on the tiny summit.

'*I'm the King of the Castle!*'

Flora looked up from below and shouted back, '*Get down, you dirty rascal!*'

'Who are you calling a dirty rascal?'

'You!' Flora slipped and, scrabbling at the rocks as she fell, landed on her bottom, sprawled in an undignified heap on a pile of seaweed. The surprise was considerable, the pain negligible, but she thought she'd cry anyway. It had the desired effect. She watched as her brother vaulted down to the ground and knelt beside her.

'Have you broken anything?' he asked eagerly.

She wailed and squeezed a grazed knee to encourage the flow of blood.

Rory stood up and wagged a finger. 'You shouldn't try to do what I do. You're only a *girl*.'

'But I *want* to do what you do. If I don't keep up with you, you'll leave me behind!'

'No, I won't. I'll never do that. I'll always wait for you.'

When the tonic bottle was half empty I topped it up to the brim with vodka. I spilt a little on my coat but it didn't show because by then it had started to rain. I thought of going back to the house but felt exhausted at the thought of moving, so I just turned up my collar. I'd lost the top off the vodka bottle so I scraped a hollow in the pebbles and wedged it upright with more stones.

The rain fell steadily and the waves thrashed at the shore leaving behind a dirty white scum which foamed over the stones. There was no way of telling what time it was. On the horizon leaden sea met leaden sky.

The tonic bottle was empty now. I had a little rest and then lifted the vodka.

1952

'What shall we do with the drunken sailor?
   What shall we do with the drunken sailor?
   What shall we do with the drunken sailor
   Ear-ly in the morning?'

Rory sat in the grounded wreck of the rowing boat, singing to Flora and pulling at invisible oars.

   'Put him in the longboat till he's sober—'

'What's that mean?'

'What?'

'Sober.'

'I don't know. The opposite of drunk, I think.'

Flora baled rainwater from the bottom of the boat with a rusting tin can. 'How did the sailor get drunk in the first place?'

'Don't know. He gets drunk before the song starts.'

'They should just throw him overboard,' Flora said cheerfully. 'Then they wouldn't have to sing all those boring verses.'

Rory stared, astonished by his sister's ruthless logic, then he laughed and started to row again.

When the sea began to boil like molten metal, I sang. Nursery rhymes, hymns, hits from the shows. I couldn't remember all the words of 'Jerusalem' *so I did* 'Abide with me' *instead:* 'When other helpers fail, and comforts flee...' *It seemed appropriate.*

I didn't notice Rory until he knocked the vodka bottle over. I lunged and caught it just in time.

'For God's sake, Rory – where've you been?' He said nothing but sat down beside me, the bottle between us. 'You gave me a scare back there. I really thought you were leaving me! You're so bloody selfish!'

He ignored me and stared out to sea.

'Are you listening? Rory, did you hear what I said?'

Still ignoring me, he got up and walked down the beach and into the sea. Except that he didn't walk into the sea, he walked on it, didn't he, like bloody Jesus. He walked out over the sea towards the fishing boats.

When he was well out to sea he turned round and looked back towards the beach, then had the nerve to wave at me. He waved his hand slowly in the air above his head, then turned and carried on walking.

I was livid. I stood up and hurled the empty tonic bottle after him. 'I hope you bloody well drown!'

Who is born to be hanged, will never be drowned.

He just kept walking, his figure becoming smaller and smaller as he strode out to sea. 'This is it, Rory! This is the end! Don't come crawling back to me because I won't want to know. I don't need you! I don't even want you any more! I'll be fine on my own, d'you hear me? Just fine! So you and Hugh and Grace – and all your bloody children! – you can all go fuck yourselves. And each other! I've had enough of you, the whole bloody lot of you – and that includes you, Rory Dunbar – d'you hear? I want to be on my own, so piss off and leave me in peace!'

But Rory was a speck on the horizon. Sinking down on to the wet stones, I screwed my fists into my eye-sockets until orange sparks shattered the darkness. I cried out and opened my eyes. He was gone.

Above the moaning of the wind and the roar of the waves I could hear a convulsive rattle. It sounded like somebody's teeth chattering. I stood up again, unsteady on the shifting pebbles, my legs numb with cold, my hand shaking uncontrollably as I reached for the bottle.

It will be easier to hate him, I thought.

Love has failed me.

You know where you are with hate.

There was a crunch of pebbles behind me. I wheeled round, clutching my bottle. A couple of young men in walking gear with rucksacks stood a few paces away, peering at me, hesitating, trying to decide if I needed help. One of them stepped forward, his hands raised to indicate he was harmless.

'You OK, love? Are you lost?'

I didn't answer but stood swaying, trying to decide how many men there were. I thought it was two but sometimes there were four. I said, conversationally, 'The wicked are like the troubled sea, when it cannot rest... Whose waters cast up mire and dirt...' I wiped my nose on the back of my frozen wet hand. 'Mire... and dirt.'

A pair of red-haired twins stepped forward and spoke in unison. 'Can we give you a lift somewhere?'

I shook my head. 'No. No, thanks... There is no peace,' I explained, 'Unto the wicked...'

One of the twins suddenly vanished into thin air. The other one said, 'Och, will you no' go in out of the rain? You look awfu' cold and wet, hen.'

I turned my palm upwards and laughed. 'Rory will be getting wet too! Serves him right.'

The young men looked at each other. One whispered something to the other, then turned back to me. 'Do you live round here, love?'

'No, I don't.' I thought hard for a long time and then it came to me. 'I don't live anywhere, actually. I'm squatting in a house nearby. I think technically,' – the word was an effort – 'I'm homeless.'

They looked at each other, alarmed. Their good turn was getting out of hand. 'Is there anyone we can contact? Husband? Children?'

'No.'

'A friend?'

'Haven't got any.'

'Isn't there anyone?'

'No, there isn't. Not any more.' I straightened up and tossed my dripping hair out of my eyes. 'There you have it – in a nutshell!' I lifted the bottle and declaimed: 'O God! I could be bounded in a nutshell and count myself a king of infinite space, were it not that I have... bad dreams.'

Someone started to whimper. Or perhaps it was the wind. I held the bottle out towards them. 'Would you care to join me for a drink, gentlemen? I'm afraid I had the last of the tonic some time ago...'

Rory told me what to do.

He was sitting on the stairs waiting for me when I got back to the house. He was draped in seaweed but his clothes and hair were dry. His eyes looked dead and I could see that the bad news and all the shouting had really taken it out of him.

I was so relieved he'd decided to come back, I didn't ask why we were carrying the paraffin stove upstairs. I thought he just wanted us to be warm. I thought we were going to bed. It must have been very late by then and we were both exhausted.

But we didn't go to bed. I watched as Rory lifted the paraffin stove on to the bed, unscrewed the cap of the fuel tank, then pushed the whole thing over. There was a slopping sound as paraffin splashed over the bedding and on to the floor.

I said, 'Now where are we going to sleep?'

Rory didn't answer but up-ended the stove, shaking it over the bedding. It was very awkward for him and I had to help because I could see it was hurting his bad hand. He pointed to the mantelpiece where the matches were and I handed them to him. He stood back from the bed and motioned me to do the same. I stood beside him and waited. He struck a match, waited for it to burn properly, then tossed it on to the bed.

There was a "woomph" and a big flash. I started to laugh. It was so exciting, like bonfire night. We didn't have any fireworks and we didn't have a Guy, but it was a lovely fire. The smoke didn't seem to bother Rory, but it filled my lungs and made me cough. My eyes were smarting so much, I couldn't really see. I reached for Rory's hand to pull him out of the room, but the smoke was so thick, I couldn't find him.

I missed my footing at the top of the stairs and fell but I managed to clutch at the banister halfway down and break my fall. I found I couldn't put weight on one of my ankles, so I crawled towards the front door, coughing, calling Rory's name. I looked back at the upstairs landing but there was no sign of him. Flames filled the bedroom doorway now and were creeping along the hall carpet.

The front door opened and I heard voices. They seemed familiar but I couldn't see who it was because of all the smoke. A man almost fell over me on the floor. He bent down and tried to help me to my feet. I cried out as my ankle took my weight. The man swore, then said, 'You'll be OK now, hen. Hold tight!' and then he lifted me up in his arms. He staggered towards the front door and I shouted, 'My brother! He's upstairs! You have to go and get him!' My rescuer stopped in the doorway and looked at his companion. They both turned and looked upstairs. The landing was a now a wall of flame.

The men said nothing and carried me outside, struggling and screaming.

I don't really remember much more. Not in any detail. Not after Tigh na Mara. *My story becomes… blurred.*

It ended then for me. The rest was just tying up ends. The end of my tether, mainly. There was no happy ending. There never could have been. Not for Rory and me.

He tried very hard to find me. He and Hugh. It was Hugh who identified my body. They asked him because he was still my husband, though Rory was of course my next of kin.

A little more than kin and less than kind.

Rory insisted on going with him and Hugh didn't try to stop him. He knew Rory would never accept I was dead unless he'd seen my body. That was the first time I saw Rory from my current perspective. I mean, Rory being alive and me being dead. Finally we were separate. It was a strange feeling, though even then I wouldn't concede defeat.

It was only after that final separation that I discovered how my brother really felt about me. I suppose I'd always known in a way, but it was still a terrible shock, to be the cause of such grief. It was unbearable. For both of us. I think it nearly killed Rory. If I'd been alive the spectacle would have killed me. To see him suffer so and not be able to comfort him… And I'd thought death would be the end of my torment. It was just another beginning.

World without end. Amen.

Hugh held him. He held him up with his massive hands while Rory sagged in his arms like a rag doll, sinking towards the floor, as if his skeleton had been removed. He looked like Raggy Aggie, the rag doll Ettie had made for me as a child. Rory decided one day, with arbitrary cruelty, that we should 'execute' Aggie. He got a penknife and stabbed her where her heart would have been. We watched with morbid fascination as Aggie leaked sawdust on to the ground, slowly emptying herself until she was nothing but a handful of worn, grubby rags sewn together.

That's what happened to Rory. As I watched, grief emptied him. He collapsed in on himself, cried out, swore, sobbed until he retched. Hugh just held his limp form and said nothing, his face impassive. As a clergyman, Hugh had seen his share of death, but in any case his entire mind and body were bent on supporting Rory, willing strength and love into him. Into what was left of him.

Hugh and I fought a battle for Rory then and I believe Hugh knew it. I was willing Rory to join me – God knows, it was what he wanted!

– but Hugh refused to let him go. He wouldn't give up. His solidity, his physical and moral strength, his bloody-minded determination anchored Rory, tethered him to his body. Rory stood on the brink and looked down, but Hugh dragged him back.

So Hugh won.

Perhaps because he loved Rory even more than I did.

Did he? I've never been sure. It depends what you mean by love. Hugh never needed him as I did. He wouldn't have killed for Rory, as I would have. But he loved him enough to let him go, to let him be. Until the end. My end. Hugh wouldn't let him go then. He held on to Rory and wouldn't let him go.

We all have our limits, I suppose. Love too has its limits, though they are not – as I discovered – temporal or geographical. Rory and I never accepted those limits, didn't even really know what they were. When you don't even know where you end and someone else begins, you grow up with a hazy understanding of boundaries. You might not know you've crossed a line that should never have been crossed. You don't even see the line.

If I'd died at Tigh na Mara, would it have been a better end? If I'd died in a domestic conflagration like mad Mrs Danvers or the equally mad Mrs Rochester? If I'd gone out with a bang and a puff of smoke like the Demon King? It would have spared my family a great deal if it had all been over and done with then. But being one of life's bloody survivors, I still had a good few years to run. It wasn't yet my cue to bow out. My incendiary brush with death was just a false alarm.

A dress rehearsal, you might say, for my farewell performance.

1987

At around midnight Rory and Hugh stopped at a motorway service station. Hugh had been dozing while Rory drove. He sat up and looked around the car park.

'Where are we?'

'England,' was Rory's laconic reply.

In the brash and noisy cafeteria Hugh brought tea and bacon rolls to a table where Rory sat slumped, staring into space.

'I'm not hungry.'

'Eat it anyway. You must either eat or sleep. You can't dispense with both and continue to function.'

Rory picked up the roll and chewed without enthusiasm.

After a while Hugh said, 'One wonders whether this music is provided for the benefit of the customers or the staff. There's no escape, even in the lavatory. You must find this kind of musical vandalism more of a trial than most people.'

Rory swallowed a mouthful of tea, his face expressionless. 'I can shut it out. I play Beethoven in my head. Or I think about which poor sods prostituted their art to pay the mortgage and whether I'd rather not play at all than have to play such crap.'

'And what conclusion do you come to?'

'That I'd have liked the luxury of choice.'

They finished their meal in silence then walked back to the car. As Hugh got behind the wheel Rory said suddenly, 'You realise I only went to Flora to prove it couldn't work, that it was over before it even began. She never would have accepted it without... proof.'

'I don't think she does, even now.'

'We should have brought her home.'

'We did try.'

'I thought of knocking her out. Abducting her.'

'So did I, funnily enough. But I couldn't bring myself to batter my wife. I know it's very hard, but Flora must be allowed to choose her own path.'

'Do you choose insanity?' Rory asked as he fastened his seat-belt. 'Or does it choose you?'

'A bit of both I suppose. Like homosexuality. We do the best we can with what we're given.' Rory turned his head and gave Hugh a look that would have blistered paint. 'Sorry. I'm sermonising, aren't I? Old habits die hard.' Hugh put the key in the ignition. 'What were you going to do afterwards?'

'Afterwards?'

'After you'd made your point. Convinced Flora you had no future together. Would you have gone home?'

'No. I told Grace we were finished.'

'Is that true?'

Rory paused. 'I don't know.'

'So... afterwards?'

'Unfinished business. Finishing something I started a long time ago.'

Hugh was silent for a moment. 'Then you and Theo are quits. You

333

gave him life... and he gave you back yours.'

'I didn't want it.'

Hugh sighed. 'I rather fear Theo might feel the same way once he knows.'

'Does he really have to know?'

'Charlotte does. You must tell her.'

'And she'll tell Theo.'

'No, if you don't mind, Rory, *I'll* tell Theo.'

I woke up in a hospital bed. I didn't know where I was. I didn't know who I was.

They asked me my name and I said 'Joan.' The nurse said 'Joan what?' and I said, 'Just Joan... Saint Joan, if you must know.' She went away and came back with a hatchet-faced Sister who asked a lot of questions. I didn't bother to answer. They told me I was being treated for superficial burns and asked if I knew how the fire had started. I said I couldn't remember. But I did. I knew I had to find Rory and see if he was all right.

I sat up in bed and told them I had to leave immediately. They said I was being kept in for observation. I told them, no, I bloody wasn't and asked for my clothes back. The Sister and I had a row and I won by yelling loud enough to upset the other patients. When they finally brought me my clothes, they smelled of smoke. And Rory.

I discharged myself, stepped outside the hospital into the rain and realised I didn't have a coat. I started looking around for a bus or a taxi. It was only then it occurred to me I didn't have any money either. I wasn't going to go back in and let that snotty cow laugh at me, so I started walking, keeping an eye open for a phone-box. I thought I could ring Colin. I could reverse the charges and he'd come in a taxi and pick me up. I was trying to remember his number when I noticed that the buses were the wrong colour.

I wasn't in London. I stared in disbelief at the names on the front of the buses. Culloden. Aviemore. Grantown on Spey.

I wasn't even in England.

I'd been taken to Inverness. I'd just discharged myself from Raigmore Hospital, Inverness. I didn't have a coat and I didn't have any money, not even a coin with which to make a phone call. I was standing in the rain in the short summer dress and sandals I'd thrown on earlier that day at Tigh na Mara. *I was six hundred miles from anyone I knew.*

So I kept walking.

I stopped and asked a woman if I was going the right way to the station. I wondered how far I could get without a ticket, if I could even get on a train without one. Fighting panic, I decided when I got to the station I would ring Orchard Farm, reverse the charges and ask Hugh what to do. Then it occurred to me Hugh wouldn't be there.

How did I know that?...

I'd seen Hugh recently. Today, in fact. Or was it yesterday? When I'd left the hospital I'd thought it was daytime but now I knew how far north I was I realised it could in fact be quite late, even though it was only just beginning to get dark.

I knew Hugh wasn't in Suffolk. He'd been to see me. Rory and me. Then he'd left. With Rory. But Rory had come back. Hadn't he?

Where was Rory?

I stood in a phone-box, sheltering from the rain, shivering, rehearsing the words I would say to my mother when she picked up the phone. But there was some reason I couldn't ring Ma, I knew there was. Some really important reason, only I couldn't remember what it was. Then it came to me. The shock was so bad I was nearly sick on the spot.

Ma knew.

She knew about Rory and me. Had known for years. She even knew about Theo. Hugh had said. He'd gone home to tell her he'd found us. That he'd found me in bed with my brother.

My mother knew.

She knew, but she'd never understand.

I stumbled out of the phone-box shaking uncontrollably. I started walking again, fast, to keep warm, but my feet were hurting. The streets got darker, there were fewer shops, fewer people. I stood under a lamp-post and looked up and down the road, trying to decide what to do. I was hungry and I needed to pee. I thought I'd look for a pub but I had no idea what time it was. I hadn't seen a bus for nearly an hour and I suspected the pubs were shut. A car pulled up and the window slid down. I thought for a moment it was Hugh – the driver was a big man and he had thick grey hair. I stepped towards the car and leaned in at the window, smiling.

It wasn't Hugh.

The man didn't smile at me. His manner was quite curt. He asked me something. I thought it was about directions but his accent was so thick I didn't catch what he said until he told me to 'Stop fucking about and get in the car'.

Then for some reason I remembered the man with the sweets. The barley sugars. The man who'd been kind when it was raining and offered me a lift home from the park. Who'd touched me with his warm, rough hands, hands that shook while I unwrapped my barley sugar. I never told Ma. She would have been so angry. And I knew she wouldn't have understood...

I told the man my name was Joan. He said, 'Get in,' and pulled away from the kerb before I'd even closed the door.

1987

Rory turned the key in his own front door, bracing himself. As he entered, Grace called out from the kitchen.

'Lottie, don't go out leaving me to do your washing-up! How many times do I have to tell you? And if you must burn scrambled egg,' She turned away from the sink, wrestling with rubber gloves. 'Do you think you could – oh my God – Rory!'

Standing in the doorway, he watched her curb the impulse to take him in her arms; noted in a distant annexe of his exhausted brain where stimuli still registered faintly, that he wanted to take her in his. Grace scowled, her usual stratagem for avoiding tears. 'You've got a bloody nerve. After that letter!'

'I know. I'm sorry. Where's Lottie?'

'At Orchard Farm.'

'She's sleeping there?'

'Yes. Things have moved on a bit in your absence.'

'I know. We need to talk, Grace.'

'Too bloody right we do. Where the hell have you been?'

'No. Talk about Lottie. And Theo.'

'How about talking about Rory and Grace? If you've come back to lay down the law about those two, you can just bugger off again. They're deliriously happy and I won't have you spreading any more of your wretched misery. This family deserves some happiness! We've paid our dues, Rory. We've suffered with you and for you, but it's time we all moved on.'

'Grace, please – I've been on the road for fourteen hours. Will you stop ranting and sit down? There's something I need to tell you—'

'Where on earth have you been?'

'At *Tigh na Mara*.'

'Dear God.' Her hand flew to her mouth.

'I went to see Flora. She was staying there.'

'Did you bring her back with you?'

'No. She's still there.'

'God, I hope not.'

'What do you mean?'

'*Tigh na Mara's* burned down. It's destroyed. Dora was on the phone an hour ago. The police have been in touch. They said it looked like arson. Dora's been out of her mind with worry. She must have known Flora was there... Rory? Where are you going? Rory! Come back! There's nothing you can do now!'

Grace watched as the front door slammed.

Chapter 26

At some point I died. Not in the fire at Tigh na Mara, *although I believe some part of me must have died there. The person on the road, on the streets, the person who ended up in London was... damaged.*

Damaged goods.

She wasn't whole. There was something missing, something important...

It is better for thee to enter into life halt or maimed, rather than having two hands or two feet to be cast into everlasting fire.

Rory...

A single soul dwelling in two bodies.

I got back to London. Eventually. I thought I could ask Colin for money, just a loan until I got straight, but when I went back to his house they said he'd moved. They wrote down the telephone number for me on a piece of paper but I lost it. I went back again the next day but there was no answer.

I found a hostel. A bag lady told me where to go. She was kind. People are. People on the streets are very kind. They look out for each other. Even the crazy ones.

In the early months I got work now and again, but the trouble was, when I did get work I spent the money on booze. Then I lost the job. It was a vicious circle. I was only ever drunk when I was working. Sally used to say, 'Oh Joan, what are *we going to do with you?' then she'd laugh and show a set of large yellow teeth that always made me think of piano keys.*

What shall we do with the drunken sailor?
What shall we do with the drunken sailor?
What shall we do with the drunken sailor
Ear-ly in the morning?
Or indeed at any other time?

Sally found me crying in a doorway. That wasn't her name. She was called Evangeline or Adeline — something grand. I called her Sally because she belonged to the Salvation Army. She didn't mind. In fact she laughed. Sally laughed a lot. She was the jolly sort. It got a bit wearing after a while, but she was very kind.

Sally talked to me. Well, mostly she listened. She tried to persuade me to contact my family. She said they'd be very worried about me. I told her it just wasn't possible and she seemed to understand. Then we had a nice chat about Jesus and how he would always look after me. But it was Sally who got me into another hostel, not Jesus. (There was a man there who said he was Jesus, but he wasn't.)

I never liked mixed hostels. I never felt really safe. Men looked at me. The way Rory sometimes looked at me. And Hugh never did.

I tell thee, churlish priest,
A ministering angel shall my sister be,
When thou liest howling.

I didn't stay at that hostel long. I preferred to keep moving on.

The wicked are like the troubled sea, when it cannot rest...

1987

'It's at times like this that I wish I smoked.' Grace placed her hand over her mouth and her eyes filled. Seated on the piano stool, his back towards the instrument, Rory looked away. She composed herself and went on in a low voice, 'I've always known you weren't faithful. I'd learned to live with that. It wasn't easy. But then nothing about loving you has ever been easy.'

Rory said nothing and they sat in silence.

'Hugh loves you as well, doesn't he?' Rory looked up, astonished, his lips moving soundlessly. 'Oh, I guessed years ago. After Flora left him. He was totally immune to the charms of various attractive widows who made it clear they were available. I don't think Hugh even saw them. I wasn't sure if you realised, if I should tell you...' A thought struck her and she put her head on one side, regarding Rory with narrowed eyes. 'Did you sleep with Hugh as well?'

'No, of course not!'

'So you do draw the line somewhere. That's comforting.'

'And that was cheap.'

'Yes, it was, wasn't it?' Grace gave him a tight little smile and leaned back in her chair. 'But I think I'm allowed a little bad behaviour as well, don't you? I've surely earned the right?'

'Yes, I suppose you have.'

'Did Flora sleep with you because of Hugh? She must have known. Was it spite?'

'No. She loves me. She's always loved me. But she married Hugh.'

'And you always loved her.'

'Yes.'

'And married me. Did you ever love me?'

'Yes.'

'Do you still?'

He hesitated. 'Yes.'

'Why should I believe you?'

His grey eyes were candid. 'Because it's true?'

'You left me for Flora.'

'No. I left you to... finish things. Finish with Flora, finish with life. I'd had enough. And it got Colin off the hook. That was what you wanted, wasn't it?'

'But it isn't finished. Flora almost certainly isn't dead. They haven't found a body. It isn't over yet.'

'It is. She won't come back now. She's lost. She's living in her head. In the past. She's in her own private hell – where she's no doubt making new friends. People always take pity on Flora. She looks so helpless.'

'God, you're callous!'

'Only if you regard me as a human being. For a music machine I'm quite sensitive.' He spun round on the music stool, put his foot on the sustaining pedal, and, spreading the fingers of his left hand, played a soft, low chord. The harmony echoed in the dining room, persisting for many seconds. As the sound died away he said, 'The trouble is, I'm neither one thing nor the other now. Hugh's been giving me lessons in humanity. I'm not a very apt pupil, but fortunately he's a dedicated teacher.'

'The man's a bloody saint.'

'Yes, I think he probably is. No wonder Flora found him

impossible to live with. She preferred lying in the moral gutter with me.' Putting his foot on the pedal again, Rory raised his damaged hand to the keyboard, formed a question mark with his index finger and picked out a succession of notes, one by one. They hung in the air, vibrating with each other, forming an eerie chord.

Grace said nothing for a while, then, as if with an effort, she breathed, 'Poor Flora. I don't know why I should blame her for loving you or expect her to be able to stop… I've never managed to do it.'

Rory stared down at the keyboard, his head bowed, his spine rigid. Grace rose from her chair, moved forward and took him, unresisting, in her arms.

Rory was right. As usual. He'd said I'd get offers. From men.
Plenty of them.
I did.
Mire and dirt…
How can loving someone be wrong?
It's not the love that's wrong, Flor, it's what love makes us do.

I saw Rory once. On a television screen. It was winter. It might have been Christmas. I remember the streets twinkled and there were fairy lights in all the shops. I was walking to get warm – it was too cold to sit and beg – and I passed an electrical shop with a bank of television screens. I stopped to watch. I often used to do that. It passed the time.

It was Rory. He was conducting something. I'd never seen him conduct before, didn't even know he could do it. It looked like a young people's orchestra. I couldn't hear anything of course. Rory was just waving the baton about, like a conjuror doing tricks.

He looked exactly the same. More lined, but basically it was the same old Rory I remembered. He slowly disappeared as my breath condensed on the cold plate glass. By the time I'd wiped it with my sleeve he'd gone. There was a man talking to camera but it wasn't Rory, so I moved on.

Colin practically tripped over me. Not long before I died. Well, it might have been months, I don't really remember, but it wasn't years. It was all the same to me by then.

I was begging on Waterloo Bridge, on the steps as you go down to the South Bank. It's nice and sheltered there. People come upon you suddenly, rounding the corner and they feel embarrassed. Sometimes they give you their small change. The thing is, you see, you mustn't beg aggressively. You mustn't give people a reason to despise you, to think, 'Well, she wouldn't be on the streets if there weren't a very good reason.'

(What would be a good reason, I wonder?)

People want to think it's your fault. It helps them cope with their guilt and shame, shame that people like me exist. So you must never look angry, or mad, or as if you expect them to give you anything. You just have to look hopeful. And grateful. Grateful in advance of receiving anything. It's quite a tricky balance to get right.

I think it helped that I'd been an actress. And of course simply being a woman was good training. I'd spent years cultivating a hopeful-but-grateful, 'for what we are about to receive' expression as a clergy wife and I found it stood me in good stead for most of the situations I found myself in, including sex with total strangers and begging on Waterloo Bridge.

Which is where I was sitting when I saw this pair of legs go by, then stop. I looked up cautiously and saw that the man had turned back to look at me, was staring at me, in fact. (They don't do that. They almost never do eye contact, even when they give you money. They're ashamed it's not more, that they aren't emptying the contents of their Italian leather wallets into your lap.)

It was Colin. I looked down and started coughing violently. (That drives people away. They think you're going to give them TB or something.) As soon as Colin was out of sight I gathered up my things and moved on.

I never went back. Shame. It was a good pitch and I used to like watching the actors and actresses going down to the National Theatre. Some of them were quite generous. I suppose they knew what it was like to fall on hard times. I saw Jack Cunningham once. Jack, my student Hamlet, my first love. (Apart from Rory.) He'd put on weight and really gone to seed. I was quite shocked.

He didn't look at me. Well, Jack never looked at me, did he, even when I was worth looking at. Jack was gay and I never realised, *stupid bitch. I was wasting my time there. Jack was bent, like my bloody husband.*

It is better to marry than to burn.

Oh, really? Not a lot to choose between them if you ask me.

I wish it was me. I'd fuck you to kingdom come.

Is that what you did, Rory? Did you fuck me to kingdom come?

You said it was what you'd always wanted, Flor... That's what you said. You said you wanted me. Me... Always...

I burn...

I burn...

1987

When Flora woke her hand was resting in the small of Rory's back. Without opening her eyes she identified the downy hollow and spread her fingers slowly till her hand filled the warm, moist concavity. She ran her hand along the ridge of his spine and buried her fingers in the tangle of damp hair at the nape of his neck.

She opened her eyes. Grey light. The dingy bare walls of the bedroom looked bleak. 'We should have had sun, Rory,' she thought. She looked at him, lying on his front, his face pillowed in his arms. She traced the curve of his arm and shoulder with her fingertips, then moved down over his shoulder-blade, feeling the projection of bone through the scant covering of flesh.

Rory stirred and opened his eyes. He said nothing but lay still, staring at her as if he were fixing something in his memory. Then he propped himself up, bent his head and kissed her gently on the mouth. Flora rolled on to her back and he kissed her again, his lips travelling down over her throat. She kissed his hair, cradled him against her breasts, inhaled the smell of him, her heart and womb leaping.

He lifted his head and smiled sleepily. Slipping an arm under her waist he lifted her bodily towards and under him, marvelling at the lightness of her. As he raised himself over her she nuzzled him gently with her thigh. He was already hard. She moaned softly as her thighs took the now familiar weight of his body. Rory hesitated, her small, thin body under his, so pale, so fragile, but she grasped the bones of his hips and pulled him down and into her. As her body arched up towards him she gasped, then whimpered like some crazed, injured animal. He lifted his head and looked down at her, pinned and splayed like a butterfly. She writhed and looked away, ashamed of her ecstasy.

'Look at me, Flor.' She felt the vibrations of his voice deep inside her, felt his ribcage move against hers as he breathed deeply. 'Look at me...'

He wanted, more than anything, he wanted her to trust him again, as she had once, when they were children. She looked up at him, askance, embarrassed. Gazing down into her fearful eyes, willing her not to break the contact, he started to thrust, gently at first, then harder. She began to relax, succumb to his rhythm, her eyes narrow with pleasure.

'Stay with me, Flor... Look at me!'

Her slack mouth moved, opening and closing as if trying to form words. She lifted both hands and touched his face, then spread her fingers in his hair. She tugged at it gently and held his head a moment, cupped in her hands, looking at him, then pulled his face down to hers. He silenced her sobs with the pressure of his mouth.

Hugh wrote me a letter. I don't know how many times he must have photocopied it. Several of them found their way to me. Because of the photo I suppose. It was a good likeness.

The letter begged me to let somebody in the family know I was alive and well. (The Salvation Army and Shelter won't tell families where you are. They respect your decision. Your right to privacy. They took Hugh's letter and passed it on, but they wouldn't have told him they'd seen me. They're good like that.)

Hugh didn't actually ask me to come home, which I imagine was out of deference to Theo. He said Dora was now very frail; Charlotte had gone abroad to work as an au pair *and had plans to go to Australia. He gave me no news of Theo other than that he was still living and working at Orchard Farm. He told me Rory was still living with Grace and he gave me their telephone number, asking me to contact Rory if I didn't feel I could ring Orchard Farm.*

It was a nice letter. Kindly meant. I kept it with all my newspaper cuttings in a big envelope safety-pinned to the lining of my coat. (Sally got me a very good coat. 100% wool and almost new. It was too big for me but that didn't matter so much in the winter because I wore so many layers of clothing. Insulation is the key to survival. Layers that trap the air and keep you warm, layers of material or newspaper.)

I wasn't surprised to hear that Rory had gone back to Grace. Where else was he to go after we'd burned down Tigh na Mara? *I told him it was a stupid idea but he wouldn't listen. Rory never listened to anybody. Except perhaps Hugh. You had to listen to Hugh. For a clergyman, he talked a lot of sense.*

1987

His hands far from steady, Hugh unpacked sandwiches on to the picnic rug and poured tea from a Thermos. He passed the plastic cup to Theo, perched on a tomb in the lee of Blythburgh Church, his long legs extended, his eyes downcast. Theo took the cup without speaking but didn't drink. He was studying the activities of a ladybird greedily devouring aphids on an adjacent rosebush. He looked away in disgust but the image of the ladybird conjured from some mental jukebox the children's rhyme:

Ladybird, ladybird, fly away home.
Your house is on fire and your children are gone.

Theo thought briefly of *Tigh na Mara,* of children yet unborn, then became aware that Hugh was speaking.

'...the work of vandals, undoubtedly. Nothing's sacred any more. I gather people steal them to put in their back gardens. With the gnomes.' Hugh was pointing to a broken statue of an angel, a tasteless monument to Victorian vulgarity erected over a child's grave. After a pause, he said in a low voice, 'If I'd been a better husband to her, Flora would never have known whose child you were. She would have enjoyed the luxury of doubt. And therefore hope.'

Theo sipped his tea in silence.

Hugh indicated the packet of sandwiches that lay untouched. 'Don't suppose you want to eat?'

Theo shook his head, then said, 'So she passed me off as yours. For how long?'

'Eight years.'

'*Jesus...*'

'I think those years must have been very hard for her. She never stopped loving Rory. She never has. I don't think she ever will. I would have told you long before now that I wasn't your father if it weren't that telling that particular truth would have required me to tell others, even less palatable. Neither Rory nor Flora wanted you to know about your parentage and I respected that. I suppose I didn't want you to know either. I wanted you to think you were my son. But in any case, none of us could ever see any reason why you would need to know. There was only one, of course, and I suppose we should have seen that coming. Perhaps if we'd told you who you really were, it might have altered your feelings for Charlotte. But Rory and Flora always knew their love was impossible and, as far as I can tell, it never made the slightest difference to how they felt. Merely increased the guilt factor.'

Theo looked up. 'Does Charlotte know? About me?'

'No, not yet. If you don't want to tell her yourself, Grace has said she'll do it.'

'*Grace?* She knows too?'

'Yes. Apart from it being an appalling shock for her too, she was very upset on your behalf. She's very fond of you, Theo. Always has been.'

'Chip off the old block, I suppose,' Theo said with a derisive laugh.

Hugh's expression was pained. 'For whatever reason, Grace thought you and Charlotte were good for each other. It's my impression that she's never had any illusions about Rory's fidelity, but she had no idea about Flora.'

Theo was silent for a few moments, then said, 'Grace must hate my mother.'

'Yes, she probably does now. It wasn't always so. They were friends once, many years ago. Before Flora and Colin ...'

'Ah, yes, Flora and *Colin*. Not content with stealing Grace's husband she has to sleep with her son as well. God, my mother is a *monster*!' Theo flung his tea at the rosebush and tossed the cup back down on the rug. He folded his arms across his chest and bowed his head.

Hugh looked up and saw Theo's eyes shut tight, his lips compressed to a thin line. In a deliberate, measured tone he said, 'Flora must have been lonely in London. Frustrated. Hard up. She'd turned her back on everyone, including Rory... Colin is a likeable young man. Good-looking. They were both adults. I think her affair with Colin was probably an ill-advised attempt to get over Rory, to start again. I believe she meant well. Flora never did anything with the intention of hurting you or Charlotte. Nor did Rory. You have just been caught, very badly, in the cross-fire.'

Theo looked up, his face contorted with anguish. 'You should never have told us!'

'Possibly not. We gave it a great deal of thought. Many harsh words were said.' Controlling his breath with some difficulty, Hugh continued, 'Flora didn't want either of you to know. But Rory wanted Charlotte to know, so I had a casting vote, so to speak. I thought you both had a right to know.'

'We had a right *not* to know!'

'Yes, that's what Flora said. She did have your interests at heart, you see. She wanted you to be happy. She saw no reason why *you* should pay for her sins. But if Charlotte conceived your child it would be the product of two generations of brother-sister incest. I think you must accept that she had a right to know.'

Theo was silent. Eventually he nodded.

Hugh continued. 'It's up to Charlotte now what she decides to do. It all depends on how much she wants a child, I suppose.'

'You mean, if she wants a child more than she wants me.'

'Yes, to put it baldly. Leaving aside the moral and legal issues, it boils down to that. And I think you should prepare yourself for the worst, Theo. It isn't possible for men to understand how much a woman may want and *need* a baby. Your mother wanted one so desperately she was prepared to keep her brother's.'

'But Flora never *loved* me, did she?'

For a moment Hugh wrestled with a strong temptation to lie, then braced himself. 'She tried. I think she tried very hard. Life was so difficult for her. Perhaps if you'd looked less like Rory... People were always commenting on the resemblance – quite innocently of course. But Flora heard reproach in those comments. She saw you as the living embodiment of her sin. You know, she was very devout when she was young. And she was a clergy wife. God didn't exactly cut her a lot of slack. I think she *tried* to love you, but shame got in the way. In the end she left – and I gave her my full support to do so – because she thought it would be the lesser of two evils. And she knew she could rely on me to look after you. She knew I would make a better job of it than she would.'

Theo stared at the elderly man he'd always believed to be his father. 'Did Flora ever love *you*?'

'Oh, yes, I believe so.' Hugh's smile was ghostly, ironic. 'She loved me – as she loved Colin, I suppose – with what was left over. After Rory.'

You had to be resourceful, living on the streets. Especially in the winter. It reminded me of when I was at the vicarage: hiding booze, stealing money, the daily challenges I had to meet, just to get by.

Food wasn't really a problem. There were soup kitchens and in the summer people would leave perfectly good food lying around in parks or on café tables. I used to steal fruit from an Asian grocer's. As I walked past I'd palm apples and oranges from his displays outside the shop. He caught me at it once and gave me a really good talking to. I told him I missed fresh fruit and that all you could scrounge, all you were ever given as hand-outs was junk. He thought this was shocking, made a speech about vitamins and told me to call by at the end of the day when he would give me a bag of bruised fruit. He even gave me a knife to cut out the bruised bits.

His name was Mr Patel and he was very kind. If it weren't for Mr Patel I might have died of scurvy.

1987

When Rory walked into the pub Hugh was already seated at a table studying a pint of Guinness, barely touched. Rory ordered at the bar, then joined him, dispensing with formalities.

'What did he say?' Hugh opened his mouth to speak but Rory forestalled him. 'I want to know what he said, not what you wish he'd said.'

Hugh stared into his Guinness, disconsolate. 'He doesn't want anything to do with you. He doesn't want to see you and he doesn't want to talk about it.'

'He hates me.'

'He didn't say that.'

'But he does. My God, I've fathered three children,' Rory muttered, 'and they all hate me.'

'It will take time.'

Rory lifted his pint. 'He also said – but you're far too kind-hearted to tell me – that you're the only father he's ever known, the only father he's ever wanted and that it makes absolutely no difference to him.' He drank deep while Hugh gazed at him, open-mouthed.

'Yes. He did. How did you know that?'

'I know Theo. He's a nice kid. Well done, Hugh. You won the jackpot. It couldn't happen to a nicer chap. I take it you didn't tell him about the love of *your* life?'

'No, I didn't,' Hugh said faintly. 'I thought the poor boy had suffered enough for one day.'

Chapter 27

1987

Rory was waiting for Theo in the music room at Orchard Farm, standing by the French windows, looking out on to the terrace. When his son entered Rory turned and, noting Theo's belligerent look, said, 'Thank you for agreeing to see me.'

Theo regarded his father, shorter by several inches, and said, 'I'd like to knock you down.'

Rory spread his hands. 'Go ahead. Break every bone in my body if you think it'll help. We could smash up the piano together in an act of therapeutic vandalism.'

Theo folded his arms and said, 'Can we get this over with?'

'Certainly. I won't insult you by claiming I know how you feel, but obviously I of all people *do* have some idea. I won't pretend it'll get easier. It never did for me. Or Flora.' Rory pushed his hands into his jacket pockets and looked down at the floor. 'I haven't been a good father to my children – *any* of my children – but in my defective, emotionally crippled way, I do love them.' He looked up at Theo, steely grey eyes meeting icy blue. 'Lottie had to be told. Which meant you had to be told. It was our intention – Flora's, Hugh's and mine – that you should never know your parentage. Since you'd acquired the world's best father in exchange for your own, we didn't see why you ever should. I thought you'd actually got a much better deal. When – *if* – you ever stop being angry with me, I think you'll agree.'

Rory paused, regarded Theo's handsome and impassive face for a moment, then continued. 'I hoped Lottie would have you anyway, but she seems to have inherited some sort of over-active conscience. Nothing to do with her Dunbar genes, it must come from Grace's side of the family, I suppose. To spare her feelings, I've refrained from pointing out that when I was a music student I donated sperm – as lots of us did – to raise cash. Theoretically, Lottie could travel halfway round the world and fall in love with another of my children. So could you. It's all a bloody lottery.'

Theo said nothing but Rory thought he detected a softening around the mouth. His eyes had widened and Rory knew he was listening intently. If he'd taught his son anything it was how to listen – to birds, to insects, to music. 'The only thing that matters as far as I can see is to try not to *hurt* each other. If you can, find a way to love each other still, retain some of what you had. But if she wants to let go, Theo, then just... let her go. Don't bully her. You'll probably find you're able to live without Lottie – eventually – but I doubt you'll be able to live with having hurt her, having made her do something she didn't really want to do.' Rory took a deep breath. 'I did that to Flora... That's why you exist. You mustn't blame your mother. It was all my fault. She just... *loved* me.'

'I loved you too. Even though you were only my uncle, I really loved you.'

'Yes, I know,' Rory said, his voice unsteady. 'Everybody seems to. God knows why, since I've always gone out of my way to be thoroughly obnoxious. But I can't be held responsible for the perversity of human nature, can I? Well, only my own... Anyway, there's nothing more I wanted to say. Thank you for your time and patience.' He turned towards the French windows and, fumbling slightly, opened them.

'Rory?'

He turned back, his face drained, no longer veiled by a sardonic smile. 'Yes?'

'Where *is* Flora?'

'Apart from inside my head, you mean? I haven't the slightest idea. But she's alive.'

'How can you know?'

He shrugged. 'I just know. And the thing that bloody petrifies me is I'll know when she isn't.'

I kept up with my family's exploits through newspapers and magazines. I picked up papers wherever I found them, read them, then used them to insulate my clothing, make pillows and bedding. In winter I sat in reading rooms until librarians kicked me out. I became known in my circle as quite an astute political commentator, renowned for my sense of balance – acquired no doubt as a result of my omnivorous reading habit. I devoured everything, from the Financial Times *to the* Morning Star.

I had a precious pair of scissors that I kept on a piece of elastic round my neck. These were mainly for self-defence but I also used them to clip out articles and pictures of the family or anything else that took my fancy. I saved reviews of Colin's novels and a lengthy profile of him from the Guardian when he was short-listed for a literary prize. (I always knew that boy would go far. He was wasted as an actor.) I came across an article about the Chelsea Flower Show in a gardening magazine with a photo of a prize-winning wildlife garden, designed by 'father and son team, Hugh and Theo Wentworth'. The photograph showed them standing side by side, Theo not quite as tall as Hugh, both of them tanned, smiling, looking fit as fleas. I never found a photograph of Rory but I collected several music articles written by him and reviews of concerts he conducted. He seemed to devote a lot of energy to youth orchestras.

I kept everything, carefully filed by subject, in manila envelopes safety-pinned to the inside of my coat. Over the years it became quite an archive. I used to rustle as I walked.

My family kept me warm. They kept me company.

Then, unfortunately, they killed me.

1987

Charlotte and Theo sat in the summerhouse at Orchard Farm in two battered Lloyd Loom chairs, facing each other, but not touching. The gloomy interior was lit only by the last of the evening sunlight as it filtered through a window almost obscured by rampant honeysuckle, the scent of which mingled with the smell of mice and rotting wood. Theo sat with an old picnic hamper at his feet and was leafing blindly through a pile of leather-bound notebooks. He opened one randomly and his eye fell upon an entry in Rory's hand.

May 26th 1975
Fox seen around dawn, strolling across lawn. Bloody mouth containing remains of chicken. Vixen killing for cubs?
Theo – watch the woodpile. Wren is nesting there.

Theo tossed the book back into the basket and said, 'I just can't bear to think we made love for the last time and—' His mouth opened, then closed again and he spread his hands. 'I didn't even know.'

'I can't bear to think we made love,' Charlotte murmured.

'Lottie, don't. Please don't take that away from me. Don't take everything.'

She looked down at the basket and nudged it with her foot. 'What *are* those?'

'The wildlife diaries. Don't you remember them? They go way back. Hugh and Dora sometimes sit in here and go through them, comparing notes about the garden.' He lifted a journal and opened it. 'This is the very first one. Your spelling was hilarious.'

Charlotte held out her hand. 'Show me.' The yellowed pages crackled as she turned them and a pressed flower, a snakeshead fritillary, transparent with age, fluttered to the ground. '1975 was the year after the accident, wasn't it?'

'Yes. Rory wasn't speaking then. He used to communicate in writing.'

'He's written half a page about barn owls here... He must have written all this for you, you know. Colin couldn't have cared less. And I was only interested because you were. Maybe I was in love with you even then.'

'You can't be in love at seven.'

'No, I suppose not. But you were special to me. Even then.'

'Self-interest. I stopped Colin beating you up.'

'No, I think I felt some deep connection with you.'

'Perhaps you sensed I was your brother.'

'*Half*-brother. Don't make it worse than it is. I didn't feel it with Colin. I still don't. He and I don't have anything in common apart from genes.' Charlotte tossed the notebook back on to the pile.

Leaning back in his chair Theo said, 'You know, there must be millions of people out there who are products of incest and they don't know it. Their parents might know, but they don't.'

'We do.'

'And that makes a difference?'

'Of course it does.'

'I don't see why. It's either wrong or it's not. I can't see that *knowing* makes any difference to the morality of it.'

'We would know what we were doing was wrong.'

'So it's OK to act immorally, so long as you don't know what you're doing?'

'Oh, you know what I mean! You couldn't be *blamed*, could you? If you didn't know?'

'Who's going to blame us? Our father? My mother?'

'It would be wrong, Theo. You know it.'

'If we never had kids, would it matter?'

Charlotte frowned. 'Being brother and sister?'

'No – being childless.'

'It would matter to me. *Knowing* I could never have them.'

'You could be infertile anyway. Or I might be.'

'Yes, but the point is the knowing, isn't it? Knowing in advance. And I'd always be worried about getting pregnant. I'm sure I could never go through with an abortion. Flora couldn't, could she?'

'I'd get sterilised.'

'It's called a vasectomy if you're a bloke.'

'Well, I'd have one of those.'

'Supposing we broke up? You might want kids with someone else.'

'I wouldn't. I've no intention of reproducing my genes. *Ever*. It wouldn't be fair. On my partner or the child.'

Charlotte was silent. Theo watched as she bent her head and withdrew a tissue from the pocket of her jeans. As she dabbed at her eyes he said, 'If you really wanted a child you could get pregnant by somebody else. I wouldn't mind.'

'Don't be sick, Theo!'

'What would it matter? If a child is all that stands between us?'

'It isn't all – don't you see? I feel differently now! I feel... *ashamed*. I feel dirty! I can't just pretend I don't know!' He didn't reply. 'I'm sorry, Theo.'

'Well, we probably would have split up one day anyway. Nothing lasts for ever. *Till death do us part* doesn't really mean much nowadays, does it?'

'I'll always be your friend.'

'No, you'll always be my sister. Till death do us part.'

Charlotte blew her nose, forced a smile and said, 'Maybe there's no incest in Heaven.'

'Or alternatively, we could try the other place where no doubt anything goes.' Theo stood and went over to the window. He leaned on the wooden sill and, his mop of hair gathering cobwebs, gazed up at the sky. 'Pipistrelles. Look at them! Such a beautiful word for such an ugly creature.' He watched the careering bats for a while, then turned back to the hamper, rifled through the notebooks and withdrew one. Picking up a short stub of pencil, he sat down again, turned the pages then began to write.

'You called that your special pencil,' Charlotte murmured. 'Rory gave it to you, didn't he?' He nodded and continued to write. 'Theo... I still love you.'

The pencil lead snapped. Staring down at the words he'd written, Theo said, 'And I still love you.' He looked up, his blue eyes – Rory's eyes – fierce and bright. 'But that's hardly the point, is it?'

She raised a hand to his head, threaded her fingers through a curl and removed a spider. 'It *should* have been.'

If I hadn't rung Rory... If I hadn't been drunk... If I'd spent the night in a hostel... No point in speculating now. What's done is done. I always met trouble halfway.

I didn't stay in a hostel because it was the height of summer and at the best of times those places stank of inadequate sanitation, vomit and unwashed bodies. I preferred to sleep out under the sky, the little bit of sky I could see between office blocks and multi-storey car parks.

I was drunk because a charitable crank had given me a tenner. Well, that's not strictly true. He'd given me £10 but I was drunk because I'd phoned Rory. I'd heard his voice. After thirteen years. I couldn't speak, but he knew it was me. He said my name. He begged me to come home. But I couldn't answer. Words wouldn't come. I just listened, then I cried.

I'd rung him because it was our birthday. I'd picked up a paper and noticed the date. June 20th. We were fifty-eight. (I couldn't imagine what Rory looked like at fifty-eight. Whenever I thought of him – and I thought of him every single day – he was always about twenty-two.) So I'd rung him to wish him a happy birthday.

But it was a waste of time because when he answered I couldn't speak.

2000

Rory sat at the foot of the stairs, clutching the telephone. The dining room door opened and Theo put his head round.

'Grace says, are you going to come and blow out all these candles? She thinks fifty-eight constitutes a fire hazard.'

Rory looked up, his eyes unseeing. 'That was Flora.'

Theo stepped into the hall, closing the door behind him. 'Bad news?'

'Yes.'

'What did she say?'

'Nothing... Nothing at all...'

There's a knack to getting a good night's sleep on the streets. The inexperienced sleep in doorways, improvising Wendy houses, but that's a big mistake. People dump the remains of their takeaways on you, then you get bothered by rats later. Sometimes men urinate on you. They're too drunk to see you or too drunk to care. Some bastards do it deliberately. So you don't go sleeping in doorways, not if you've got any sense.

I used to like sleeping in out-of-the-way places, off the main thoroughfare. It's safer for women to sleep during the day and keep on the move at night, but you learn to sleep lightly and I always used to wake at the first hint of trouble.

Except when I was drunk.

I'd found an abandoned sofa in a side street. I think it must have been thrown out by some club or office. There was nothing wrong with it. Last year's colour, I suppose. No one else had found it yet and I was able to lie down, almost full length, on this lovely comfy sofa. It was Heaven. I'd have slept like a log, even without all the vodka.

They probably thought I was a bundle of old clothes. Or maybe they did it deliberately. Someone's idea of a bit of fun.

I must have spilt some vodka. My coat was full of newspaper. Some kid probably tossed a match. What does it matter now? When I woke up I found I was burning. I was burning and I was already screaming. My hair was on fire and my lungs were full of smoke and I was choking and when I wasn't choking I was screaming. I jumped off the sofa and beat at my clothes, trying to put out the fire, but as I moved, whirling like a dervish, the draft just fanned the flames.

My last thought was for Rory. That I hadn't wished him a happy birthday and now I never would.

2000

Rory sat up in bed with a strangled cry. Grace woke immediately. Before she'd even turned on the bedside light, he was sitting on the edge of the bed, reaching for the phone.

'What is it? What's the matter?'

'Flora. She's in pain. In danger... Somewhere – I don't know...' He sounded confused and was jabbing a finger at number pads on the phone.

'Who are you ringing?'

'An ambulance.'

'But what are you going to say? You don't know where she is! No one does.' Rory's finger hovered above the phone. Grace put an arm round his shoulders and registered that he was shaking. 'Darling, I think you just had a nightmare. Put the phone down and get back into bed. Even if Flora is in danger, there's absolutely nothing you can do about it. But you're probably just imagining things.'

'No, I'm bloody not!' He started to cough, then doubled over, choking. He closed his eyes but couldn't shut out a vision of Flora, like a glorious avenging angel, a fiery halo round her head, her golden hair burning, her garments made of flame.

Grace held him till the screaming stopped, then, as he seemed barely conscious, she rang for an ambulance.

My family gathered at Orchard Farm to discuss my funeral, all of them except Charlotte who, I discovered, had been in Australia for many years. It was a shock seeing them all. I hadn't seen Rory for thirteen years, except once on a TV screen. I hadn't seen Grace for twenty. If we'd ever met I might not have recognised her. The years hadn't been kind. But far kinder to her than to me.

No one was looking their best, but Rory looked like a corpse. The bones of his face stood out as if his skull were trying to force its way through his skin. I couldn't bear to look, so I sat beside him on the sofa, in the space between him and Colin – my lovers, father and son.

They discussed the details of my cremation. Hugh asked Rory if he had any suggestions for music for the ceremony. He just shook his head listlessly. Dora requested that everything should be as simple as possible and suggested a couple of my favourite hymns. I was touched she remembered which they were.

The conversation dwindled and in the ensuing silence my mother started to weep. Theo was instantly at her side, his arm round her, his long fingers, so like his father's, stroking her sparse, white curls.

'Poor Flora... We failed her, didn't we?' my mother asked between sobs.

No one answered, then Hugh said, 'I know I did. But try as I might, I can't think what more we could have done.'

Dora squeezed Theo's hand. 'Loved her more, I suppose.'

'Or loved her less.'

It was the first time Rory had spoken. Heads turned to look at him, then silence descended again, punctuated by Dora's quiet weeping. Theo looked up at Hugh who nodded, then my son lifted my mother gently, easily, as if she were a doll, and carried her out of the room.

Colin passed a hand across his face, then leaned forwards in his chair, tense fingers laced together. He exhaled, then said randomly, 'What do you actually die of if you're badly burned?'

Grace hissed, 'For God's sake, Colin!' Hugh looked at him for a moment, glanced across at Rory, then said, 'Shock, I believe. Shock caused by a massive loss of fluid.'

'Oh. I see.' Colin leaned back in his chair again, looking even more uncomfortable.

'Flora died of shame.'

No one looked at Rory. No one spoke.

I laid the ghost of my hand on his, his poor crippled hand. His head jerked and he looked down suddenly, disbelieving.

I knew then that the pain must have stopped.

Epilogue

2000

Theo strides up the garden path towards the house, raising a hand in salutation to Hugh and Dora. He pauses to watch as Dora, enthroned on her electric cart, points to a rogue purple phlox in the middle of the white bed. Hugh wades into the undergrowth with deadly intent.

Theo is kicking off gumboots outside the back door when the phone rings. He pads indoors in stockinged feet to answer it.

'Orchard Farm Nursery.' He hears a low murmur of voices, the sounds of cutlery, musak. 'Hello?'

No one answers and he's about to replace the receiver when a tentative female voice says, 'Theo?'

'Speaking.'

Silence again. Then, 'It's Charlotte. Lottie... Theo, are you still there?'

A long pause. 'Yes, I'm here. I was – I was just... very surprised.'

'I got your postcard. About the funeral. I was very sorry... to hear about Flora.'

He sinks into a chair. 'Did Grace explain?'

'Yes.'

'I hadn't seen her for years. Not sure if that made it better or worse. Why are you ringing, Lottie?'

'Because I want to see you.' Theo doesn't reply but leans on the table, his bowed head supported by his free hand. 'I want to buy you a ticket to Sydney. I can't face coming back and Mum says you don't have much spare cash—'

'Lottie, are out of your mind? It took me bloody *years* to get over you!'

'Please come. Just for a holiday. It will do you good to get away from the family.'

'Lottie, I have a business to run and, as Grace so helpfully pointed out, it's not making me a rich man. I can't just drop everything.'

'Yes, you can. Come for two weeks. Mum says your staff will manage.'

'I'll kill that woman! Have you discussed all this with her already?'

'Only the practicalities. Not how I feel.'

'Which is?'

'I no longer care who or what you are. What I am. I just want to *see* you... Will you come?' He doesn't answer. 'Theo, will you come?'

'I don't know... I'll think about it.'

'There's something else. Something I wanted you to know.'

'What?'

A silence. He hears her intake of breath, then, 'I have a child now. A son. He's two.' The line crackles. 'Are you still there?'

'Yes. I'm here. Who – who's the father?'

'A friend. A good friend. I wanted a child, he obliged. He's a nice guy. But that's all.'

'What's he called? Your son, I mean.'

'Hughie.'

Eventually Theo says, 'Does he take after you?'

'No, he looks rather like Dad.' Her voice catches. 'Which means he looks a lot like you... Theo, will you *come*?'

'Lottie—'

'Theo, *please!*'

'Yes, I'll come.'

Theo finds Hugh in one of the glasshouses, busy with a watering-can.

'I just had a phone-call.'

'Oh?'

'From Lottie.'

'Good grief!' Hugh straightens up with difficulty. '*Our* Lottie?'

Theo's grin is sudden, lopsided. 'Is there more than one?'

'Was she all right?'

'Seemed to be. She's had a baby.'

Hugh beams and nods. 'She's told you then?'

'You *knew*?'

'Oh, yes. I've got a photo somewhere,' he says vaguely. 'Delightful-looking child. Curly blond hair. She named him after me, you know. I was very touched.'

'Why did no one *tell* me?'

'She told us not to. Thought you might be hurt. She knew you'd never have children of your own, you see. If you don't mind my asking, why did she ring?'

'She wants me to go out to Sydney to see her. Have a holiday. She's offered to pay.'

'Splendid! Well, don't worry about me. I'll manage perfectly. I dare say Rory will help out with the nursery. High time you had a holiday. You did say you'd go?'

'Yes. I did.' Theo drags his hand backwards through his hair. 'I said I'd go and see her...God help me.'

'Oh, He probably will.' Hugh bends to his watering again. 'He very probably will.'

I burn... I burn...

You think it's finished, Rory. You think I'm dead and gone. Ashes to ashes...

But I'm not.

I'm still here. Waiting.

I waited all my life for you. I can wait some more.

As long as it takes.

~~~

Author's Note

Music plays a large part in this book and in my life, although I don't play an instrument, nor can I read music. My inspiration and constant companions in the writing of A LIFETIME BURNING were the recordings of pianists Vladimir Ashkenazy, Daniel Barenboim and Paul Lewis.

These are the pieces that Rory plays in the course of the novel:

BEETHOVEN Cello sonata in A, Op. 69
BEETHOVEN Piano sonata No. 21 in C, Op.53, *Waldstein*
SCOTT JOPLIN *Maple Leaf Rag*
RAVEL Piano trio in A minor
SCHUBERT Piano sonata D.960 in B flat
SHOSTAKOVICH Piano Concerto No. 2 in F, Op.102
SHOSTAKOVICH Prelude & Fugue No. 1 in C

Acknowledgements

I would like to thank:

My daughter and husband, Amy and Philip Glover who always asked for more.
Linda Priestley who offered a sharp critical eye at the eleventh hour.
Stephen Harrison who answered my musical questions.
My agent, Tina Betts who praised and encouraged.
Nikki Read and Giles Lewis of Transita, the original publisher of this novel.

Other books by **Linda Gillard**...

HOUSE OF SILENCE

Selected by Amazon for *Top Ten BEST OF 2011* in the Indie author category.

"My friends describe me as frighteningly sensible, not at all the sort of woman who would fall for an actor. And his home. And his family."

Orphaned by drink, drugs and rock'n'roll, Gwen Rowland is invited to spend Christmas at her boyfriend Alfie's family home, Creake Hall – a ramshackle Tudor manor in Norfolk. Soon after she arrives, Gwen senses something isn't quite right. Alfie acts strangely toward his family and is reluctant to talk about the past. His mother, a celebrated children's author, keeps to her room, living in a twilight world, unable to distinguish between past and present, fact and fiction.

When Gwen discovers fragments of forgotten family letters sewn into an old patchwork quilt, she starts to piece together the jigsaw of the past and realises there's more to the family history than she's been told. It seems there are things people don't want her to know.

And one of those people is Alfie...

REVIEWS

"HOUSE OF SILENCE is one of those books you'll put everything else on hold for."
CORNFLOWER BOOKS BLOG

"The family turns out to have more secrets than the Pentagon. I enjoyed every minute of this book."
KATHLEEN JONES (Margaret Forster: A Life in Books)

UNTYING THE KNOT

Awarded a Medallion by the *Book Readers Appreciation Group*
www.bragmedallion.com

Marrying a war hero was a big mistake.

So was divorcing him.

A wife is meant to stand by her man. Especially an army wife. But Fay didn't. She walked away - from Magnus, her traumatised war hero husband and from the home he was restoring: Tullibardine Tower, a ruined 16th-century castle on a Perthshire hillside.

Now their daughter Emily is getting married. But she's marrying someone she shouldn't.

And so is Magnus...

REVIEWS

"This author is funny, smart, sensitive, and has a great feel for romance... Highly recommended!"
RHAPSODYINBOOKS book blog

"Daring to write characters like this is brave. And it works. Beautifully."
INDIE EBOOK REVIEW

"Another deeply moving and skilfully executed novel by Linda Gillard. I am totally in awe of this author. Once again, she had me committed to her characters and caught up in their lives from the first few pages, then weeping for joy at the end."
Tahlia Newland, AWESOME INDIES